Ripping

DEDICATED

To aviators and families of aviators everywhere…

INTRODUCTION 2017

I was a bit cynical about publishing 'Minds of the Empire' again. After all, it's been twenty two years since the book was first published. How would it fair in a very different world? Well, I decided to carefully read and edit the original manuscript and over this period I came to a conclusion - the younger me did good... I see why the 'Dyason' series became a bit of a cult classic. Surprisingly perhaps, the 'good vs evil' story, comes across as a bit of 'light relief' in our modern, complex and confusing world.

After a prolonged break (to raise a family), I'm delighted to be back in the 'Ripping' saddle!   As my younger self once said, *'Put your feet up, grab a beer and enjoy a 'Ripping' story!'*

Warren James Palmer 2017

Note to younger self : Three kids sonny - not 2.2.... But you're still flying - so not all bad... Lost your hair though...

INTRODUCTION 1995

As a kid I was fed a diet of pulp fiction, war comics, Star Trek and Biggles. They obviously had quite an effect on me because here I am in my thirtieth year and I'm still a pulp fiction addict. I also find it hard to come to terms with the idea that I should have a steady job, mortgage, 2.2 kids, wife and semi-detached. Don't get me wrong, I have absolutely nothing against any of these things. It's just that I'd rather be flying! I guess I'm a bit sad like that.

Anyway, this book is nothing but pure adventure, a *'Ripping Yarn'*. All the technical stuff is loosely based on current scientific thinking, but then current scientific thinking seems to be based on the philosophy of 'Yeah, well it could happen!' So that doesn't mean much — I mean what with quantum physics and all … Sorry I'm rambling again.

I hope you'll enjoy this book and will go on to read others in the series. I've got lots more adventures for Moss, Jenson, Myrddin and the gang, to come yet! I also hope you'll support what *'Ripping'* stands for — books for anyone who believes life's too short *not* to fill it to the brim with adventure!

So put your feet up, grab a beer and enjoy a 'Ripping' story!

Cheers
Warren James Palmer   1995

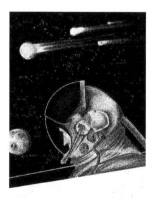

MINDS OF THE EMPIRE

BOOK ONE
OF THE DYASON

WARREN JAMES PALMER

CHAPTER ONE

STRATEGIC DEFENCE COMMAND EUROPE.
LUXEMBOURG, MARCH 15TH, 2045. 15.33GMT.

Major Lorien leaned back in the comfortably padded commander's chair and stretched his legs out under the console. He gazed at the three dimensional holographic image of the Earth that dominated the centre of the operations room. It was a mass of colour with deep blue oceans, brown land masses and white weather patterns that swam through the atmosphere. He sighed deeply; it looked like it was going to be another quiet afternoon shift.

From his position on the circular gantry that surrounded the globe Lorien could clearly see the position of each of the laser platforms that orbited above the image of the Earth. Different colours marked separate platforms, and cones of light spread from each position towards the Earth's surface, showing the area of fire covered by the lasers sitting in geo-stationary orbit. Only the laser platforms in position above Europe were shown in detail on the hologram. Other areas of the globe such as the Pacific Basin or the Americas were controlled from other similar control rooms placed within their own spheres of operation.

Lorien often marveled at the technology that had created not just this, but all the OPCs (operation control rooms) that were part of the newly created United Nations Laser Defence Network. The concept of weapons in space that could fire at will upon any object on the planet below was nothing new. The United States attempted to convince the Soviet Union they were capable of such weapons back in the 1980's. But it had taken giant leaps in technology and worldwide co-operation to produce the present network.

The old actor President Reagan had harboured the dream of space-born weapons that could shoot down incoming Soviet missiles at a time when the phrase 'Super Power' still had some meaning. However, politics and technology had moved beyond the former president's dream. Now the technology for such a defence network existed, but the coverage of the 'shield' was global. Today, Lorien and his command crew were out to stop any aggression, of any kind, in any country. This was the basis upon which the World Defence Force (WDF) could work. If no other country could move its forces without being gunned down from space, then there could be no aggression.

So it was Major Lorien's job to sit in the semidarkness of the battle room, and watch the movements of all Europe's and Western Russia's military forces including satellites and space stations. Monitors on the control desk in front of Lorien allowed him to view any specific point within his area. A flick of a button could raise a view of the new European Alliance space station, a view of the Baltic home defence airfields, or any other point in orbit or on Earth within his area of operations. If he observed any unauthorised military activity he could use the digital communication links to make inquiries. If he believed it necessary, he could order the firing of the battle lasers. Then the huge platforms would realign their orbital positions, lock onto co-ordinates sent by the battle centre and fire the needle lasers that could take out aircraft, men and machinery regardless of weather conditions.

However it was rare for Lorien to be called upon to use any of the powerful hardware at his fingertips. The last time the adrenaline of action had surged through his veins was when Iran attempted to enter the Southern Muslim states of the Russian Commonwealth. Then the aggression had been stopped in its tracks within the first hour, but only after nine strike aircraft plus a column of tanks and personnel carriers had been destroyed. Since that time, the region had been quiet, with Iran claiming the attack had been organised by army extremists.

And so it was on that March afternoon that Lorien and his crew were less than fully attentive. It was a pleasant afternoon outside the bunker and they'd all eaten well. Now they went through their schedules automatically, without really paying much attention to their equipment and all looking forward to a party organised for that evening. After all what was the point? Nothing ever happened, and if it did, the warning klaxons would sound anyway.

Had any of them been more observant they may have seen the strange image appearing on the video camera of laser platform 034. The object didn't register on any of the sensors, but if they had been watching the video monitor closely they would have just been able to discern a dark silhouette move against the background of stars. Unfortunately it was only when platform 034 blinked off the holographic globe, warning lights lit up the control room monitors and the klaxons did sound that their attention was raised.

Damn! Lorien thought to himself, that's the third time this week that the sensors on one of the platforms had failed. Now he would have to order a remote robot to initiate a check and repair program. Lorien hit the klaxon reset, stood and turned to one of his crew to give the order to send out a repair drone, but he hadn't even opened his mouth when a second platform winked out, disappearing from it's position above the hologram.

'Sir,' another crewman called out, 'Platform 012 has gone off network. Sensors on the Orion satellite register a large energy release from that area. It looks like 012 blew up!'

It took a moment for what had been said to register with Lorien and when it did all thoughts of a quiet afternoon disappeared in an instant. He was fully attentive now. 'What do you mean blew up?' he snapped at the crewman sitting before his panel, 'Don't be bloody stupid man! It can't have just blown up! You must have misread the sensors!'

The crewman turned to face Lorien, a flush rising up his face from the rebuke, but sticking to his analysis nevertheless. 'Sir, I'm sorry but I am definitely reading a large energy release. Where the platform should be, there's nothing but debris registering on the radar!'

Lorien moved to the station and quickly read the monitor readings. The man was right, damn it! 'Well bugger me! What about 034? What happened there?' he demanded.

The crewman quickly pulled up a different graphic and Lorien interpreted the information. Damn again! The same thing had happened to that platform as well! Now he was worried. Platforms had gone out of commission for various reasons before, but they'd never exploded, and not just one but two of the buggers! What the hell was going on? It was inconceivable that they were under attack so it must be some sort of bizarre malfunction. They could observe any missiles launched from any spot on Earth and their scanners showed that there were no other objects in orbit within several hundred kilometres of their platforms. So just what the hell was happening? He sat back down at his desk and opened a secure line to the Group Commander's office. It was time to pass the buck.

'General, this is Major Lorien at the command centre, sir,' Lorien spoke into his head mike. 'We've lost two platforms in the past few minutes. It seems they just disintegrated... yes sir, I am sure of that. We're down-loading the data to your tablet now... yes sir, we are registering energy releases in those areas, the Orion satellite is confirming that...hold on sir...holy shit!'

Lorien was watching the bank of monitors while he spoke to the general. As he watched another platform winked out, leaving a major gap in the defence network.

'Sir, we have just lost a third platform. If you watch your monitors now, you can see the data. The same thing happened again. Unless I knew better sir, I would say that they'd all been taken out. No sir, radar has not shown any objects within their areas. But sir, we must be under attack! There's no other reason for what's happening, but from whom and from what I can't say!'

Lorien finally noticed a dark silhouette moving against the stars on the video monitor of platform 016. 'Hold on sir, something strange is happening. I'm looking at platform 016's video monitor. There is a large unidentified object approaching the platform, there are no lights, it's hard to judge the size, but I would estimate it to be at least 500 metres. Nothing is reading on the ECM sensors and there is no radar signature. Yes sir I confirm, there is no fault with the video monitor. There...'

Major Lorien was cut short and could only register a brief moment of disbelief before the fireball swept across the command centre, the heat vaporising everything it touched, including the Major's body. Above Luxembourg rose a huge mushroom shaped cloud.

UNITED STATES STATION 3, EARTH ORBIT. MARCH 15TH, 2045. 15.35, GMT

Kowolski hated EVA. Sure, it was well paid, and when he returned home for shore leave he always had the credits for a wild time. Women and drugs aplenty, he'd enjoyed nearly all the fleshpots on Earth when not marooned in orbit. In fact it wasn't the job so much. Working on the outside of the station on a multitude of tasks allowed him a view of heaven and Earth that other people would kill for. No, if he was honest, it was the smell he couldn't stand. That mixture of sweat, canned air and electrical ozone all EVA suits had got right up his nose, literally. The problem was the last occupant.

The new suits were miniature space vehicles in their own right. Hard shells enclosed a self-contained propulsion and atmospheric conditioning unit. Long articulated arms, with touch sensitive servo-operated claws allowed the occupant to work in a shirt sleeve environment, without all the drama of putting on one of the antique space suits of the twentieth century. The only problem was the smell. Nobody had bothered to fit scrubbers that gave off the fresh smell of pine. Instead there was just that sickly sweet smell of the previous driver. As the station was always short of water, few personnel bothered with hygiene in the Earthside sense, so everybody stank. This was Kowolski's big gripe.

However, he buried his misery under the pressure of work, and at this particular moment he needed all his concentration to control the movements of the loose infrared probe. As usual the last repair was a bodge job; less than six weeks after the last scheduled maintenance the whole housing and antenna unit needed replacing. Privately Kowolski thought it was time the station was turned into meteorite fodder. Built at the turn of the century, the place was showing its age. If they got rid of it, he might get transferred to one of the newer, more luxurious United Nation's space stations.

Something caught Kowolski's eye and he paused from his work to look up at the bright backdrop of stars. It was strange, he was sure he'd seen something move out of the corner of his eye, but now it was gone. No, hold on a moment, there it was again, in fact a whole patch of space seemed to be blanked out. Where once there were stars there was now only an empty darkness.

Kowolski thought he must be hallucinating, it wasn't possible for the stars to disappear. Maybe that tab he'd swallowed before coming on shift was having more than the usual effect on him. Other than the station there wasn't anything else in orbit for hundreds of kilometers. No shuttles were due, so that didn't explain it. He must be working too hard. He looked again... no, there was definitely something there. What was it? Now he knew where to look, he could just make out a shape almost invisible against the backdrop of space. But whereas sunlight reflected off the metal of the station, this thing reflected no light at all. So what the hell was it...? It was definitely getting nearer!

He clicked open his comm channel to call control, but all that came out was a gasp of shock. A searing flash of light momentarily blinded him and when his vision returned the space station was beginning to tumble out of control, a plume of vapour erupting from a huge gash in the hull. Kowolski could only register brief disbelief, before the shock wave of a massive explosion sent his pod spinning helplessly into the void. Nobody heard his dying scream.

ABOVE THE SOUTHERN STATES OF THE RUSSIAN FEDERATION. 15.35 GMT

Vladimar Kirchistki pushed the throttle of his new Sukhoi 45 to the gates, and the small interceptor leapt towards the darkness of the outer atmosphere.

By injecting hydrogen and oxygen into the Sukhoi's hybrid engine, Valdimar could push his aircraft to the very verges of space itself, reaching hypersonic speeds. Indeed it had only been six minutes since take off and already the blue of the Earth's atmosphere was fading to the black of outer space.

To anybody else the flight would have been an exhilarating experience, but for Valdimar it was a pain; quite literally, in his head. Unfortunately, his earlier hangover, caused by an over-indulgence of the local southern vodka, had not cleared sufficiently before the onset of G forces set his brain pounding. His mood was not improved by the fact that he was chasing yet another shadow across the local WDF monitors. In fact this was the third time this month he'd been scrambled to chase space junk that showed up on some idiot's screen as an alien invasion!

Abruptly, the acceleration that forced his head into the padded seat ceased and the interceptor floated in low Earth orbit. The sun shone through the tinted canopy heating the tiny cockpit and making Valdimar sweat, until cooling units cut in to compensate. Despite the incredible view of Asia floating below a layer of broken clouds and the curve of the Earth contrasting sharply with the vastness of deep space, his mood didn't improve dramatically. He was constantly aware that the only thing that kept his eyeballs from being sucked out his head was his flimsy pressure suit and the thin carbon-fiber walls and canopy of the cockpit. Even through his gloves, if he touched the perspex above him, he could feel the cold of outer space.

Well, he was in the right place and as to be expected here was nothing to see, except the curve of the planet below. Nothing reading on any of the sensors, nothing much anywhere at all. 'Control, this is Delta Foxtrot 37, in the target area,' Vladimar spoke into his mike. 'Nothing to report. Sensors read nothing, over."

'Delta Foxtrot 37, this is control,' came the reply. 'Are you sure there is no sign of space junk on your monitors in the area? We definitely picked up a positive reading of something quite large. Over." Vladimar lost his patience and snapped into his mike, 'Look control, you want to get your balls squashed and launch up here to take a look? There's nothing here. Nothing on any of my sensors. No infrared signature... No radar signature... Nothing... Bugger all! And I can see bugger all except for a few billion stars! Over!'

'Roger 37, copy that. Sorry, must be another glitch in the equipment. Come down for dinner. Over.'

'Roger control. Glad you see it my way. Next re-entry window in fifteen minutes.Over.'

'Okay 37. See you on the ground, have a good trip. Out.'

Arsehole, thought Vladimar. They ought to replace those damn antique units with some new Chinese kit. Those old radar and infrared monitors almost dated back to the old Soviet Union days.

Casually Vladimar rolled the interceptor in preparation for re-entry, a bumpy, noisy and unpleasant affair. As the stars above rolled past he noticed an area where they appeared to be missing, they simply did not shine. He halted the roll to look more closely. The blotted out area appeared to be getting larger. It was strange, if he looked carefully he could vaguely make out a shape even though there were no reflections, just a deep darkness.

Then the tiniest glint of light showed Vladimar a metallic form and in an instant he realised what he was looking at. Surely, it wasn't possible, nothing that big existed! Without warning a fireball of light shot towards his craft. He only had time to shout 'Oh God No!' into his mike, before his interceptor was turned into a flaming meteor falling to the Earth below.

WORLD DEFENCE FORCE HEADQUARTERS, PARIS. 15.40 GMT

The situation room was in a state of disorganised panic. People in various uniforms ran around, wildly pointing at computer monitors and gesticulating frantically. No matter how many times they practiced crisis situations, when it came to the real thing, the first few crucial minutes always ended up in chaos.

In the midst of shouting people, flashing monitors and holograms, sat General Thompson, previously of the Canadian Air Force, now commander in Chief of the World Defence Force. Tall and lean, with a body like that of a marathon runner despite his 60 years, he sat like an immovable object in the command chair overlooking the whole crisis centre. For several minutes he had watched the incredulous reaction of his staff as the situation developed. Eventually he decided the panic had lasted long enough, stood to his full lean height and bellowed, 'Everybody shut the hell up!'

Immediately the room became silent, bodies froze and faces turned expectantly to the General.

'Now everybody sit down and wait their turn to give me a status report. A couple of you continue to monitor traffic, the rest of you listen up! Schmitt, give me a brief resume of events.'

Schmitt, a short immaculately dressed German, remained standing as everybody else sheepishly sat down. In his hand he held a tablet computer from which he began to read.

'Well sir,' he began mumbling.

'Speak up boy!' bellowed the General.

'Well sir,' Schmitt began again, a little louder, 'the first events took place at 15.29 GMT just over fifteen minutes ago when several tracking and surveillance stations worldwide reported unidentified shadows on their monitors. Usually we put these down to glitches in the equipment, however, the shadows bore some similarity to the signature of our own stealth aircraft, if more effective. So the matter was reported.

Then at 15.34 GMT our laser platforms started to go out of action, apparently from attacks on the platforms themselves. Our sentry sats showed large focused missile strikes against the platforms. Since then the entire laser defence network has been entirely destroyed outright or disabled. Currently, our satellite surveillance and comms network is also under attack. In fact, all the satellites are rapidly being taken out one by one, and that includes the commercial sats, not just our own. We can't confirm what is hitting them, and without the laser platforms we have no defence against them.

At 15.35 GMT all five space stations, that is the three United Nation's, one American and one Japanese, were destroyed. Again we're getting readings of large energy dissipation and debris from their orbital positions. Only the Japanese station managed to send out an SOS before they went off air. The message was; " Hostile manoeuvres by unidentified vessel. We are coming under attack. Station disintegrating. Massive missile strike. Lord have mercy..." there the message abruptly ended...' Schmitt paused, sighed heavily as though he carried an enormous weight, then said sadly, 'Worse of all, the cities of Luxembourg, Perth, Singapore, Honolulu, Toronto and St Petersburg have all been hit by what appear to be nuclear strikes. There were WDF bases in or near each of these cities. Reports of casualties are still coming in, but I'm afraid they'll run into tens, maybe hundreds of thousands.' He looked up from his computer and studied the sad, frightened faces of the assembled men and women. He had to swallow a lump in his throat and quell his stomach before he concluded, 'As yet we don't have a fix on where the strikes originated or who the aggressors are. That is the situation at present, although new information is coming in all the time.' Schmitt looked straight at General Thompson, fear in his eyes. 'Basically, General, we're under attack Worldwide, but as yet we don't know who the enemy is!'

He sat down heavily, his face a picture of misery. Beyond the glass walls the operations room was still in a state of panic, but within the conference room it was deathly silent. General Thompson said nothing, simply sat and scowled for a moment before turning to another of his aides. 'Jefferson, your report now,' he snapped.

Jefferson stood at the other end of the conference room. He was short, academic looking and wore a pair of small round spectacles in preference to having his eyes surgically corrected. Absent-mindedly he adjusted his uniform jacket over his paunch before speaking. Nervously, he cleared his throat then said in an almost strangled voice, 'Well sir, initial readings from Luxembourg and the other struck cities show an absence of radiation fallout. This would indicate a strike by some form of weapon other than nuclear. While the last readings from the destroyed laser platforms and space stations indicate some sort of missile strike...'

'Wait a minute,' the General interrupted 'you're telling me that the nuke strikes were not in fact nuke strikes, and our laser defence network has been obliterated by some sort of other space-born attack system?'

Jefferson squirmed uncomfortably under the stare of the General. 'That's about right sir,' he muttered.

'So we're under worldwide attack from somebody with more hardware than the combined countries of the WDF, being nuked by something other than nukes!' General Thompson's strained voiced rose several octaves. An uncomfortable silence fell over the room. Jefferson was at a loss for words. In a nutshell the General had summed up the contents of his report without even hearing it. He sat back down without saying another word. As he sat, a civilian, in a wrinkled suit slowly stood up and addressed Thompson. 'Ah... General,' he muttered.

'Who the hell are you?!' Thompson bellowed in exasperation.

'Smith, Sir. Space observation team, Sir,' Smith mumbled. General Thompson narrowed his eyes in suspicion at this nasty piece of slime out of uniform. 'Well spit it out then Smith!' he ordered.

'The nuke strikes aren't nuke strikes at all Sir. They're asteroid strikes...'

'Bullshit!' blurted out an officer sitting nearby.

'Um n...n...no, not quite,' Smith stuttered 'N...No, I'm afraid our observations show that several large asteroids are being dropped from high Earth orbit onto our cities, the effect being almost identical to a large nuclear strike. Whatever is attacking us is using stealth technology to cloak their movements. However, the falling rocks or asteroids are leaving easily readable radar signatures. Further, we're receiving eye witness reports from survivors of these things falling onto our cities like comets. The trailing flames created by their entry into the atmosphere are easily visible even in bright daylight!'

Muttering broke out among the assembled team. General Thompson's narrowed eyes bored into the eyes of the unfortunate man from the space observation team. The General was a man used to talking nuke strikes and the rapid deployment of mobile forces. Somehow being told you were being decimated by somebody hurling large boulders at you didn't seem quite right.

'I guess you're about to tell me that this attack comes from an alien race?' He said in a barely controlled voice.

Smith vainly tried to avoid the General's stare. He instinctively knew the General was only a hair's breadth from exploding in frustration and confusion, indeed he found his own conclusions hard to accept himself, so he wasn't surprised by Thompson's hostility. But he was determined to speak his mind, he knew there was only one conclusion to be drawn from the data coming in. When he did finally speak, his voice was nothing more than a whisper.

'As there is no single nation on Earth with the hardware to utilise such large objects as projectiles, then that is unfortunately...the logical conclusion. It would take the construction of a huge vessel to tow large enough boulders out of the asteroid belt to Earth's orbit. The ATELL shuttle constructed by the Pacific Union is the largest spacecraft on Earth, and certainly is nowhere near capable of moving such a huge payload. It would be impossible to keep the construction of such a craft secret, and we've had no such intelligence reports. We must accept the possibility that the attack is not human in origin.'

General Thompson simply sat and stared at Smith, his face expressionless. The seconds ticked by, sweat dripped off Smith's brow, the tension visible on his face as he stood waiting for the inevitable onslaught. However, the outburst never came. Without moving his stare from Smith, the General addressed Schmitt on the other side of the room.

'Schmitt, what do you make of this Bullshit!'

'Well,' came the uneasy reply, 'I've seen the information supplied by Smith and I believe he is correct about the asteroid strikes. That would explain the lack of radiation fallout. A space-born force using stealth technology would also explain the ghost shadows on our monitors. As to whether the attack is from an alien species...well I just don't know, sir. But, what I do know is that whoever they are, they now have the upper hand. With complete control of the highest ground, so to speak, we are at a great disadvantage.'

These words seemed to pull General Thompson out of himself, much to the visible relief of Smith, who collapsed into a chair like a sack of potatoes and mopped his brow. The General pulled himself upright, adjusted his tunic and addressed the room.

'Okay, so we may or may not be under attack from the little green men from Mars,' he bellowed with authority. 'That aside we must act now while we still have some satellite communications and some combat capability. Lockhart!' a woman staff officer stood to attention, 'Send out mobilisation orders to all WDF forces, even though most of them already have. General orders to all units to disperse from their main bases. Let's not make it easy for the enemy. Regional commanders to take command in the event of a communication breakdown. Worldwide alert. Civilians to stay indoors etc, etc. You know the drill. Keep the media in the dark for now, though God knows, they probably know more than we do. Oh yeah, send up those new interceptors to low Earth orbit, see if we can't get a pot shot at the fuckers.'

20

'We already have sir,' Lockhart interrupted. 'Six Russian Sukhoi's are missing.'

'Oh, bloody marvellous!' the General cursed. 'Okay forget that for now, let's stick to limiting our losses. Get the United Nations' President and his motley crew into the Switzerland Haven. And that applies to everybody here too. You've got ten minutes to send out the orders, then everybody boards the VTOL transports. General evacuation. Okay move!'

The room erupted into activity as orders were snapped down the communication links and up to whatever comm-sats were still in operation. Those without anything more to do closed down their consoles and headed for the rooftop landing pad. 'Oh crap...' the General cursed to nobody in particular.

POLAR RIDGE WDF AIRFIELD, GREENLAND. 16.35 GMT.

The sweat trickled down Squadron Leader Jenson's spine despite the freezing temperature of the Arctic air. He'd been sitting strapped into the cockpit of his McDonnell F3 Thunderball for over twenty minutes with the turbines ticking over on auxiliary. Now in the Arctic sun that warmed him through the perspex canopy he was beginning to feel very uncomfortable. The whole base had been placed on full alert since the general orders were sent from London some forty-five minutes ago. So the whole squadron had to sit in their cockpits waiting for the order to scramble. The only problem was that since the satellite link to command headquarters had been severed, nobody knew where to scramble to. Everyone knew of the reports of a worldwide attack by an unknown force, of nuke strikes on WDF bases, and the destruction of the star wars network. Unfortunately, with all incoming radio signals being crudely jammed by wide-band blocking, none of the reports had been confirmed. Nothing showed up on any of the sensors within the Arctic area. Until something did, they had to carry on waiting.

Jenson wasn't the only person beginning to feel uncomfortable. Around the base perimeter he could just make out the missile emplacements of the airfield defence units, while scattered over a wide area, each partially hidden by their blast pens, sat the other Thunderballs of 511 Squadron. Jenson knew that everybody felt the pressure of waiting. Stomach muscles tensed, sometimes there was an overwhelming urge to relieve yourself, even though you'd been just ten minutes before. Everybody felt it, that strange feeling, waiting for combat, that fear. Of course it all disappeared in an instant once the action began. The surge of adrenaline made sure of that. But for the moment there was just that tightened gut feeling... fear. He'd been in the WDF Airforce since he left college more than ten years ago. As a kid he'd planned to join the Canadian Airforce, but when Canada joined the WDF and turned her forces over to their control, it seemed logical to join the new service instead. Now he commanded his own squadron, 511 Squadron. They'd spent the winter in Greenland on arctic warfare exercises and had been due to return to their home base near Montreal in a couple of weeks' time. Right at this moment, Jenson wasn't even sure that Montreal was still there! As he waited he fretted, how would his squadron perform? They were all hardened and highly trained after the long winter of exercises, but none of them had ever been in real combat. It wasn't as if they knew what they were up against... just what the hell was happening out there? Was this all just another exercise? Another test dreamed up by North Atlantic Command? How could it be, with reports coming in from all over the place, including commercial television, of worldwide attacks? His stomach twisted into an even tighter knot of apprehension and fear. Fear not for his life, but of failure, of somehow not making the grade when it really mattered.

Jenson didn't have to wait much longer. Without warning there was a loud explosion and a pall of smoke from the far end of the airfield. One of the Thunderball fighters blew apart. The gut feeling disappeared in an instant as the adrenaline surged through his body. My God! They were under attack and for bloody real! All his multiple radar and ECM (electronic counter measure) sensors were blank, read nothing, but they were definitely under attack, holy shit!

Further explosions and palls of smoke appeared all over the airfield. Without even waiting for control clearance he flicked his mike to the squadron channel and ordered in a frantic voice. 'Squadron scramble, scramble! We're under attack, all aircraft scramble! Clear the area! There's nothing reading on any of the scanners, so ignore them. Keep your eyes peeled and clear the airfield! Get those engines fired up and get off the ground. Rendezvous at GPS reference three-seven-nine-alpha, height, angels four-five.'

Then he desperately waved with one hand for his ground crew to disconnect the umbilical connector, while closing the canopy and opening the throttles with his other hand. The turbines whined louder and louder until within a few seconds, the engines were giving off their enormous full thrust. As the ground crew rushed for shelter Jenson thumbed the vectored thrust control to vertical and the Thunderball literally leapt off the concrete and into the air.

Before he was even twenty metres off the ground there was another explosion, this time very nearby and the Thunderball felt as if it were about to collapse back onto the ground. However, the blast pen absorbed much of the impact and Jenson just managed to hold the bucking aircraft. As soon as he gained some measure of control, he thumbed the vector control towards horizontal and the full force of the turbines shoved the aircraft forward. Rapidly, the airspeed increased, and as the swept forward wings bit into the air, he pulled the Thunderball into a near ninety degree bank, and hauled it away from the airfield. Then he pulled the nose upwards and roared into the Arctic sky.

He continued to accelerate in a near vertical climb until he reached 15,000 metres. Then he throttled back and pushed the control stick forward so that the Thunderball was cruising away from the airfield, heading for the rendezvous point. While trying to calm his furiously beating heart, he scanned his controls. He seemed to have escaped unscathed and he could see two other Thunderballs forming up on his port and starboard wing tips. The numbers painted on their twin fins identified them as Sandpiper and Davies. Jenson tried his radio but only got an earful of screeching. He tried another channel, but got the same result. He punched the number for North Atlantic Control, but again he got nothing but an earful of screeching. Somebody nearby was crudely jamming all the frequencies with a transmitter so powerful his own was swamped. Off his starboard wing Sandpiper pointed to his helmet and shook his head, indicating that he too could hear nothing. Jenson nodded his head in acknowledgment and indicated with his hands for them to stay in formation. If all their frequencies were jammed, there was no way of knowing if any of the other Thunderballs had heard his call and got off the ground. He saw at least two take hits as he scrambled. For a moment he was almost gripped by panic at the thought that he may have lost nearly his whole squadron before they could even get airborne, but then his training took hold. There would be time for panic and fear later. He would just have to hope that some got away and were making for the main bases in Canada. Right now there were three of them armed and airborne with an aggressor down there on the ground. At this point in time that was all that mattered. He ordered his on board computer to scan the surrounding area for hostiles of any nature and register them on the head-up display.

Much to his surprise, the computer replied that there were no hostiles, or other aircraft within a two hundred kilometre radius. This was worrying; unless the 360 degree pulse radar was being affected by the jamming it meant two things, neither of them good. Firstly it confirmed his worst fear that out of the squadron's fifteen aircraft only the three of them managed to get away. Secondly it meant that whoever was instigating the attack was using only ground forces effectively 'cloaked' under some sort of stealth capability. Having said that, the wide-band jamming of the type being used was effective but hardly the latest in stealth technology. Jenson asked the onboard AI unit to locate the source of the jamming. He wasn't surprised when it came back with the epicentre of the transmissions centred on the airfield itself. The WDF base was obviously the objective of the attack. He could have sworn though, that the initial attack on the airfield was by shelling rather than 'smart bombing' or missile attack, which is what he would have expected. The fact that he got away, albeit by a very narrow margin and Sandpiper and Davies also managed to scramble clear, would support that theory. If he had lead such a surprise attack, nobody would have survived. Mind you, three aircraft out of fifteen wasn't exactly getting away without losses. Then again it struck him like an ice pick to the heart that it was possible that they might be the only ones to get away. God, there were hundreds of men and women who worked on the base! What was happening to them! Whoever or whatever instigated the attack, Jenson was determined were about to get their arses kicked. The three of them had no choice but to return to the airfield and counter-attack. With that thought, he hauled his Thunderball into a tight bank, back towards the airfield, with Sandpiper and Davies keeping tight formation.

They dived towards the Earth until they were hugging the ground, flying at 500 knots only ten metres above the snow, following the undulating ground. With any luck, at this height and speed, and with the electronic interference going on, they should hit the attacking force without being seen until it was too late. The jamming worked both ways; they couldn't get a resolution on the aggressors, but then they couldn't see the three of them either. Jenson quickly glanced both sides to check his wing men were still with him as they rapidly approached the plain between the mountain ranges on which the airfield was built.

Ahead of them small clouds of black smoke appeared around their speeding Thunderballs. Well, that was the end to any thoughts of a surprise counterattack...Anti-aircraft units had obviously been placed on the ridge above the airfield. In an attempt to avoid the anti-aircraft fire all three aircraft started jigging wildly. Jenson tensed ready to pull full Gs at the first hint of a SAM (surface-to-air) missile. But after a while, when nothing happened and his threat indicators remained clear, he began to wonder why they were not being attacked by other aircraft or missiles. Obviously they were relying solely upon anti-aircraft fire, fast-firing Gatling guns were spewing explosive shells at them, but as the ECM threat indicators remained clear, it meant that none of it was radar guided...thank God! Still a shell could turn him into a fireball just as easily as a missile.

Jenson had to leave that particular train of thought as his computer AI attack unit warned him that the last ridge before the airfield was coming up. Rapidly he went round the cockpit checking his weapons systems and verbally ordering the computer to arm the ordinance. He was carrying three laser "smart warheads." Four air-to-ground Blackstreak missiles, two Slipstream air-to-air missiles, and 3,000 rounds in the Gatling cannon. The three aircraft gained height slightly to clear the ridge then shot down into the valley. The Polar Ridge Airfield appeared below them. Jenson scanned the devastation with a professional eye, but certainly wasn't prepared for what he saw. Underneath his oxygen mask his jaw dropped in surprise and horror. Sitting astride two runways, the distance between each being more than half a kilometre, sat a huge metal vessel in the shape of a dome. A large black dome, a dome that seemed to absorb light. It sat in the middle of the airfield dwarfing nearby buildings and hangars. At its highest point it must have been at least seven storeys high. Around the edges of the dome, the ground had turned black, scorched by intense heat. In fact Jenson could see the melted remains of several aircraft and personnel carriers. He just couldn't take in the sheer size of the thing. The surface at first appeared to be seamless, but on second appraisal Jenson noticed several blisters spaced equally around the dome, and from the tracer fire emitting from them, he could only presume that they were some kind of gun emplacements. Whatever, or whoever, had attacked the airfield had arrived in that sphere, and they were now in the process of mopping up resistance. In one section of the field perimeter Jenson could make out a few WDF troops under attack from some sort of troop carriers.

Any further inspection was dramatically postponed when the dome's guns turned on the rapidly approaching aircraft. This certainly focused Jenson's attention on the job at hand and he began to weave madly, followed closely by Sandpiper and Davies in an attempt to avoid the worst of the renewed flak. There was loads of it, God it was like flying through a wall of fire! The Thunderball was rocked by nearby explosions and the sky was so thick with smoke and shrapnel you could almost get out and walk on it. The sound of shrapnel hitting the belly of the aircraft made him duck instinctively in the cockpit, even though it was a futile and pointless thing to do. Damn! They didn't need missiles with this much crap being thrown at them! While pulling hard Gs he spoke to his onboard computer, asking for a lock on the Dome. He could only curse when the reply came as "Target unidentified". Well whatever jamming methods they employed, they were still working as his AI unit was also being affected. He flicked the laser designator to manual and aimed his helmet monitor towards the target and ordered "lock-on". Jenson could only hope that Sandpiper and Davies were doing the same. Quickly he checked the threat indicator ... no other aircraft or pulse scans on them. Part of his mind registered the fact that this was very strange, every force on Earth now relied heavily on electronic scanners to "lock" onto a target, but this bunch relied on crude manually aimed flak. Even so, the anti-aircraft fire being thrown up was getting closer every second. There would be only the one pass, so Jenson ordered the computer to direct the smart bombs to the sphere thing, while the air-to-ground missiles would launch against the enemy personnel carriers and tanks streaming out of the machine.

The computer acknowledged manual lock-on and started to count down from ten to release "pickle" point. This was the hard part ... Jenson would have to over fly the target and remain straight and level for the last five seconds. The computer counted, ten, nine, eight, seven, six, five... Jenson straightened the Thunderball, behind him and Sandpiper and Davies did the same. The three jets roared towards the dome, low, fast and level. The computer registered "ordinance released and tracking". Then everything happened at once, and to Jenson's mind, in slow motion. He could feel the flak hitting the Thunderball somewhere in the belly, and immediately he felt the twin turbines scream in protest before dying. The controls went loose and the computer blasted into his ear, "Terminal damage... Eject. Eject!" Bolts exploded and the slipstream whipped the canopy away, while clamps automatically secured his arms and legs before hurling him and his attached seat two 200 metres into the air. Below him, the missiles and bombs of the three aircraft reached the targets with dramatic consequences.

The shock waves from the multiple impacts hit the ejector seat as it tumbled through the atmosphere, and Jenson blacked out as the air was squeezed from his lungs. It was some time before he became aware of his surroundings again, by which time the parachute canopy had opened and he found himself slowly sinking towards the ground. Towards the horizon he could just make out the dwindling shapes of the two remaining Thunderballs as they disappeared into the Arctic wasteland after successfully completing their attack. Silently, Jenson wished Sandpiper and Davies good luck. Hopefully they would find an unoccupied airfield in Canada before their fuel ran out. His attention moved to the scene of devastation below him. The smart bombs had obviously hit their target. There were several ragged holes in the surface of the large dome where the bombs had penetrated the skin, and smoke poured out of numerous orifices.The gun emplacements were silent; one of them appeared to have been blown from its mountings and hung like a discarded toy, while the remainder were blackened and unmoving. However, the blow hadn't been fatal, Jenson could see troops and vehicles of some description swarming around the base of the dome, like ants evacuating an inflamed nest. They may have knocked a hole in the weird craft, but there were still plenty of enemy troops left.

The ground was approaching rapidly, so Jenson pulled on the control cords of his parachute canopy and turned into the wind. He was drifting towards the perimeter, where the Blackstreak missiles had taken out the enemy tanks and personnel carriers. All that remained of them were burning hulks while the CBU 34s (cluster bombs which release several hundred small anti-personnel bomblets) dropped by Sandpiper and Davies had caused havoc among the unidentified attacking troops. Now he could actually see his own airfield troops dug into defence positions beyond the carnage and pulled the shroud cords to steer towards them.Then as he passed over the burning hulks and trenches, he bent his knees pulled the envelope cords hard and neatly landed on the compacted snow. He took the shock in his bent knees, collapsed and rolled, at the same time twisting and pulling on the canopy to collapse the silk. As the air spilled out of the chute, he hit the harness release and spotted the ejector seat lying in the snow some distance to his left. He would need the emergency provisions kept with the seat if he was to survive in the Arctic conditions. Either that or find his own side, otherwise he would have to surrender to the dome bunch and as he had just put a nasty hole in it, that option was not very appealing!

A shuffling noise behind him struck his heightened senses and he hit the snow, pulling out his automatic all in one fluid movement. Several troops were hurrying towards him, their white combat gear making them hard to distinguish against the snow. Only the crunching of combat boots on crisp snow gave them away. Much to Jenson's relief he recognised the white smocks. They belonged to 511 Squadron field defence. He let out an audible sigh of relief and lowered his automatic.

'Sir,' the leading trooper waved and shouted to him, 'if you're unhurt please follow us, there's no time to waste. We're about to evacuate!'

Jenson waved in acknowledgment and trudged towards the four troops. When he got closer he recognised the corporal who was leading the group. His face was worn and smeared with blood, and he limped slightly, favouring his left leg, which had a bloody bandage around it.

'Corporal Peters what the hell is going on here?!' he demanded when he stood before them.

'Glad to see you in one piece, skipper.' The corporal replied. 'Well sir, as you saw that saucer thing attacked and took out the rest of the squadron aircraft before they could get off the ground. Only you, Davies and Sandpiper got away. Then they landed and troops swarmed out from the inside of the thing. We didn't stand a chance sir, there were so many of them. Our group was the last to resist, and we were doomed until you came along. You bought us time sir, but only that. They're already regrouping for another attack. So Captain Black is using the confusion to withdraw. We've got snowmobiles behind those drifts, and we're to meet up with him as soon as possible sir!'

'God, what a mess!' Jenson exclaimed with feeling. He began to shiver from the cold and shock, and hugged himself tightly. 'So where the hell does Black think we can run to? We're over 800 kilometres from the nearest WDF base. The ridge airfield was meant to be the last post before the Arctic, not Piccadilly Circus!'

'I don't know sir, but I guess the Captain has got plans of some sort. All I know is we can't stay here, we're beaten.'

Jenson didn't bother to reply and with that sober thought, they trudged over to the snowmobiles and headed towards the armoured vehicles, already beginning to move from their fortified positions, while there was a lull in the fighting. The remnants of the airfield defence force looked in bad shape. There were just three personnel carriers and two snow leopard tanks moving away from the airfield. Behind them was a scene of devastation. Smoke rose into the sky from numerous gutted tanks and APC's, bodies lay prone in the snow, their blood staining the virgin whiteness. But Jenson could see their defence was not entirely in vain, for there were even more bodies and wrecked vehicles in front of the trenches. The uniforms of these troops were black, and smoke poured from tanks of a design Jenson had never seen before. In the distance the dome still belched thick black smoke where their bombs had hit. For now there was no further fire from the gun emplacements, but it was only a matter of time before they came after the survivors of the WDF force.

The snowmobile pulled alongside a battle cruiser, a hatch opened on the turret and a weary face appeared. 'Jenson, you're a sight for sore eyes! Thank God you and the others came when you did. Our number was about to come up! Climb aboard!' Black shouted. Jenson climbed off the snowmobile and clambered aboard the huge battle cruiser. The interior smelled of sweat and cordite but was deceptively spacious. Black led him to a jump seat at the rear of the cruiser and sat opposite.

'You okay kid? You look a bit shaken.'

'Yeah, I guess so. Just a bit cold.'

'It's the shock, it hits you like that after a while'.

'You don't look so good yourself, you know,' Jenson managed to smile.

'Cheers mate,' come the reply. 'Corporal! Get a medic over here. Check the Squadron Leader for ejection injuries!' Black ordered.

Jenson became sombre, and while a medic checked him over he asked 'So where we going? Are we all that's left?'

'I'm afraid so,' Black relied. 'Your three aircraft were the only ones that got away. They took us completely by surprise. I mean we just couldn't believe the size of that thing, it just appeared from nowhere. One minute it wasn't there the next it was bombing and shelling us. No missiles or the like, mind you, just good old-fashioned high explosives.'

'Yeah, I know,' Jenson interrupted. 'We noticed the same thing. No SAM's or other aircraft. Just loads of Flak.'

'Bad shit! It was only our relative distance from them that saved us. We had a chance to gather our wits. Everyone else got fried either by the dome's landing blast or later artillery.'

'God, what a frigging mess!' Jenson said with feeling. 'So as I said, where in hell are we going now?'

'Got to head for the hills man while they're still confused by your counterattack. We've got some supplies hidden away in some caves a few clicks beyond the first ridge. We set them up a few months ago for Arctic survival training. There's a plateau halfway up a mountain with a large cave we expanded and kitted out. That's where we'll hole up for now.' Jenson simply nodded in agreement, too tired to reply. He'd heard of the caves used for arctic training and warfare exercises. It was as good a bolt hole as anywhere.

'You just sit tight there and have a doze. I've got to organise the orderly retreat. God, what a joke!' finished Black. Jenson sat and watched the retreating back of the captain as he climbed into the turret and began to issue orders. The cruiser lurched forward and Jenson's stomach with it. The look in Black's eyes said it all. They were defeated and on the run. It was time to head for the hills. He began to shiver uncontrollably. The small column sped across the snow and tundra, leaving behind the bodies of their friends to an unknown enemy.

WDF RETREAT, SWISS ALPS.
MARCH 25TH 2045 0800GMT

General Thompson shuffled down the long granite corridor, the light panels casting deep shadows under his eyes. Shadows that had appeared since he had been at the retreat. His uniform, once crisp and starched, was now creased and sweat stained. He hadn't slept in over thirty-six hours, and he felt like death warmed up. Under his arm he carried the morning report on the war being played out on the surface several miles above his head. It was a depressing report to be read to the United Nations' president Jean-Paul Ricard and his ministers. A bunch of bloody bureaucrats as useful as refrigeration to an Eskimo.

Thompson had suffered the agony of split loyalties many times over the past ten days since the beginning of the invasion. His job was to organise resistance from the security of the "retreat" a large underground complex hidden deep below the Swiss Alps. It was the last bolt hole for world leaders, the irony of which never escaped him. Here they all were buried under a Swiss mountain, an impenetrable fortress, trying to win a war against an unidentified enemy. Nearly all the world's leaders had fled their countries and arrived here at the retreat, their tails between their legs. They could see the writing on the wall, the way the war was going, soon there wouldn't be anywhere left for them to rule. He despised the cowardice of them all, for while brave young men and women fought desperate battles, the politicians wined and dined, waiting for the day when they could pick up the pieces. Like Nero, they fiddled while Rome burned. How he longed to be on the surface, giving orders from the front, wherever that may be, suffering as his troops suffered, fighting the enemy face to face. Alas he was doomed to this underground prison.

He stopped before the large double doors of the main conference room. Two armed troops carefully checked his palm prints in the computer memory before opening the doors. Taking a deep breath he absent-mindedly adjusted his uniform and entered the room. He paused at the threshold surprised to find the room empty, except for a small solitary figure, slouched at the end of the long conference table. His hair was disheveled and stubble darkened his face while his once fashionable suit was creased and stained by sweat.

President Jean-Paul Ricard looked up and nodded to him. 'Oh it's you General,' he said in a small high voice. 'Please come and join me.'

Thompson stepped to the table feeling a little confused ... this was meant to be a full ministerial meeting and briefing. 'I believed this was meant to be a full briefing Mr. President. Where is everybody?' he asked.

'I sent them all away' the President replied with a dismissive wave of his hand, 'The time for talk is over, now I have to make a decision. A decision only you can help me with. It is pointless asking those spineless fools for their advice, they have none.'

Ricard tapped his fingers on the table and stared into the middle distance. 'Do you know that in one hour I have a meeting with the general assembly? I have to decide what to advise them, and only you are in a position to give me the information I need. That, General, is why we are having this meeting alone.' He turned and looked at the general expectantly.

Thompson paused, unsure of what to do or say next. Jean-Paul Ricard was famous for never making decisions alone. He always had a flock of advisers in tow, even when he went to the can. He wondered if perhaps the pressure had taken its toll on the diminutive President. He wouldn't be the first to crack. Already several politicians, after seeing their towns and cities mercilessly destroyed, had crossed that fine line between sanity and madness.

'It's okay General, I haven't lost my mind, yet,' said the President reading Thompson's face. He motioned for him to take a chair. 'There's plenty of time for that later, but not now. Please come and sit next to me. I need you to see this video, received by micro-net earlier this morning.'

Somewhat cautiously, Thompson sat in a chair opposite the President and faced the monitor. He was still unsure of what to make of this strange behaviour, but he moved his attention to the holographic monitor as the president clicked on the video link. A three-dimensional image of one of the strange enemy spheres appeared on the screen, floating above the Earth. Beside it could be seen the wreckage of space station alpha, it's twisted and blackened structure deformed almost beyond recognition. Thompson had to remind himself that over two thousand personnel had inhabited that station. They were all dead now, incinerated in the explosion, or floating lifelessly in orbit.

'This video is for the attention of President Jean-Paul Ricard of the United Nations of Earth,' began a voice in perfect English, over the image of the Dome. 'President Ricard, I am authorised by the council of Dyason, to offer your people conditions for surrender'.

On the screen the space scene faded to be replaced by a close-up of a face. A human face. A male, about fifty years old by Thompson's reckoning, with the deepest green eyes and strange red hair. He tried to place the man's origins but couldn't. His features seemed to be a mix of Anglo Saxon, Mongolian and Oriental. In fact, despite meeting all the world's shapes and sizes at the UN, he simply couldn't figure out where the guy came from.

'Who the hell is that?' he exclaimed. 'What is this, some kind of hoax. You're paying attention to somebody with a sick sense of humour who claims to speak on behalf of a bunch called the Dyason!'

President Ricard turned and looked with annoyance at the General. 'Be quiet, Thompson! This is no hoax. The message was received by micro-net transmission from a known Dome position. The message could not have come from anywhere else, nor could it have been received by anybody else,' the president snapped. On screen, the voice continued unabated. 'President Ricard, may I introduce myself. I am Admiral Tirpolz, commander of the invasion fleet of Dyason. My battle vessels now surround your planet, while destroyers and cruisers hold key cities and military installations. You are urged to order your defence forces to surrender their arms. Your position is hopeless. We have already destroyed many areas of population with asteroid strikes. If necessary we shall continue to destroy more if you do not surrender. The council of

Dyason offer reasonable terms for surrender. Earth will become a member of Imperial Dyason and an active colony under these terms. To save any further loss of life, I ask that you consider your position most carefully. I expect a reply by 1200hours GMT.'

The image pulled back from the facial close-up to show the admiral as a man of about Thompson's height, dressed in a starched heavily gilded uniform. He was surrounded by equipment, which looked surprisingly similar to the innards of an old German "U" boat. The interior was dimly lit, with pipes, conduits and visibly huge controls of some sort. There was an overwhelming impression of a lack of space, and in the background could be seen other men standing shoulder to shoulder at strange work-stations. The hologram then faded and died. Thompson sat dumbfounded, staring at the blank screen. President Ricard observed him carefully.

'Well, General, what do you make of that?' he said after a while.

'I don't know what to think Mr President. Are you sure this is no hoax?' Thompson replied shaking his head.

'It is no hoax General. That was the first thing we checked for. The location of the transmission was a particularly large Dome in geo-stationary orbit above the Pacific.'

'So who the hell are the Dyason?'

'I don't know General. All we know is what you have seen on the tape and information from our intelligence services.'

Thompson's mind raced. There had been reports of enemy troops with unusual features, and certainly the technology behind the Domes and their weapons was unfamiliar to the WDF. The few prisoners they had taken all spoke the same unidentified language. The only word the interrogators did understand was the name they called themselves ... Dyason. However, he still found it hard to grasp the concept of an invasion from "outer space". The scientists had been hinting at this scenario for several days now, but he had always dismissed the idea as too far fetched. Without their nav comm satellites, and WDF forces in full retreat, hard information was almost impossible to gather. So it was difficult to confirm or deny any diagnosis. Even so, it was a bitter pill to swallow, besides they were obviously human. Weren't aliens supposed to be bug-eyed monsters? Ricard watched him, studying his face, trying to gauge his reaction.

'General I can see you are having difficulty accepting the information given in the message. I agree it is difficult to believe. However, the fact remains that these people are in a position to hit any centre of population on the planet apparently at will. Our military forces are powerless to prevent these asteroid strikes. Soon there will be nothing left for them to destroy. Already there are signs that the dust and debris thrown into the upper atmosphere is having adverse effects on weather patterns. Not only do we face genocide, we also face ecological disaster on a scale unknown to mankind. We must find some way to stop these attacks. Not in the next few days or hours, but now! Earth and the people on it can not take much more General! Now tell me truthfully, what is our military position?! Is there a military solution?'

Surprised by this outburst from the President, Thompson pulled out his tablet and cast it's information to the monitor. He tried to rally his thoughts into some sort of coherent pattern then he cleared his throat and began.

'Well Mr President, I'm afraid the picture is no better than at last night's briefing. The United States and Canada are now almost totally in the control of the enemy. Except for small pockets of resistance in the desert and mountains, all urban areas have either capitulated or been destroyed completely. What WDF forces remain are retreating to South America. There it is hoped the topography may help to hamper the enemy.' On the monitor images flicked past of defeated and exhausted troops leaving aircraft and helicopters somewhere in South America. Graphical charts showed the number of casualties and direction of retreat.

'New York has been hit by an asteroid strike, we have no word on casualties at present, but I'm afraid they'll be high. The worst news is that a direct hit on the San Andreas Fault set off a major earthquake which has devastated the whole area from San Francisco down to Los Angeles. We've lost contact with California and I fear casualties in the civilian population will be extremely high.'

The President placed his head in his hands and gave out a low groan. 'How many General?' he murmured.

'Over a million, Mr President.'

'Oh God, is there no hope?' he pleaded.

Thompson fidgeted uncomfortably, embarrassed by the President's dismay, a dismay he felt himself. But he had to give the man some hope, he had to throw a lifeline to a drowning man.

'Well we have had some success Mr President,' he carried on. 'We've managed to repulse an attack on New Zealand, and hold our base there. In Europe we still hold mountainous areas such as the Alps, Pyrenees and much of Scotland and Ireland.'

'And what of our cities General? What of Moscow, Paris, London, Tokyo, and all the other world centres?' demanded the President.

'I'm afraid they've all fallen, Mr. President. Our cities have been the target of the enemy's major offensive. We've been forced either to withdraw our forces, or risk an asteroid strike, as at Luxembourg, New York, San Francisco and a dozen other places.'

In an uncharacteristic display of anger, the president ripped the computer file out of the monitor, which blanked out and hurled the unit against the wall. Angrily he turned on Thompson and shouted, 'Damn it man, we've lost millions of lives already, civilians and military, right across the globe! What are our real chances of winning this? Do we have any way of stopping these asteroid attacks? Unless we can halt those, everything else is pointless! You know that as well as I, General. The situation is the same as the nuclear holocaust scenarios of the last century, only we have no means of lobbing nukes back at them!'

Thompson sat silent while Ricard ranted. His mind raced trying to think what to say, but the truth could not be avoided.

'Mr President, without control of space, and with the enemy's ability to target asteroids at us, we can only retreat at present. We can hold certain less populated areas, but that is all. We must conserve our forces and hope to find a way to regain control of the higher ground,' he said, standing rigidly to attention, eyes focused on the wall above the Presidents head. 'Without our space laser platforms, comm sats and nav sats we are fighting blindfolded with one arm behind our back. Communications beyond a few hundred miles are near impossible due to the atmospheric debris and the jamming still being used by these mothers. However, our intelligence indicates that the technology used by the Dyason is nowhere near as advanced as that of the WDF. They're relying on crude ballistic weapons compared to our missiles and although they have some beam technology, it is clumsy and inefficient compared to our own. They're relying on sheer transmitter power to jam our equipment. What I'm saying, Mr President, is that these bastards aren't invincible, not by a long way. At present they have the advantage, but eventually they will all have to come down from space. They won't have the fuel or provisions to stay there for ever. When they do, that will be our time to take them out. A few nuke strikes and those leach sucking mothers are history!'

'That's what I thought,' came the whispered reply. 'What you're really saying is that we have no current defence against these- space born attacks?'

Thompson shuffled his feet embarrassed, and looked away. Christ, what did he bloody expect? Ever since the economic crash countries across the globe had been cutting defence expenditure to the point where there was barely anything left. How the blazes was he supposed to hold off a global invasion with a force a fraction of the size of the armies facing each other across the Cold War frontiers of the 1980s. They were meant to be a rapid deployment policing force, not the bloody seventh cavalry! He said none of this. There was no point so finally he muttered, 'Yes I guess I am Mr President.'

The President seemed to shrink into himself, almost visibly collapse. He buried his head into his hands for a moment before looking up at Thompson again. 'Thank you, General. That will be all. Only history can judge me now.' And with that he gave Thompson a dismissive wave.

With some measure of relief Thompson went to the door and opened it. As he stepped through and quietly closed it behind him, he could just hear the President weeping. Despite everything he thought of politicians, Thompson felt sorry for Ricard. He was close to weeping himself. He moved off down the corridor and was halfway back to the operations room when the full meaning of the President's words hit him. 'My God', he thought, 'the stupid sod's going to surrender!'

SOMEWHERE IN THE ARCTIC.
APRIL 3ᴿᴰ 2045 1200 GMT.

Jenson stood on the balcony overlooking the cavern. Below him sat three Thunderball fighters all that remained of 511 Squadron. Figures swarmed over them carrying out numerous tasks under the glare of the halogen lights suspended from the hard rock roof.

It was amazing what had been achieved in such a short space of time. They'd arrived at the series of caverns some seven hours after they'd left the ridge airfield. First carved out of an Arctic cliff face by gold miners back in the early twentieth century, the original tunnels extended in a network that reached back nearly a kilometre into the hard granite rock and connected a series of large natural caverns. A few years ago the WDF had enlarged the original tunnels and turned the mine into an Arctic survival and warfare base. Food and equipment were brought in from the Ridge airfield and the tunnels made large enough to move aircraft and machinery into the caverns which made excellent natural hangars. When the remnants of Blacks squad arrived in the surviving APC's they thankfully found the bolt-hole still well stocked with food, arms and equipment. Hanson Sandpiper and Mary Davies had figured the survivors would make for the caverns, so much to his delight, they were waiting with their aircraft when they arrived.

Since then, every one of them had toiled day and night to turn the caverns into a secure base of operations. The work had kept them all occupied and kept their minds off the terrible events that were happening across the globe. Black had ordered that the WDF wavelengths be monitored and they'd made an attempt at communication with the northern Atlantic headquarters. But they'd received no reply to their transmissions. In fact they were unable to contact anybody. The relatively low powered transmitters at the caverns were unable to break through the broad-band jamming and they suspected the comm-satellites had been destroyed.

Desperate for information, Black and Jenson had carried out a recce of the ridge airfield two nights before. They had taken one of the vehicles to within a kilometre of the ridge overlooking the airfield then carefully walked to a vantage point where they could use their infrared scopes. The strange Dome still sat in the centre of the airfield, and work crews were busy welding patches onto the hull, making repairs to the damage caused by Jenson's earlier attack. The perimeter around the strange craft was well guarded with troops and armoured vehicles, but the airfield itself seemed to be virtually deserted. Jenson guessed they simply didn't have sufficient manpower to patrol the airfield as well and believed their position to be secure anyhow. Taking advantage of this lapse in security the two men had elected to take a closer look and slipped undetected through the perimeter fence. They headed for the cover of the hangars where, to their delight, they found a serviceable Thunderball fighter, with half full fuel tanks and three more APC's.

Black began to load up one of the APC's with stores and equipment from the hangar, while Jenson took a look at the other hangars and engineering blocks. He came back half an hour later with fifteen men and women. They'd been the only other survivors of the attack and were kept under a light guard in the blockhouse which he'd quickly dispatched. Together they had all loaded up the remaining APC's then Jenson had climbed into the Thunderball while Black and the freed aircrew climbed into the vehicles. When the coast was clear they fired up the machines. The Thunderball taxied out of the hangar and launched straight into the arctic night, while the APC's gunned their engines, broke through the perimeter fence and sped off into the darkness. They were gone before the troops around the Dome knew what was happening and not a shot was fired after them. The surprise raid raised the morale of everyone, the enemy may have been successful in the first attack, but they'd proved they were far from invincible. Since then, despite several half hearted patrols by the enemy troops in strange tanks and personnel carriers the survivors of 511squadron had managed to keep their new base hidden.

There was a tap on his shoulder and he turned to find Davies standing beside him. Her brow was furrowed in a frown. 'Hello Mary, what's up?' Jenson asked.

'You'd better come and look for yourself. We've received a message from the WDF retreat.'

'I thought we couldn't get through to Switzerland because of the jamming?' he queried.

'Not any more. This came through loud and clear. I'm afraid it's not good news. I think you'd better come and see it for yourself Paul.'

With that Davies turned and headed back to the communications room. Jenson followed. Inside he found Sandpiper and Black, together with a group of airmen, all gathered around a holo-monitor.

'Skipper,' Black called, 'Come over here and take a look at this.'

Jenson moved over to where they were all grouped talking in hushed tones.

'What's going on guys? What's the panic?' he asked.

'We've received a message from General Thompson at the WDF retreat in Switzerland,' the marine captain explained with a grim face. 'The message came by wide channel, which means that anybody with a receiver can pick it up. What's more, during the time of its transmission, all global jamming ceased. However, the codes given at the start of the message match the last known WDF codes. I'm afraid it looks like the broadcast was transmitted with the agreement of the bastards who are attacking us. I can't think of any other reason why the jamming should completely clear, and the broadcast is being repeated on a continuous loop. I think you'd better prepare yourself for the worst Paul.'

Jenson's heart sank. It didn't take much imagination to figure out what the gist of the message would be. Even though he'd been expecting it, now that the time had come he still found it very hard to grasp the concept of defeat. Black turned and switched on the monitor. On the screen appeared the image of General Thompson, with the retreat control room visible in the background. His face was worn and tired, and Jenson could see him visibly hold back his emotions. He'd once met the General on a training exercise in northern Canada and knew the man to be a hard-arsed son of a bitch who until now, never even recognised the meaning of the word defeat ... it simply wasn't part of his vocabulary. However, it looked like he would have to recognise its meaning now. Christ, Jenson thought to himself, the guy must be torn to shreds inside. It was as though Thompson represented the WDF itself. Up until ten days ago he was supremely confident, sure of the equipment and personnel that made up the WDF. Now he had that hunted and haunted look, as the very foundations of his existence were being destroyed before his eyes.

'To all WDF forces, land, sea and air, across the globe; this message is for you,' the General began. 'At 1100 hours GMT, today the 3rd of April 2045, President Ricard of the United Nations formally signed a ceasefire with the Dyason race. The ceasefire was signed at the Vatican in Rome, in the presence of all surviving world leaders. At 1200 hours GMT, all hostilities are to cease. WDF forces are to return to their home ports or bases. All weapons are to be handed over to Dyason units. WDF unit commanders are ordered to cease any action against the Imperial Dyason Forces.'

The General paused again, swallowing hard as a single tear welled in his eye and fell down his cheek. 'I would like to take this opportunity to say how proud I am of the resistance all you men and women have put up against the forces which invade our home,' he croaked. 'We have all lost friends and loved ones in this short but most brutal battle in the history of mankind. However, I must urge you all to comply with the terms of the ceasefire.'

'The Dyason race, who come from a star system similar to our own, control large asteroids poised in orbit, ready to impact on all our major cities. New York, Luxembourg, San Francisco, St Petersburg and many others centres of population across the globe have already been devastated by this means of attack. Casualties run into the millions. Unless we all abide by the ceasefire, the Dyason will destroy our remaining cities.' The General paused again, pulled his shoulders back and stared into the camera. 'I'm sorry everybody, but we've lost this battle. We must conserve our civilisation as best we can. Mankind will rise again. It is the view of the strategists that for so long as these Dyason hold the higher ground in orbit around the Earth they can take out our centres of population largely at will. They have already destroyed all our space defence systems, communications and navigation satellites. This message is being relayed around the globe by the Dyason themselves. Further, our scientists tell us that unless there is a halt to these asteroid strikes, the atmosphere will suffer irreparable damage and within a few short months cease to be able to support life. Already the dust and debris in the atmosphere will cause the whole planet to suffer from a type of nuclear winter where the sun's rays can't reach the surface. How long this global winter will go on for, nobody can be sure.

'For these reasons we have had to sue for peace. I ask that you all give yourself up to the nearest Dyason garrison who are waiting for your weapons to be surrendered. There will follow after this transmission the necessary demilitarisation codes and a complete list of the Imperial Dyason demands and conditions for surrender. Once again, I am sorry to do this to you all. There can be no doubt that you all fought with courage and tenacity against an overwhelmingly superior force. My thanks go out to you all.' Then Thompson looked straight into the camera and with a tear coursing down his check said. 'I'm proud of you mothers! In the annals of history people will always remember the WDF personnel as being the bravest troops that walked the planet. None of you deserve this, but we are talking about the salvation of what is left of mankind and life on our planet.'

'This is the end of the final orders to the World Defence Forces from your Commander in Chief, President Ricard of the United Nations. I'm General Thompson, senior commander of the WDF. Good luck and God save us all.'

The screen went blank. For a while the room was silent. Everybody was lost in their own thoughts. Davies broke in tears and sobbed quietly. Sandpiper put his arm around her, his own face a picture of gloom. Jenson collapsed into a chair, devastated.

It was too much for him to take in. He'd seen the alien Dome for himself, but the concept of the whole Earth being taken over by a race of human-like aliens was something he could barely manage to grasp. How could they be defeated? How could the WDF, a force that was made up of troops and equipment from just about every nation on Earth, capitulate? It just didn't seem possible!

Finally, after several minutes, Jenson asked Black, 'There's no doubt that that's the General is there? He hasn't been caught and forced to give the codes has he? This isn't some kind of sick hoax?'

'I don't think so,' Black answered 'News vids of Ricard signing the surrender at the Vatican have been broadcast on all the social media channels, which just happened to come back on the air.'

'I guess it's no real surprise,' Sandpiper offered. 'After all, what little information we have been able to gather on UHF and long wave, points to the WDF being pretty well licked everywhere. I mean, with them having the high ground, and being able to hurl rocks at anything that moves, makes organised resistance almost impossible. But this thing of an alien invasion seems unreal. Shit, we can't be defeated! This can't be the end of it. We've seen them, they look as human as you and I. We can't just give up! How can the bastards hand over the whole sodding planet like that!' Sandpiper's voice was catching in his throat, the grief and anger he felt clearly audible.

'I know how you feel,' Black said, 'but what the hell can we do? We're stuck here in the middle of nowhere, with the aliens sitting on our airfield less than a 150 klicks away. There's fewer than a hundred of us, with three battle-scarred planes and ten worn-out APC's. The politicians have thrown in the towel, leaving us poor bastards out on a limb. Aliens or not, they're out there with the fire-power and all we've got is a few peashooters!'

Jenson could see the situation was getting out of control, his friends were on the verge of despair. Unless he could find some straw of hope to cling on to they would soon all withdraw into a bottomless pit of despondency. But the truth was, what could they do? They all had families; his were in Vancouver. Hanson Sandpiper had parents and a sister in England, and Peter Black was engaged to a beautiful young woman from Paris. Who knew when they would see any of them again? That is if any of them were still alive. Jenson could feel the first tendrils of despair gripping his own heart, but he fought to keep a clear mind. Straightening his back he addressed the group.

'Listen to me!' he commanded, 'Yes you're right, the politicians have thrown in the towel, but that doesn't mean we're defeated! We've seen that these aliens or whatever they are, aren't invincible. We gave them a bloody nose only two nights ago. Or have you forgotten that!'

'But Skipper,' said Mary Davies, wiping her tears away with the corner of her jump-suit sleeve, 'What can we do here on our own, when the whole world has given in?'

'Has the whole world given in?' Jenson asked. From somewhere in the depths of his heart came a will, a desire not to give in. Sod it, he could understand why the UN leader signed the armistice, but surely he didn't believe that mankind would just sit back and accept mass slavery and genocide. There had to be some hope. He'd be damned if he was going to jack it all in. There may not be many of them now, but how many others felt as he did? It would take time, but if they could get in touch with others who felt the same, then they could resist, regardless of what the UN said or did!

'How many others are in a position like ourselves?' he said to the others, his despair turning to anger, 'others who survived the Dyason blitzkrieg. Now they're holed up somewhere, trying to figure out what to do. Do you think they'll give up? No they won't! Across the world there must be thousands like us. At first they'll lie low, then in time they'll resist. They'll be like a thorn in the side of the occupiers, stabbing them in the side, then slipping away. Then the day will come when everybody rises up to defeat them. People have always resisted tyranny, and democracy always wins out in the end!'

'We're in a good position here, this site is easy to defend, and once winter arrives it will be almost impossible for the Dyason to find us. We can carry out more raids, gather more equipment, and eventually destroy the already damaged Dome at the Ridge. Then, with more equipment, we can make raids on Canada and so on. These creatures have shown themselves not to have any value for life. They've already slaughtered millions and they'll do it again. Are we just going to give up and let mankind slip into slavery? Or are we going to join those other groups and resist, no matter what the personal costs?!'

The room lapsed into silence as each man and woman thought about what had been said. It was quite a speech and struck a cord in them all. They knew that Jenson had said this not just to raise their morale, he genuinely believed in what he was saying and if he believed they could fight on, well that was good enough for them. Eventually Sandpiper stood up and said, 'I would rather fight and die, than become a slave. I'm with you boss!'

'And me!' cried Mary Davies. Jenson could feel the atmosphere in the room change as defeat and despondency were replaced by anger and a desperate desire to carry on, to keep fighting no matter what the odds. They weren't fighting for any one nation or for a political cause. They wanted to fight on to keep the human race from the shackles of global slavery! All their anger and frustration finally had a focus. One by one voices were added to a chant that began as a whisper until all the caverns reverberated to the sound of a hundred voices all calling out the call sign of 511 squadron. 'Arctic Fox! Arctic Fox!'

'Well Paul!' Black said, clapping his friend on the shoulder, 'That was one hell of a speech! I'm behind you all the way, but I have to say I think you've just signed our death warrants!'

Jenson looked at Black with an expressionless face and said, 'You're probably right Peter, but what choice do we have? If we don't resist and show the rest of humanity that we haven't thrown in the towel - that there's still hope no matter how desperate things may be, who will? We can't expect anyone else to fight on our behalf, when we didn't have the guts to do it ourselves!'

'Oh fuck it!' Black replied his eyes welling up. The two men embraced, knowing their futures seemed almost impossibly bleak.

CHAPTER TWO

LONDON, ENGLAND
JANUARY 18TH 2047

The sky was dark and overcast, the clouds black and threatening. The air temperature hovered at around six degrees below zero. It was one o'clock in the afternoon, but on the ground it was almost completely dark. Very little light seeped through the cloud cover, but that was nothing new. Europe and the northern hemisphere had been in the grips of an eternal winter since the invasion.

The dust and rubble from the cities destroyed by the asteroid strikes had risen into the upper atmosphere, blocking out the sun's rays. Mankind's worst fears had become reality. The world was in the grip of the worst kind of nuclear winter. The only blessing, if such a word could be used in such horrific circumstances, was that the asteroid strikes caused no radiation fallout, as would have been the case in a true nuclear war. The few tactical nukes used in the first frantic days of the invasion by the United Nation's forces had been of the low yield kind, their effects long dissipated. Not that any of this was of any comfort to the poor remnants of mankind's once proud nations, who now fought against the cruel elements to feed themselves. Millions died from starvation and exhaustion under the most savage reign of terror known to any human being ... that of the Dyason Empire.

There were very few lights on in London. Gone were the days when the glow of streets lights, homes and offices could be seen from the fields of Surrey and Kent. Only a few weak lights grouped around the once proud and fashionable West End and Chelsea areas penetrated the gloom. The rest of London was dark and now largely nothing more than rubble. The scene was reminiscent of the bombing that had destroyed much of Berlin during the

Second World War with devastation on a huge scale. The towering office blocks of the City were now skeletons of concrete and metal, their steel bones twisted and torn rising accusingly towards the turbulent heavens. Roads were indistinguishable, hidden under layers of brick, glass and mortar. From Croydon to Southwark, Highgate to High Barnet, London had been razed to the ground. Buried in the rubble, in unmarked graves lay most of her population, now food for the ever growing number of rats that eked out a living in the ruins. Most of her population, but not all, were dead. Some, a pitiful few, still survived. They were the ones who'd managed to escape the genocide brought about by the systematic bombing of London after the uprising in August of the previous year. They scraped a living among the rubble, looking for packaged food from before the war, killings dogs and cats, sometimes even eating the flesh from the half-buried human bodies frozen in the permafrost since the Dyason bombing raids. It was surprising what once civilised people would do to survive.

Somehow life went on in the ghettos, but then there was very little choice. Nobody left the ghettos ... the walls and towers of the Dyason made sure of that. Then again, perhaps it would be more precise to say that only a very few left the ghettos. There were some who managed to climb the wall and enter the bright lights of West End. The West End was where the Dyason ran things, together with the collaborators. They lived in luxury in the apartments, houses and hotels of the pre-war rich.

Perhaps this needs further explanation ... you see, it would be incorrect to say that all of London had been reduced to rubble. There were parts that had remained relatively intact ... the parts that the Dyason wanted. The Strand, Covent Garden, Westminster, The Mall and Chelsea had been spared so they could become the playgrounds of the Dyason. Officers on leave spent their time in the once proud houses of the rich, using and abusing the women who once lived in them. For the ranks, there were the brothels just off Sloane Square and the Strand for amusement. In Covent Garden the Opera House was still open, and suitable productions ran in the many theatres in the area, although the audiences were made up entirely of the Dyason and their consorts, who in turn were mainly those Londoners who openly collaborated with the invaders. The Houses of Parliament and the offices remaining intact around Westminster had become the centre for hundreds of bureaucrats that ran the Dyason Empire in northern Europe.

When the resistance led a revolt in August of the previous year the Dyason had come up with a simple solution. They systematically destroyed everything immediately outside the West End to a perimeter marked by the circular route, the M25. They did a pretty good job, barely a building remained standing anywhere within this area. To contain the survivors and to ensure they could cause no trouble again, the Dyason used slave labour to build a wall, just like the Berlin wall of the previous century. This wall made of concrete six metres high and nearly as thick, was interspersed with watch towers sprouting heavy machine guns. Mines were buried at the base of the wall and searchlights scanned the no-man's land that spread out from the wall for a further 150 metres. The wall began at Holborn and spread around the West End, down Oxford Street, along to High Street Kensington and from there down through Fulham to the river. The river Thames created a natural barrier to the south of London, with all the bridges manned and secured. Patrol boats scoured the water, shooting without question anything that swam, man or beast.

Once the M25 had been mined, wired and equipped with gun towers and tanks, the Dyason believed the only way into their playground was along the heavily guarded M4, leading right into the heart of the West End. They believed that in time the survivors in the ghettos would simply all starve to death, saving them the effort of doing the job themselves. They were very nearly right. London had become the largest prison camp in the history of mankind. The only people who did manage to cross the wall were the 'thieves' who risked all to steal from the Dyason.

Sitting in the shell of a bombed house sat a youth, warming his hands before a fire. He was about seventeen years old, 1.95 metres tall, with a robust if undernourished body. His long dank hair was pulled away from his face and tied back with a small piece of rag. He sat with his back to the wall sheltering from the incessant rain under some old beams and crudely placed metal sheeting. In his hands he held a small revolver which he carefully wiped with a small oiled rag. His face was intent with concentration as he lovingly prepared the gun. His face lifted and he stared out into the twilight. He paused for a moment, as though sniffing the air, then quietly slipped out of view behind a half collapsed wall, the gun held at the ready.

A figure appeared from out of the gloom and moved towards the fire. It was dressed in rags that hid the shape of the body, if not the height, which was short. It stood for a moment as though unsure what to do next, then it threw its hood back and looked around the ruins, revealing a young girls face, dark and drawn.

'Moss? Moss? Moss where are you?' she called quietly, peering into the dancing shadows.

'Kay! What do you want?' came the reply from the darkness.

'Moss, me ma's ill Moss. We need medicines or she'll die. Do you have any? Tablets, pills, anything Moss?' the small girl pleaded.

'Why should I have any medicine Kay? If I did why should I give you any, what have you got to pay me with?' said Moss, still hidden behind the wall.

'You must help Moss! Everyone knows you have things hidden away, from over the wall. And all those things you hid after the bombings,' said the girl pleading, a look of near despair on her pale, wan face. 'Where are you? Please come out Moss, you're scaring me.'

Moss stood up and moved away from the wall towards the fire where the girl stood shivering, steam rising from her damp rags.

'Like I said Kay, even if I did have anything why should I give you some? Besides what's wrong with her?' he asked flippantly, as though the child's mother meant nothing to him.

'She's ill Moss. Coughing and spitting blood she is. Can't get up. Been like that for three days. Please help. She helped you when the soldiers shot you in the leg last summer.'

Moss crouched beside the fire and idly poked at it. He remembered the help the woman had given him. He'd fought in the insurrection, using an ancient shotgun against tanks and helicopter gunships. The child's mother had nursed him for days when a gunshot wound in his leg went septic. She'd kept him hidden throughout the Dyason reprisal raids. In truth he owed the woman his life, and he recognised the symptoms of the illness. They called it the "Cramps" in the ghettos. It was said to be caused by all the rats. It started as coughing and the shakes, and then became excruciating cramps in the stomach. If you got it in the ghettos you were usually dead within a week.

He looked at the drawn face of the little girl with genuine pity unable to maintain his pretence at indifference. 'I'm sorry Kay, I haven't got anything for the Cramps. I've only got a few aspirin hidden away.'

Suddenly the girl burst into tears. The dampness causing white smudges on her dirty cheeks. 'Oh Moss, you must have. She can't die she's all I've got, what'll I do on me own? What can I do? Look I'll pay you back I promise'. She took off her coat then raised her filthy skirt to show painfully skinny white legs and the mound of her undeveloped womanhood. This wasn't what Moss wanted. He gently took the girl's hand and lowered her skirt. Despite himself, Moss felt pity for the small wretched child. It was a feeling he tried hard to suppress. Since the invasion he had seen many deaths, including those of all his family. They'd been shot by a Dyason death squad in reprisal for a resistance attack on the West End early on in the occupation. He'd only managed to escape by disappearing into the sewers in all the confusion.

Now he survived by hustling, finding items nobody else could find; food, clothing, medicine and weapons. He was a "thief" and one of the best. He was also one of the very few who went over the wall regularly. Nobody knew how he did it and Moss wasn't telling. What everybody did know was that it was the items that the 'thieves' stole that kept the survivors alive in the ghettos. However, Moss knew his survival depended upon trusting nobody and never, ever, showing feelings. There had been too many deaths for that. Many by his own hand. Yet he couldn't help feeling sorry for Kay. For some reason he wasn't sure of, he felt the need to place his arm around the child and protect her. Instead he gruffly said. 'Stop crying kid, it's getting on me nerves. Have you eaten?'

The girl rubbed her eyes with her knuckles and sniffed, 'No, not since me ma went ill. I can't get anything.'

Moss walked over to a corner of the room and pulled some rubble away. Then he pulled up some rotten floor boards and stuck his arm into a cavity. He pulled out a metallic bag and threw it to the girl. She managed to catch it and eagerly opened the catches. Her eyes gleamed as she saw the contents. She pulled out a package and looked at it in wonder. 'Moss these are Dyason rations!' she exclaimed.

'Shut up kid. You want everybody to know!' he snapped.

Hurriedly the girl shoved the package back into the satchel, but not before grabbing a fistful of some sort of biscuit and shoving them into her mouth.

'Now come back tomorrow night kid. If your mum's still alive, I might be able to help.' he said.

The little girl nodded her head while munching hurriedly. She shoved the satchel under her rags and disappeared into the gloom.

'Oh well, I was going over the wall tonight anyway. I guess I'll just have to add to the shopping list. Damn it; I must be getting soft,' he said to himself, sitting down and picking up the revolver again.

Just as twilight gave way to complete darkness, Moss started to make his way through the ruins. His "home" patch was the area once known as Camberwell and Kennington, though since the bombing one area looked much the same as any other. Now he headed towards the burnt out ruins of Waterloo station.

He slipped from shadow to shadow, avoiding the lights of the small open fires of the other ghetto inhabitants. On his back he carried a small backpack, while on his feet he wore a pair of para boots, 'liberated' from a dead soldier during the uprising. The revolver was tucked inside his jacket and a blade was shoved into the top of his left boot.

All around him the inhabitants of the ghetto carried on the business of survival, unaware and uncaring of his presence. He passed derelict cars and lorries that had been turned into shelters, the occupants adding sheets of metal and rubble to form crude shacks. Peddlers moved about holding racks of dead rats, bartering with the occupants for useful items in return for the rancid rodents. Packs of wild dogs howled into the night, there was the occasional scream or weeping of a tormented soul, but nobody paid any attention, except to strip a dead body of its clothes and belongings. This was life in the ghetto.

In time, Moss reached the ruins of Waterloo station. The terminus was deserted now, the station concourse open to the elements. Before the war, trains had arrived here from all over Europe via the Channel Tunnel, but now there was nothing left except the twisted metal of the tracks and the burnt-out hulks of the trains themselves. Sometimes Moss came to the station to read the newspapers and journals still to be found in the ruins of the news kiosks. He would sit there for hours, sheltering from the wind and rain, staring at the glossy photographs, dreaming of the happy days before the war. He could still vividly remember the day when his father had come home early from work because the world was at war. On that day he lost his childhood and his innocence.

London had been spared the initial holocaust that befell Luxembourg, St Petersburg, Los Angeles and a dozen other cities across the world. Rather than see the capital destroyed by another asteroid strike, or gutted in house-to-house fighting, the British government had surrendered to the Dyason without a struggle once the United Nations had capitulated. For the first few weeks after the invasion life for Moss became a strange, phoney existence. His father still went to work at the local council offices and his mother continued to work on the wards of Greenwich hospital, but when they came home at night they spoke in hushed frightened tones about the appearance of Dyason troops; men who looked as human as anyone, except for their easily recognisable flaming red hair and tight-fitting black uniforms. They also spoke of colleagues who went to meetings and never returned. However, life for Moss went on in a strange parody of his pre-war existence. He still went to school each morning and had to do his homework, but gradually the effects of the invasion seeped into his suburban life. The shelves of the supermarkets rapidly emptied until it became impossible to buy even basic foodstuffs. Eventually, rationing was introduced, but even then the amount distributed meant that Moss constantly felt the pangs of hunger cramping his stomach.

London sat under a heavy layer of thick sooty cloud that left an acrid taste at the back of the throat and caused bouts of coughing. The climate changed rapidly and dramatically so that even in high summer temperatures rarely rose more than a few degrees above freezing and it rained ... God, did it rain! Freezing, pouring rain, that went on day after day without ever stopping for more than a few hours at a time.

One night Moss was awoken by flashing blue lights casting dancing shadows across his bedroom ceil,ing. He crawled out of bed to the window and peered between the drawn curtains to the street below. Outside number forty-three were parked two police vans and a Dyason personnel carrier. The police went to the front door and smashed it off its hinges with a sledge hammer. Half a dozen men disappeared inside then reappeared a few minutes later dragging the Jordan's from their beds. Mr Jordan was thrown into the street, his legs flailing uselessly behind him. Then they pulled out Mrs Jordan and the two kids. Moss knew the children, they were a couple of years below him at school, and their dad was a councillor or something. He watched in horror as a Dyason troop butted the shouting Mr Jordan with his rifle, who promptly collapsed into the gutter with blood pouring from a gaping head wound. Mrs Jordan screamed hysterically and tried to reach her husband, but was pulled away and bundled into a van together with the two crying children. The inert body of Mr Jordan was picked up and unceremoniously thrown into the back of the van after them. Then the whole lot drove away, lights still flashing.

Next morning Moss asked his parents why the Jordan's had been dragged away in the middle of the night. They sat at the breakfast table looking uncomfortable and said nothing. Later his father took him aside and made him swear never to mention the incident again. The Jordan kids never appeared at school after that, but then school only lasted for another few weeks anyway.

But today Moss hadn't come to Waterloo to read the magazines or reflect on the past; that would achieve nothing. Instead, he'd come to cross the river. On the other side of the river was the West End. Its grand buildings were lit up, cars moved up and down the Embankment and people ate at posh restaurants. Moss knew this because he'd been there. Around them, among the rubble of ghettos, people died of disease and starvation, while the

Dyason and human collaborators lived a luxurious lifestyle. Moss hated them all to his very soul.

He didn't intend to attempt to force his way across the still intact Waterloo bridge. That would be suicidal. No, he had a much better route ... underground. Beneath London, lay another city, a city of sewers, tube tunnels and conduits. Obviously the Dyason had blocked off all the known tunnels that entered the West End, but they were so numerous it was impossible to cover them all.

Since before Victorian times, tunnels had been dug under the Thames for a variety of reasons. Two were intended as extensions of the subway network into south London, circa late 1800's, but never used. Several were ancient Roman aqueducts and sewers. In fact many didn't even appear on any sort of map, because nobody knew they existed. It was one such tunnel that Moss had discovered and now used as his route in and out of the West End.

Carefully picking his way through the glass and rubble of the Channel Tunnel platform, Moss headed down the stairs of Waterloo Underground station. He squeezed through the iron grating covering the entrance, and into the ticket hall. He shone the beam of his torch towards the far wall and headed for it. Carefully, he picked his way over the skeletons lying on the floor, their clothes in tatters, the bones picked clean by rats. Early in the revolt the Dyason had fire-bombed the underground station causing panic amongst the civilians sheltering in the tunnels. Hundreds had fled for the exit to Waterloo station, only to be confronted by another fire-storm above ground. Most had perished in the ticket hall, crushed in the panic, or consumed by the fire.

The bombing and fire had loosened old bricks and mortar so that when Moss finally plucked up the courage to explore the Underground he'd found the hidden entrance. It was a large steel door which had once been bricked up, but was now exposed. Positioned at the rear of the hall, Moss guessed it was part of the original structure, built in Victorian times.

Removing the bricks he now used to camouflage its presence Moss put all his weight behind the handle and heaved the door open. It swung open quietly on hinges that he'd carefully greased. He stepped through, pulled the door closed behind him and stood at the top of a stair-well, which despite its age was still sound. Shining his torch onto the steps, Moss headed downward. There were 430 steps in all. He knew because he'd counted them before. Which meant it went a long way down, probably deeper than the tube line.

At the bottom of the stairs Moss faced another door. This one was made of heavy steel plates welded together with a large knurled wheel at its centre, that once turned to the left, released steel pins at the top, bottom and at the sides. There was a slight hiss of air as the seal was broken and the door swung inward. He stepped into a room, flicked a switch and a bare light bulb illuminated some sort of office. There was an ancient telephone switchboard, several Bakelite telephones, and a desk on which sat not a keyboard and monitor, but an original typewriter. The ink on the ribbon had long dried out but the keys still moved, leaving blank impressions on the yellowed ancient forms left in it. On the walls were maps of south east England, with tacks in such places as Biggin Hill, West Malling, The Medway and Ashford. The date on the maps was June 1940.

This was Moss's secret hideaway and route across the wall. After exploring more rooms similar to this one, Moss had come to the conclusion that he'd stumbled across a century old secret war office from the Second World War. The equipment and files looked much like the war-vids he used to watch as a kid. As far as he could make out the centre had been sealed and forgotten at the end of 1940 when the threat of invasion from the Germans had faded. Yet the original occupants had obviously thought they may need to come back, because the electricity was still connected, obviously to some source in the West End, though he dared not think what state the wiring was in. Now, after invasion from a different enemy, it had become the centre of Moss's own clandestine operations. Beyond the bunker was another tunnel. However, in contrast it was putrid, half filled with sewerage, full of rats, but still sound. This tunnel led under the river to another hidden entrance in Embankment Underground station.

Nobody else knew of the existence of the rooms, and Moss intended to keep it that way. He moved through the office and opened a side door into another room. He put on the light and surveyed his stores. Here was where he kept his hoard. There was food, medicine and clothing, nearly all of it acquired from the West End, from under the nose of the Dyason. Some of it though was retrieved from the war centre itself. The whole place had been remarkably well preserved, probably because of the airtight doors. So when he'd stumbled across the store of ancient weapons he'd been pleased to find them in good condition. Their covering of light oil and wax paper had been sufficient to keep any corrosion at bay.

Moss had chosen for himself a revolver, which he now kept with him at all times, tucked under his armpit in a holster he'd fashioned himself. He also kept at the ready an ancient Lee-Enfield rifle together with its .303 ammunition. It was an old bolt-action weapon that despite having a five-round magazine, needed to have its bolt manually pulled back to insert the cartridge and prime the firing pin. It was heavy, with a stock of solid wood and a recoil that bruised the shoulder. Yet, it was still a formidable and accurate weapon, with a slug that would fell an elephant. He'd practised his marksmanship out in the rubble of the ghettos and was now a crack shot with both weapons. He picked up the rifle and slung it over his shoulder then from a locker he picked out a box of bullets for the revolver and the Lee-Enfield. Then he left the room. Back in the main office he checked his kit once more, and when satisfied, headed for the tunnel. He opened a second airtight door, releasing the securing bolts he'd carefully greased before. Switching on the pencil beam of his LED torch he shone the light down the tunnel.

Several inches of rank, filthy water lay at the bottom of the tunnel which he would have to wade through, and numerous rats squealed and ran from the light. It was revolting, but if the rats were still there, then he could be fairly sure that the tunnel ahead lay undisturbed. He sealed the door behind him and with one last check of his equipment set off. It was time to enter the realm of the Dyason.

CHAPTER THREE

BUCKINGHAM PALACE, LONDON, ENGLAND
JANUARY 18TH 2047

Security Leader Gulag stood before the full-length mirror and adjusted his uniform. His all-black tunic and trousers had been carefully ironed by his batman, and his knee-length leather boots gleamed in a manner that only hours of careful polishing could achieve. Not that he'd ever polished them himself. He was thirty-one years of age, young to be in his high-ranking position. His eyes were narrow with an intense stare that some females found attractive, but most simply found chilling, in fact downright frightening. His closely cropped hair was jet black, unusual for a Dyason, while his high cheek bones led to a small thin mouth. He smiled at his reflection, it looked more like a snarl.

Tonight was an important night In his career and he was determined to make a good impression. This was the first visit to London by the head of the Earth occupation forces, Marshal Topaz, and he, Security Leader Gulag, was to escort the Marshal to the theatre. It had only been recently that the Marshal's headquarters had deemed London and Britain safe for a visit. Previously it was felt that the risk of terrorism by the resistance, or unrest among the proletariat, precluded any moral boosting tour. However, since Gulag had suppressed the local population, headquarters had reviewed the matter, and now the Marshal himself had arrived. In fact, it was Topaz himself who had ordered the visit, so that he could observe at close quarters the work of Gulag and his staff.

Gulag again stared at his reflection. His chest swelled with pride when he reflected on his position as Security Leader for Britain, and all he had achieved in the suppression of this barbaric race. He'd shown no mercy, just as a good Dyason officer should, and he'd got the necessary results. He placed his ceremonial helmet, which shone bright silver and was topped by the feathers of the Palagnee bird of prey, under his arm. Then he checked his appearance once more before stepping through the ornamental doors to the Marshal's suite.

He entered a large room with a high ceiling and marble floor. Along the walls were gilt-framed portraits of the kings and queens who had once ruled this country. The furniture was antique and ornamental; footmen stood along the walls wearing traditional costume. For a barbaric race, Buckingham Palace was surprisingly civilised. Beside a huge fireplace Marshal Topaz stood drinking cocktails, talking and laughing with his entourage of army officers. He was tall and thin, except for a protruding stomach that his uniform failed to hide, with a mass of red hair tied back in the traditional pigtail. His hands constantly brushed a long thin moustache that was attached to his face below a rather large angular nose. Deep red cheeks and a red nose were testament to the fact that Topaz enjoyed the pleasures of the flesh rather more than hard work and physical exercise.

Gulag snapped to attention and waited to be noticed.

'Ah Gulag,' said Topaz. 'Good man! Ready to move to the theatre are we? Excellent!'

'Yes Sir,' replied Gulag. 'If you would all kindly follow me, the cars are ready."

'Right, let's go then gentlemen, I'm looking forward to seeing what this pitiful country has to offer in the way of entertainment. And I don't mean men in stockings!' said Topaz jovially.

The entourage all laughed heartily at the feeble joke. Gulag cringed. Then they started to file out of the room. The Marshal beckoned to Gulag. 'Gulag, I would like to have a quiet word with you. Perhaps you would care to join me in my car," he said.

'Of course sir!' he replied, his heart beating faster, 'It would be an honour!' An honour indeed, he thought, the Marshal must want to praise him personally for his achievement in this foul country. Perhaps there was even another promotion in the offing! Before he took command of the occupying forces in Britain, production was down and the resistance was a constant thorn in the side of the imperial forces. Now, after months of hard work production was double its previous levels and the terrorists were at least contained, if not completely eradicated. Tonight, he would finally receive the recognition he so rightly deserved.

However, Gulag was too good an imperial officer to let his face betray his thoughts, so with a face set in stone he followed the Marshal to the waiting limousine. Before getting into the rear of the car with the Marshal, he looked around once more to check his men were in position at the front and rear of the entourage. There was always a small risk that the terrorists might take a pot shot at them and Gulag was determined there would be no hitch in the evening's proceedings. Satisfied all was as it should be, he got in and sat opposite Topaz on a small jump seat.

The car started and swept out of Buckingham Palace and down Pall Mall. Outside, standing in the pouring sleet and gloom, crowds waved and cheered in a desultory fashion, Gulag didn't even have to look to know they were cheering. He'd ordered all the privileged native workers to line the streets and cheer, or be deported to the ghettos. Of course, they all cheered.

For a few minutes the Marshal gazed thoughtfully out at the crowds, constantly playing at his moustache. Then he said quietly, 'Well Gulag, I'm very impressed. You seem to have the local population very well tamed. Even got rent-a-crowd out eh?'

Gulag coughed diplomatically. The crowds weren't really an attempt at showing the local populace as Dyason loving people; everyone knew that the Earth-born people hated all of them to their very core. It was simply a case of those here in the West End having chosen to bury their hate in return for food and shelter. It was either that or join the miserable wretches on the other side of the wall. No, the crowds here were more a subtle reminder to the Marshal of the control Gulag had over the population, and of course Topaz had got the message.

'Err, yes sir. I felt they should show you the necessary respect and gratitude,' he replied.

The Marshal chuckled, he wasn't fooled for an instant. 'Never mind Gulag, You've still done a good job. In fact your work here in this country has not gone unnoticed at headquarters. I've heard good things about you. However, I always like to hear things from the man's own mouth, as they say. So let's have your report; no white wash mind you...just the truth. How are things here in London and Britain?'

Gulag had to swallow hard with a dry throat before answering. He gave a small cough to give himself time to construct his thoughts. He would have to tread lightly here. Topaz would already have been carefully briefed on the state of the regions occupation, and would be probing him for an answer that matched his brief. It would be a mistake on his part to make a report that was too glossy, but by the same token there were definitely some matters that were best not raised at all.

He looked the Marshal in the eye and said, 'Well sir, matters are under control. The natives either work for us here in the West End or they are kept in the ghettos. Estimates now put the numbers of Earth-born in London at thirty percent of the pre-war number and falling. We are confident that we can rebuild and re-colonise the ghettos within eighteen months.'

'So I understand,' interrupted Topaz, 'but have you eradicated the resistance? So long as there is organised resistance, there is hope for the natives. To crush their spirit utterly there must be no hope.'

'The resistance has been a problem I admit,' continued Gulag, 'especially during the uprising of last year, but we feel we have the matter under control now. However, there is a problem in the rest of the country with food. We cannot keep up levels of production of our goods and weapons unless we can feed the human workers. With the constant cloud cover, very little food can be grown'.

'Our scientists estimate that the debris in the upper atmosphere will disperse within twelve to fourteen months. Anyway, it is of no consequence if some of the native humans perish. There are far too many of them anyway,' said Topaz dismissively. 'Surely you're not getting soft Gulag?

'No of course not sir', Gulag replied hurriedly 'My concern is only to achieve the production quotas.'

'Glad to hear it,' continued Topaz. 'Production must not fall. Our home world is calling out for the goods and materials. Freight cruisers are leaving every day and they must be filled, and there is the new fleet to consider. Do I make myself clear Gulag?'

He nodded his head in agreement. Topaz stared out of the window again. 'There is another problem,' he continued, 'One of a sensitive nature'.

'Yes Sir?' Gulag politely enquired.

'It has come to our notice that there are a number mental operants among the Earth's people. I believe you are partially operant yourself. Is that right?'

Gulag hesitated. He'd always repressed his so-called 'extra-sensory' powers. On Dyason such talents were very rare and generally regarded by the Imperial Forces as being skills supplied by the devil, rather than talents blessed by the Gods. So Gulag had always kept his abilities a closely guarded secret, despite using it on occasion to further his career. How the Marshal knew of this he didn't know.

With a flush rising to his checks he mumbled, 'Ahem, I have a marginal ability sir. Not that I've ever used it Sir'.

'Yes of course," replied Topaz with a knowing look. 'Whatever... We want those native operants. They pose a threat to our rule, but can be useful if turned'.

'So what can I do sir?' he asked guardedly.

'I want you to set up a special squad to search out all operants of whatever level in these islands. When you find them you are to pass them on to headquarters. Do not exterminate them! Is that clear?'

'It is sir, but may I be so bold as to ask why you want them alive? I have heard reports that in the past twenty Earth years or so, incidents of telepathic talent has risen dramatically amongst the planet's native population. I wasn't aware that that posed some sort of threat to out security. Surely if they are a threat it would be better simply to eradicate them?' Gulag asked.

'No, you may not ask! Suffice to say, that we have plans for them. Now, enough of this talk. Tell me about these native women to be displayed later tonight!' Topaz snapped in irritation.

And so Gulag started to describe the perverse strip show the Marshal was to see after the theatre performance, while part of his mind wondered why headquarters wanted the use of dangerous Earth operants.

Outside the Adelphi theatre the crowds stood in the freezing rain waiting for the convoy of cars. Their faces were a picture of abject misery. After toiling all day in offices, shops and restaurants, serving their Dyason masters, they now had to stand, soaked to the skin, ready to cheer an alien they hated to their core. Some of the weaker swayed, suffering from cold and hunger. Others were being propped up by their neighbours. Behind them all stood Dyason troops. Occasionally they prodded a body, the rain gleaming off their automatic rifles. They were the force behind rent-a-crowd.

However, not everybody felt the cold and rain. Two fugitive figures stood watching the whole scene intently. One was of average build the other was small and stocky. Beneath their overcoats were hidden small weapons; a blade, a one-shot pistol. Around them, others shifted nervously in the crowd seeming to sense the strangers were somehow different.

Neither figure looked at the other, but if you could tune in to their minds, you would hear a discussion.

'What sorry bunch. They look drowned rats. You bet cheer like visit by king. Bastards', drifted one thought across the strange ether in which mind patterns existed.

'What choice for them. Ghettos or here. They rather here in West. Not choice cheer either, Cheer or bullet in back,' thought the other.

'We should Marshal shoot ', from the first.

'No, Orders remember. Observe only. Resistance need report urgent', came the reply.

'Would like to shoot'.

'Silence, Observe. Car appears', the thought ended.

From around the comer the cavalcade appeared. On cue the crowd started to cheer and scream maniacally. The soldiers prodded more bodies to encourage them along. The vehicles pulled up outside the theatre and troops poured out of the leading cars to take position around the entrance. With keen eyes they watched the crowd, their automatics at the ready.

Gulag got out of the limousine, walked around to the nearside and opened the door for Marshal Topaz. The Marshal stood up straight and the cheering intensified. He turned and smiled at the people, gently waving his hands like a benevolent monarch. There was a crack, just audible above the noise of the crowd. A neat hole appeared in the forehead of Marshal Topaz. His smiled collapsed, his body folded and he fell to the ground in a heap. The crowds roared.

Moss crept across the rooftop keeping his body low, his movements slow and deliberate. He moved like an alley cat, poised and silent. Already he'd slipped into the kitchens of the Savoy Hotel on the Strand, and had stolen loaves of bread and fresh meat. He'd also broken in through the skylight of a Dyason pharmacy and acquired the drugs needed by Kay's mother. Now he was moving from rooftop to rooftop in search of other booty.

Moss had seen the crowds lining the streets below him and had originally been alarmed by the number of soldiers watching the crowds from the rooftops. But so far he'd managed to slip quietly past them. It wasn't that he was invisible it was simply that he had the knack of occupying the blind spot in their eyes. His mother had called it the 'gift'; in the ghettos he was simply a 'head', an operant.

He'd never had any proper training in using his powers. His mother had once talked of sending him to the 'mind' academy in Switzerland, established at the turn of the century when the number of definite, ESP gifted, people suddenly blossomed. But the war put an end to that. Now he used his talents to survive; making himself 'invisible' to others was his forte.

Nearing the edge of the flat roof of the office block, Moss lay on his stomach and crawled to the parapet. From this vantage point he could see directly below him a large crowd outside a theatre in Drury Lane. The collaborators standing in the rain looked miserable and cold. Moss felt no sympathy for them. They should come and live in the ghettos and find out what real misery was about.

On top of the building opposite Moss could see Dyason riflemen watching the crowd below through their liquid crystal field binoculars. They paid no heed to Moss. Curiosity overcame caution; Moss unclipped his backpack and rifle and made himself comfortable. With this many people and troops about, something important was about to happen and he wanted to know what it was.

He didn't have to wait for long. A long cavalcade of big limousines, gleaming in the rain, lit by the street lamps, turned off the Strand and into Drury lane. The leading car came to a halt and Dyason troops leapt from it to take up positions around a theatre entrance. They held their automatics at the ready, sweeping the crowds with their muzzles. The largest of the limos then stopped beside the theatre and two figures stepped out. Moss's heart suddenly began to beat furiously. He recognised one of the Dyason officers. Despite all the tin and ribbons he wore on his uniform, Moss would never forget that alien face. It was a face he hated more than anything else in the universe. It was the face of the man who ordered the murder of his parents and family.

Even from this distance he recognised the sharp nose, Mongoloid eyes and sickly pale skin. How he hated that arrogant pose, and those cold black eyes. Visions of that day in the ghettos when the death squads arrived flicked past Moss's eyes, like a rerun of an old movie. He could still hear the screams of his mother and sister as they were dragged from their house. He could still hear the pleading of his father, begging for their lives. He could still hear the gunfire. But more than anything else he could remember seeing the face of the officer who gave the order. From his hiding place he had seen it all. Now it was time for revenge.

Without thinking Moss unclipped his ancient rifle and pulled back the bolt, placing a round into the chamber. He shoved the stock tightly into his shoulder and carefully adjusted the rear sights. The target turned and faced the crowd. He breathed shallowly, evenly and as the barrel rose slightly, the target came into his sights. Gently, he squeezed the trigger. The .303 round sped faster than the speed of sound and hit Marshal Topaz squarely in the forehead. On the rooftop Moss cursed violently. He'd hit the wrong bloody bastard!

Gulag saw the body of Topaz collapse onto the wet pavement, but could not will his body to move for the first vital seconds as shock immobilised his body. Then his brain overcame his immobility and he grabbed at the Marshal's lapels. He pulled the upper torso off the ground, placed his palm over the chest and felt for a pulse from the older man's heart. But he knew from the sightless eyes it was pointless.

In one swift movement he let the corpse fall back onto the pavement and pulled his small automatic out of his ceremonial holster. As panic and anger forced adrenaline into his veins, he turned and faced the crowd, searching for the assassin. Already his guard were turning their weapons on the crowd and blocking exits. Other officers from the entourage started to fuss over the dead Marshals body bleating for a doctor.

Gulag was furious, he couldn't believe this had happened. A few seconds ago he was a proud security officer escorting his superior officer. Now the Marshal had a bullet in the head and his career was in ruins. How could the slime be so stupid? Did the resistance really think they could get away with a murder like this? My God, but they would pay for this atrocity. Yet, how could his own troops let somebody with a weapon get within range of the Marshal? He swore to himself that they too would pay.

Pandemonium broke out all around the theatre. The crowds had stopped cheering and seeing what had happened were now pushing and shoving to get as far away as possible from the scene of the assassination. The Dyason guards were pushing them back, clubbing and hacking at the crowds with the butts of their rifles. There were shouts and screams and in the distance a siren howled.

Gulag scanned the crowds. Where was he? Where was the assassin? He must find the bastard - he would be found! He must be close by, maybe one of the humans standing on the opposite side of the street. Out of the comer of his eye he saw some movement, a human was forcing his way through the panic-stricken crowds towards Covent Garden. Without thinking he raised his pistol and let off several rounds. Several humans fell to the ground, but his target slipped around the comer. Screams broke out and the panic intensified. Gulag cursed. He turned to one of his subordinates and shouted, 'Nobody leaves the area, shoot any native who tries to escape, do you hear me? Nobody leaves here. I want that assassin!'

The subaltern nodded and ran off shouting orders at the troops who were shooting above the crowds, in an attempt to control them. Gulag began to feel an unfamiliar pressure at the back of his head, it was as though he could almost feel somebody else there. He couldn't explain it but he was aware of another presence nearby. He looked up in the direction of where he thought the feeling was coming from and saw on a rooftop opposite a figure clutching a rifle. That was him! The assassin. He raised his pistol again and let fly. Chipped masonry flew around the figure, but he didn't fall. Gulag screamed at his guards gesticulating wildly at the building opposite.

'There on the rooftop. There, go on after him. There you idiots, fire at him!'

Several of the troops saw where he was pointing and started firing themselves. Gulag turned and grabbed a lieutenant by his tunic. 'You grab three men and follow me. I want that man!'

He turned and forced his way through the humans towards the building, shoving and clubbing his way through the panicking people. On the rooftop, the figure dropped the rifle which fell tumbling towards the ground. Then it turned and disappeared from sight. Gulag swore, shot a man blocking his way and finally reached the entrance to the office block.

The two strange figures standing in the crowd watched in shock as the Dyason leader fell to the ground and the Security Leader knelt beside the prone body.

'Jesus! Assassin kill Dyason! Who order this?' thought one to the other.

'Know not. Big shit trouble for this. But orders I know nothing.' came the reply. *'Inform group of this now '.*

With a frown of concentration on his forehead one of the men threw his thoughts into the ether. *'Group, priority one. Do you understand?'*

A third stream of thought entered the men's receptive minds. *'Group responding. What is position?*

'From outside theatre. Dyason arrive, but Topaz shot. Dead! Not by us. Other. What orders?' one of the men asked, relaying a mental replay of the assassination.

'Dead? Shot by who? We not order assassination! ' came the Urgent question into their minds.

'Know not answer. Not from us – shot from rooftop we think, definitely not one us!' replied the other man.

There was a pause while the anonymous third mind conferred vocally with others the pair could not see nor hear.

'Orders are, find assassin from rooftop. Orders for assassination come not from resistance. Repercussions serious. Threat to security; find killer. Keep control informed'. Then the third thought link faded from their minds.

'I head for back of building. You slow Dyason,' one linked to the other. *'Acknowledged!'*

The three-way conference took a mere second and the two figures returned their attention to the scene in front, just as the security chief rose, scanned the crowd and drew his weapon. One of the pair slipped through the now panic-stricken crowd to the edge of an office block. The other headed for the main entrance. They heard the shots fired at the crowds, one saw and reported the people around him who fell to the ground, blood pouring from gaping wounds. The other saw the Dyason forcing their way through the crowds towards the office block. Suddenly he found himself trapped by the surging people, with the Dyason security chief heading straight for him. He could only send out a brief thought of surprise when he was shot through the heart.

On the rooftop, Moss frantically tried to pull the bolt back on his rifle so he could place another round into the chamber. But the ancient rifle had chosen this moment to jam and no matter how hard he tried, it would not budge. From below he could hear the screams of the crowd and the shouts of the Dyason troops. He felt something hit his cheek and realised he was being shot at. Bullets were flying around him and chipped masonry had cut his face.

In a blind panic he dropped his rifle over the ledge and ducked below the parapet. He realised that in the excitement he'd let his cloaking thoughts wander so that he'd become visible to everybody. From below he could hear shouts to storm the office block he was on top of, and across the street the troops sitting on the opposite roof were aware of his existence and putting up a withering fire. Masonry, bits of brick and mortar flew around his prone body, but mercifully no shots found their mark. It was definitely time to get the hell out of there!

Pushing his knapsack in front of him he crawled flat on his stomach, below the level of the parapet. If he could make it to the other side of the roof, he could make his getaway across the rooftops, across Covent Garden and down to the Embankment. Bullets were still flying around the parapet, but by keeping flat he could keep out of sight. Slowly, he crept round until he was protected by the air conditioning ducts. Then he stood and ran for the far ledge. Just as he reached the edge, a maintenance door beside the air conditioning units sprang open, and out dashed a Dyason brandishing a pistol, followed closely by three troops. It was the bastard he'd been trying to kill! The officer shouted at

Moss, in English, then raised his weapon and pointed at him. Moss wasn't about to hang around to find out what was going to happen next and without taking a second glance, he clutched his knapsack to his chest and leapt off the edge of the office block.

Gulag forced open the rooftop door and sprang onto the roof itself. He saw the assassin, a thin wretched native boy, standing on the edge of the far parapet. He shouted, 'Stop or I fire! Stand where you are boy!' and raised his pistol. Behind him the troops who'd followed him up the stairs raised their automatics, but before any of them could react, the native leapt off the building. Gulag raced to the edge and peered over. Below him was a four storey drop to the ground with no sign of the wretch. He stood stock still for several minutes combing the dark alley below with his eyes, but saw nothing. *Bugger*, he wanted the little creep alive! Now it looked as though he had fallen to his death. Too bloody quick! He could see nothing in the rain and gloom. By the gods he was in the shit now! He turned to the guard officer who had followed him.

'Search the alley. I want his body, and the weapon he used. Find them *now* and take some of the people who were in the crowds and execute them. Some of the shits must have been involved!'

'Sir, Yes Sir!' snapped the Dyason guard, 'How many would the Security Leader like us to execute?

'God, I don't know man!' snapped Gulag. 'As many as your ammunition will allow. Several hundred at least!' Then with a dismissive wave he stomped to the stairwell and swore revenge against the resistance. The swine would suffer dearly for this evening's treachery. He would not be made a fool of! He stopped at the top of the stairwell and paused. At the back of his mind he felt a strange, yet familiar sensation.

CHAPTER FOUR

Somehow Moss had leapt the twenty metre gap across the alleyway and landed relatively softly on a fire escape landing. It had been a jump made of desperation. In normal circumstances there would be no way he could reach such a distance. Yet somehow his body had reacted to his panic-stricken surge of adrenaline and he'd landed with only a slight twist to his left ankle. He sat there for ages, carefully using his mind to cloak his position until the searching troops had moved on. When they found the body of the other poor wretch behind the skips, Moss couldn't believe his luck. If he'd believed in God or providence he would have thanked Him, as it was he figured he was just plain bloody lucky. The Dyason would be thrown off the scent, but not for long. The dead body looked about his age and build; it must have been some other poor bastard who had run the gauntlet to get to the West End, but died of cold and hunger despite having got there. There was no doubt that the Dyason would make a thorough examination of the corpse, and when they did, they would realise they'd got the wrong body and all hell would break loose. However, until then, the pouring rain and enveloping gloom had for once also been his ally and he managed to hide himself without too much difficulty.

When the troops had finished searching the alley below him and he'd finally plucked up the courage to move, he climbed up the fire escape and onto the rooftops again. As he moved from roof to roof, he heard and saw the screams of pain and fear as troops rounded up groups of people and indiscriminately fired on them. Bodies fell to the ground in piles, the streets became awash with blood that stained the wet tarmac. Men, women, children, it made no matter, the Dyason murdered them all in reprisal, like automated killing machines. When no one was left standing, they moved through the mounds of bodies firing single shots at anything that groaned or still moved. Moss saw all this from his vantage point on the rooftops, but the horror of the atrocity taking place failed to register in his mind. He'd seen too much death in the ghettos to feel for these collaborators. It wasn't that he was unaware of the consequences of his actions, it was simply that he was incapable feeling compassion or guilt. Life in the ghetto had been reduced to individual survival for the likes of Moss, and the death of others no longer struck such a strong chord.

With his mind cloaking his movements as before, he avoided the carnage and Dyason troops until he reached the derelict Charing Cross station. Then he climbed down to ground level again and into Embankment Underground station. Unseen and some distance behind him, from the shadows of a small dark doorway, a small man stood and watched him.

The group entered the Underground chamber and immediately spread out, searching each room one by one. They opened the cupboards and removed the rations, they took down the ancient weapons and ammunition, and they carefully examined the antiquated maps and telephone systems. Once they had made a complete sweep of the bunker they reported back to a tall-well built man wearing combat fatigues. His face was rugged and weather beaten, possibly even handsome. Despite his stern military demeanour, his eyes betrayed humanity rare in such appalling times. He was the type of person who men immediately respected. His troops would follow him to hell and back and often did.

'The area is secured Squadron Leader. We found some old weapons, ammunition and a whole hoard of food clothing and medicine. Most of it Dyason, No booby traps though,' said another wearing combat fatigues. Jenson nodded in acknowledgement. 'Quite a hideaway the kid has here. What is it? An old World War Two bunker?' he asked.

'Looks like it sir. Though my history isn't very good.'

'Never mind sergeant, just make sure the welcoming committee is ready. This kid is a slippery brat, he made short measure of the Dyason troops. Let's make sure he doesn't slip through our fingers as well. I take it Jennings is still tracing his movements?' he said.

'Yes sir. He's still in mind link with Anderson there,' said the sergeant pointing to a thin man in fatigues.

'Okay, let's get on with it then.'

Moss walked along the old tunnel, his torch giving out a weak beam of light for him to follow. His heart was still racing a bit; the recent events had shaken him a lot. In retrospect, he realised just how stupid he'd been. He'd nearly got himself killed trying to take out that murderer in such an open place. All he'd managed to achieve was to shoot another Dyason officer and make it impossible for him to go back into the West. They would have his description now. Once they figured out they'd got the wrong corpse, they would pull out all the stops to find him. It didn't take a psychic to figure out that he'd shot some important bastard. In fact he would have to escape from the ghettos as well. You could bet that they'd be sending death squads into the ghettos for reprisals, and you could also bet that somebody would squeal on him. Yes, he would have to get out. It would be sure death to stay. The only question was how?

Still deep in thought Moss finally reached the entrance to the bunker. He heaved open the door and walked through. He flicked on the light and a dozen automatics were raised and pointed straight at his head.

'Surprise, surprise kid," someone called.

Jenson looked the kid over. He reckoned he was about seventeen years old. Thin, like all ghetto kids, with long greasy hair tied back with a piece of rag. His clothes were a mix of old WDF kit, Dyason boots and civilian jumpers, finished off by a black leather jacket. It was the eyes that Jenson noticed the most. They were a deep, deep blue, sunk into a lean face like spotlights. The kid stood there with a look of shock on his face, not fear Jenson noted, just surprise.

'Close your mouth kid, it's unhygienic,' said Jenson.

Moss stopped gaping, but stood immobilised with surprise. Nobody knew of his hideaway, how had they found him? A thousand thoughts went through his mind at the speed of light; escape, who had followed him, who were these people? They obviously weren't Dyason. A thousand questions, but only one answer - the resistance had found him!

'Sarge get the kid a chair and secure the bunker. Jennings and Anderson report to Group,' Jenson ordered. The other men left the room leaving just Jenson, Moss and a guard who stood quietly in one comer.

'I've been wanting to have a chat with you for quite a while kid', began Jenson.

'What's the resistance doing in my shelter? What have you done with my things? Let me go!' Moss started yelling.

'Heh, heh...simmer down kid,' said Jenson in a calm voice. 'You're in no position to demand anything. Especially after tonight's doings.'

Moss suddenly went quiet. It came to him in an instant that they knew of what had happened outside the theatre and this was why they were here. Yet they were the resistance, surely they should be pleased at what he had done?

'How do you know?' he asked.

'Come on kid. You don't think you're the only operant that slips into the West do you? We had men watching the whole thing, one of whom is now dead thanks to you. You've really stirred up a hornets nest. Do you know that?' Jenson demanded anger showing on his face.

'So I shot a stupid officer. So what, they're the enemy aren't they? Who cares? Why aren't you killing more of them? You're supposed to be the resistance aren't you? Or are you all just collaborators? And how did you find me here?' Moss shouted back angrily, but still cautious of this resistance man and his fighters. Something in his manner told him he was in no immediate danger, but he had a look that warned him to tread carefully. There was fairness and honesty in his eyes, but also a hard streak that he recognised. When it came to the crunch, this man was a killer.

'That wasn't just any officer, you little turd!' Jenson shouted back in his loudest barrack square voice. He was getting angry, despite his promise to himself to remain calm. 'That was Marshal Topaz, Chief of Staff to the Dyason occupation forces! He was here on a visit, and now thanks to you, the whole of the Dyason security services are going to descend on Britain on a rampage of genocide as reprisals. Death squads are already roaming the ghettos killing at random, and Covent Garden is filled with the corpses of innocent people, murdered in revenge for your thoughtless action. As to your last question, we've known about your little hoard for a long time. It's simply been in our interests to allow your little forages into the West. But not any more kid. You're in deep shit!'

'Oh,' whispered Moss. He felt as if the wind had been taken from his sails. If what he said was true, then he really was in it up to his neck. They'd not leave a stone unturned until they found him, and then he could expect a long and very painful death. The real bugger of it was he hadn't even been aiming for him, it was only because that other bastard had moved at the last second that Topaz had been hit.

'"Oh", is that all you've got to say? "Oh"!' asked Jenson. 'Come on, kid you can do better than that. What the hell possessed you? You're not stupid, you know the rules. Why'd you do it?'

For a minute Moss said nothing. He sat staring into space lost in thought. Then he turned to Jenson and said, 'He killed my parents!'

'Who?' demanded Jenson 'Topaz? He's responsible for a lot of deaths, but we don't all go out and assassinate him!'

'No, not him,' said Moss 'The other one standing next to him. I was aiming to kill the other one. He was there when they killed my parents.'

'What, Gulag? Jenson asked in surprise.

'I don't know, whatever his name was.'

Suddenly it all became clear in Jenson's mind. God, the irony of it all! The kid hadn't been aiming for Topaz at all, but for Gulag, head of the Dyason death squads. Gulag must have killed the kid's parents in one of his death sprees in the ghettos. So, Moss had tried to shoot Gulag and missed, killing the Dyason leader instead, with dire consequences. God, how bloody ironic! Now thousands more innocent people would die in an orgy of reprisal killings.

The anger drained out of Jenson. The truth was he couldn't really blame the kid. He would probably have tried to do the same. An infinite sadness and weariness overcame him. The kid was simply a product of the horror and madness that had descended upon the world. Jenson turned away from Moss and shouted for the sergeant, but before he could open his mouth there was an explosion and the room filled with smoke, so thick he couldn't see his hand in front of him.

'Sarge, sarge! Quick get the kid' he bellowed coughing and spluttering.

Jenson lurched towards where the kid had been standing a moment ago, but the smoke was so thick he couldn't see a thing. Choking unable to breathe he reluctantly moved away and, grabbing the guard, got out of the room. Some minutes later, when the smoke finally began to dissipate they searched the room. There was no sign of the kid. He'd somehow found another exit and slipped away again. Jenson cursed.

CHAPTER FIVE

GULAG

Gulag paced up and down his office in Buckingham Palace, his face a picture of dark fury. In front of his desk three junior officers stood rigidly to attention, eyes front, faces expressionless.

'What do you mean the wrong body! I personally saw him jump from the top of that office block. There is no way that he could have survived such a fall and I saw them drag a body from behind some rubbish skips. Now you're telling me that it was the body of some other little bastard?' He shouted in fury.

'No.., I mean, yes Security Leader!' The centre and most senior officer snapped in confusion. 'The pathologist tells us that the body had been lying there for several weeks and was in a certain state of decomposition. We found the assassin's rifle and spent cartridges. However, the body had no trace of gunpowder, supporting the pathologists report.

I'm sorry sir, but there can be no doubt, it was not the corpse of the assassin. The area was searched most thoroughly and then completely sealed. Nobody got in or out of the Covent Garden area without our knowledge, I can assure you. The assassin must have survived the fall and managed to mingle with the crowds at street level. The chances are his corpse is among the bodies of those killed in the reprisals. Either that, or he is amongst the group brought in for questioning.'

'So you're telling me that this terrorist may or may not be amongst the dead, but then again he may be one of those in interrogation? Well that's just bloody great isn't it! Surely your complete incompetence would indicate that he got clean away, and even now is laughing at us from some squalid bolt hole in the ghettos? Maybe I should have you all executed now for dereliction of duty, and save us all the effort of a court martial?' Gulag spat at the unfortunate officer, his face so close he could feel Gulag's rancid breath.

'Sir, with respect, we have done everything that can be done. We are systematically searching all the buildings in the sealed area. All surviving humans have been detained for questioning and we are carefully searching through the bodies of those terminated. It is only a matter of time before we find him, if he is still alive, or we find his body. I'm confident that he hasn't escaped our net and slipped back into the ghettos,' a second officer said, his voice quavering from tension, eyes looking straight ahead, fixed on some far point of the room.

Menacingly, Gulag marched up to the officer until once again his face was only centimetres in front of his. He knew the assassin had escaped, he felt it, that feeling in the back of his mind had been there ever since. He was sure now that somehow the strange sensation was linked to the human assassin. Only someone with extraordinary abilities could have got away, of that he was sure. The thought of it made his blood boil.

When he spoke it was with a quiet, deliberate and threatening voice. 'You may be confident, but I am not. All I have to say is that you had better pray that he is found! Because if he is not, I'm going to remove your sex organs with a blunt knife and throw you into a cell to rot for the remainder of your miserable lives on this miserable planet! An execution would be too good for you... You have all let me down! I trusted you to carry out your orders. You have failed. Now I am answerable for the murder of our Commander in Chief. And if I go down because of it, the three of you will go with me. Do I make myself clear?'

'Yes Security Leader!' the officers cried in unison.

'Very well! Now I want every surviving human in the vicinity of the theatre to talk. I admit that perhaps we were a little hasty in our reprisals and should have searched the crowds more carefully before their termination, but it's too late for that now. Interrogate the survivors, and I want them to *talk*, not give out a load of bollocks in some trumped-up confession. If you think they're lying, add some volts to their testicles or tits, or whatever, but make sure they *talk*. I want to know where the resistance is now, *who* helped them into the West, and *who* organised the murder; and I want to know by the morning. Finally, I want squads moved into the ghettos. Get more of the wretched humans and find out who's helping the resistance scum. If you kill a few of them along the way even better, I want reprisals and I want a body count! Now get your ugly faces out of my sight before I'm physically sick!'

The three officers snapped to attention again, bowed in salute and marched out of the office, relief at leaving the vicinity of their commander written all over their faces. As they walked out, Gulag's adjutant tentatively knocked on the door.

'Yes adj. what is it?' Gulag shouted, his anger still broiling.

The adjutant, a small rather timid Dyason officer who was clearly terrified of his superior, placed one foot inside the room, and one foot in the corridor, ready to flee in an instant. It was something he'd done a few times before, so he was well practised by now.

'There's a message from Dyason command sir. Ready for viewing in the communications room sir,' he blurted.

Gulag swore. He'd been expecting this, but that didn't make it any easier. Command would throw the book at him for this evening's events which would surely spell the end of his career. If he were lucky, he would be sent to command some hell hole on the far side of the planet, but it was more likely that he would be shipped back to Dyason for a court martial and public execution. His mind told him to ignore the comm link and flee, but years of military training overcame that urge. Instead he simply said, 'Oh by the gods, I'm in the merde now! All right adj. I'm on my way.'

He nervously adjusted his uniform and followed the small Dyason down the corridors of Buckingham Palace to the communications room. One side of the room was filled by large cabinets of equipment bristling with large dials, meters and switch relays. On the opposite side of the room were a small holographic viewer and a small digital telecommunications unit. Gulag moved to the holographic viewer. The enormous cabinet cases of wires and valves were the Dyason state of art technology, the small micro-circuitry equipment was made here on Earth. He hated to admit it, but the human equipment was far superior to their own.

The adjutant ushered the technicians from the room and left Gulag alone to receive the message. He hit the receive button on the holo. The image flickered into life and the recently, very recently, promoted Marshal Mettar stood before him. Gulag bowed in salute.

'Ah Gulag, about time too," said the image of the new Marshal, a sneer of contempt fixed on his aristocratic Dyason features. 'You've made rather a mess of things I hear!'

Gulag coughed nervously and tugged at his uniform again. 'We are confident of capturing the murderer within the next twelve hours sir!' he began in his defence, but was cut off before he could say more.

'A lot of good that will do Gulag! The Marshal is already dead!' Mettar snapped.

'Err, yes sir. However, I am sure we can destroy the resistance cell responsible. Reprisals are already underway!' Gulag desperately went on, envisioning a very rapid end to his career, and possibly even his life. Failure in the Dyason imperial Corp was usually dealt with by rapid removal of the offender's head.

'Gulag, do shut up you pathetic wretch!' the new Marshal snapped again. 'Your excuses are tiresome. There are matters here that are far more important than your tiny mind can perceive. The death of a few pathetic humans, already on their way out of life, is hardly going to bring Topaz magically from the grave is it?' Sarcasm dripped off his tongue. Gulag stiffened at the insult, but kept quiet.

'Now then,' Mettar continued, 'operants here at Group have been observing London, and feel there is a strong disturbance in what they call the "mind dimension". God knows why, but orders from our home world are that we must learn as much as possible about these human mutants. There is at least one, maybe more operant humans within the London ghettos. He, she or they, are to be found at all costs and shipped here to Group. That was the purpose of Topaz's visit to your miserable province. Unfortunately, it appears that the operant, singular or plural, found him first. Now I know that you hate admitting to being a freak yourself Gulag, but I want you to use your abominable talents to find the source of this so-called "disturbance". However, you are to curb your blood-letting instincts and when you find the wretch, deliver him alive and intact to us here at headquarters. Those are your new orders. Topaz is gone, thankfully, I'm glad to say. Deliver the human bastard to us in one piece and no blame will be placed on you for recent events. Fail in this and I can assure you Gulag, that your demise will be long and extremely painful!'

Gulag hid his surprise. For some reason the Dyason command had decided to gather together the human mutant telepaths. Traditionally, the Dyason had viewed any signs of ESP or the like, as possession by the devil and treated it as such. Yet, now he was being actively encouraged to use his own abilities—which he had suppressed for so long—so that he could find the location of just one human mutant. Until that evening, he thought his talents were a closely guarded secret. Now it seemed that everybody knew of them. Something definitely untoward was going on. In fact more than just untoward, it was incredible, The Dyason high command was renowned for its unforgiving nature, defeats were attributed directly to a unit's commanding officer rather than any fault with the higher command structure. Many of his associates (not friends

MINDS OF THE EMPIRE

- he didn't have any) had quietly and sometimes not so quietly, been removed from their units after a setback.

The murder of Topaz could be said to be more than just a minor setback, it was a bloody disaster! By all rights he should be dragged off for an immediate court martial, but Mettar shrugged it off as though it were of no consequence. Admittedly, the demise of Topaz had made him the overall commander of the occupation forces, but even so, Mettar made no bones about disliking Gulag intensely. Yet, he was to be given another chance! He had heard Mettar right, if he found the human his record would be cleared... He must find the little bastard, it was either that or a summary trial and death!

'May I be so bold as to ask why these operants are so vital my Lord?' Gulag chanced, probing for more information.

'You may, but the only answer you'll get is that they are essential to the future of the Dyason Empire,' the new Marshal answered abruptly his face contorted into an arrogant sneer. 'That's all you need to know Gulag. You're being given another chance. We recognise that you didn't know the nature of what you faced. Topaz should have been more careful. However, I shall make it perfectly clear that I do not like you or your barbaric methods. Make another mistake and the consequences will be dire, nothing would make me happier than to see your neck swing from a rope!'

'Yes sir!' Gulag responded automatically, stiffening to attention and staring at a point on the wall beyond the holographic image, 'and may I congratulate you on your promotion my Lord!'

'Don't be such a creep Gulag,' said Mettar. The image faded and died.

Gulag stood and thought for a moment. Obviously there was more to Topaz's visit than he'd realised. He should have placed more importance on what he was told in the limousine. Instinct told him that events were moving rapidly, and worryingly, beyond his control. Mettar really did loathe him, so the order for him to be given another chance must have come from somewhere else. Which was an interesting thought, because with flights to Dyason taking over a month each way, and radio communication being impossible, who was more senior than the Marshal of the Imperial occupation forces? Whatever else though, he had a chance to redeem himself, and he must seize the initiative. He would find the human terrorist dead or alive, and he would look carefully into the use of human operants and his own talents. To someone somewhere, these matters were of the utmost importance and it was in his interest to find out why.

He strode out of the communications room and bellowed, 'Adjutant get over here. New orders!'

The adjutant scurried towards him and at the back of Gulag's head, his mind tingled.

The little girl tossed and turned fitfully, unable to sleep properly as she listened to the sound of her mother coughing and wheezing. She lay next to her thin body trying to keep her mother warm with her own, hugging the threadbare blanket around them. For much of the day she'd been doubled over with agonising stomach cramps and vomiting and now she'd slipped into a coma from which the little girl couldn't wake her. The little girl knew it was only a question of time. By the morning she feared her mother would be dead, and she would be left to live or die in the ghettos alone. Outside the damp cellar the rain fell heavily on the rubble.

At times the little girl couldn't be sure if she was awake, or in that twilight area between sleep and consciousness. Images of a youth appearing in the doorway to the hovel entered her mind. He stood there water pouring off his tattered jacket and jeans, pausing as if to sniff the air. Then he deposited a package enclosed in a satchel beside her. He laid a hand against her brow, bent over her mother, then turned and slipped into the black of night. She tried to wake up, to get up and see if this dream had any substance, but her eyes were too heavy, and she only caught fleeting glimpses of the figure looking back one last time before disappearing into the gloom. Later she fell into a deep sleep, deeper than at any time since the war.

As the grey tendrils of dawn moved over the ruins of London, Kay awoke to find her mother sleeping peacefully, the fever diminished. In a satchel beside her, Kay found food and medicine, sufficient for several weeks. Her dreams had been for real, but her saviour had come and gone without her thanking him. When later in the morning she searched in the usual places for Moss, he was nowhere to be found.

Slipping from shadow to shadow Moss moved through the ruins of London. He'd been on the move since his escape from the resistance. He dare not stop, with both the Dyason and the resistance after him he knew he was in deep trouble. He had to get out of London. Sure, the ghettos covered a huge area and he could hide out for some time without ever being seen, but eventually he would have to emerge to scavenge for food and supplies. By that time every sneak and collaborator would have his identity tattooed on their foreheads, just waiting for him to reappear. Then he would find himself pursued again, not just by the Dyason bastards, but by the resistance as well. No, there was nothing for it, he would have to get out of London altogether. In fact, he would have to go to a place where he could be sure of his safety. He'd heard the rumours that the far north was still free and in British hands, perhaps that was where he should head for? Moss reckoned he had a couple of hours lead on the resistance. It would take them time to find the hidden doorway he'd used to escape the bunker rooms, and then they would have to discover which way he was heading. That was unless they were already tracking him in the same way they did when he was fleeing the West End.

Moss knew there were other operants in the world beside himself, but he'd never met any before. Certainly he'd never considered that he could be tracked by his own thought emissions, like a radio tracking beacon. Now he would have to be careful not to use his powers unless absolutely necessary, and then try to shield them, He had the idea of how to do that, he just needed to refine the method a bit. You sort of directed your thoughts at the person you wanted to reach, rather than broadcast in general, like a popular music station. Whatever, he would need to be very careful in future.

Moss was heading southwest. His first inclination had been to head for the old M4 and try to stow-away on a Dyason lorry heading out of the West End. This was the main supply route that cut through the ghettos. But he soon ditched that idea, many had tried and failed. It was too well guarded, with regular check points, mines, floodlights, gun posts and vehicle searches. The Dyason, and probably the resistance, would be expecting him to head that way which would make matters worse. So instead he was heading for what was once the old A3, the route that before the war was the main southwest exit from London, which went all the way to Portsmouth and the South coast. At first his progress was slow, as he headed from Waterloo through Vauxhall, Battersea and towards Wandsworth. There were now hordes of Dyason patrols that had entered the ghettos, their armoured cars ploughing through the rubble and shanty towns of the ghetto dwellers. Several times he had seen groups of wretched men and women lined up and summarily shot, he guessed as some kind of reprisal. God, but if only he'd not hit the wrong bastard! Perhaps the resistance bloke had a point, the consequences of his impulsive actions did indeed mean death for numerous others.

But then again, death was something Moss had long come to terms with. The ghetto was one huge death camp, where men and women killed each other like savages for scraps of food, and gangs of children roamed around looking for easy prey, the sick and dying. When they found a suitable victim they would murder them and take whatever meagre food and possessions they had. This winter was particularly bad, and the gangs had taken to not just killing their victims, but eating them as well, and so taking the final step into barbarism. It was hard to feel concerned about Dyason death squads when the ghettos of London were already filled by the dead and dying. Survival was all that mattered, and survival now meant escape.

By keeping to the shadows and being able to "feel" the presence of others, Moss was able to move without being detected, He could feel the presence of the Dyason patrols before he saw them, and merged into the rubble whenever one came anywhere near him. In the same way he avoided the groups of wretches huddling around small fires sheltering from the howling wind and rain. That was until he stumbled through the deserted factory. By the early hours of morning Moss was completely exhausted, and soaked to the skin. He knew instinctively he needed to find some shelter from the raw elements before his body temperature plummeted too low, and lethal hypothermia set in. So he entered the burnt-out shell of a small industrial unit situated just before the start of the A3 on the edge of what was once Wandsworth High Street. The interior of the factory had been gutted, anything useful having long ago been taken by the ghetto survivors. However, parts of the roof remained intact offering at least some shelter. Positioning himself in one corner, out of the wind and rain, Moss gathered some small scraps of timber and using one of his precious matches and tinder, lit a small fire, which he hoped would be out of view to anybody outside the ruins. Eagerly, he warmed his numbed hands over the fire and rubbed himself vigorously, attempting to get some warmth back into his body. Then he sat there chewing on some of the Dyason food he'd stolen earlier.

After a while his eyes became heavy and inevitably he ended up falling asleep. He didn't know how long he'd been asleep for, it couldn't have been more than a few minutes at most. Indeed, he didn't know why he awoke when he did, maybe part of him never slept, that part that had ensured his survival in all his months in the ghetto. Whatever it was, he came to just as the sledge hammer was being raised over his head. In an instant Moss was wide awake and rolled clear as the hammer impacted the concrete where only a moment ago he'd been sleeping. He leapt to his feet and faced his attacker, pulling the long blade of his bowie knife out of the top of his boot in one fluid movement. The assailant was a small boy, no more than ten or eleven, dressed in filthy rags, his face contorted with rage and given an evil look by the dancing flames of the fire. The boy was struggling to raise the hammer to strike at Moss again, but before he could raise it even a few millimetres off the ground, Moss leapt into a counterattack. With a leaping bound he leapt across the fire and landed a thrust kick to the child's head. The boy reeled back from the blow and slumped against the wall unconscious. Moss nimbly landed on his feet and immediately turned to face the darkness beyond the fire.

From out of the darkness came catcalls and animal-like growls. Moss knew that the rest of the pack of kids lay out there ready to beat him to a pulp. How many he couldn't be sure, but more than the number of rounds he had in his ancient Webley revolver, which he pulled out of the other boot top. Standing in the classic street fighter's stance, Moss waved the knife before him, not in a jabbing motion, but in a side-to-side swiping motion, ready to slit an attacker from ear to ear. Which was exactly what he did as another child, vaguely recognisable as a young girl, leapt at him from his left thrusting a piece of metal railing at him, as though it were a spear. Blocking her blow with his forearm, Moss swept his bowie knife across the arm of the child as she sailed past him. She collapsed against the wall beside the other child, screaming loudly as the blood poured out of the open wound.

Two more assailants launched themselves at Moss, this time from his right. Before they reached the fire's perimeter he felled them with two snap shots from his revolver. Then suddenly the whole factory was dazzlingly lit, and Moss could see that there were at least another twenty children out there, ready to take the place of their fallen pack members. Instinctively Moss hurled himself towards some corrugated iron and timber that offered some shelter. It was just as well as a machine gun cut many of the remaining pack members to ribbons. Outside the factory, Moss could just make out the silhouette of a Dyason chopper, hovering a few feet above the half-collapsed roof. It opened fire with its nose-mounted Gatling gun, tracer lighting up the night sky arcing towards the child pack. Through a hole in the wall, Moss slipped away into the wind and rain, leaving the screams of the dying kids behind him, his heart pounding. It had been a close call.

From the ruins of the factory he moved rapidly along the old A3 itself. There he could move quickly from car wreck to car wreck. In the last days of the revolt, before the Dyason had subdued London by pounding it to ruins, many had tried to escape by car using the last drops of their preciously hoarded petrol. The result had been the grid lock of every route out of London. When the Dyason gunships arrived these cars turned into death traps as the storm-troopers systematically went about the business of turning all the trapped vehicles into blazing wrecks, strafing and napalming the defenceless refugees. Thousands had died, trapped inside by the other vehicles around them. The A3 became nothing more than a huge scrap yard of fused metal and carnage.

As he moved from one burnt-out hulk to another Moss came across many gruesome sights. Bodies were nothing more than lumps of barely recognisable charcoal, their limbs imploringly reaching out of twisted and torn metal. Beside the road hundreds of other skeletons lay, their bones picked clean by scavenging dogs. Some had heads or limbs clearly blown apart by the cannon fire of the Dyason aircraft as they'd strafed the refugees. Others were half skeletal, half burned flesh, as if only splashed rather than consumed by the napalm.

The sight of these poor souls made Moss retch and empty his stomach of its meagre contents. Even by his standards it was a horrific scene of carnage. However, the wrecks made good cover and a new-found superstition kept other ghetto dwellers away. So, he forced himself to keep moving, running from the shelter of one twisted hulk to another. Eventually, he came within sight of the skeletal remains of the Tolworth Tower. From here on, he knew the Dyason had cleared the wrecks from the carriageway of the A3 as a buffer zone up to the boundary that was the M25.

So, without sufficient cover, he was forced to move through the ruined suburban streets of Worcester Park, Ewell and Epsom. The once neat and tidy rows of suburban houses were now nothing more than heaps of rubble. Here and there stood a building on its own, standing up like an oasis in a desert of devastation. Moss stopped to look over a couple of such places, but each was completely gutted, already stripped of anything vaguely useful. Nobody lived in these outlying areas any more. After the Dyason created the ghettos, disease spread rapidly through the surviving inhabitants, like a medieval plague and people had died in their thousands. Those that remained once the wild-fire sickness had taken its toll now huddled together in the areas closer to the river, where there was at least a ready supply of fresh water. Despite the savagery of the inner ghettos, people naturally grouped together for whatever meagre food and protection they could get. Hence these outlying areas were virtually deserted, especially as the area was regularly used for target practice by Dyason Death Squads and training regiments. The only inhabitants of the sad remains of suburbia were roaming packs of wild dogs, and the occasional gang of murderous children, led by their teenage 'Barons'.

Moss managed to avoid these groups without further incident, and although still desperately tired he kept on moving, afraid of falling asleep again. Finally, in the grey light of dawn, he crept through a deserted and withered wood, only a half a kilometre from the M25, the fortified boundary that encircled London. He only had to cross that border and he could make his way to unoccupied northern Scotland, and some sort of freedom.

It was childhood memories that had led Moss to this place. They were memories of happy days flying model gliders from Reigate Hill, just the other side of the boundary. In those halcyon times he'd come here with his father to spend many happy hours flying his radio-controlled glider from the steep slope that formed the beautiful North Downs.

What was important about this place was that at this point the fortified M25 ran between several large escarpments, in a man-made cutting some thirty metres deep. If his memory served him correctly, there was a small pedestrian bridge over the M25 just beyond the woods. This bridge, if it still stood, lead to Reigate Hill and out of the London ghetto. If he could get across this bridge and the hill, Moss knew he stood a chance. This was his plan, if you could call it that. He reckoned nobody would figure he would head southwest and attempt to cross the heavily fortified M25. He just hoped the bridge was still there. He wouldn't attempt the crossing during the day though, he would wait until nightfall. So, Moss looked for a hiding place, somewhere among the skeletal remains of the trees. Eventually, he found a small trench with an old drainage pipe at the bottom. The pipe was just big enough for him to squeeze into and, after poking about with a stick to check it wasn't already occupied by man or beast, he gratefully crawled inside. He took out some of his meagre rations and made himself comfortable, chewing on the stolen Dyason bread and dried meat. Inevitably his eyes became heavy again, but feeling his position was more secure than in the old factory he allowed himself the luxury of nodding off. Within minutes he had fallen into an exhausted troubled sleep.

From the exterior it looked nothing more than the shell of a derelict office block. Its windows were blown out and many of its girders reached towards the tormented sky, twisted and warped by the heat and impact of numerous explosions. It was just one more ruin among the many that once made up the business centre of Croydon, south London. But deep within the basement, hidden by a complex system of camouflage and doors that looked like large pieces of concrete rubble, was an advanced communications complex. This was the UK headquarters of the resistance.

The complex had originally been set up as a civil defence centre during the Cold War years of the mid-twentieth century. After the invasion it was rediscovered and extended by the resistance. Now it housed barracks, stores, medical facilities and communications equipment. Without knowing it the Dyason had by sealing much of London and creating the ghettos, given the resistance the ideal place for their centre of British operations. Any Dyason incursion into the ghettos was known by the resistance as soon as it happened, giving them time to hide and secure their positions.

Jenson sat with his boots on a metal table leaning back in his chair staring at the blank concrete wall. The glaring fluorescent tubes above his head and his lack of sleep gave him a headache. Events had moved on rapidly through the night. After the kid's escape they'd fanned out and searched the area, but to no avail. Even the operants now tuned to the youth's mind wavelength couldn't trace him. He'd got wise to their method of tracking and was carefully shielding his thoughts. There'd been reports from informants among the ghettos dwellers of a youth matching Moss's description in Battersea and Wandsworth. Unfortunately, when they'd arrived there the kid had already moved on. What made matters worse was that the Dyason were now moving into the ghettos in force. In fact, they were ploughing their way through in greater numbers than at any time since the revolt. They were all looking for the same thing, a thin youth with long dank hair; and if you said you hadn't seen him, they simply shot you. Christ, that kid had really stirred up a load of trouble!

There was a knock at the door, and a young woman dressed in faded combat fatigues entered the room. 'Squadron Leader Jenson sir!' she snapped to attention.

'It's okay Jenny, take it easy,' he said. Jenny Anderson was typical of the breed that made up the resistance. All her family had been killed in the early days of the war when street to street fighting took place around the naval base at Portsmouth. The Dyason hadn't discriminated between civilians and the military and her family had been butchered in a sweep through the residential areas of the city. Jenny and a group of youths had managed to get away, joining the embryonic resistance movement soon after. Just out of her teens, she was young, beautiful and deadly with at least a dozen Dyason dispatched personally by her bowie knife.

The young woman relaxed her posture and said, 'The operants say they have contact with Arctic Command, skipper. They're ready for you now.'

'Okay,' said Jenson, taking his combat boots off the table and standing up with a stretch. 'Let's do it.'

He followed her out of the door and down a corridor to another room in the complex. Inside it was subdued, lit only by the light of several monitors and control pads, which cast a soft glow across two couches. On these couches lay a man and a woman each with a headset looking much like the early virtual reality helmets sitting on their craniums. They lay back eyes closed, apparently asleep.

Jenson sat down at a control console next to a thin young man who watched the displays monitoring the pair's vital functions. He looked at the many pulse graphs and numerous touch sensitive controls, then looked at the man beside him and said, 'So all this stuff actually works?'

Josh looked up from what he was doing, the lights from the monitors giving his face a pale wan look.

'They sure do skipper!' he replied with enthusiasm. 'These wavelength amplifiers work a treat—we can now contact any operant, anywhere around the globe. There is no way that the Dyason can intercept our messages!'

'Because the transmissions are made up of thought waves?' asked Jenson.

'That's right skipper," Josh continued. 'You see what we're really doing is linking telepaths, so any message we send can't be read by any conventional radio equipment, because we aren't sending out radio waves. No, what we are sending are brain "waves", pulses of pure thought energy.'

Jenson looked at all the computers and equipment linked up to the headsets worn by the pair lying on the couches. 'And all this equipment,' he asked, 'is here to amplify their thought patterns so that they can reach further?'

Josh nodded, 'Dead right, this kit simply increases the power of the thought patterns. In that sense, telepathy is just like radio, the strength of the signal is entirely related to the distance from the transmitter. The greater the output from the sender, the further away the receiver can receive the thoughts.'

'Well, bugger me, it's hard to believe such stuff is possible,' whistled Jenson, shaking his head from side to side, 'So what do I do now?'

'Simply direct your questions at the senders there,' Josh explained pointing towards the telepaths. 'They'll pass your message on and articulate the reply. You might find it a little strange at first, but you'll quickly get used to it.'

Shifting a little uncomfortably in his chair for a moment Jenson thought about what had to be said, then in a clear voice gave a description of recent events to the telepaths, who relayed his words. Once he'd finished his report there was barely a moments hesitation before a reply was returned.

'Squadron Leader, there have been reports from around the globe of a strong disturbance in the "mind" dimension,' came the clear if somewhat uncanny reply from the female telepath. 'Indications are that the youth who evaded your capture is the source of these emissions. We are aware that the Dyason who, despite having no known ESP ability of their own, are carrying out experiments using human operants.

'We believe their experiments are looking at the potential military use of ESP talents. Your report supports this supposition. It is clear that their search for the youth is not solely due to the assassination of Topaz. It is imperative that the boy is found and brought into resistance protection before the Dyason can get their hands on him. That is now your number one priority. Spare no resources to find him...Message ends.'

Jenson sat in silence for a moment, thinking over what had been said. Well, tell me something I don't know, he thought to himself. Somehow he just knew that getting his hands on the kid would be easier said than done, but the thought of Dyason meddling in the use of operants was frightening. Could it be that they already knew of the resistance means of communication? Was that the direction of their research? Perhaps they were looking for a way to counter the use of operants in the resistance.

Slapping Josh on the back he said, 'Well done. This kit will prove invaluable. At no time since the Dyason took out all our comm sats have we had the capability of global communication; even if it is a little unconventional. Keep it up, and make sure all the other units know how to produce this kit.'

Then, returning Josh's pleased grin, he left the room, deep in thought.

Gulag paced up and down his office like a trapped animal. He was oblivious to the antique desk, priceless paintings and carpet, which was rapidly wearing out from the ceaseless pounding of his combat boots. In another time and place, the main study of the executed King of England would have filled anyone with awe, but today, Gulag's mind was far away from the ostentatious opulence of Buckingham Palace.

His mind grappled with the problem of finding the native youth. The little bastard had already slipped from his grasp once, he wasn't about to do it again! Or at least he wasn't once he had got his hands on him again. Damn! The brat had been standing not ten metres away from him on that rooftop. How by the gods had he managed to survive that leap? He'd been back to survey the scene himself and knew that no man could have walked away from a fall from the several storey building. Nor could he have leapt the gap to the adjacent building, it was simply too large. Yet for all that, the murderer had not only survived, but apparently made his escape out of the West End! For not the first time Gulag felt he was up against no ordinary Earth-born human.

Mettar had told him to use his own talents to locate the youth, but Gulag had never tried to use his abilities to do something like this before. In fact he knew of no other Dyason with operant talents. It was possible there were others like him, but they kept their skills carefully hidden, just as he had, because they were fearful of the reaction they would get from their peers. So he had no experience or precedent to guide him. In frustration Gulag poured himself a large dose of the drink they called Scotch, and collapsed onto a cot placed against one wall of the room.

Perhaps he was approaching the problem from the wrong angle. That strange tingling sensation at the base of his skull was still there, as it had been since he confronted the youth in Covent Garden. He lay back, closed his eyes and concentrated on the sensation. As he did so it seemed to become more prominent, to expand in his consciousness until it filled his mind. A kaleidoscope of colour swirled before his eyes, unsubstantial, like multi-coloured mists. At times, they seemed almost to take on recognisable shapes, to take form. He thought he could make out voices, murmurings, like Chinese whispers, snippets of conversation blowing on the wind.

He felt his mind roam these mists, fleeting as if from cloud to cloud, until he came across one that appeared more substantial than the others. Gulag floated towards it, and as he did so it took form, became substantial, until, without warning, he saw everything with startling clarity. Through eyes he knew were not his own, he saw a room, dimly lit. He looked down and stared at hands that were not his! By the gods, was he hallucinating, or had he really entered another body! Without attempting to move anything except his eyes, Gulag looked around the room. The body he inhabited was lying on a couch, strapped up to some strange apparatus, with some bizarre device on its head. A woman lay on a couch next to him, similarly wired up to a head device. She was talking in a clear voice. The language was definitely not Dyason, but unmistakably English. Sitting behind a nearby console sat a young man, thin, studious looking. Beside him sat an older man wearing combat fatigues. The type of combat fatigues that were worn by the resistance!

My God, what was this place? It was obviously the lair of some resistance cell, but where? The head moved without Gulag's volition and began to speak. So he wasn't in complete control of this body, it was as if he were alongside the occupant's own soul, looking in, only able to suggest, not to control. Damn it, he must find out where this place was!

A thought came to him, if he were sharing this person's mind, could he also share the knowledge? Tentatively he began to probe, looking for access to the memory. He searched around blindly for a while lost in an unfamiliar soul, until almost by accident he came across what he was looking for. The memories flowed past at an incredible rate, flashes of childhood, school, death, the war, all swept by in an instant, and Gulag fed on it all as if it were the food of life itself. Almost overwhelmed, he absorbed the host's knowledge and memories into his own, all in a time span less than the blink of an eye.

Having gorged himself Gulag left the host body, leaving the hapless victim unaware his mind had been invaded. Through the mists of this strange dimension he followed his path back until, with a shock that sent a spasm throughout his nervous system, body and soul were reunited. He lay still for a moment breathing heavily until he could focus his own eyes again.

My God, who would have believed such a thing was possible? Such power, domination! To enter another mind, rape it of knowledge and incorporate it into your own! Somewhat shakily, he rose from the cot, staggered to his desk and flicked on the intercom.

'Adj., prepare the regiment, we're moving out!' he flicked the intercom off again, not bothering to wait for an answer. He knew the location of the resistance. He now knew the importance of the human operants. To think Mettar wanted him to use his own talents to further that bastard's career! Oh no, not now, not with his new-found knowledge. How many more minds were out there? Minds he could absorb, becoming stronger, more powerful every time? Gulag could see a whole new landscape of opportunity opening out in front of him. He would take the resistance headquarters, make the operants he had seen captive, take all their minds for his own! He would find the bastard murdering youth and when he did, he would take his mind also, just before he crushed the swine. Then he would destroy the resistance once and for all. Nobody and nothing could stop him - not now! He knew the secret, the secret his superiors had been trying to keep from him! He would be redeemed. Promotion was assured, but more than that, with his new-found talents, he could rise to the very top. Not just Marshal of the Earth Imperial forces, but supreme commander of all Dyason forces! He had the resistance now, this was the end for them and the start of the next stage in his career. He would do it, nothing could stop him!

Jenson poured over a map of London under the glare of a single light bulb. With a pen he marked areas of South London.

'So these are the places where the kid was possibly sighted. Battersea, Wandsworth and the Raynes Park section of the A3', he said. 'Now he's obviously going to try and get out of the ghettos and he's not heading for the M4. So where's he going to make his break?'

'Well skipper, I doubt if he's going to try and follow the A3 all the way. It's heavily guarded from the Tolworth roundabout onwards. He'd never make it,' said a resistance member wearing the pips of a sub lieutenant. 'Still, he's been seen heading in that direction, so he must be aiming to get out somewhere along the south west border.'

Jenson stood in thought for a moment staring out the map. Gradually an idea formed in his mind. 'Hang on a moment,' he finally said. 'I think I've got it.' He pointed to an area, on the map between Westerham and Epsom Downs. 'Look at this point, the M25 rises up the north Downs, but actually goes along a cutting. So although the motorway itself is patrolled heavily, and the south side of the downs is like a fortress, on the North side it's only patrolled irregularly.'

'You think he may try to cross the cutting sir?' enquired the sub lieutenant.

'Sure why not,' Jenson continued. 'If he's situated above the fortifications and the M25 he stands a better chance of finding a weak spot. I mean, there must be loads of old pedestrian bridges, you know the small ones for farmers and the like. If he could find one that was lightly guarded, he might be able to slip past. After all he's shown he's talented enough at that!'

'You may be right sir! Certainly it makes more sense than him trying to get out by one of the major routes.'

'Well sub, it's the best lead we've got. So organise a squad, spread the word, and search the whole of that area especially, but keep the other patrols checking the places we know he's been through. I want the kid found before somebody else does!'

'Yes sir." With that the lieutenant left the room.

Jenson rolled up the map, put it back in its tube and left the room after him. In the corridor outside, he headed towards his office when there was a distant rumble and dust filled the air. A klaxon starting blaring, the main lights went out, and the red emergency lamps started flashing. Jenson turned and ran for the operations room. The corridor rapidly filled with resistance troops all running for their positions. He recognised an officer fighting his way towards him where they met at the door to the operations room. 'Hanson,' he yelled above the sound of the klaxons. 'What the hell's going on?'

'Dyason skipper! Several chopper loads of the bastards, all armed to the teeth! They came straight here and are even now blasting their way through the perimeter defences. We're being swamped!' Hanson Sandpiper yelled urgently.

'Shit, some bloody bastards blown us out!' exclaimed Jenson just as they burst into the operations room. Inside it was a scene of pandemonium. Operators sat before comm units desperately trying to get hard information from fighting squads. A fire co-ordinator tried to plot the attacks on a holo-board showing the complex. Jenson turned to him and asked urgently, 'What's the situation?'

The man looked at him with a slight look of panic on his face. 'It's bad Squadron Leader. The reports are very confusing but it appears that at least a battalion is attacking the complex from three sides. Choppers have landed the Dyason troops right beside the main entrance points. They took heavy casualties at first but now they've broken into the outer corridors. They must know where the hidden entry points are, they went straight for them!'

The comms officer briefly listened to an incoming message on his headset then carried on, 'Helicopter gunships are scoring hits on our surface emplacements. It's as if they know exactly where our weak spots are. I'm afraid it's only a matter of time sir. We never expected to defend ourselves against such a large scale attack.'

Jenson's heart sank. Somebody, somewhere had given the Dyason all the information they needed. If they were already inside the outer corridors it was only a matter of time before they reached the inner complex. There was another rumble, louder than the previous one, and more dust rose from the floor causing several of the operators to cough and splutter. 'Where the hell did they get the choppers from? I thought the Dyason had nothing except the Domes and the shuttles?' he asked.

'They look like ex WDF sir. The squads report that the old insignia have been painted out and Dyason markings put on.'

'Oh great, screwed by our own hardware!' Sandpiper said sarcastically.

One of the radio operators frantically turned to the fire-control officer. Spilling out from her headset Jenson could hear the desperate calls of squads coming under heavy fire, calling out for support; support they weren't going to get. All the units were already committed trying to hold a weak defensive perimeter. It was a rapidly deteriorating situation.

'Sir!' the operator called out trying to keep her voice calm and level but only partially succeeding, 'squad seven report that the Dyason have broken into the main complex at the northern sector. They're taking heavy casualties and being forced to retreat. What shall I tell them sir?'

The fire-control officer swore and began to talk rapidly into his headset. Sandpiper took hold of Jenson's arm and looked into his face. 'It's time to *go* skipper! The situation's falling apart, and we may have only a few minutes in which to evacuate! We've got to save what we can. And we *must* get the operants out before they fall into Dyason hands, otherwise the whole resistance is in jeopardy. They know the location of all the other resistance cells!'

Jenson knew his friend was right. In the past they'd always relied on the secrecy of their hideaway to keep the Dyason forces away. Although the complex was fortified, they didn't have nearly enough troops and hardware to fend off a major assault such as this. Someone, somewhere had given the game away and if he ever caught the individual, he would personally rip their limbs off. Damn it! They had no choice but to evacuate and salvage what they could in the short time they had before they were overrun, which looked like it may only be a matter of minutes.

He turned and grabbed the fire-control officer who was still quick firing orders into his headset. 'Is the VTOL bay still clear?' he demanded. The officer checked his situation board which showed a holographic map of the complex with the areas still in their control marked in blue. These areas were changing to red one by one, even as they spoke.

'Yes sir. For how long for I don't know, but that sector is holding for now,' he confirmed.

'Right,' said Jenson, 'here are your orders. The bay is to be held secure for as long as possible; that is essential. All the operants are to be escorted to the bay, and loaded onto the transports. Sandpiper and I will take them out.'

'You will hold the complex until the transports are away. Then make for the third transport which we will leave. Get as many as possible on board and head for the rendezvous point. The rest of the squads are then to disengage and slip into the ghettos as best as they can. We'll pick them up from the safe houses later. Is that clear? Remember, the operants must get away at all costs! Oh yeah, blow the gear as you leave.'

The fire-control officer nodded his head frantically, 'You got it skipper. You'd better go now. We'll hold the fort until you get away. Good luck!' At that he turned back to his holo-board and started snapping off orders into his mike. Sandpiper and Jenson turned and quickly left the room.

Jenson turned to Sandpiper. 'Han, you go and collect the operants and meet me in the bay. I'm going to blow the mind transmitters. It's a bugger 'cause they're the prototypes, but we can't afford to let them get into hands of the Dyason. We'll just have to build some more. If it looks like the flight bay is going to be overrun before I get there, leave without me. I'll take my chances with me others. Okay?' Sandpiper nodded and sped off up the corridor. Jenson turned and headed in the other direction.

The klaxons were still screaming, the emergency lights flickering and everywhere was hidden by clouds of dust and smoke that made breathing difficult. More by feel than sight Jenson found the room where he'd spoken earlier to the operants. There in the corner, were the vast electronic mind expansion machines. Jenson took two H.E. grenades from his battle pouch and tossed them into the room, quickly pulling the reinforced door closed afterwards. There were two dull crumps. He opened the door again and looked in. There was nothing left but smoldering wire and distorted metal; that was the end of the transmitters. Then he turned and began to run in the direction of the flight bay.

It had only been a matter of minutes since he'd left the operations room, but already he could hear the sound of gunfire getting closer every second. He didn't have long before the base would be completely overrun. As he turned a corner he ran straight into a squad of resistance in full flight.

'What the *hells* going on?' he yelled as they collided in a heap. The troops all looked panic stricken, their faces dirty, smudged with sweat and blood, their eyes wide. Their battle fatigues were stained and torn and hung loose on the young bodies that were barely out of adolescence.

'Dyason, Dyason!' one young lad shouted. 'They've broken through! We couldn't stop them, there were too many! The sarge bought it, and Smith!' He tried to pull away, but Jenson hung on tightly to the lad's sleeve. He recognised sheer panic had stricken the squad, and only the strongest of wills would break through their overwhelming desire to flee. Jenson knew there was nowhere to go.

'Okay, calm down,' he said in a strong steady voice, 'Where have they broken through?'

'I don't know sir, it was so confusing! We didn't stand a chance. Sector eleven I think. We've got to get away or we're done for!' a young girl rambled, barely able to carry the heavy automatic cradled loosely in her arms.

Shit, Jenson thought, if she was right, that cut off his main route to the bay. The Dyason were advancing even quicker than he had first thought. No wonder this group had broken and run, he would probably have done the same had he been in their hopeless position. That meant his only chance was to go through the service conduit by sector twelve and he would need their help to get there. He only hoped he could get past their fear and break their instinct to run blindly.

'Okay, now listen!' he ordered. 'We'll all get out if you listen to me. There's not much time so we're going to go through the service conduit and into the flight bay. There's a transport waiting to take us out, but you must pull yourselves together. We may have to fight our way to get there. Do you understand?'

The half dozen troops looked at each other then nodded, trying to hold their courage together. Jenson looked into the eyes of the lad who's arm he still held in a vice-like grip; their eyes met for a moment. The young fighter pulled back his shoulders and nodded once. That was what Jenson was looking for.

'Good!' Jenson said, letting go of the arm, 'now have your weapons at the ready, keep an eye out, and follow me!' He turned and ran back down the corridor, the squad following him, relieved that finally someone was being decisive and taking the lead. They took several turns at a pace then halted before a large metal mesh set in the concrete corridor wall. The overhead bulbs flickered then died. Cursing, Jenson pulled out a flashlight, as did the rest of the squad. With the help of some of the others, he started to lever the mesh off with the barrel of his automatic, but before they'd even half pulled it away from its rusted mounting there was an explosion further down the corridor. A large steel door collapsed to the floor, smoke and rubble moving ahead of it in a cloud. For a moment a silence descended before, with a shout, soldiers in black uniforms, firing from the waist, poured through the opening, One of the young resistance fighters immediately fell, blood pouring from a bullet wound in his thigh, screaming in agony. The rest of the squad fell to the floor and began to return fire wildly at the advancing Dyason troops. Someone with the presence of mind called out to douse the flashlights, which they did, making it harder for the Dyason to fire accurately, while leaving themselves clearly visible.

Jenson swore and ignoring the fire fight going on around him, doubled his energies in attempting to lever off the service shaft cover. He heaved and pulled as automatic fire chipped the concrete all around him. The young fighter he'd held onto earlier clambered up beside him and added his weight to the job. After what seemed an age and with a final clang, the cover broke from its mountings and fell to the floor.

'Quick, everybody inside the shaft! Come on move!' he cried.

Needing no second invitation, the squad leapt for the cover of the service shaft, pulling their injured comrade with them. Jenson turned his automatic on the Dyason troops, now lying prone on the corridor floor, and returned fire, covering the young resistance fighters as they jumped in ones and twos into the lip of the shaft. Then several arms grabbed and hauled him into the shaft as well. As he got unsteadily to his feet one of the squad pulled the pin on two grenades and rolled them back into the corridor. There were shouts of anguish from the Dyason troops, then two loud crumps! Immediately the firing ceased.

'Good lad!' said Jenson. 'That should hold them for the moment. Now let's move, we haven't got much time!' They set off down the service shaft, following the gentle slope downward at a steady trot. There was a bleep in Jenson's headset and a crackling voice spoke to him urgently. 'Skipper! Where the hell are you? Skipper? Come in!'

'Hanson!' he answered breathlessly into his throat mike. 'I'm in the service shaft, heading for the flight bay. Where are you?'

'I'm in the transport', replied Sandpiper, his voice still breaking up slightly because of the poor reception. 'We're all ready to leave. All the operants and research teams are on board. The operations group have evacuated and are on board transporter two. We're only holding the flight bay and part of sector thirteen now. Everywhere else has been overrun!'

'Shit!' Jenson swore as he ran, leaping over a conduit crossing the service shaft. They were cutting it too fine. If the Dyason got hold of the information in the heads of those personnel it could mean the end of the whole resistance. 'Listen Han! Get those transporters out of here, don't wait for us! You must get those operants away. We'll take our chances. Do you hear me? Take off now!' he shouted frantically into his mike.

'What was that skipper? You're breaking up! We'll hold them off till you get here!' came the faint reply.

'Han...! Han! Don't give me any crap, take off now! You can bloody well hear me!' Jenson yelled, but there was no reply, just static. 'Shit!' The squad turned a comer, ducking under a pipe in the process, and came to the end of the shaft. Three of them kicked frantically at the mesh cover, which after several boots, fell noisily to the floor. Quickly they all clambered out. Ahead of them sat the three vertical take off transports, their turbines whining ready for take-off. Jenson waved to Sandpiper, sitting in the cockpit of the first, who waved back grinning. Then he ran towards the boarding ramp of the third transport, the squad following on his heels. Just as they reached the bottom of the ramp, the sound of automatic fire came from the far end of the flight bay and Jenson saw resistance fighters retreating in full flight from a horde of Dyason troops.

He cursed, ran up the lowered boarding ramp and through the fuselage, literally falling into the pilot's seat. Behind him the rest of the squad started to return fire at the Dyason troops from the top of the transport ramp. Fingers flying rapidly over the control panel he started the flight initiation sequence.

'Glad to see you skipper!' came a voice behind him. Jenson turned to see the grinning face of his friend. 'Hanson! For Christ's sake what are you playing at? Get those transporters out!' he yelled.

Sandpiper fell into the co-pilots seat and started flicking switches. 'They're on their way skipper. I figured you'd never get out without my help though!' he replied glibly. Jenson looked out of the window and saw the other two transporters rising towards the opening sky hatch. Now wasn't the time to argue. They'd cut it fine, too fine, before launching, but he had to admit to himself he was glad his chum was here; it felt like the odds were marginally more in their favour.

'Okay Han! You hold off those bastards while I get this thing in the air!' he said.

'Will do skipper," Sandpiper replied, aiming the remote cannon under the transporters nose and letting loose a withering fire towards the advancing Dyason troops, who hit the ground and spread out in all directions.

Seeing their chance, the retreating resistance fighters ran for the boarding ramp and began to pour into the cavernous hold, guided by Jenson's squad. Peering over his shoulder into the hold, Jenson waited until the last man was on board, then closed the boarding ramp and opened the throttles, in one movement. The turbines rose in speed until their screaming thrust lifted the transport off the ground and towards the flight bay opening. Sandpiper continued to pour cannon fire onto the Dyason troops who were wildly firing at the aircraft. The sound of light weapons hitting the armoured skin reverberated through the fuselage.

As soon as they had cleared the flight bay, Jenson slammed the vectored thrust to full forward and the transport accelerated rapidly into the darkening sky. They were less than a thousand metres away when from below came a series of violent explosions that shot flame and debris into the sky. The self-destruct charges had ignited, marking the final demise of their base. Grimly, Jenson banked away and disappeared into the cloud cover, flicking on the active stealth cloaking device. On the ground, the three transporters disappeared from the Dyason radar. The resistance cell was destroyed, but the bulk of the fighters had escaped to fight another day.

The blow from the rifle butt hit the resistance fighter squarely on the jaw and his head snapped back. He fell in a sprawl onto the hard concrete floor. Two Dyason troops grabbed him by the armpits and dragged him up so that he hung limply between them, blood streaming from his face, his left eye swollen closed.

'Where are the operants? Terrorist! Come on talk you bastard! Where are they? Where's the assassin?' screamed a Dyason officer, raising his rifle again, ready to strike. Gulag watched impassively from the doorway. The officer shoved the butt into the resistance fighter's face, a scream of pain forcing its way past the beaten man's swollen lips.

'Ahhh! I don't know," he cried spitting blood and teeth onto the floor. 'They left in the transporters. I swear I don't know where they're going!'

'Come on vermin! You can do better than that! I want to know where they're going. What's their flight plan, and who was responsible for Marshal Topaz's murder? You're holding out on me... Come on talk!' he raised the rifle ready to strike a third time.

Gulag raised his hand, and stopped the descending rifle. 'Enough', he said to the officer, 'I have a better method!'

He walked over to the pathetic figure hanging limply between the two storm troopers. The lights from the LED lanterns brought in to illuminate the subterranean control room cast surreal shadows across the man's beaten face and highlighted his injuries. Pulling his gloves off, Gulag placed his hand onto the human's blood-stained forehead. He opened his mind, gathered his will and thrust into the man's brain, spearing through his thoughts mercilessly, forcing his way in past the feeble attempts to keep him out. The resistance fighter seemed to shrink in horror from the touch of the alien mind, but Gulag moved further and further into the core of thought, peeling away layers of memory.

The man could feel the rape of his mind and screamed and writhed under the iron grip of the storm troopers. Gulag ignored him and continued searching, feeling his own strength increase in proportion to the diminishing native mind. Yet, he was not finding what he needed to know. Damn it, the truth was, the scum genuinely didn't know where the operants had fled to, only the location of some resistance safe house he was supposed to flee to. Hang on... wait a moment, what was this? Maybe he had found something after all? Gulag recoiled in horror, fleeing the human mind. He turned to the officer and shouted at him.

'Out... get out! Get everybody out of the complex now! Come on, move. Out now! Leave the bastard, move your arses! Don't ask any questions, just move!'

He ran to the door of the bunker and fled down the corridor, the storm troopers and officer close on his heels wondering what the panic was about. Gulag shouted to other troops as he went, hollering at them to leave their weapons and flee the resistance complex. Lying on the cold floor of the bunker, the resistance fighter lay in a pool of blood. But his mind registered a brief moment of satisfaction before the demolition charges exploded, sending him into peaceful oblivion.

CHAPTER SIX

SOUTH LONDON, ENGLAND

Standing in the shadow of a clump of trees, Moss watched the explosions that lit up the darkening sky. Flames shot up into the clouds like a horde of pyrotechnics, and the ground shook under his feet. He'd slept for most of the day, hidden inside the pipe, but as the grey daylight faded, he was awoken by the sound of artillery in the distance. So he'd packed his knapsack and moved to the top of a nearby hill. There he watched the flash of explosions silhouette the surrounding desolate landscape, sounds of gunfire drifting on the wind.

Moss just couldn't shrug off the feeling that in some way the fighting that was going on in south London was something to do with him. The Dyason seemed to be pulling out all stops to find him, so maybe they were looking in the wrong place and had found something else instead. Either way it meant trouble, but even if some poor bastard was copping a packet because of him, there was nothing he could do about it. No, it was time for him to try and make it to the other side. So, slinging his pack over his shoulder he headed for Reigate Hill.

Moving silently from shadow to shadow, Moss moved towards the ravine that marked the position of the M25 motorway, the fortified boundary around London. After about twenty-five minutes he reached the small wood which edged the ravine. Slinking from tree to tree, he headed for where he remembered the pedestrian bridge to be. Occasionally, like flashes of lightning, the skyline was lit up by distant explosions, bringing the landscape into momentary sharp relief and helping him find his way across the numerous felled trees and splintered stumps that were all that remained of the woods after they'd been napalmed a few times. He crept along by the edge of a path, until eventually he lay prone at the edge of the ravine, with the M25 below him, and looming only a few metres away, the dark bulk of the bridge.

He looked down at the M25 in dismay - it was lit up like a Christmas tree. Armoured vehicles patrolled the old motorway, their turrets turning to and fro. Barbed wire lay in thick clumps on the hard shoulder, while at regular intervals stood tall watch towers. Inside the towers, Moss could make out several Dyason troops manning machine guns and search lights. Yet, most weren't looking at the motorway at all, they were concentrating on the series of explosions that were still lighting up the sky in the north east.

This thought Moss could just be the distraction he was looking for. If the pyrotechnics continued long enough, the bastards might just be distracted enough for him to slip across, using his mind to cloak himself, just as he had when entering the West End. Using his talents might warrant risking attention from other unwelcome sources, but he got the impression that the resistance were a little busy just now.

He turned his attention to the pedestrian bridge spanning the ravine. From his position Moss could make out just two Dyason troops sitting behind some sort of pill box at the far end of the bridge, but his heart sank when he saw the amount of barbed wire strung with mines that had been placed across the span. There was no way that he could easily creep past that; he would have to find another method.

Lying prone, moving one limb at a time, he crept closer to the bridge until he lay just below the concrete girder of the first arch. It was just possible that he could climb under the bridge itself. Although the underside was smooth concrete, there were several conduits that must carry power or telephone wires, and he reckoned he could haul himself along these. What's more, it looked pretty certain that they hadn't bothered to mine the underside. So, not wanting to waste any more time, he grabbed hold of one of the conduits and started to pull himself along, hands gripping at the front, legs wrapped around the pipes at the back. Centimetre by centimetre, Moss pulled himself along, not daring to look down to the bottom of the ravine fifty metres below, eyes fixed solidly on where he was going.

He was about halfway across when he was rocked by the concussion of a huge explosion. It lit up the whole of the sky, bringing everything into sharp focus as if it were daylight. The bridge shook violently and he could feel the force of the shock waves being transmitted through the conduit he was desperately clinging onto. He felt his feet begin to slip, then lose their grip. His legs fell away leaving him hanging precariously, just by his hands, while his body swayed sickeningly above the ravine as further shock waves rippled through the structure. He held onto his grip for grim life, shut his eyes and waited for the shock waves to disappear.

It felt like an eternity before the bridge eased its swaying. Through narrowed eyes he looked for the huge mushroom cloud he was half-expecting. There wasn't one, just a broiling mass of smoke and flames shooting up hundreds of metres into the air. That was the biggest explosion Moss had seen since the invasion and it had nearly taken him with it. Working hard to overcome his fear, he tensed his muscles and hauled himself back up onto the relative safety of the conduit. He then lay there motionless for some time, waiting for his heart to stop tapping a rave rhythm on his heaving chest. When he looked down at his hands, blood seeped through gashes caused by rusted metal cutting through his palms. He cursed, ignored the pain and moved on.

When he did eventually look up, Moss saw the pandemonium around him. All the vehicles on the motorway had stopped, the crews had climbed out and were gesticulating wildly at the flames from the aftermath of the explosion, which were lighting up the horizon. The Dyason in the watchtowers were also calling to each other excitedly, laughing and pointing at the flames. As to the troops on the bridge, they'd left the pill box to stand on top of it to get a better view of the pyrotechnics.

This was Moss's chance. In a burst of energy he hauled himself to the end of the bridge, dropped off into the grass below the final arch and disappeared into the darkness. The troops never even heard the rustle in the undergrowth. Moss's heart soared, he was across the fortified M25 and out of the London ghettos! From here on it was plain sailing to freedom!

What little he knew…

He could see very little once the glow from the floodlights of the M25 barricade faded behind him. Everywhere was dark, a deep all-enveloping darkness that hung like a cloak over the landscape. It was in stark contrast to the ghettos; there the sky was always aglow with the lights of the West End reflected off the low clouds. Small fires lit by huddles of ghetto dwellers cast deep shadows over the ruins of south London and searchlights from patrolling helicopter gunships roved across the rubble. It was a twilight world of shadow and death, but out here there was nothing. No distant glow on the horizon, no street lights in a nearby village, no solitary lamp in the window of a farmhouse. Moss felt the blackness closing in on him; never before had he felt so desolate.

By expanding his mind as if he were pushing out in front of his body, he found he could perceive what was in front of him up to a few metres away. It was a bit like looking at an infrared image, or perhaps a negative; everything was a vague outline, barely recognisable for what it was. However, it was sufficient for his needs, and despite being a little concerned that using his talents might attract more unwanted attention, he didn't really have much choice if he wanted to put some distance between the ghettos and himself before daylight. Besides, he really was using very little of his mind to see in the dark and felt fairly sure that he wasn't broadcasting sufficiently to be tracked, by Man or Dyason.

Throughout that night Moss walked through the empty fields, the rain and cold causing every bone in his body to ache. He walked for hours, only stopping briefly to take a mouthful of his meagre rations, until by the grey light of dawn the following day, Moss reckoned he was a good forty kilometres from Reigate Hill. He was also on the verge of exhaustion. If he didn't stop soon to get dry and warm, he knew he was at risk from hypothermia, slipping into a sleep from which he would never awaken. Already, he'd caught himself stumbling, and the urge to collapse into a heap was almost overwhelming. His clothes were completely sodden and he was beginning to shiver uncontrollably. Now he needed to find somewhere to rest; not only because he'd used up his reserves of energy in crossing the M25 and marching through the night, but also because he dared not move while it was light. Out here, away from the ruins of London, cover was sparse, and a stranger would stick out like a sore thumb among any locals.

After looking around without any joy for half an hour Moss eventually came to a small barn, made of rusting sheet metal, in a comer of a field occupied by thin and desultory looking sheep. Carefully, he checked for signs of human occupation and finding none, forced his way inside. The barn was a store for poor-quality hay and animal feed and despite being a little smelly an ideal place for Moss to shelter from the wind and rain. It looked as if it hadn't been visited since the beginning of the war. The remaining bales of hay were beginning to rot as water dripped in a steady stream from the wooden beams. One corner of the metal sheet roofing had worked loose and kept lifting up and crashing down as the wind caught it, letting in a spray of rain every time.

None of this mattered though, it was luxury compared to some of the places Moss had been forced to sleep in before. From a corner he retrieved several empty sacks, then wormed his way into a gap between piles of feed and covered himself with the sacks. The stress of the past couple of days was finally beginning to catch-up with him and within minutes he fell into a deep exhausted sleep.

It wasn't long before images swam across his disturbed mind like fleeting montages of horror. He dreamed of the young girl and her mother playing happily on a hillside overlooking a London unblemished by war and death. She skipped and played, laughing and singing happily in the warm evening sunlight, as her mother looked on smiling warmly. Then, without warning, a small hole appeared in the centre of the mother's forehead and bright crimson blood oozed and dripped into her eyes. Her smile faded, soundlessly her legs gave way beneath her and she collapsed onto the ground like a broken doll.

The little girl screamed loudly, ran over and began pulling on her mothers arm shouting 'Get up Mummy! Get up Mummy! They're coming! Please get up!' Behind her the sun was swamped by broiling black clouds that hurled lightning bolts to the ground. The skyline of London changed into rubble and ruin, as though the earlier image was nothing more than a poor hologram, and this was the way it should really look. Up the hill ran a squad of Dyason storm troopers that immediately surrounded the little girl and her dead mother. Each pulled back the firing pin of their automatics and raised the muzzles until they pointed at the girl. Two of the troops parted to let an arrogant officer swagger into the circle they'd created. The little girl looked up at the officer and pleaded 'Please help me. I can't get my Mummy to wake up!' The officer looked down at her, opened his mouth and laughed hysterically. It was a laugh Moss knew well, it could belong to only one Dyason, the one he hated more than any other. In his dream he raised his old Lee-Enfield to his shoulder, took aim, and squeezed the trigger. However, the Dyason didn't fall down, instead blood gushed out of the chest of the little girl. Her hands vainly attempted to stop the flow of blood, and she too slowly collapsed to the ground beside her mother. The Dyason officer looked up, and in his mind's eye stared directly at him. Then, once again, he laughed maniacally.

Moss was filled with horror. It felt as if his brain was expanding, squeezing against his skull as if it was going to explode. He hadn't meant to miss, it was only a dream, so why did he feel so horrified? Why did he feel as if the responsibility for millions of lives suddenly lay in his lap? He felt as if the weight of guilt and responsibility was forcing him into the ground.

Then the pressure was gone. Where there was horror and guilt, now there was the feeling of a higher presence, a benevolent presence, standing beside him, guiding him through this maze of horror. He couldn't see who or what it was that was helping him. It was as if he couldn't turn around to see. The horrific image in his mind faded and was replaced by a field surrounded by huge upright stones. The sun was shining on a warm summer's day, and a skylark sang close by. Immediately Moss felt tranquil, calm, and a voice whispered in his ear that he should not fight his destiny, to go with his instincts, and follow the path set before him. It was a kindly voice, a voice he could trust. The voice told him to beware the minds searching for him, to only follow his instincts and find the stones. But when he tried to question the voice, it faded and disappeared, to be replaced by the grinning evil face of a Dyason officer, the face of the alien bastard who'd killed his parents and family in cold blood.

The Dyason was laughing at him once again, telling him that it was futile to resist. The evil face filled his vision, laughing hysterically, as Moss felt himself falling deeper and deeper into a bottomless pit. Now Moss was terrified, there was nobody to help him, he was falling... He woke with a start, his clothes drenched with sweat. Opening his eyes he leapt up in surprise. Standing above him, staring with wide serious eyes, was a small boy.

'My dad says I'm not to talk to any strange men. Especially, if they've been near them aliens,' piped up a small voice. He was young, no more than eight or nine years. His hair was a tangled mess, with bits of twigs and straw sticking out in all directions and his face was smeared with dirt. He wore a vastly oversized pair of trousers, held up at the waist by a piece of string; whilst on his feet were an ancient pair of boots, many times too big for his small feet. Water dripped from his soaked clothes making a small puddle on the barn floor. Shaking off the effects of sleep, shivering in his sweat-soaked clothes, Moss stood up and swayed slightly, surprised and unsure what to do. He was still thrown off balance by his nightmares.

'I'm not a strange man,' he finally mumbled, and immediately wished he hadn't. It was a lousy introduction. 'My name is Moss Penn,' he tried again.

'My name is Ambrose,' replied the child, staring at him intensely, with large curious eyes, 'Why are you sleeping in me dad's barn? Haven't you got anywhere to go? He'll be mad when he finds out.'

Moss blinked blankly and said nothing. Outside the shack the incessant wind and rain beat a tattoo on the corrugated roof. The loose sheet constantly slammed against a wooden post, creating a surreal rhythm that merged with the other sounds of yet another storm. Just what was he going to do with the little boy? He was still far too exhausted to bolt for the door and make a run for it. Besides, it was still daylight outside. If he let the child go, he would more than probably tell somebody of his whereabouts and the game would be up. Yet, he also knew that he didn't have it in him to hurt the lad. Moss was a killer, he'd proved that time and time again over the past months, but only against those who directly threatened him. He would never raise a hand or lay a finger against the weak and innocent. It was a strange set of morals to have in a time when only survival mattered, but Moss figured you had to draw the line somewhere, or you simply became as evil as those you despised. So he was caught in a dilemma. There was something strange about the boy though; something in his eyes. They were a deep brown colour and looked old; it was as if he had the body of a child, but the eyes of somebody much older. They were eyes that had witnessed many, many things. Moss shook his head, it must have been the dreams, his mind was still scrambled, he was thinking nonsense. Yet, somewhere deep in his mind, at an instinctive level, he knew he could trust this boy, and this meeting was in some way important. He didn't know why he felt this, but he did. So, perhaps he should risk confiding in the boy and winning his trust.

He took a deep breath and said, `I've crossed the wire from the ghettos and I'm on the run from the Dyason. I needed sleep and rest, so I took shelter in this shack. I'm trying to make my way to Scotland.'

'No you haven't' the child exclaimed pointing an accusing finger at his face. 'They say that everybody who lived in London is dead now. There are only ghosts there, and they work for the devil!'

Moss smiled grimly at that. In some ways there were only ghosts left there, and many of them had sold themselves to the devil. He kept that thought to himself though, and said, 'Err, no, not quite Ambrose. Many of the people who lived there before the war are dead. But some survived, they scratch out a survival in the ruins. I'm one of those survivors.'

'If you're from London, then you must work for the devil then!' said the boy, again jabbing a finger at Moss who suddenly, without really knowing why, laughed.

'If only I did Ambrose!' he finally replied, 'Then maybe I wouldn't be in the mess I'm in now. Besides, I hardly look like a devil do I? I admit I might look a little bit scruffy, but then we could both do with a good bath.'

Ambrose still eyed him suspiciously, 'No, I suppose not, but if you did escape from London, how did you do it, and why are you going to Scotland?'

'Whoa. Hold on a moment! One question at a time.' Moss got the distinct impression that the lad was always one step ahead of him. He needed to slow the conversation down and make it less like an interrogation otherwise he would end up saying too much.

'Look I'll tell you what. I'm hungry, what say we sit down, light a small fire, dry our clothes out, and I'll tell you everything you want to know?'

'You got food for me then?' Ambrose demanded.

'Well a little,' replied Moss, a little concerned at sharing his meagre rations and protectively pulling his small satchel of provisions towards him.

'Okay then!' the boy chirped and ran off to the far corner of the barn where there sat a small, ancient, wood burning stove stood. 'Over here! he called.

With a shrug of his shoulders, Moss gathered his bits together and walked over. There was a good store of chopped wood piled nearby and within a few minutes Moss and the small boy were hungrily munching on the dry bread and chocolate, scrounged from the West End, warming themselves in front of the stove. Outside the rain beat an incessant rhythm on the tin roof as the dreary day wore on.

'So why are you running away?' Ambrose asked Moss once he'd finished eating.

'Always the inquisitive one aren't you?' Moss replied munching on the last biscuit.

'What's inquisitive?

And so Moss began to tell the small boy his story. Not all of it, he didn't want to put the child at risk by giving him information the Dyason would want, but enough to give the small boy a picture of life in the ghettos of London.

Ambrose sat almost motionless, his eyes full of wonder for almost an hour as the story unfolded. Occasionally, he would ask surprisingly intelligent questions which Moss would try to answer as simply as possible, but at times he found himself forgetting he was talking to a child and not an adult, such was the level of the conversation. When the tale was told Ambrose sketched an impression of life in the Surrey hills, although he was very reluctant to say anything too specific about his family and past. So Moss diplomatically avoided the subjec,t fearing the child had lost some of his family during the invasion.

Eventually, Moss dug out the well-worn pre-war road map he was planning to use to guide himself to Scotland and Ambrose showed him the rough position of the barn. It turned out that they were near the village of Shere, some six or seven kilometres from Guildford. For the first time Moss started to think seriously about how he intended to make his way to Scotland. Escaping from London was one thing, making his way across hundreds of kilometres of occupied territory was another. The truth was he had made his escape by luck, but luck alone wouldn't get him to Scotland. Besides, it was only a rumour that Scotland was relatively unoccupied by the Dyason. He didn't know of anybody who had actually been there, so there was no real way of telling. It was a long way to go, just to discover it was nothing but a rumour.

Ambrose was sitting on an old fertiliser container swinging his legs when he suddenly piped up. 'The Bristol Channel Moss! You've got to head for the Bristol Channel'.

Moss looked up from checking over his provisions with a slightly puzzled expression. 'Why the Bristol Channel?' he asked curiously, not making the connection between there and Scotland.

''Cause you can steal a small boat and make your way up the coastline to Scotland. If you pick a small enough boat and travel at night the Dyason patrols will never find you.'

Ambrose traced a route on the map with a small digit then triumphantly crossed his arms and sat back down again, a small grin on his face.

Moss looked thoughtfully at the map. The child's idea had some merit to it. If he cut west avoiding main routes, he could cross Salisbury plain and head for the Bristol Channel. Then, by travelling at night and hugging the coastline, he could make his way north. Admittedly he hadn't been near a boat since before the war, but he could still remember sunny afternoons on his dingy, sailing up and down the Medway river. Yes, there was definitely some merit to the idea! It would be dangerous, what with all the storms that seemed to batter the country constantly, but he reckoned he stood a better chance that way, than trying to cross hundreds kilometres on foot. The storms would also work to his advantage by helping to conceal him from Dyason patrols.

In fact, the more he thought about it, the more merit the kid's idea possessed. Moss turned to Ambrose and gave him a wink and a broad grin. 'You know, you might just have something there kid!' he said.

Ambrose looked at him with a smug expression on his face. 'Told you!' he retorted.

Then together they pored over the road map of Britain again, looking in more detail at the possible route he could take up the west coast of England and Wales. It was some hours later when the child got up, turned and looked out of the barn door at the gathering dusk. A change of mood came over him; a more withdrawn, sad expression creased his little head, and once again Moss felt as if he were looking at someone much older than a young child.

'It's time for me to go, or I'll be in real trouble, bye...' he said abruptly. 'Oh, you can stay here tonight, it's safe, nobody ever comes here,' and without giving Moss a chance to say another word, he ran for the door, gave a brief wave and disappeared into the gloom.

Moss walked over to the entrance, a little surprised at the rapid departure, and peered into the gloom trying to make out where his new friend had gone to. But there was nothing to be seen in the rain and enveloping dark. For a brief interlude, something good had entered his life, like a ray of sunshine bursting between storm clouds. Now it was gone and winter had returned to his soul. He couldn't help feeling that there had been something a little strange about the child. Without knowing how or why, the visit had left Moss feeling more confident, less frightened than before. The idea of heading for the Bristol Channel was far better than anything he'd thought of for himself, but more than that, talking to the child had been like therapy. He'd been forced to calm down and look at his predicament clearly. After their initial meeting, the thought of being discovered by a Dyason patrol hadn't even crossed his mind, in fact he was sure that he was still secure inside the ramshackle barn, being warmed by the slowly burning logs - at least until the following day. Moss sat down again beside the small stove. Weariness crept over him and his eyes began to feel heavy. He made himself comfortable among the old sacks and soon fell into a deep and dreamless sleep.

He woke next morning feeling more relaxed and refreshed than at any time he could remember since the invasion. Blearily, he rubbed the sleep out of his eyes and discovered a small parcel wrapped in an old shopping bag lying beside him. Certain it hadn't been there the night before, Moss opened it with curiosity. Inside he found a small compass, an ordnance map of the West Country showing far greater detail than his old road map, and some bread and salted meat. His little friend had left him a present during the night and he'd never even stirred! Moss felt a surge of gratitude to the small boy and mentally wished him well. Then, placing the parcel in his rucksack he tightened his boots, checked his weapons and strode out of the barn into the dull winter morning.

The hypersonic transport landed at Tokyo international airport and taxied to a corner of the busy airfield. The hatch opened and Gulag stepped out onto the concrete. The air was much warmer here than in Britain, he noted. Indeed the sun was almost breaking through the cloud cover, showing that the dust in the stratosphere here was settling faster than in Western Europe. Maybe there was hope that the climate on this god awful planet was finally showing the early signs of recovery. Anything was better than the incessant wind and rain he had to endure in Britain.

The air was full of the sound of turbines and vectors as various aircraft took off and landed at the airport every few seconds. Tokyo was the chosen location for the Colonial Dyason headquarters, and the amount of air traffic reflected this. Many of the aircraft taking off were Earth-built airliners, moving Dyason personnel from country to country. Dyason-built shuttles also took off from an adjacent runway, using their jet engines and stubby wings to get them up into the upper atmosphere before igniting their rocket engines for the last leap into space and docking with the orbiting Domes. A flight of helicopter gunships took off nearby, causing Gulag to grab hold of his cap before it got blown away in the rotor wash. The gunships swept out towards the distant mountains, obviously on another anti-terrorist mission.

He felt a certain amount of satisfaction that even here, at the centre of Dyason operations, native terrorists were still an unresolved problem. So much for the subjugation of the local populace! After a few minutes a Japanese built limousine crossed the apron and stopped before the shuttle. Two Dyason officers wearing the uniforms of central command, climbed out the back and marched over to Gulag. They saluted stiffly and snapped out the formal greeting.

'The Emperor and mother planet!'

'Glory in her conquests,' Gulag replied dryly. He took an instant dislike to the desk-bound warriors, and didn't make any attempt to hide his feelings.

'If you would care to follow me Security Leader, we have accommodation prepared for you. The Marshal will see you tomorrow,' one of the officers said with a sneer.

Gulag nodded in reply, not bothering to say anything, and got into the back of the limo flanked each side by the officers. Smoothly the car moved towards the airport exit. At the checkpoint they were waved through, and with an escort of Dyason motorcycle riders, they sped through the streets of Tokyo, lights flashing. Gulag saw very little of the indigenous Japanese population, most of the people on the streets were Dyason troops and officials. There had been stories of the Japanese people killing themselves en-mass rather than suffer the dishonour of capitulation. Although Gulag rather thought this was an excuse for the mass killings undertaken by the Dyason population control squads.

After about ten minutes the car pulled into a large hotel, now used as a billet for Dyason officers. Thankfully, his escort left in the car after depositing him and his luggage in the foyer, telling him they would pick him up at 0700 local time the following morning. The hotel foyer was filled with officers from all services, but all of senior rank. They milled around aimlessly, chatting in small groups, sipping tea and fondling young Japanese women wearing traditional kimonos. One such woman rose from a low table and approached him, her silk gown whispering along the polished floor.

'Security Leader Gulag, I am known simply as Blossom' the woman introduced herself in heavily accented Dyason. Her young doll like face was heavily made up in the traditional Japanese way and beneath the silk gowns he could just discern a small lithe body. 'I am ordered to prepare your room and entertain you,' she said, then gave a small bow, picked up his small case and headed for the lifts.

It had been a long flight and Gulag was physically tired, but his pent-up stress and anger needed venting, so with a hungry look of anticipation in his eyes he followed the diminutive woman to the lift.

Night was falling as Gulag stood staring out of the window, watching the drizzle fall lightly over Tokyo. Bright neon signs flashed from the tops of skyscrapers making small popping sounds as the fine rain drops fell onto the hot tubes. Once they had advertised Japanese televisions, camcorders and computers. Now they pronounced Dyason slogans of undying support for the home world and Emperor.

Behind him the Japanese girl slept fitfully on the bed, exhausted after Gulag had spent his lust and frustration. He felt better for the copulation, even if it was with an Earth-born female. He'd been surprised at his pent-up rage the brunt of which the Japanese woman had taken. It would be some weeks before her numerous bruises and small cuts healed. If he was honest with himself, his stress was caused by his apprehension over his forthcoming audience with Marshal Mettar that morning. The order to travel to Tokyo had come as soon as he'd reported the destruction of the resistance base in Croydon. There'd been no explanation with the orders. Gulag feared that Mettar may have discovered that the operant youth who was responsible for Topaz's murder was still at large.

Gulag knew that the youth was not in the bunker when it was destroyed together with several hundred of his best storm troopers. He knew because that familiar tingle at the base of his neck was still there, as it had been ever since he faced the youth on the rooftop in Covent Garden. His talent had been reawakened and intensified beyond measure in the past few weeks. It was as if he were opening his eyes and seeing clearly for the first time in his life. He realised now that he'd been mistaken to suppress his powers in the past. However, he was still not strong enough to pinpoint the location of the murderer, only to feel his life force. Now he'd been ordered here and he had no misconceptions about the reason for the audience. He knew that despite the destruction of a major resistance cell, Mettar had it in for him. He was in trouble. Just how much trouble he was in, he would have to wait until the morning to find out.

Gulag felt his loins stirring from a mixture of lust frustration again. He turned and moved towards the girl on the bed. It was time to force himself upon her again and he would enjoy making her suffer.

The escort arrived early the next morning and took Gulag to Marshal Mettar's offices which were situated in the palace of the ex-Emperor of Japan. There Gulag found himself kept waiting for nearly an hour, on a hard-backed chair in the corridor, outside the Marshal's office. The unsmiling face of the adjutant sitting at his desk in front of the huge gilded double doors was little comfort.

Finally, the intercom on the adjutant's desk beeped. The small mean-faced Dyason looked up at Gulag then beckoned him to go through to the Marshal's office.

Gulag opened one of the ornate doors and marched through. Inside the room was huge, with large bay windows that opened onto the palace gardens. The walls were decorated with Japanese works of art, while the floor was of deeply veined marble. Marshal Mettar sat at a huge desk at the far end of the room, his head bowed over a folder he was studying. Mettar was short and squat with a square bold cranium that sank directly into huge broad shoulders. His well tailored uniform did little to hide the bulge of well-toned muscles. Despite his fifty years or so, Mettar was one mean son of a bitch.

Gulag marched down the length of the room his gleaming boots making a staccato rhythm on the marble floor. He stopped two feet in front of the desk and snapped to attention. Mettar ignored him and continued to read the folder. Gulag stood rigidly to attention staring at a fixed point somewhere above his superior's head. Finally, after several minutes, Mettar put the folder down and looked up at Gulag. His face was set like granite except for a single vein pulsing on his shiny forehead, the only visible sign of emotion.

'I don't like you Gulag' Mettar opened in a deadpan voice. 'You've made matters extremely complicated. Not only did you allow the resistance to murder my predecessor, you managed to lose half a brigade of the finest storm troopers in a futile attempt to capture a handful of human operants.'

'With respect sir!' Gulag unwisely interrupted in a rather futile attempt to defend his actions from the very beginning. 'We totally destroyed the resistance headquarters!'

'Don't be naive Gulag! We *already* knew of the location of their headquarters. We spent months installing informants into the complex, only to have you and your thugs ruin *everything*!' Mettar snapped.

Gulag visibly paled. Damn the bastard! He hadn't even considered the possibility that command might already know of the base, let alone have informants placed there. What the hell had been going on? He should have been the first to know the whereabouts of the terrorists, and been the one to liaise directly with informants. If Mettar was telling the truth, then he'd been purposely kept in the dark. What else had been going on under his very nose that he hadn't been told about? A flush of anger rose up his face, but he kept his mouth shut. He was supposed to be the bloody area Security Officer, for God's sake!

'Further, your methods of controlling the British population by mass killings are crude and ineffective. Topaz may have been impressed by your sadistic behaviour; I am not!' Mettar continued unabated. 'However, these are all matters we can discuss in more detail later. As much as I would like to see your ugly face in front of a court martial, I am forced to subdue my feelings.' Mettar paused and looked back at the folder. Gulag felt confused, he was braced to take the full force of the Marshal's fury. What was going on? Was he about to be sacrificed, removed in some unofficial manner other than the public disgrace of a court martial? His heart beating faster, his fate would become clear any minute now.

'Gulag, the colonial force is already aware of your operant powers, despite your attempts to keep them hidden from the psychiatrists during training,' Mettar continued. 'I am aware that the use of "mind powers" is considered by many old wives back on Dyason, as a gift from the devil, and certainly in your case I can believe it. However Gulag, the empire has need of such powers. So I want to hear from your own lips, what are the limits to your talents?'

Gulag froze; the question had come straight out of the blue. Mettar appeared to have gone off at a complete tangent, or had he? Was he about to be stripped of his rank and privileges or not? This was the second time Mettar had made reference to his operancy, the first being during the holo-communication in London. He'd always been told as a child that his talents were a gift from the devil, so he'd learnt to keep them secret, only using them when he felt there was no chance of discovery. This was an instinct he had carried with him into the colonial service, and now he was being told to divulge all his secrets. Should he tell the truth? Definitely not—he must not let the old bastard know of his recent surge of power, nor his method of discovering the resistance base. Besides, why should he be co-operative? The bastard hated his guts anyway, so he certainly wasn't about to add any ammunition that might send himself to the gallows.

After some moments of hesitation he replied, 'I don't know sir. I've never really used my operancy talents for the reasons you've already stated. However, I can feel what appears to be some disturbance in the place where thought works. I've felt uneasy since the murder of Marshal Topaz. To be truthful sir, I have never tested the parameters of my skills. I have always relied upon my "normal" abilities.'

Mettar examined him thoughtfully for a moment, waved a dismissive hand then stared out of the bay windows at the drizzle. 'Sit down Gulag,' he said. Gulag sat on another hard-backed chair opposite the Marshal and waited as patiently as he could for Mettar to return his attention to him.

'What I am about to tell you is highly classified. Under no circumstances are you to utter a word about it to anyone.'

'No sir' Gulag replied dryly, wondering what was coming next.

'Do you recall the journey from Dyason to Earth?' Mettar asked.

'Yes sir, we spent six months in transit on one of the cruisers that made the first attack on Earth,' Gulag replied.

'Yes, but do you recall the method of how we travelled across the light years to reach Earth?' Mettar urged.

'I recall one of the cruiser's crew telling me something about hyperspace and the fabric of the cosmos. But to be honest I didn't really understand it,' said Gulag searching for the significance of this to his operancy and being purposely vague about how much he really knew. There was no point in showing any of his cards at this stage of the game. Let Mettar ramble on for a while.

'Right,' continued Mettar, 'well, all you really need to know is that some years ago astronomers on Dyason discovered a hole in space, within our star system.'

'You mean a fault in the fabric of space itself, like that described by the crewman?' Gulag asked again playing slightly dumb.

'Exactly,' confirmed Mettar. 'The fault was very small, affecting gravity only within a few thousand klicks of itself. It was decided to send a manned probe through that rip. This, as you will remember, was done and to our surprise, the probe and her crew returned a year later with information on the fault and the star system that existed on other side.'

'It transpired that the fault was a two-way hole through space, a tunnel if you like, leading to the star system we are in now. Obviously, we conquered this world as part of the Dyason Empire once we knew of its existence. However, astronomers and physicists have recently discovered that the hyperspace tunnel is becoming unstable and liable to collapse in the near future. Obviously, we cannot allow our links with Dyason to be severed, so we must find a way to stabilise the hole, or discover another way to transverse space. This is where operants like yourself come in...'

'I fail to see how I can be of help sir?' Gulag said, probing carefully, looking for a link between Mettar's rather basic understanding of astrophysics and his operancy. It occurred to him that perhaps he should scan Mettar's mind and take the knowledge he needed directly. But he couldn't be sure of doing this without Mettar realising what was happening. There was no point in making his situation any worse, so he would just have to be patient with the old sod.

Mettar ignored him and continued, 'The scientists believe it's possible to distort the fabric of space and time through mental operancy. It transpires that Earth operants have been working towards this goal for quite some time.'

Circuits began to switch on in Gulag's mind as he finally made the connection. 'I see!' he interrupted. 'You want the human operants to open another space tunnel.'

'Very nearly Gulag, very nearly,' Mettar replied getting up from his desk and moving towards the bay windows before turning and saying, 'It may be possible for every Cruiser to have an operant on board who could open the door to hyperspace allowing that Cruiser to traverse the galaxy. That's why we need all native human operants, so that experiments can be carried out on them. Now we have reports from operants about a new mind, far more powerful than those gone before. That mind belongs to a youth in Britain, possibly the same youth that assassinated my predecessor. We need to find that youth, because he may be the first of a new generation of humans with sufficient mental operancy to perceive the fourth dimension of hyperspace. It will take an operant to find an operant, and you are the only Dyason operant on Earth. ....*so far.*'

The last jigsaw piece fell into place in Gulag's mind. Realisation burst forth. The youth who killed Topaz was the operant and Mettar wanted the youth's mind to open up hyperspace. No wonder he was ordered to find but not kill the little bastard.

The Marshal looked away from the window and stared at Gulag 'I see by the look on your face that you are beginning to understand the situation,' Mettar observed.

'Indeed I do sir!' Gulag replied, trying to keep his face expressionless, despite his mind racing ahead, examining all the possibilities of this new information.

'Good!' Mettar continued, still eyeballing Gulag, 'because as much as it galls me to say so, you are the only Dyason we can trust to find the human youth, and all the other remaining human operants... Stand to attention!'

Gulag stood up automatically and snapped to attention. 'As of now Gulag, you are relieved of your command in London. You will receive training to improve your operancy skills then you will head a Dyason team to find human operants, the youth in particular. You will report directly to myself alone, and be given full access to all imperial men and materials. Don't fail me Gulag! Remember, these orders come from the Emperor himself. If it were up to me I would have you flogged and hanged... Fail in this task that is exactly what I shall do... Be sure of that! Now get your foul body out of here. You will receive your written orders from the adjutant!'

Gulag clicked his heels, turned and strode towards the doors. A warm glow of excitement flowed through his body. The gods were smiling favourably, things couldn't have worked out better! He would find the murdering youth, but he wouldn't let him live... As to the opening of the hyperspace link, well given the right knowledge he felt confident enough to achieve that as well, somehow. It was all falling into place. To imagine that only a few weeks ago his talents were subdued, dormant, waiting for a time and place to manifest themselves. Well, now was the time, and here on this bloody awful planet was the place. Destiny was leading him down a path to greatness, and nothing and nobody was going to stand in his way. Mettar had unwittingly sown the seeds of Gulag's future; now there would be no turning back!

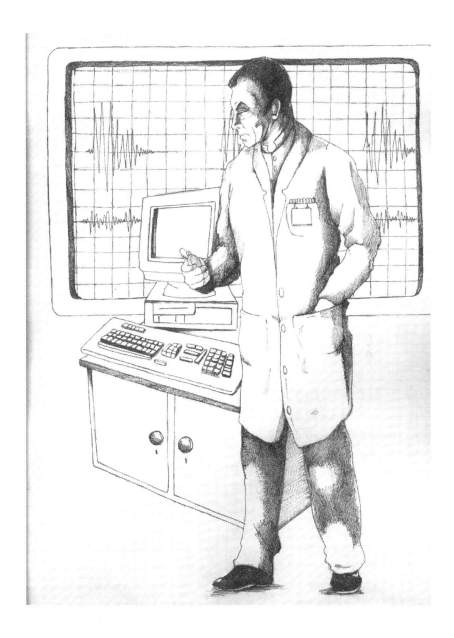

Brabazon was a thin, gaunt man. His bifocal glasses and narrow face gave him the look of a haunted weasel; which was exactly how he felt. He sat in front of a holo-monitor, carefully examining the sine curves and graphs that flowed before him. Occasionally he tapped at the keyboard, re-examined the results then looked up to where an Asian man sat in a laboratory chair in an isolation room, wired up like a Christmas tree. The subject was approaching the barrier the others had come up against. His ESP trace was beginning to peak and trough to the very top and bottom of the scale. Inside the isolation room he twitched and tossed more violently until he was pulling against the restraining straps, moaning loudly. Brabazon adjusted the graph scales to compensate for the increased activity, but even at minimum sensitivity, the peaks were off the scale. Suddenly the man arched his back violently pulling against all the straps so hard that one of the arm restraints broke and his arm flailed around his head. He gave out a long piercing scream, a scream that reached down to the very depths of the soul and placed an icy hand around one's heart. It was a scream of terror and a scream of death. Abruptly all the traces fell back to their baselines, the man's body went limp and his vital signs died. With a sigh, Brabazon powered down the instruments. He didn't even bother to go and check the body of the Asian, he already knew they'd failed. He'd consigned another human being to hell.

Abruptly the lab door opened and two Dyason officers walked in. Shit, that was all he needed, more witnesses to his failure. It was Zibber, his supervisor, and some other Dyason he hadn't seen before.

'Ah Brabazon,' said Zibber in heavily accented English. 'Here you are. Glad to see you're working hard for the Empire. Pity the experiment didn't work, but then the price for ultimate knowledge is always a high one - eh?' Brabazon wished he could strap the bastard in the chair and frazzle his brains. 'There's someone here I'd like you to meet'. He turned to introduce the second officer who'd already stepped forward to reach for Brabazon's hand, pumping it up and down. The officer was athletically built, chisel featured, but with deep dark eyes, and a thin mean mouth.

'Good afternoon Brabazon.' The Dyason said in perfect English keeping a tight hold on his hand, staring intently into his eyes. 'I hear you've been making a great contribution to the Imperial cause. Let me introduce myself; my name is Security Leader Gulag. We shall be working closely together in the future.'

Brabazon began to murmur a reply, but before he could open his lips, his mind froze. Beads of sweat began to appear on his forehead. Unbidden into his mind came the words, '*I agree my friend we should strap him in the chair and frazzle his brains too! Ah, I see you are surprised that I can read your thoughts. Yes human, I too can rove the world beyond the body. I can read your mind at will, peel away your thoughts one by one. There will be no secrets between us. After all you wouldn't like your young wife to be sent to a slave factory would you? Maybe that young body of hers could be used to satisfy the glorious troops!*'

Brabazon's face paled, he felt faint and weak at the knees, but unable to tear his eyes away from the evil stare of this Dyason. The hairs on his neck stood on end and a shiver of fear ran down his spine. The one thing above all that he feared the most, faced him not a metre away, the one thing that could finally spell the demise of everyone born on earth - a Dyason operant.

'Ah, still here Zibber?' Gulag asked the other officer without looking at him, his eyes still boring into Brabazon. 'I shall be spending the rest of the day with the good doctor here. Your presence is no longer required. Thank you for bringing me here.'

Zibber went red in the face, opened his mouth to retort, but thought better of it. Instead he turned on his heels and marched out of the lab, slamming the door behind him. Gulag held Brabazon in his stare, like a coiled cobra mesmerising its prey before striking. 'We're going to get to know each other very well, human, *Very* well indeed!' he said in a voice that dripped malice.

At that moment Brabazon knew his soul was forever lost in Dante's innermost circle of hell.

It was the early hours of the morning by the time Brabazon returned to the small apartment block he was allocated within the military zone of Tokyo. He showed his pass to the bored guard at the entrance, underwent a cursory search, and took the elevator to his floor. Once inside the tiny studio apartment he headed straight for the bottle of Saki he kept in the bathroom cabinet then fell in exhaustion onto his bed. His hands shook as he took a slug of the alcohol straight from the bottle. Despite his physical tiredness, his mind was still reeling, swirling from the drama of the day's events.

He felt stripped and gutted, mentally raped. The Dyason Gulag had spent all day questioning him on every aspect of his life and research into ESP, or the "higher faculties". Not all the questions had been verbal, At times the Dyason had simply ripped the information he needed straight from his mind, while he'd been powerless to resist, his own feeble mind too weak to block the powerful Dyason. Brabazon wasn't sure which was the more terrifying, the fact that this man Gulag now knew everything about his experiments, including those matters he'd previously managed to keep secret, or the fact that for the first time he'd met a Dyason with awesome mind powers; something no Dyason had previously shown any talent for.

He couldn't get the bastards threat out of his mind. The threat against the one person he cared for above all else. Flashbacks, like old video tapes again came unbidden into his mind as he recalled his wife and the past he had been forced to leave behind. He remembered as a young boy sending "secret" messages to his twin brother. Since birth he and his identical twin had been bound by far more than appearance. Even before they could walk and talk, they were intrinsically linked in thought and feelings. If one of them became sick, Brabazon remembered that the other would feel the pain. He could even remember that when one of them suckled at their mother's breast, the other would feel the transmitted warmth and security. One could argue that this was nothing more than the normal bonding between identical twins, but when he was eight years old, they proved that their links were far stronger than normal siblings.

That summer he'd been playing in the old oak tree that stood beside the creek, about half a kilometre from their home in New Hampshire. For some reason he couldn't remember, he'd clambered out onto the limb that hung over the creek. The branch had broken under his weight and he'd fallen into the water. Unable to swim, he'd floundered about, panic stricken, calling out for help, but nobody came. Every time his head disappeared under the water it took him that bit longer to struggle to the surface again, and he knew he was slowly drowning. In a last desperate call for help he concentrated his mind and flung his thoughts at his brother sitting at home, and it was he who, a few minutes later, climbed out on another limb of the tree and hauled him half drowned out of the creek.

At the local high school, the twins had shown a real flair for science subjects and always got top grades in their examinations, not just because they were extremely intelligent, but also because on exam day two heads are better than one, and even if the examiners were suspicious that their papers were very similar, they could prove nothing. By their late teens the mental rapport between Luke and Josh Brabazon was fully matured. They went everywhere together and shared everything, including girlfriends, but they were always careful to conceal their talents from the adults around them. They were too bright to fall into the trap of becoming media sideshow freaks. That was until the fateful day they went to a lecture on ESP given by Dr Dusard. It was a lecture that was to change the course of their lives.

Dusard was a parapsychologist at Boston University and led the field in research into telepathy and the paranormal. For years science had relegated such research to the "lunatic fringe", considering the very concept of extra sensory perception to be on a par with alchemy. However, by the last years of the Twentieth Century the science community was forced, under a deluge of irrefutable evidence, to bring parapsychology into mainstream science and Dusard had led the renaissance. In his lecture he had talked of the growing number of cases of humans with "extra faculties", around the globe, and how he predicted that humanity was on the verge of a new evolutionary step. An evolutionary step in the direction of telepathy and ESP. After the lecture the twins had sought out Dr Dusard at his laboratory and confronted him with their own powers of telepathy. Dusard then promptly recruited the twins to join his research faculty at the university.

As the "higher faculty" movement grew, the Brabazon brothers were at the forefront of the experiments being carried out to discover the limits of mankind's new-found skills. Unfortunately, the twins soon discovered that their own skills were limited to telepathy between themselves. Even so, they were able to contribute greatly to the mounting documented knowledge of ESP, and created the unit of Dusard, named after their mentor, as a standard by which higher faculty powers could be measured.

Then one day the world changed forever; the war began. The fighting itself was over very quickly, and largely missed the university campus. However, the skies over America were soon broiling as the sun disappeared under a layer of ash and smoke, and thousands of sick and homeless refugees came in search of aid. It was during those few frantic weeks after the invasion that Brabazon met his young wife Lucinda. She was a student, desperately trying to care for the sick and hungry. Brabazon fell in love with her beauty and compassion. Their romance was brief and passionate and this time he had no intention of sharing the affair with his brother. The marriage took place in the university chapel and their honeymoon was a night of passion in Brabazon's small quarters.

One day, some six weeks or so after the invasion, the Dyason finally came to the university campus. They arrived in a convoy of armoured cars and cattle lorries. All the refugees and most of the campus town's inhabitants were herded onto the lorries and driven away, never to be seen again. The twins had never felt so helpless. A garrison of Dyason troops occupied the town and the higher faculty department was brought before the commander. To their surprise they were offered every courtesy and asked to resume their research as before, submitting regular reports to the Dyason high command. They were dumbfounded. What possible value could their research into parapsychology be to the Dyason? However, they had little option but to agree to their terms, so the research continued as it did before the war. As the dark months went by, much discussion took place as to why they alone were being allowed to continue their lives, much as they had before the war. Information filtered down from the telepaths among them of how, across the globe, universities were being allowed to continue research into certain subjects, such as engineering, electronics and ESP, albeit under strict Dyason supervision. As to the rest of humanity, it seemed that the world was being enslaved as rumours of labour camps and prison cities emerged.

Brabazon had argued that, despite this, if humanity was to throw off the shackles of the Dyason, they would need the powers of the 'higher faculties' so the research must continue. His brother Josh had vehemently rejected this, claiming the only reason they were spared from the slavery that ensnared the rest of humanity, was because it suited the Dyason needs. For the first time in their lives the twins could not agree on something. A wedge had been placed between them. With hindsight, he realised that his marriage to Lucinda had largely been behind their discord. He would do anything to keep his wife safe, and that meant doing the enemy's bidding. Josh, without such responsibilities, couldn't work under such circumstances. One cold morning, after a particularly bad argument with his brother, Brabazon arrived at the lab to find him gone, along with half the department's younger staff. There was only a short note left to give a clue as to where he had gone. It'd simply said, "Can no longer carry out the devil's work. Have left to join the resistance." Brabazon had attempted many times since to reach Josh through their telepathic links, but without any joy. To this day he didn't know whether Josh was alive or dead.

The garrison commander was furious at the desertions and shot Professor Dusard, and several of the department staff on the spot. The rest of them were packed onto lorries and driven to a camp in New Jersey. There, Brabazon, his wife and the remains of the research team were forced to carry on with their research under more squalid conditions and even closer scrutiny. Then eight months ago they came during the night and took Brabazon away and brought him here to Tokyo. He had to leave his wife in New Jersey and they hadn't been in contact since. Cast out into an emotional wilderness, lost without the two most important people in his life, he resigned himself to working as hard as possible, in the hope that the Dyason might at least let his wife join him sometime in the near future.

In Tokyo, Brabazon found himself in good company. All the leading scientists in the field of ESP research were also there, He was ordered to co-ordinate research on a particular project, using the facilities of Tokyo university. The project however, was almost beyond belief and filled him with despair. He was ordered to carry out research into the possible ability of operants to visualise the fourth dimension. For some years now, scientists had speculated that mental operancy took place in a dimension beyond the known three-dimensional universe, a theory supported by the fact that it didn't rely on the electromagnetic spectrum in the same manner as telecommunications or light waves. The theoretical fourth dimension does not adhere to the accepted rules of space and time, so mental operancy appeared to fit within this hypothesis. Just before the invasion, Dr Dusard printed a paper on the hypothetical link between the fourth dimension and mental operancy. He believed that as humans operancy talents expanded, it may be possible in the future to map the fourth dimension, and this mapping could be the key to interstellar navigation. A distant star may be billions of light years away in the three-dimensional universe, but in the fourth dimension the rules don't apply, so that distance no longer exists. Well, that at least was the theory, putting such concepts into practice would take another few thousand years of human evolution - so thought Dusard.

The Dyason unfortunately weren't willing to wait that long. They wanted to know if there was a link between operancy and the fourth dimension straightaway, so they set Brabazon and his team on the job. At first the task seemed impossible, and if it weren't for his desperation to see his wife again, he would have given up the task and taken the consequences. But he'd kept at it for more than twelve hours a day, seven days a week, until eight months later, to everybody's amazement, not least his own, his research team had some limited success. Some of the operants were indeed able to mentally visualise the very fabric of space itself, if only for a fraction of a second. Unfortunately, after those few seconds their minds were reduced to porridge by the sheer enormity of what they saw.

It didn't take much to figure out why the Dyason were so interested in this field of research. Speculation during the war had been rife among scientists that the Dyason had come to Earth through a fault in hyperspace, that somehow connected the two solar systems. Without the aid of the four-dimensional fault, they would have been incapable of travelling such huge distances. From what he'd seen of Dyason technology, Brabazon knew that in most respects their technology was no more advanced than that on Earth. Certainly in fields such as electronics they were years behind, but in other areas such as rocket propulsion, they had the advantage. But not such an advantage that they could carry out journeys beyond their star system without the aid of a space-time fault, hence their interest in operancy research. If the Dyason could open up their own links to the fourth dimension, then they could travel to any place in the universe without relying on an unstable phenomenon. An appalling thought! However, it would need mental skills far more powerful than those possessed by their current research subjects. Now though, there seemed to be a new generation of operants emerging in the world and it might just be that one of these new minds could bring the Dyason goal within their grasp.

Today Brabazon had met the first Dyason to ever display mental operancy and by God what power! There could be no doubt that this creature; Gulag, possessed awesome, untamed and totally evil power, not even aware yet of his full potential. There were other minds that also stood out from all others; one had been traced to the country Gulag had just left, England. But here the mind belonged to a male youth; young, raw but also full of potential. At first this mind had radiated thoughts like a radio beacon across the fourth dimension. None of them easily read; the human mind sped from one thought concept to another too fast for that, but easy to track. Lately though, this mind had gone quiet. Not dead, as they had first supposed, more sort of subdued, as though suppressed and guarded. There was one other power making itself felt. It was the most powerful of them all, but nobody had managed to pinpoint it. Like background static on the airwaves, it was always there on every wavelength.

And so the Dyason had sent their own operant to oversee the project. A creature who would stop at nothing to achieve his aims. A creature instinctively aware of his human competition far away in England, and now he'd been given the tools to fulfil his desires. Brabazon felt he was nothing more than a pawn in a game being played out by unseen competitors, with the whole solar system as the game board and quite frankly, he was terrified! The empty bottle of Saki fell onto the floor and he fell into a drunken, fitful sleep.

CHAPTER SEVEN

BEYOND THE WALLS OF LONDON

Under cover of darkness Moss moved steadily across the deserted tracks and footpaths firstly of Surrey, then Hampshire and Wiltshire. As the nights passed by he became attuned to the sounds and thoughts of the creatures around him. He learnt to 'passively' tune into the minds of the pitiful few survivors of the English countryside. He could feel the thoughts of foxes intent on scavenging for food to stave off hunger, wishing they were in their warm dry dens. He could feel the confusion of small birds hunting for berries that never grew, their minds unable to grasp why the sun never shone and spring never seemed to arrive, as their genes told them it should. He could even feel the primeval instincts of the dogs that roamed in packs hunting as their ancestors had done, now their human masters were gone.

But more than anything Moss could feel the utter desolation of the landscape he travelled through. Fields were bare of crops, farmyards empty of people and livestock, and everywhere lay the rotting carcasses of dead sheep, cattle and horses, their flesh taut across empty stomachs, their eyeballs shredded by hungry birds. Only very occasionally did he come anywhere near a farm that was still occupied, and when he did, the few surviving cows and sheep he saw looked like living skeletons. It was all very different from the countryside of fields of ripening wheat, neat thatched cottages, and friendly farm dogs that Moss remembered as a child.

At times he would come across a small village or hamlet, each as deserted and desolate as the surrounding woods and fields. Whenever possible, as night fell, Moss would enter an empty house or barn and scavenge for old cans of food, usually without any success. He would nibble on the disappearing rations the child Ambrose had given him then fall into a fitful sleep, listening to the howling of dog packs in the distance. One night as he crossed into the Hampshire borders Moss came across a farmhouse and outbuildings nestled behind a clump of bare oak trees. It had in better times, he had no doubt, been the home of a prosperous farmer. At least 150 years old, the buildings were traditional brick and wooden frame, while the remains of a thatch still covered the roof of the farmhouse. He forced his way in through a window and made his way to the kitchen in the hope of finding stored food, but instead he found the mummified remains of a small girl, no older than three or four. She lay next to the open door of a fridge surrounded by empty cartons of milk and biscuits. The child must have been left to fend for herself when the Dyason came and took her parents away. He figured the child had died of starvation and the cold, while the enclosed environment of the house had preserved the body. Moss had seen more dead bodies than he could count in the ghettos of London, but for some reason, seeing the remains of the girl struck a cord in his heart. Maybe it was because the rest of the farm was so nearly untouched. He could almost smell the aroma of newly baked bread, hear the barking of dogs and the cries of laughter from a happy family, sensations and feelings that belonged to a better time. A tear welled in his eye then became a torrent that went on and on, as he sat for some time beside the tiny body, purging his soul of pent-up grief. Later, Moss wrapped the child up in an old blanket and buried her at the back of the house. That night he ignored the comfortable bed in the house and slept in the barn.

After ten days and nights Moss neared Salisbury Plain, a high, flat and bleak place, some ninety or so kilometres from London. By now he had just about finished all the food in his knapsack, and was becoming seriously weak and hungry, his condition made worse by the freezing wind and rains. He'd tried trapping birds, rabbits and the like, but Moss was an urban child and failed miserably in his attempts. Nor could he risk wasting ammunition on hunting as that would only attract unwanted attention. Besides there were barely any birds to catch, and he hadn't seen any rabbits at all. Like so many other creatures, they were victims of the war and repression.

As to the small villages he had travelled through—they were all deserted, with nearly every dwelling picked clean of anything edible. He dared not head for any of the larger towns for fear of being caught by a Dyason patrol, but the situation was becoming desperate. He would have to do something soon.

As dusk fell on the eleventh day, Moss approached a mass of buildings, surrounded by a huge wire fence, placed in isolation on the middle of Salisbury Plain. Smoke poured from several tall towers, while a constant stream of lorries went in and out of the complex. The place was huge, covering hundreds of acres, larger than a small town and was lit up like a Christmas tree. In the centre of it all stood an enormous structure shaped like an aircraft hangar, but bigger than anything he'd ever seen before. Out of curiosity he stealthily approached the perimeter, using shrubs and bracken to hide his movement, until he could see the watch towers and machine guns lining the fence. This, he surmised was one of the rumoured Dyason slave factories.

Up until this point, he'd carefully avoid areas of population for fear of being seen, but hunger can be a powerful force. Moss knew he had to get more provisions, or succumb to the freezing wind and rain, so he reluctantly decided he had no choice but to risk breaking into the complex and head for the kitchens. He could have tried one of the larger local towns, but you could be sure they would be expecting him to try that. No it would have to be the camp - if he could get in and out of the West End, he could get in and out this place.

Once it was dark, he crept towards the single road that entered and left the slave factory, carefully observing the movement of the lorries and the layout of the complex. The road led to a barbed wire fence, interspersed with huge watch-towers and brightly floodlit. Behind the wire were several low buildings, or rather huts, from which humans were being escorted under Dyason guard. This at least explained why most of the villages and hamlets he had come across were deserted. It looked like much of the surviving local population were here. Beyond the huts were another wire fence, and then the factory itself, which was an amazing complex of pipes, huge buildings, and towers that belched smoke into the stormy night sky. Everywhere was brightly lit, and steam swirled from numerous vents and pipes. In the centre of it all sat the huge hangar, standing like the hub of a wheel from which all the other structures were connected like spokes. Moss was awe struck.

Off to one side of the complex was another series of huts, but this time they were occupied by Dyason. One larger hut was brightly lit with the sounds of music coming from it. When a Dyason lurched out the door, pulling a hapless human woman with him, he realised that this was where the guards quarters were, and this was where the food would be. All he had to do now was figure out how to get into the complex without becoming a permanent resident. Moss settled down behind a clump of bushes, and began to make his plans.

By a little after midnight, he reckoned he'd found the way in and out. The fence was out because you could be sure it would be electrified, with mines and booby traps around it. That narrowed it down to just the single road that led into the compound. Connected to the A303 several miles away, the road led to a check-point where

The lorries were given a cursory check before entering the compound. The guards weren't very thorough, after all who the hell would try to break into the place? The search was far more thorough for the vehicles leaving the compound, but nothing Moss couldn't handle. Several lorries at any one time were queued up waiting to go in, so it would be an easy matter to silently climb aboard one of the container lorries, hiding behind the cab. Once inside he would then just have to wait for the lorry to stop, slip out from his hiding place and make his way to the kitchen area. Then, as he had done in London, he would have to scavenge for food, making any Dyason who saw him "forget" he was there. He was a little concerned that using his talents this way would attract the attention of other operants again, but he figured the nearest "head" was miles from this God-forsaken place, so the risk would be minimal. Besides, he didn't have much choice; he must fill his stomach or perish, it was a risk he would just have to take. Getting out should be much the same as getting in. Anyway that was the plan, it wasn't much, but hunger was a very motivating force.

Using what cover he could, Moss moved nearer to the compound, following the edge of the road. He hid where the last lorries stopped, waiting to go through the check-point. Then when one of the driver's attention was distracted by the security guard checking the lorry in front, he ran up to the rear of the cabin. The lorry was of the trailer and power unit type and as Moss had already observed, it had a large bin at the rear of the cabin containing tools and equipment. He threw his knapsack inside the bin and climbed inside himself. By making himself as small as possible he could just close the lid. It took several minutes for the lorry to move to the head of the queue and he had to wriggle his toes in his boots to stave off cramp. After what seemed an age, the driver stopped beside the check-point, and from his hiding place Moss could just make out the sounds of the driver jovially talking in Dyason to the guards. After a brief pause there was a jolt and the lorry moved into the compound. Lifting the lid up just a fraction Moss saw the boundary fence and checkpoint disappear around a bend - so far, so good. However, the lorry continued to drive through the inner compound without any signs of coming to a halt as he had expected it to. He could see that the place was very brightly lit, with Dyason milling around everywhere, despite the late hour, so he couldn't risk jumping out. He would just have to stay where he was and wait until the lorry reached its destination.

As they went through the second security fence into the inner compound, Moss's heart sank. His plans were rapidly falling apart. The inner compound was full of machinery of all kinds, with huge vents belching smoke and choking fumes. Humans wearing rags toiled under the cruel eyes of Dyason guards, who regularly brought the butts of their assault rifles down onto the heads of some poor wretch. Moss gritted his teeth in anger. The lorry continued on, turned behind a large building and into a warehouse, where it finally came to a halt. The engine died and the driver climbed down out of the cab. Moss quickly pulled the lid closed until he heard the steps fade away then he cautiously peered out and examined his surroundings. The warehouse was brightly lit with overhead LED floods and contained between ten to fifteen lorries, dispersed in loading bays. Prisoners drove fork-lift trucks or manhandled large crates out of the back of the containers under the watchful glare of Dyason guards.

There seemed no obvious way out of the warehouse without being seen, yet he knew he couldn't stay where he was, his muscles were already crying out from cramp. Moss spotted the driver walking back to the lorry, followed by a work gang of humans and a fork-lift truck. They opened the large double doors and began to haul crates onto the pallet carried by the fork-lift truck. Seeing his opportunity, he slipped out of the bin and down between the axle, to the underside of the lorry. His face contorted in pain as blood agonisingly swept back into his cramped muscles. Silently, he massaged them back to life then crawled on his stomach towards the end of the lorry where the fork-lift waited. With most of the work detail inside the container, that left just the truck operator waiting for the pallet to be loaded. Now if he could just form the impression in his mind of not being there, and project it forward... like that... there! Moss clambered out from underneath the lorry, leapt onto the pallet carried by the fork-lift and slipped between a small gap between two crates.

For a moment the driver sitting astride the gas-powered truck thought he saw something leap from below the lorry onto the pallet in front of him, but when he blinked and looked again, there was nothing to be seen. He rubbed his eyes tiredly; it had been over ten hours since he had eaten his meagre ration of potato soup and there were another four hours until his rest period. He was seeing things.

Moss quietly pulled a canvas tarpaulin over the gap he sat in while the slaves stacked more crates onto the pallet. With a lurch the lorry began to move and from a rip in the canvas Moss could see they were heading towards a passageway at the end of the warehouse. The fork-lift moved down a long corridor, passing other fork-lifts coming back the other way then passed through large double swing doors, and from his restricted viewpoint Moss could see that they had entered one of the large hangar type buildings. The lights were incredibly bright, and the noise of men and machinery, very loud.

The fork-lift came to a halt, the pallet rose up, taking Moss with it, and was deposited on a stack of similar crates and pallets. It moved away, turned and returned down the corridor it had just travelled up from. Moss waited several minutes to see if anything else was going to happen, then when he judged the coast to be clear, lifted the canvas and nimbly jumped down from his hiding place then turned and looked around him. What he saw made him stop in his tracks and his jaw drop in amazement. From the corner the crates were stacked in, the warehouse was several hundred meters wide and disappeared into the distance as far as he could see. Men and machines moved around like ants swarming through a nest, every soul intent on what they were doing. Cranes moved across huge gantries lifting enormous sheets of metal, and sparks shot into the air from numerous welding torches. But what sent his senses reeling more than any of this, was what they were constructing, Huge scaffolding and protective sheets of plastic partially hid two gigantic shapes, but they were still easily recognisable as Dyason Dome spacecraft.

Hundreds of humans toiling under Dyason guard were busy hauling and welding the huge steel plates onto a skeleton structure of girders that soared to the roof. The sparks of arc welders flashed everywhere and dozens of small trucks fetched materials from stock-piles at the edges of the warehouse then disappeared with them into the cavernous interiors of the craft. No wonder all the local population had disappeared, thought Moss, they were being forced to build a new space fleet for the Dyason! All thoughts of hunger were swept aside by the excitement of what he'd discovered. He had to see more of these incredible contraptions! His usual sense of self-preservation was overtaken by curiosity. Never before had he been so close to one of the alien crafts, and he knew he must find out how the Dyason built these gargantuan machines!

Another fork-lift swept towards the stack of crates, so Moss ducked down out of sight. It picked up a nearby pallet of crates and as the driver turned around to reverse, Moss again took the opportunity to slip into a gap between two crates. The truck rapidly moved across the huge factory floor back towards the huge skeleton of the Dome then went up a ramp and into the heart of the craft. It sped along dim corridors, lit only by bare construction flood lighting, then emerged into an inner cavern several metres wide and tall. The pallet was deposited and the truck sped away again. Cautiously, Moss slipped out from his hiding place once more, but abruptly froze when a voice yelled at him.

'You there, what you think you doing?' Moss slowly turned around, his heart beating like a hammer on an anvil and faced a Dyason guard pointing an automatic rifle at him.

'Yes you, arse licker! What the sod you think you do?' the guard demanded in poor English, waving the muzzle of his automatic in his general direction. 'Get with sodding work. Come on, pick-up bar, open up those crates. Move it slave!'

Moss realised the guard had mistaken him for one of the prison labourers. Briefly, he contemplated making a run for it, or trying to make the guard "forget" he had seen him, but he couldn't be sure that he could do either in his current state of hunger. So slowly he bent down, picked up a crow bar lying on top of some nearby machinery and began to open the recently deposited crates. The guard grunted, turned to a small group of slaves entering through a bulkhead and ordered them to start unloading the crates as well.

Moss cursed under his breath - for the time being he was trapped and he would just have to play out the role of slave until he could make good his escape. The group of prisoners came over to where he was working and started opening the wooden crates, unpacking electrical equipment tightly wrapped in protective plastic. The poor wretch working beside Moss was a short man of about fifty, his face worn and grimy. A once-smart business suit now ripped, tattered and held together with string, hung loosely on his half-starved body. As the man worked he kept looking at Moss with sideways glances, a frown creasing his forehead. After a few minutes he sidled up to him and while pretending to unpack equipment, urgently whispered to him. 'I haven't seen you before. Who are you?'

Moss continued to open crates ignoring the unwelcome attention, but the man persisted. 'Have you just come from outside?' he pressed, 'Have you any news? When is the army coming to liberate us? Have you seen my wife, you must have, she's in Tatsfield, Mrs Johnson? You must have seen her, is she well?'

Moss ignored him again, the poor bastard was obviously at the end of his tether as none of his questions made any sense, but this time the man grabbed his arm and shook it violently. 'Answer me dammit!' he almost shouted, his eyes wide and vacant. The commotion attracted the guards attention who strode over, much to Moss's dismay. The Dyason raised his rifle butt above the man ready to strike. 'What hell's going over here with two shits? No talking slave! How many times you motherfuckers told!' he screamed abusively, his face contorted in an arrogant snarl.

The man looked up in horror, saw the guard and fell to the floor, cowering under an upraised arm and immediately defecated himself. 'Please don't hurt me! Not again! I don't want to be hit again...Please I'll do anything you say...No more pain...Please!' the cowering man whimpered. Moss felt sorry for the poor sod, God knows how many times he must have been beaten in the past to reduce him to this quivering wreck.

The eyes of the Dyason glinted evilly and the rifle began to descend in a long arc towards the cowering mans exposed skull. This was more than Moss could take, his sense of self-preservation was swamped under a towering rage at the treatment the poor bastard had obviously received. Without thinking, he grabbed the guards arm and at the same time raised his leg in a side thrust kick straight into the Dyason's stomach.

The guard shot back and collapsed against a bulkhead, fighting for breath. The group of slaves stopped dead, their mouths gaping, staring in awe at Moss. The guards intended victim still lay on the floor, looking first at Moss then at the guard in astonishment. However, the guard was only winded, and while holding his abdomen with one hand, he raised the automatic with the other.

'You slimy Terran filth... Nobody does that to me and lives! Prepare to meet your god arsehole!' the Dyason spat between clenched teeth.

For a moment Moss stood rooted to the spot staring down the muzzle of the rifle pointed at his head. Then without any conscious thought, pure power and anger seemed to surge down his back from his head into his arm and then to his hand. It felt as if his whole body was charged with a million volts of pure energy, like some huge capacitor. Where that power came from, he couldn't say, it was as if it came from the very roots of his soul. From head to toe, every hair on his body stood stock upright as if charged with static electricity. Without even knowing the reason why, he raised his hand and pointed at the guard with one finger.

Just as the guard's finger tightened on the trigger, a deep blue flame, like an intense aura, shot out from Moss's hand and engulfed the Dyason. The guard's face rapidly changed from evil anticipation to shock, then fear, as the blue flame enveloped him. Moss just stood there, the raging power pouring out from his left hand as the Dyason began to scream in fear and agony. The blue aura surrounded him in a dancing shimmering light that played up and down his body making him writhe in pain. His clothes began to smolder then his very flesh erupted into flames, enveloping the body. He screamed with pain unable to escape the blue flames. The energy just kept on pouring out of Moss's hand and the guard pleaded for mercy, his hands feebly attempting to keep the enveloping flames away from his face. It was all in vain, as the very flesh of his face melted and fell away in dripping burning clumps, showing the white bone beneath it. After what seemed an eternity the screaming finally died. The guard was nothing more that an unrecognisable lump of scorched, burnt flesh. Moss lowered his hand and the aura faded.

The prisoners, who had been rooted to the spot, now looked at Moss in horror, turned as one and fled down a corridor towards the exterior of the craft. Moss staggered, sat down heavily on a crate and stared at the Dyason's smouldering remains, appalled at what he'd done. How had he done that? What had possessed him? He didn't know he could do that. My God...what had taken power of him? Just what the hell was that blue flame? A thousand thoughts flashed through his mind, the image of the Dyason writhing in flames, pleading for mercy, replaying over and over again. What kind of creature had he turned into?

A klaxon began wailing somewhere outside the craft in the giant hangar. Along the corridors, the sound of boots pounding on metal plates rang through the hull of the partially completed Dome. The cat was out the bag, it was time for Moss to depart. Trying to pull himself together, resisting the urge to vomit and not daring to look at the smouldering remains of the Dyason, he grabbed his knapsack, pulled out his small automatic, several clips of ammunition, and fled down a corridor in the opposite direction to the approaching troops.

The corridor twisted and turned, but always headed towards the heart of the huge craft. His feet pounded on the steel mesh floors and the swaying bare fluorescent tubes cast an eerie glow. Human slaves working at various tasks, stepped smartly out of his way, expressions of fear permanent features on their half-starved faces. Moss turned right at a junction and suddenly saw several Dyason guards ploughing towards him. Sod it! Moss thought, this was no time for more fancy pyrotechnics, instead he raised his pistol and loosed off several rounds. One guard collapsed to the floor, but another guard raised his automatic and let fly. Bullets ricocheted off the bulkhead behind him. Double shit! He turned and belted down the corridor in the opposite direction. The firing abruptly stopped and he could just make out one of the guards yelling in Dyason, 'Don't shoot you idiot! You might hit something vital. The orders are to apprehend him. No shooting inside the Dome any of you!'

Well that was something to bear in mind. He just hoped all the other guards had the same orders. Moss ran past the junction he'd come through only moments before, and saw another squad of Dyason running towards him. That left just one other corridor. He took a left and ran on again, the Dyason squads close on his heels. The passageway went through several ninety-degree bends then ended at a solid bulkhead. Moss looked about frantically, but couldn't find any hatch or exit - it was a complete dead end. Turning around he saw at least twelve Dyason pounding towards him.

His heart pounded. *Sod it he was trapped*!... This was the end! There was no way out, and he couldn't expect mercy from this bunch, not after what he'd just done! Instinctively he knew he wasn't up to a repeat performance of the blue aura, even if he knew how he'd done it. The Dyason began to slow down as they saw their prey trapped, evil grins spreading across their faces. Slowly they came to a halt some five metres in front of Moss, spread across the corridor. The guard in the middle turned to his squad and said, 'Looks like we have the little turd cornered. Time to repay our comrade, he's not going to burn a Dyason again. Forget the orders not to open fire, take aim lads...We'll simply tell the captain the evil little shit resisted arrest!' then he smiled malevolently.

'Screw you arsehole!' Moss replied in Dyason. He shot the guard between the eyes and watched the body promptly fall in a pile onto the mesh floor, staining the new metal. The remainder of the guards fell prone and raised their automatics. Moss closed his eyes, said a quick prayer, and awaited his death volley. The guards fired as one, and hundreds of bullets filled the air, ricocheting off the metal bulkheads. When the smoke and ringing had gone, they expected to see a bloody body smeared across the metal. What they saw was nothing! No body, no blood, just hundreds of impact marks and empty cartridge cases!

Moss felt himself falling, tumbling down a long chute, round and round, like a helter-skelter. He tried to slow himself down, but the momentum and ultra-smooth metal was too much, and he slid down at an ever-increasing speed. He saw light at the end of the chute, which rapidly came closer then he was flying through the air itself for a second, before landing with a blow, onto a pile of plastic packaging material. He lay there for a moment, too winded to move, unable to believe his lucky escape.

Something tugged at his leg. He looked down and saw a filthy-looking human girl pulling at his trousers saying, 'Quick, don't just *lie* there! They'll be here any moment! Come on *get up!*'

She slid down the pile of plastic, gesticulating wildly. Not knowing what else to do, Moss sat up with a groan and began to follow the girl. They were in some sort of refuse area, with old crates, plastic and used metal everywhere. He kicked at a rat that ran in front of him and headed to the far side of the large bin they seemed to be in. There the girl spun a large wheel on a bulkhead door and opened it. She gesticulated at him to go through, so with pistol at the ready Moss cautiously stepped through. The girl followed and closed the door behind her.

The corridor was concrete, and higher than the metal grid ones of the Dome somewhere above them. He guessed they were now outside the hull of the Dome, probably below the level of the hangar, and that he had, by fortune or with help, slid down a refuse chute that lead out of the craft and into that bin.

The girl, although now Moss had seen her more closely, he should say, young woman, was dressed in rags, her jeans patched with canvas. A sheet of plastic with holes for her head and arms covered her upper torso, under which she wore a filthy T-shirt. She whispered urgently to Moss. 'Quickly, there's no time, you must follow me!' She set off at a trot down the passageway. Cautiously he followed her, presuming, or rather hoping, she was an ally rather than a foe.

'Hang on!' he called after her. 'Who the hell are you? Did you open the chute door? Where are we going?'

'There's no time. Fatman will explain everything. Come on quicker!' she shouted back.

Fatman? 'Who the hell is Fatman?' he yelled back, but she didn't reply, just kept on running, and rounded a corner. Moss ran to catch up.

For ten minutes or so they cut down passageways lined with steaming pipes and conduits. They went down ladders and crawled along ventilation shafts. Eventually, just as Moss was about to call out that he'd had enough, they came to a halt. The two of them stood before what Moss thought was a solid bulkhead. The girl rapped on it, in some sort of rapid code, and to his surprise a crack appeared and a small hatch opened, just big enough for them to crawl through. Moss barely had time to realise that the bulkhead was a very clever camouflage job before the girl

began to shove him through the opening. He started to crawl through, then felt himself being hauled by several pairs of hands. Before he could resist, he found himself inside a small room, apparently made from the internals of some ancient boiler, lit by a single bare bulb, and held firmly in the hands of several men. They took his pistol and knapsack then forced him to sit at a table made of crates and metal sheet. Moss, now nearly totally exhausted by hunger and his recent ordeal, couldn't and didn't resist. The girl who had led him there whispered urgently to a man standing in the shadows at the edge of the room, frequently glancing in Moss's direction. Yet he didn't feel he was in any immediate danger. These were humans not Dyason and obviously slaves by the look of the rags they wore. Perhaps they'd organised themselves into some sort of resistance, and this was where they held out, somewhere in the foundations of the hangar and factory.

'Who are you people? Where is this place? What's going on?' Moss demanded of the men who held him in the chair. They didn't reply, but the figure in the shadows moved forward into the light spread by the single bulb. The man was tall and wily, at least six foot seven and as thin as a bean pole. He was, Moss judged, in his late thirties, balding, with greying temples. He .wore what appeared to be home-made canvas trousers and jacket, crudely stitched together, with the remains of a biker's leather jacket on top. On his feet he wore an old pair of boots.

'I think,' the man said to Moss, 'that we should be the ones asking the questions.'

'You're the Fatman I presume? Moss asked.

Fatman smiled weakly. 'A childish name I admit,' he answered, 'but it serves its uses. The Dyason don't have much imagination. That's enough of me. Who might you be young man? Certainly you're not one of the new slave intake. You look far too healthy for that. Where have you come from?'

Moss thought for a moment about making up a fictitious name and story, but he could see no real advantage in that. If he was to get out of this place, he would need their assistance, so he took a gamble and told the truth. 'My name is Moss. I'm on the run from the Dyason. I escaped from London he said.

One of the men holding Moss snorted. 'Pah, he's lying. Nobody escapes from London 'cause they're all dead! Everyone knows that! I say we kill him. He's a plant I tell you.' There were murmurs of agreement from around the room, and Moss's heart began to beat faster once again.

The Fatman raised his hand to silence them. Then he beckoned the girl over and asked, 'Are your sure he's the one?

The girl simply nodded.

'The one what? Moss demanded. 'I tell you, I escaped from London and entered this miserable hell hole to search for food, but got more than I bargained for. It's true I tell you!'

Fatman came over to Moss and peered intently at his face as if seeing it for the first time. The rest of the room watched in silence. Finally he said, 'I don't doubt you, young man. In fact we've been told to look out for you.' Then it dawned on Moss, these weren't just prisoners, they were resistance! He began to struggle against the grip of the men restraining him. Shit! The resistance wanted his hide as badly as the Dyason!

'Steady on there young man,' Fatman said, placing his huge hands on Moss's head and forcing him back into the chair. 'We're not here to harm you. It's just that your little show incinerating that guard, could be heard by operants right across the globe. Now you can be assured that *everybody* knows you're here and that includes the Dyason. Any time now the hordes will be coming to this spot and will move heaven and Earth to find you. You've become a very important person, the hottest property in town, I might say. It's just a shame your arrival couldn't have been a little more subtle. Hardly the way to 'impress everyone' was it now?'

Moss stopped struggling, curiosity overcoming his fear. 'What the *hell* are you going on about?' He asked suspiciously.

Fatman ignored his question, went to the far side of the room opened a flask, and poured out a bowl of broth. This he placed in front of Moss before sitting down before him. Moss spooned the broth greedily into his mouth and tore at what could just about pass for bread.

'The resistance' Fatman finally said, 'has cells across the world. Our aim is to finally defeat the Dyason and free mankind from genocide and slavery in the traditional heroic manner.'

'Very noble,' Moss said between mouthfuls. 'What's that got to do with me?'

Fatman raised a hand. 'Please be patient, I'm coming to that,' he continued. 'Now, as you discovered in your blundering, the Dyason are creating a new fleet of craft in factories across the world. Of which this is one. At the moment the Dyason have only a relatively few craft ferrying goods and men between Earth and their home world. These new vessels are meant to be faster and more efficient than those built on their home-world. They incorporate all the technology the Dyason have stolen from us. If these craft are completed, their stranglehold on Earth will be even greater as their navy will have swelled enormously. Therefore, it is imperative they do not complete these new ships—hence the resistance presence.'

'I still don't see what this has got to do with me?' Moss again asked.

'Ah! That's the interesting thing lad. You see, your escapade in London has stirred up a real hornet's nest, and the method of your escape has raised some suspicion. The Dyason are finally realising the danger to them from human operants, to which my lad, you give a whole new meaning. The Dyason are pulling out all stops to find you, and in the process have destroyed our cell in

London and are generally making life very unpleasant for everyone.'

'So that's what the explosions were! It was the Dyason taking out your hideout!' Moss said, connecting what he had been told to recent events.

'Indeed!' continued Fatman. 'The question now on everyone's lips is, could there be a connection between yourself, the Dyason, the new craft and the disturbance all the operants are reporting? Why is it that you should be showing so much talent, at just the time that the Dyason are showing an interest in operancy? Could it be that you are in the pay of an unknown master? Either way you're too dangerous on the loose, therefore, we must find some way to get you out of here and into a safe resistance haven.'

It took a moment for the information Fatman was feeding Moss to sink in. Then a sudden realisation came to him. 'Jesus!' he exclaimed. 'You're not really suggesting that the Dyason are intending to use human operants to steer these things are you?'

'I've said too much already, young man,' Fatman said with a dismissive wave of his hand. 'I'm sure your bright mind can appreciate the importance of keeping you out of their hands, despite your best efforts to get yourself captured and lobotomised. And we haven't even begun to go into that little incident back there...'

Moss began to feel himself caught up in a web that extended far beyond his own horizons. He started to shiver, partly from exhaustion, partly from shock. Only part of his mind registered the importance of what he had been told, the rest of him couldn't escape the thought that he wasn't safe and he couldn't let himself fall into anyones hands, including the resistance. There was a nagging fear at the edge of his conscience, something about this hideaway and the girl who led him here. Then there was what he had done to that guard...there was too much happening at once. He needed time to think things through, to sort out what was happening to him, but that was a luxury he wasn't going to get. His immediate survival was the most important thing at present.

The girl moved out of the shadows and came towards him shyly, while the Fatman turned to the men who'd been holding him and conferred with them. Moss hoped they weren't about to carry out the threat to dispose of him; he didn't feel he had the energy to resist if they did. The girl placed a hand on his arm, her deep blue eyes wide with a look of astonishment on her face. Moss heard a whispering in his mind. *'You are the one. I can feel it,'* it said.

Moss raised his weary eyes and looked into the girl's face. The thoughts came from her... Somehow he wasn't surprised, but he asked out aloud, 'the one what?'

Before she could reply there was an explosion that threw him out of the chair, the blast forcing the air out of his lungs. The hideaway filled with smoke and Moss found himself prone on the floor, with the girl beside him, while automatic fire emanated from the far side of the room. Fatman also lay on the concrete floor, but his

eyes were wide and unseeing, staring accusingly at Moss, a neat round hole in his forehead.

Several others lay dead on the floor half buried in a nibble of concrete and steel, but a few were still alive, firing their weapons at a hole in the concrete wall at the far end of the hideaway, through which Dyason where now blasting back at them. For the moment at least, they were keeping them at bay, but Moss knew that wouldn't and couldn't last long.

The resistance fighter who only a minute ago, had been ready to butcher Moss scrambled over to where he and the girl lay. At first Moss thought he was going to carry out his threat when he raised his automatic, but instead he shoved the rifle into Moss's hands, together with his knapsack. Then he turned to the girl and shouted above the din of flying bullets and shrapnel. 'The Dyason, they bloody followed him here! If it was up to me I'd let them have him, but the little bastard's too important for that! Go girl, get him out of here, get him away! The data-fobs, they're in his sack. Whatever happens they must get to the resistance!. Do you understand?' He took her by the shoulders and shook her violently, her eyes were wide with horror, but she nodded and scrambled to her hands and knees, grabbing Moss's arm. The rebel slave turned back to the melee and began shouting orders to the few fighters still fending off the Dyason.

Moss scrabbled on his hands and knees after the girl, again not knowing what else to do, as she headed for a ventilation shaft at the opposite end of the hideout from the fighting. Through the dust and dancing light of tracer rounds, he saw her open the vent of the shaft and enter, then turn, grab his arm and pull him towards the shaft lip. Moss just got a quick glimpse of the slaves making their final stand, before he threw his rifle and knapsack into the shaft and climbed in himself.

Inside, the shaft was dimly lit from somewhere at its end, and Moss could see that its smooth walls were horizontal for the first few metres, then rose vertically. The girl moved rapidly to the bend, constantly looking behind to check he was following then stood upright at the ninety-degree junction. By placing one leg and one arm on each side of the conduit, she hauled herself up the shaft, like a climber going up between two rocks. Slinging the rifle over his shoulder, Moss followed her while the sounds of gunfire reverberated painfully through the metal.

His tired muscles cried out for relief as he awkwardly followed the girl up the shaft, shunting one arm, then one leg, then the other arm and other leg. Metre by metre they rose towards the light entering through a grille at the top of the shaft until, as they neared the end, the sound of gunfire died from below. Panic swept through Moss. There was no way that the rebel slaves could have held off the Dyason. The end of the fire-fight could mean only one thing.

'Oh Shit, get a move on girl,' he yelled urgently, 'They're right below us. Come on *move!*'

With a grunt of effort the girl reached the top of the shaft, forced open the grille with one hand then pulled herself through. Moss attempted to follow, but in his haste he lost his grip on the lip of the shaft. He felt he was about to fall, but with surprising strength, the girl grabbed his slipping arm and helped heave him out of the shaft. They collapsed in a pile on the concrete floor surrounding the shaft just before a muffled crump and a plume of smoke rose from the vent. So much for wanting to take him alive! That was a grenade lobbed into the vent.

Despite the shiver of fear that rippled through the girl's body as Moss lay on top of her, it was only moments before she threw him off and bounded down yet another corridor, yelling at him to follow. Shaking and stumbling, his ears ringing from concussion he wearily rose from the floor and set off after her.

It seemed as if time slowed down, each minute lasting an eternity as they ran down corridors, under pipes and between huge machines. From the distance came the sound of wailing sirens, but they encountered neither Dyason nor human. Eventually, they arrived at another vent which they squeezed through, but this time it went only a small distance before terminating. With practised ease the girl kicked at the grille, which came loose and they squeezed through and dropped to the ground.

With some surprise Moss realised they were outside the main complex. He could see clouds racing across the sky and feel driving rain against his cheeks. He could also see where they'd come from. The main hangar was about a hundred metres to their right, and they'd obviously climbed from below ground level, through power and ventilation ducts to the outbuilding which they now crouched beside. Across the complex they could see Dyason guards rushing to the main hangar the tone of sirens rising and falling eerily. Searchlights swept across the compound, forcing them to duck behind a low wall, as the lights passed them.

Moss turned to the girl.

'Now where do we go? What's the plan to get out of here?' he whispered urgently. The girl turned to face him, her eyes wide.

'I don't know! This is as far as I've ever come before. Nobody's ever got out of the compound itself,' she replied, a tone of defeat in her voice. 'They're all dead aren't they? Fatman, Bracknell and the others. I don't know what to do now... You tell me, you're the one with the powers! Can't you zap them or something?' She wiped away a mass of tangled hair from her eyes in exasperation and stared hard at him.

Zap them! Moss didn't feel he even had the energy to slap a Dyason, let alone repeat his performance of the burning aura. He felt utterly exhausted, and despite eating the broth only a short while ago, his stomach still ached from hunger. Yet for all the punishment and abuse his body had taken, from somewhere deep inside him came the urge to carry on, a determination to escape from this hell hole. At all costs, he must carry on, to survive... survival was all.

A glimmer of an idea came to him as he watched the Dyason mill around the outer compound, like ants whose nest has been stirred with a stick. Several of the guards were racing around the perimeter fence on trail bikes, looking for them no doubt. The bikes were standard Japanese models with big rough country tyres and two-wheel drive. The riders all wore flak jackets and visored helmets with sub-machine guns slung around their necks. Moss grabbed the girl by the hand and headed for the perimeter of the inner fence, using whatever cover he could find, lying prone every time a searchlight swept anywhere near them, praying nobody was using night scopes. A few metres from the fence he stopped and pulled the girl down beside him, into a slight dip in the ground. She started to open her mouth to speak, but he quickly silenced her with a stare. He felt her mind tentatively probe his, about to frame a question, but this wasn't the time or the place, so he shut her out of his head forcefully. Her face fell, but she said nothing. Damn the girl! She was a bloody distraction, for under all the grime was a shapely young body, and despite the dirt and tattered rags, her odour stirred something deep inside Moss - desires he didn't want to admit to himself, at least not right now.

From around the back of the main complex, another rider appeared and headed straight for where they lay. Silently, Moss grabbed the rifle by the barrel so that the old wooden stock was furthest away from him. He watched the approach of the bike with steady eyes, trying to ignore his exhaustion and hunger. It raced nearer and nearer to them, until when it was almost on top of them, Moss leapt up and with a short swing of his arms, swept the rifle butt into the visor of the helmeted rider.

The Dyason tumbled unconscious from the machine, which carried on for a metre or two before falling to the ground, its engine still running. Seeing what Moss was doing the girl leapt from where she lay and in a flash of movement swept a vicious carving knife out from the folds of her rags. Without any hesitation, she swept the blade across the trooper's throat and neatly gutted the Dyason's neck. He lay on the ground quietly gurgling as his blood poured from the terminal wound, and then he expired.

With fumbling hands, Moss pulled off the helmet and stuck it on his own head, then clumsily pulled off the rider's flak jacket, which was far too big for him but fitted neatly over his own leathers. He stumbled to the bike, lifted it off the floor and sat astride it. As he'd thought, it was a standard five-gear model commandeered by the Dyason. He kicked it into gear and held the clutch in, He looked around, peering awkwardly through the visor to see if the girl was behind him, but felt her arms around his waist before he could turn his head sufficiently. 'How are we going to get past the gates like this? Anyone can see that you're not a Dyason,' she asked, not by speech, but through his mind.

Moss snapped back, also in thought. *'Keep out my bloody head will you! Just shut up and watch!'*

And with that they roared towards the compound and first gate.

As they swept past, squads of guards hurried towards the hangar complex, rounding up groups of slaves as they went. Moss ignored them and carefully created an image in his mind. The image was that of a senior Dyason officer, sitting astride a bike, alone, with an important message for the regional Dyason HQ. Once he'd framed the image then, as he had done so many times before, he radiated it like a beacon from his mind. The effort made the pores on his head open up, and sweat dripped painfully into his gritty eyes, but nobody paid them any attention as they rode across the apron. They reached the inner gate and a junior officer stepped forward and peered suspiciously at him, a frown creasing his brow. For a moment Moss felt the image almost collapse, like a wall with a crack in it, but he managed to hold the thought in his mind.

'I have an important message for regional group, squad leader!' he snapped at the Dyason. 'Stand aside trooper!'

For a moment the Dyason seemed unsure, as though he couldn't quite make out why this group leader was on a motorbike. Then he shook his head, saluted awkwardly and motioned for the other guards to open the gate. Moss swept through, with a sigh of relief, but he couldn't let the image slip, not yet. They still had to get through the outer gate. They roared down the road that ran through the outer compound, swerving past squads of Dyason milling about in confusion, but all thankfully ignoring them. Then they swept around a bend between two smaller hangars and screeched to a halt before the outer gate. Another Dyason squad leader stepped forward and peered suspiciously at him, and once again Moss snapped out that he must get to group HQ.

'Sir,' the squad leader continued to peer suspiciously at Moss, trying to make out the face behind the visor. 'It's not safe to travel by that machine at present. With reported resistance activity in the area it would be best to travel by armoured car. I shall arrange a vehicle immediately for you sir.'

Inwardly Moss cursed, this wasn't going to be so easy, and he was having real difficulty holding the image together in his head. Any moment they would become visible for who they really were and the game would be up. Trying to make his voice sound authoritative Moss replied, 'Thank you, but that won't be necessary squad leader. I've travelled the route many times and know it well. Matters are too important to wait for another vehicle and transmissions might be intercepted. It is vital I leave now, and you're delaying me. Now stand aside'.

'Sorry sir, but I must check with control' the squad leader answered stubbornly, and moved slightly away from the bike to talk into his shoulder-mounted radio. Moss began to sweat uncontrollably, it poured into his eyes and down his neck, despite the freezing wind and rain. He couldn't keep the image up any longer. He felt it beginning to crumble and fade like a damaged vid, but just as he was trying to patch it all together he felt the girl enter his mind, *'Tell me what to do. Let me help!'* she cried desperately.

'Jesus, shut up you stupid bitch', Moss screamed in his head. The image he'd been working so hard to maintain instantly collapsed and he knew they were visible to all for who they really were.

The Dyason guard looked up from talking into his radio with astonishment. Immediately he reached for his automatic, but Moss didn't wait for him to react any further. He revved the bike up, kicked it into gear and they accelerated towards the closed wire and metal framed gate. The girl screamed out loud in horror as they roared towards the solidly locked gates, but as before, Moss felt a surge of unknown power rise up from his spine and surge through his head and down to his hand. He raised his arm and the same blue flame shot out from his from his fingertips and danced over the wire-framed gates. This time the flame was short and intense; the gate buckled and sprang apart just before the motorbike swept through and on into the night, away from the installation.

With delayed reaction the guards raised their weapons and fired after the retreating machine, but it was too late. With the lights switched off the little machine soon disappeared into the gloom and driving rain. For the moment Moss and his new ally had escaped.

CHAPTER EIGHT

TOKYO

Brabazon analysed another set of figures, while massaging a massive migraine that seemed to have appeared from nowhere. There was a commotion at the other end of the lab, he looked up from his work, and the all too familiar feelings of dismay and fear twisted his stomach into knots. Ploughing his way past other human scientists was a Dyason officer his face wet with perspiration and flushed a deep red with excitement.

'Out of the way you fools!' He cried shoving aside an assistant carrying a box of fragile probes. 'Brabazon, Brabazon! Where the hell are you? You sniveling excuse for a human being!'

Resisting an urge to hide, Brabazon wearily waved his hand in Gulag's direction. Gulag fixed his stare on him and homed in like a torpedo. He leaned over the desk and stuck his face to within a few millimetres of Brabazon's. The Dyason's breath was rank, his uniform dark with sweat and a wild look haunted his eyes.

'I've found him, Brabazon! I've found him!' You thought I couldn't do it didn't you? Everyone thought he'd got the better of me, but no, I've found the little turd and he will suffer. Yes, he *will* suffer! Oh yes, I've got him now!' he ranted.

Brabazon stared with confusion into the eyes of the Dyason. Gulag was increasingly showing signs of psychosis. The Dyason kept insisting on pushing the mental boundaries, putting his mind under incredible stress and it was beginning to show.

'Who exactly have you found Group Leader Gulag?' he stammered nervously, He was both repulsed and fascinated by this evil alien.

'The youth you idiot!' The one who escaped me in London! He got away that time, but by all the gods he won't get away this time. I can feel him, even now. His thoughts are uncontrolled, pathetic, but I know exactly where he is now!' Gulag raved.

Brabazon tried to make sense of what the Dyason was going on about. 'What youth is that sir?' he again stammered 'Do you mean the human Operant you came up against in England?' He asked hopefully,

'Of course I do you fool!' Gulag shouted back, spitting in Brabazon's face, his eyes rolling wildly. 'Who else would I be going on about? You mean you *can't* feel him? He's like a sore in the other dimension, he's in my head now. I can feel what he's doing, what he's thinking. For whatever reason, he's blown his cover and I know where the little bastard is!'

Brabazon stole a quick glance at one of the human operants on the other side of the room, standing with the others nervously watching Gulag. The man gave a small nod.

My God, Brabazon thought, could it be true? Could it be that the youth's mind had become so strong that Gulag could feel him? Or was it that the Dyason had become so strong? Either way, there was a strong commotion taking place in the other dimension. If he thought about it, perhaps he'd noticed it a few minutes previously. That would explain the migraine. He returned his eyes to Gulag who fixed him with a stare.

'One of us. There can only be one of us,' he carried on, a snarl curling his lips back in animal fashion. 'But I know where he is now and we're going to find him, you and I. When we do he's going to die! Forget about bringing him in to study, Brabazon, the boy is going to die... Pack your kit man! The hypersonic leaves in half an hour'. With that the Dyason turned on his heels and with a small giggle, skipped towards the door.

The blood drained from Brabazon's face and his head collapsed into his hands. His worst fears were becoming a reality.

Gulag was clearly becoming unhinged, even by Dyason standards, and he was dragging them both into a bottomless pit of madness and despair. He was being forced to help the mad Dyason officer hunt down some unknown British boy, who seemed to possess, an even more awesome, operancy ability. When they found him, Brabazon would become an accessory to the murder of the one person who could inspire hope in mankind. The history books would surely brand him as a traitor. His stomach contracted even tighter forcing him to lean over the corner of his desk and retch violently into the waste-basket.

RESISTANCE HEADQUARTERS, SOMEWHERE IN THE ARCTIC

They'd been gathering for the past several days from the four corners of the world. At great personal risk the resistance leaders of each regional cell had travelled to the arctic base. They all knew each other from reputation and communication through the operants, but this was the first time they'd gathered together. Until now it had always been perceived as being too great a risk for them all to be in the same place at once, but times were changing. Events were moving ahead at a pace and it was vital that each cell leader was fully briefed without the Dyason getting wind of their plans. Now that the Dyason were using operants themselves, nobody could be entirely sure that the mental links hadn't been compromised, so the resistance leaders were gathered around the large stone table cut by laser from the sheer rock of the mountain from which the base had been created. Jenson couldn't help feeling that despite the recent defeat and loss of their main base in England, there was some hope for humanity. This base and those people who occupied it were testament to that and now it was time to prepare the counterattack that would once and for all throw off the shackles of the Dyason empire.

He could still vividly remember the early days when he, Sandpiper, Davies and Black had come here with the remnants of his squadron to hide from the Dyason who had taken their airfield in a devastating surprise attack. For months they'd not dared leave the confines of the rough and ready cavern retreat. Their only contact with the outside world was through watching the official holo broadcasts from Canada and the United States. The vids were enough to see how the Dyason were forcing humanity into slavery, but they were helpless to do anything, all they could do was expand their retreat and bide their time. Over the dark winter months, they toiled unceasingly to create the huge system of tunnels and caverns that became the secure northern resistance headquarters. One day, when daylight finally returned to the arctic, a patrol returned with the news that the Dyason had left their former airfield. At first Jenson thought the patrol must have got it wrong, but when he went back with them he saw, through blizzards of snow and ash, that the airfield was indeed deserted. The huge skeletal remains of the Dome he'd crippled in the attack still sat in the centre of the airfield, its hemispherical shape blurred under a blanket of snow, but it had been stripped bare of anything useful, as had the rest of the base. Jenson figured that the Dyason considered them to be no longer a threat, so not having sufficient manpower to maintain a permanent garrison so far north, they had given up with repairs on the Dome and evacuated. To his surprise though, they left much of the original WDF kit. There had been half-hearted attempts to wreck equipment, but not knowing what much of it was for, they'd left a lot of it behind intact. Most of the stuff was easily repaired and over a period of weeks, they'd moved all the airfield's remaining equipment, including snow cats and leopard tanks, up to the cavern hideaway. So, free of Dyason interference, Jenson and his group formed their resistance cell.

Jenson knew now, from talking to those who occupied this room that a similar tale was to be told of groups across the globe. In New Zealand, Ukraine, India, the Amazon, and dozens of other locations, men and women had taken up the struggle against the Dyason. Now for the first time, the leaders of these groups had come together, to plan the Dyason downfall.

His thoughts were interrupted by a sharp rap on the table by the conference president, head of the Pacific region resistance, Yi Wang.

'Ladies and gentlemen,' he began. 'This is a sombre moment in history, the beginning of the end of the race called Dyason, who hold mankind in slavery.'

There was a smattering of applause from around the table. Yi Wang waited a moment then continued. 'I thank each and every person here for making the perilous journey to this land of ice for this conference. I know that many of you have had to overcome many dangers to be here. I am confident that you will not regret your decisions to attend. Although we have all spoken before, through the telepathic network of operants set up by the good doctor,' Yi Wang pointed to Josh Brabazon at the far end of the large oval table, who nodded in acknowledgement, 'it was felt too dangerous to discuss long-term strategic plans over such a network, especially as it would appear that the Dyason are making use of human operants for their own evil deeds. Therefore, it is my pleasure to declare this conference in progress and I hand over to our host Squadron Leader Jenson, head of the North Atlantic resistance cell.'

Jenson stood up and self-consciously adjusted his old WDF uniform as he strode to the display screen at the head of the conference table. He turned and faced the various resistance leaders. They were a mixed and diverse group. The young woman who led the African cell sat next to the ex-teacher from Connecticut, who now led the American cell, despite the number of ex-WDF generals that were a part of that resistance group. On the other side of the table, the Russian leader Gurikev sat next to the Muslim fundamentalist who led the Middle East cell. Before the invasion, many of these people would be at each other's throats, rather than sitting next to each other around a table. The desire to defeat the Dyason was the driving force that unified them and turned old enemies into firm allies.

Jenson cleared his throat and began his carefully prepared statement. 'May I repeat the thanks of the conference president Yi Wang for making the great effort to reach this desolate place. As inhospitable as we may find the Arctic, you can be sure that the Dyason will be even less keen to come here to pay us a visit.'

Twenty-four pairs of eyes were focused on Jenson, and despite his many morale boosting speeches to the troops, he felt a flush rise uncomfortably up his face. He turned to the globe being displayed on the 3D holo-viewer to hide his embarrassment. 'I would like to begin this conference by summarising what we know about the current placement of the Dyason,' he continued. 'We now know that at the time of the invasion, the Dyason attacked the Earth with twenty large craft, known as "Domes", and fifty smaller vessels we call cruisers. They approached the Earth under the cloak of a stealth device that, although crude by our own standards, was effective. By destroying the laser battle stations that once covered the globe under UN control, the Dyason were able to carry out a pre-emptive strike with relatively little risk to themselves.'

'At some stage during their voyage to the Earth, the Dyason fleet had taken in tow quite large numbers of asteroids, ranging from a few tons, to several thousand tons in weight. These, they were able to nudge into a re-entry course, terminating at targets of their choice.' As Jenson spoke, the holo-viewer showed different views of the laser station first, then the Domes, and finally shots of the devastated cities hit by the Dyason asteroids.

'The effect,' he went on, 'was dramatic. Each asteroid impact had the effect of a thermonuclear device. Most large WDF bases were immediately destroyed. Smaller bases were rapidly occupied by Dyason cruisers, which were able to initiate surprise attacks without being discovered by radar or any other active detection device. Quite how they achieved this remains a mystery at present. After many large cities across the globe had been destroyed, and millions murdered, the United Nations leader, Jean Paul Ricard formally surrendered to the Dyason.'

At this angry, murmuring erupted from several of the group. Jenson could sympathise with them. Jean Paul Ricard would go down in history as the man who sold out the human race. Yet Jenson knew the man had been placed in an impossible position. If he hadn't surrendered, the Dyason would have carried on hurling rocks at the planet, until it surrendered, or there was nothing left to pound. Perhaps mercifully, Ricard had committed suicide soon after signing the surrender.

'Organised resistance collapsed soon after the treaty was signed. The Dyason immediately embarked upon a programme of genocide, killing anyone who might possibly be a threat to them, and creating huge slave factories to produce diverse goods for themselves. However, as most of us in this room soon realised, the Dyason were not numerous enough to occupy all areas of the globe. They have repeated the classic strategic mistake of stretching their lines of supply too far. We've noted that large areas of several continents are relatively free of Dyason occupation. Even so, all areas of the globe still come under surveillance from their own network of satellites, or at least those that can penetrate the debris-cluttered atmosphere.'

'By taking on so much territory, the Dyason may have created the weak link we're looking for. This, ladies and gentlemen, is their Achilles heel.'

The Russian delegate Gurikev interrupted Jenson. 'That may well be the case sir,' he spoke out in heavily accented English, 'but, if we make any large-scale move against the Dyason they will simply drop more lumps of space rock on us. Then we'll all be back at square one.'

Jenson was quick to reply. 'Not necessarily. There are several factors which now reduce this risk. Firstly, the Dyason have established themselves in many of our cities. For example, they've made their main base in Tokyo where they have the advantage of being at the Pacific Rim's centre of manufacturing technology. They also have heavy troop concentrations in other centres of industry and technology across the planet. The wide distribution of their forces means that any asteroid attack would cause heavy casualties among their own people. '

'The second factor is the ash which came from the debris of the initial Dyason attack. This as we all know, has created a kind of nuclear winter in which food has been almost impossible to grow. I'm sure I don't need to remind you of the millions who have perished from starvation. The cloud cover does, however, have one advantage in our favour. It makes observation of the earth from space far more difficult. Only some of the Dyason satellites are able to penetrate the cloud cover, so at present, large parts of the Earths surface are free from orbital reconnaissance.'

'There are signs, though, that the debris is finally beginning to fall back to Earth. There has been a notable thinning of the cloud cover in the southern hemisphere and it's expected that there will be a similar thinning in the northern hemisphere soon. The nuclear winter is finally coming to an end. But before it does, we must strike against the Dyason. Once the cloud cover goes, all our military activities will be visible to them. Our scientists believe we have six months before the cloud cover thins sufficiently for accurate worldwide satellite reconnaissance.'

The Connecticut teacher, Dantalon, politely interrupted Jenson at this point. 'Excuse me Squadron Leader, but it seems to me that six months is a very short space of time in which to mount a massive counterattack against the Dyason. What makes you think we're capable of such a feat?'

'If at this stage I could bring in our science coordinator, Joshua Brabazon, to brief you on the background of the Dyason which we believe will indicate several weak spots in their armour,' Jenson replied.

From the other side of the room the thin, lanky Josh Brabazon stood up and moved forward to where Jenson stood. He coughed nervously then addressed the room. 'Ladies and gentlemen, as

Squadron Leader Jenson says, we've been able to make a close study of the Dyason since the invasion, and our understanding of this alien race may be our greatest weapon.'

He turned to the viewer and pointed to a hologram of a blue and white planet, similar to Earth but with unfamiliar continents, floating through space. There were gasps of surprise and murmuring from several of the group.

'This,' he continued, 'we believe to be the Dyason home planet. It's been animated from information taken at great risk from Dyason library files. As you can see, it bears a remarkable resemblance to our own Earth. You will have also noticed that aside from their unusual facial features, the Dyason are physically very similar to humans. Indeed their biological make-up is almost identical to our own, the only noticeable differences being that their blood corpuscles are slightly different, and they have a marginally different immune system.'

'The statistical probability of a race evolving on another planet in another solar system, in an almost identical manner to humankind, is infinitely small. Therefore, we can only come to the conclusion that at some time in the past, Dyason and humans shared a common ancestry!'

The room erupted in a chorus of questions and demands. Jenson stepped forward and with palms downward tried to quieten the delegates.

'Please,' he said, 'hear the Doctor out! I know the idea may seem absurd, but I can assure you that once you have heard the evidence you will believe the theory. We will be happy to answer questions later, but for the moment please be patient. Quiet please!'

After a while the room quietened down again and Josh Brabazon, his face crimson with embarrassment, looked down at his tablet computer for a moment before facing his audience again.

'I know how hard it is to absorb,' he continued, 'but the evidence overwhelmingly points to some sort of common background. First, let's look at how the Dyason travelled to our planet...' he pointed again to the holo-viewer, which this time showed a graphical image of the Dyason home world and star system.

'We cannot be sure of the exact position of the Dyason home system, but we do know it's not one of our nearer neighbouring stars. Therefore, their fleet must have travelled many thousands of light years to reach Earth. At first, it was presumed that the Dyason had perfected some sort of hyperspace drive, which would allow them to traverse such a distance in a reasonable space of time. However, after careful observation of our own solar system, astronomers have come up with what they think is the answer.'

The image on the holo-projector changed to show a view of the solar system, with a blinking marker close to due orbit of Jupiter. 'An anomaly has been discovered near the orbit of Jupiter. This anomaly takes the form of a fault in the fabric of space. Not so much a black hole, which is the remains of a collapsed star, as a pinprick in the many dimensional frequencies that form space itself!'

The holo-viewer showed an animated close-up of the anomaly, which took the form of a black circle of nothing, surrounded by stars and the light of Jupiter itself.

'We now believe that this hole is a tunnel, a thread through time and space, with an exit that leads to the Dyason home system, along which they have travelled. To confirm this, we have the flight records of several Domes showing their approach to this spot and then their disappearance. In return, several Dome flights have originated in our system from the point where they disappeared. This would explain how they can travel such distances without any apparent effects from quantum mechanics.'

By this time the conference room was totally silent except for the voice of Josh Brabazon. Now he held all the delegates in rapt attention. Again, the image on the holo-viewer changed to show a complex three-dimensional graphic. Josh continued his lecture with more confidence. 'Once we had discovered and confirmed the existence of such a fault, other theories as to the origin of the Dyason became possibilities. The appliance of quantum mechanics and the standard model suggests the possible existence of parallel universes. Many of you will be familiar with this theory, but for those who are not, I shall attempt to explain it in the most simple of terms.'

'Imagine,' he continued, again referring to the holo-projector, which now showed old newsreel from the early part of the twentieth century, 'that the German dictator Adolf Hitler had been killed in the trenches of the First World War, where he was once a corporal. If this had happened, then the Second World War may never have taken place, and modern history would be very different. In the theory of parallel universes, Adolf Hitler was indeed killed in the trenches, and the Second World War never did take place. It's simply that this version of the Earth's history took place on a world the same as ours, but occupying a parallel but different position in the universe.'

'At every point in humankind's history there have been several roads along which history could travel. The theory of parallel universes dictates that history did indeed follow these roads, as well as our own. It's simply that we occupy a world that took one particular route. The Dyason perhaps occupy a world that took several alternative roads at important junctions in their history. One theory is that the Dyason come from a world that once followed the same path of evolution as man did. By studying their culture and history, we have discovered many parallels between our past and theirs, but somewhere in relatively recent history the paths diverged. We took the path of world government via the United Nations, and our technology become electronic based with the development of computers, super conductors and advanced micro-electronics. This has not been the case with the Dyason. Our research shows that one country dominated their whole planet after a prolonged worldwide war. Their technology was always military based, time and funds being spent on the development of huge war machines, rather than consumables for their population, as in our own world. The result is a warrior culture, that has no regard for civilians, and has not developed the electronics-based consumer economy of our own world. The Dyason are murderous and aggressive warriors, however, their grasp on modern Earth technology is very poor. This is an advantage that has yet to be exploited'

Brabazon stopped with a dramatic flourish, having delivered his bombshell to the resistance. He was prepared for another barrage of outrage and questions, but was instead greeted by stunned silence. Eventually, the conference president Yi Wang spoke up. 'Thank you Joshua Brabazon,' he said a little uncertainly, 'for that astonishing theory. It is something I feel we shall all need to think long and hard about, and I look forward to reading your report on it. Indeed your theories may lead us to find more weak spots in our enemy's armour.'

'However,' he continued moving on to safer ground, 'perhaps we should go on to the more certain topic of the Dyason's use of human operants, something of which I believe you have first-hand experience?'

Josh Brabazon shuffled uncomfortably, not wanting to meet the stare of the Asian resistance leader. He couldn't hide his disappointment that the conference didn't share his enthusiasm for the new theories they were exploring. Admittedly, none of the men and women sitting around the table had a scientific background, but surely the concept wasn't that hard to grasp? The problem, he admitted to himself, was that they were people of action and theorising was a luxury none of them could afford. They were only concerned with facts, and now they wanted to drag the spectre of his collaborating brother from the past. To his relief Jenson moved over and addressed the conference before he could say anything.

'Ladies and gentlemen,' he said. 'At this stage I am sure that Dr Brabazon wouldn't object if I answer this question for him. You see Dr Brabazon's brother is being forced to work for the Dyason operant project...'

'I heard he was leading the project and collaborating them!' interrupted the Muslim Mohammed.

'We cannot confirm that,' replied Jenson, attempting to avert a confrontation. 'Even if it is true, it has no bearing on the work that Dr Brabazon is carrying out for the resistance.' Mohammed stared hard at Brabazon, but said nothing more.

'Now to return to the matter in hand,' Jenson continued. 'As we're all aware, telepaths have proved invaluable to the resistance as a means by which, we can all communicate securely without resorting to radio, Internet or microwave. All of which are open to monitoring by the Dyason. The thought amplification equipment is a great aid to this.'

'Since the invasion, the Dyason, who until recently have never shown any operancy talents of their own, have been forcing human research teams from universities around the world to continue research into human operancy. For a long time, we couldn't figure out why. '

'However, we can now link the research to two other factors. First, the Dyason have built a large number of heavy plant factories, using human slave labour. Some of these factories are producing weapons and goods that are being shipped back to Dyason itself. Others, we can now confirm are building a new fleet of 'Dome' cruisers and battleships. Their research is closely related to the formation of this new fleet.'

There were several small gasps and grunts from the conference room at this. Rumours had been flying around for some time now about the creation of new vessels incorporating the more advanced Earth micro-technology. Now their suspicions were confirmed.

'The second factor,' Jenson continued, 'arises from observations of the space fault through which the Dyason travel. Our own scientists are now sure that the fault itself is very unstable. Its existence is only temporary and it's likely to collapse and close at any time. This won't have any effect upon the Earth itself, but obviously

it would cut off the Dyason here from their home world.'

'When is this likely to occur?' asked the African leader.

'We cannot be certain,' replied Jenson. 'But we estimate between six to twelve months, certainly no more than eighteen months.'

'This is indeed marvellous news, Squadron Leader,' said the African. 'But how does it relate to the Dyason interest in human operants?'

'Dr Brabazon and his team,' Jenson replied, 'have managed to contact an operant among the Dyason research group. Their information is that the Dyason are looking for a means to navigate through space-time faults. They intend to use operants to visualise the very structure of space itself.'

'This is *preposterous*!' exclaimed the Russian Gurikev. 'Are you trying to tell us that it is possible to travel through space using the mind alone?' he snorted.

'All I'm telling you is what the Dyason are trying to achieve,' retorted Jenson. 'Whether they succeed or not is another matter, but it makes no difference to us! We must stop the Dyason building another fleet of Domes. If they succeed, they will be able to continue their stranglehold on Earth, with or without, a link to their home world. Therefore, we must strike before the new fleet is ready, and certainly before the Dyason can possibly progress any further with their research!'

The room erupted once again into a barrage of questions and debates, as the delegates argued amongst themselves over what they had been briefed. Jenson felt exhausted, and stood down from the podium. A hand tapped him on the shoulder and he turned to face Sandpiper.

'We've got a problem skipper!' he said.

'What is it Han, can't it wait?' Jenson asked.

'No, I'm afraid it can't. Can you step outside a moment? Black has agreed to take your place here for the time being.' Captain Black stepped up to the podium and faced the conference room, nodding to Jenson.

'Okay, let's go' said Jenson. They stepped out into the corridor and Jenson saw Josh Brabazon slumped against the smooth laser-bored rock, in deep conversation with an operant Jenson recognised from the doctor's staff. Jenson walked up to them.

'What's up Josh?' he asked. 'Can't it wait until after the meeting?'

Josh looked up at Jenson, his face flushed and beaded in sweat. The operant also looked flushed and sweaty. 'I'm sorry Squadron Leader,' he replied, 'but this is very important to us all. We have located the British youth, the one the Dyason are so desperate to find.'

'You have? That's great where is he?' Jenson asked.

'He's escaped from a slave factory built on Salisbury Plain, but there's more to it than that. There's been an event.'

Jenson looked at the man questioningly.

'The youth,' Brabazon continued, 'unleashed awesome powers in order to escape. The shock waves have reverberated through the mind dimension. Every operant on the planet was able to feel it, as if they were there themselves. His talents are far greater than we ever expected. Now he's on the run again, and the Dyason Gulag is on his way to get him.' He grabbed hold of Jenson's tunic and looked him in the eye.

'They must not get hold of him Paul! If they do, they may achieve their aims! The Dyason Gulag must be killed. He's their first known operant and may possess talents as great as the youth's! We must rescue the youth, and kill Gulag, otherwise consequences will be disastrous!'

Jenson looked at the tension in Brabazon's face and knew he was stating the truth. God, but that kid was a walking time bomb! It seemed at times as if the whole future depended upon this one snot-nosed, spotty youth. Well, he didn't have much choice did he? He turned to Sandpiper.

'You heard the man - let's go get the kid out of there!' They turned and set off at a run towards the flight bay.

CHAPTER NINE

SALISBURY PLAIN

The driving rain hit Moss painfully in the face, and it was all he could do to make out the vague outline of the track ahead, as the first fingers of a grey dawn spread across the desolate landscape. The girl behind him gripped his waist tightly, but had remained silent since their dramatic escape from the compound. Above the whine of the motorbike engine he could hear other, heavier engines, and he was in no doubt, that the Dyason were in hot pursuit in their armoured personnel carriers. They had the advantage of being able to see under the blaze of their headlights.

At the moment Moss and the girl had a small lead, the small bike was fast and it would take time for the APCs to gain on them. He leant further over the handlebars and opened the throttle wider. The bike screamed down the undulating road and across the plains, but above the noise of wind, rain, and engine, Moss heard the sound he'd dreaded the most, the whip, whip of rotor blades. He risked turning his head backwards and saw behind them, the lights of a gunship, low above the horizon and heading rapidly towards them. He began to swerve the bike across the carriageway in an attempt to present a more difficult target, though he realised that if they had an infra-red sight, they were surely dead meat. In a moment the gunship was hovering above them and they were swamped by the light of its searchlight.

'Stop or we open fire!' came the demand from a loud hailer.

Moss ignored it and swerved the bike across to the other side of the road again, in an attempt to escape the blazing light. The chopper followed and they were stuck under the light again.

'Stop! We will not give another warning!' came the repeated demand. This time there was a small burst of gunfire and the ground erupted just in front of the bike. Moss nearly lost control of the machine but somehow managed to swerve the bike away from the pitted tarmac and rode up and then down the grass verge.

'When I say, swerve the bike over to the grass verge and stop as quickly as possible,' came the thought from the girl behind him.

'Why?' What are you going to do? Moss demanded also in thought.

'Never mind! Just do as I say!' came the reply.

Without any plan of his own, Moss had no choice but to go along with the girl. He prepared to swing the bike over. The chopper moved until it was directly over them again and another burst of fire shredded the tarmac in front of them.

'Now!' came the loud thought from behind.

Moss heaved the machine over to the opposite grass verge and hauled on the brakes. The bike began to go into a skid, but Moss deftly countered the swing and the machine came to a halt. Behind him he felt the girl leap off the bike, grabbing the automatic from the clip alongside the frame. Above them the chopper, surprised by the move overshot and leapt ahead of them. Quickly the girl raised the automatic to her shoulder and let out a long burst that at such short range couldn't miss the Dyason helicopter. The explosive cartridges cut a swath through the fuselage and rotor blades. The chopper raised up into the sky like an alarmed horse, then madly began to rotate around the rotor axis, smoke pouring from its turbines. For a moment it hung in the sky then plummeted towards the ground, exploding in a fireball in a field alongside the road.

The girl pulled Moss onto the ground as debris shot over their heads. They lay there looking at each other, until the flames subsided a little, then still aware that the APCs were not far behind them. Moss picked the bike up off the ground, kicked the engine into life, and motioned for the girl to remount. He kicked the bike into gear, but instead of carrying on down the old A303 as the nearby sign declared, he rode onto the plain itself, guided by the light of the burning helicopter.

Jenson decelerated the F28 stealth fighter from its hypersonic speed, to just over 500 knots, and dropped the aircraft through the murk, towards the ground. Sandpiper also dropped his machine through the rain, maintaining close formation. It had taken them barely ninety minutes to fly the distance from Greenland to England, relying on the Stealth capability of the F28 to hide their presence from the Dyason. Jenson had to admit he didn't have much of a plan. His rear navigator's seat was empty, so he could pick up the youth who seemed to wreak havoc everywhere he went. Sandpiper carried Josh Brabazon in the back of his fighter in the hope that he'd be able to pinpoint him telepathically, while their vertical take off and landing capability should give them the ability to land near the kid's position. As they dropped lower Jenson could make out the shape of the Dyason slave factory on the thermal scanner.

'Okay]osh,' he called over the RT, 'we're over the factory now, can you be more precise as to the kids position? If he's still in the factory, we don't stand a chance of getting him out.'

'I don't think he's in the compound anymore...' Brabazon replied. 'There was another big disturbance in the dimension on our way here. I think he got out, but he's on the run.'

'Hang on skipper,' Sandpiper interrupted. 'I'm getting a thermal reading a few miles west from here, along the A303 route. It looks like a number of APC's and the burning remains of a chopper. It could be the Dyason pursuit team.'

'Well done, Hanson mate,' Jenson said. 'That's got to be where they are... Only the kid could leave such a trail of chaos! Let's high-tail it over there and even the odds a little.'

Jenson banked the F28 over, and sped towards the Dyason APC's.

They'd lost their lead in the exchange with the chopper. Now Moss could clearly see the tracked APC's ploughing across the fields, past the burning chopper, still in hot pursuit. It was only a matter of minutes before they were in range of their turret-mounted cannons. Their own automatic rifles would be useless against the armoured personnel carriers. There was enough light to see by now, and the rain had eased, allowing Moss to open up the throttle a little, but the APC's were just as fast across the open ground.

'*They're gaining on us*,' came the thought from the girl.

'*I know*,' he replied, '*but what the hell do you want me to do?*'

'*Can't we go any faster?*' she thought.

'*Not without falling off!*' he shot back.

They were heading up a slope, towards the dark monoliths of Stonehenge. Behind them the APC's were already starting up the slope between them. Moss stood up and leaned forward over the handlebars to keep his balance on the steep slope, the throttle wide. They were nearing the lip of the ridge when the engine began to falter.

'Oh God not now, *please* not now,' he shouted.

'What's the matter?' the girl yelled.

'I think we're nearly out of petrol' he yelled back.

'Oh Christ!'

The engine stuttered. Moss blipped the throttle. The engine roared for a minute, then began to fade again. He blipped the throttle once more, but to no avail. The engine spluttered and died. The bike rolled to a halt. The two of them leapt off, and Moss glanced back to see the APC's halfway up the slope and moving rapidly. He looked around desperately for somewhere to run to, but the plain was bare of all cover. There was nothing but the ancient monoliths. He grabbed the girl's hand and they scrambled frantically up the slope towards the stones. Behind them the floodlights of the APC's caught them in a dazzling glare that swamped the pale dawn light.

Desperately they ran for the cover of the stones, the last few metres seeming to take a lifetime, but they got there just ahead of the Dyason and flung themselves behind an oblong monolith lying flat on the ground, just as a burst of cannon fire emptied over their heads. Moss picked up the automatic and emptied the rest of the clip at the leading APC, to no effect. The explosive bullets simply bounced off the armour plating. Then, without warning, the rearmost vehicle exploded in a mass of flames and ammunition, closely followed by the APC directly in front.

Two jets screamed past the Dyason, over Stonehenge, and into the overcast sky, banking tightly ready for a second pass. Turning very fast, they dropped towards the last two APC`s, which were rapidly tracking their turrets towards the oncoming aircraft. The two jets began to jink wildly as they manoeuvred to avoid the tracer that arced towards them. They dropped lower and lower, until they skimmed over the plain at less than twenty feet. Then, almost simultaneously, they opened fire with their Gatling guns and Moss saw their tracer hit the two APC's which began to disintegrate. Within moments the return fire halted and flames began to pour out of the vehicles.

As the fighters screamed back into the sky, Dyason poured out of the rear-most of the blazing vehicles, whilst the others exploded in huge fireballs. Picking up his automatic, Moss aimed at the fleeing aliens and with a new ammo clip, picked them off one by one, until they all lay unmoving in the dirt. As quickly as it had started, the fighting had ended. Stonehenge was silent again, except for the crackling of the burning vehicles.

The sound of the jet fighters returning grabbed Moss's attention from the macabre scene and he raised his weapon again, ready to fire at the aircraft. The girl grabbed at the muzzle and forced it down.

'No you idiot! Don't fire at them, they're ours! Why else would they take out the Dyason vehicles?' she said.

Reluctantly, Moss let the girl take the weapon from his hands. The adrenaline still poured through his veins and he had to control his urge to run. There was something wrong here, although these were his own kind, he still wasn't safe. But where could he run to in this desolate place? Wiping the wet hair from his eyes he carefully watched the returning aircraft, His body beginning to shiver as shock set in.

The two jets made a slow pass over the burning APC's then turned towards Stonehenge. While one machine circled over the stones, just below the low cloud base, the other began to descend vertically on its vectored thrust engines. It descended slowly, then landed some one hundred metres in front of them. The cockpit canopy opened, the pilot climbed out, jumped to the ground and ran over to them. Moss stood up poised to grab his small revolver, but the girl kept a firm grip on his arm.

'Seems to me you're always being chased by the baddies kid!' the man said when he reached them.

Moss recognised the voice and immediately felt a strange mix of anxiety and pleasure. 'Hello, Squadron Leader Jenson. We really must stop meeting like this!' he replied wryly.

'Who's your friend?' Jenson asked, nodding to the young girl who half hid behind Moss.

'She helped me escape from the slave compound. I want you to take her with you. Thanks for helping me out. I'll be on my way now.' Moss said deadpan turning to leave.

Jenson leapt forward and grabbed him by the arm. 'Whoa! Hold on kid! Where you planning to go? Every Dyason from here to Scotland will be out looking for your hide. There's nowhere to run to. There'll be other APC's here any minute. You won't get five kilometres on your own.' he said.

'He's right Moss interrupted the girl, 'You can't run forever'.

'Besides' continued Jenson, 'I didn't come the thousands of kilometres from Greenland just to shake hands with you! You're a walking combat zone kid. It's time to take you somewhere safer!'

Moss looked at Jenson, then at the girl and a wave of exhaustion swept over him. He'd had enough of running, but he found it so hard to trust anybody. If he relied on nobody but himself then he wouldn't be disappointed, he wouldn't get hurt. He was so tired though, he'd been on the run for days. He was hungry, and nearly at the end of his physical reserves. It was a long way to the Highlands especially if it turned out they were in Dyason hands after all. The chances were he'd end up a corpse long before he got there. He hated to admit it, but they were right... He realised he couldn't go on forever, not now, not after what had happened that night. He needed time, some place quiet to think over what he'd done. What he had become. Silently, he nodded to Jenson and bent down to pick up his knapsack. He would go with him, willingly this time. As he knelt down, he thought he could hear something in the background, almost like the sound of...oh God, not again! He fell to the floor grabbing the automatic, and pulling the girl back behind the rock again in one fluid movement.

'Get down!' he yelled at Jenson who, confused by Moss's actions, instinctively pulled out his own hand blaster. Jenson took one look at them and dropped behind the monolith.

From below the level of the far ridge a helicopter gunship suddenly raised up over the lip and let loose a long blast of its Gatling gun. The ground around the monolith erupted as the explosive shells ripped up the turf, creating gouges in the ancient stone. Jenson's fighter exploded in a fireball that sent debris flying over their heads. The gunship roared over Stonehenge, its rotor blades slicing through the air making the characteristic whipping sound. Moss clearly saw its Dyason markings as it cruised over them, preparing to make a pass from the other direction.

'Christ,' exclaimed Jenson, 'where the hell did he come from? Our scopes were clear!'

'I don't know and don't care,' yelled back Moss, 'but don't just sit there we've got to move before he makes another pass. We're sitting ducks here!'

They got up in unison and ran for the cover of another monolith as the gunship turned on its axis and let rip another burst of cannon fire that exploded all around them. Jenson let out a scream of pain and collapsed against a stone, grabbing his right thigh. Moss dragged him by his flight suit under cover.

'Ahh! I've been hit!' Jenson moaned.

Moss glanced over the wound with an experienced eye as the gunship lined up for another pass. 'It's only a flesh wound, you'll live. At least until the next pass. He's got us dead in his sights this time,' he said.

'No,' Jenson moaned through gritted teeth. 'We're being played with. He could have taken us out on the first pass if he'd wanted!'

'Looks like he will this time!' Moss exclaimed, as the gunship lined up in front of them.

Sandpiper pulled a hard left as soon as he saw the gunship rise over the ridge, as surprised as Jenson at its appearance. Nothing had appeared on the scopes and he never saw the helicopter creep up through his thermal imaging sights. One thing was for sure, he had to take out the chopper before it made mincemeat of Jenson and the kid. He pulled a four 'G' climbing turn up to 1000 metres, but was dismayed to see in his rear view that the chopper had sliced up Jenson's F28 and plastered the monolith they were hiding behind. Behind him Josh Brabazon groaned, unused to the 'G' forces.

Sandpiper pushed the side control column right over and pulled at the vectored thrust at the same time. The F28 turned over onto its back and plummeted towards Stonehenge. He cursed as he saw the gunship fire it's Gatling gun once more. Jenson fell to the ground and was dragged by the kid under the cover of a monolith. The skipper was hurt!

As the F28 rapidly closed on the chopper at 350 knots, Sandpiper aimed his missiles and locked onto the gunship with the laser designator. Behind him Brabazon began to moan strangely, talking incoherently into his mike.

'For crying our loud, will you shut the fuck up Brabazon!' Sandpiper yelled, but the doctor kept on moaning. Sandpiper tried to ignore him as the computer blipped, counting down to firing position. Then several things happened at the same time... The gunship, finally aware of their counter-attack, leapt into the air, raised its Gatling gun and loosed off a burst at the rapidly approaching F28. At the same moment, Sandpiper's finger tightened on the pressure-sensitive fire button. Just as the missile was about to fire, Josh Brabazon screamed out loud, 'No... No, don't fire! That's my brother down there!' and hauled on the dual control stick in the rear cockpit, hurling the F28 wildly into a steep climb.

The missile released, but not locked onto its target, sped towards the gunship, and impacted on the plain immediately behind the rear rotor. The gunship bucked into the air, let off a burst of gunfire and spun madly. For a moment it looked as though it would crash, however, the pilot, fighting the wild pitching, managed to bring the machine back under control, though it was badly damaged.

Sandpiper was less lucky. The F28 had been hit by the burst from the gunship and was rapidly losing power in both engines. Hazard lights lit up on the control screens like lights on a Christmas tree. He pushed the stick forward to kill the climb and put the fighter in a shallow dive to keep up the falling air speed. The F28 was dying, and Sandpiper knew they had only minutes left in the air.

For a moment, Moss thought the gunship was finished as the missile hit the ground near it, but to his amazement the pilot managed to bring the smoking chopper back under control. The jet though, was obviously in great trouble, as it disappeared over the ridge, trailing a long plume of smoke. Jenson looked at the falling plane and groaned loudly. Crap, Moss thought, so much for a rescue! He knew there was something wrong when Jenson landed! The cavalry had become victims themselves, and for all their good intentions, a millstone around his neck. And to think a moment ago he was about to meekly tag along with these guys!

His attention returned to the chopper which was attempting to manoeuvre nearer to them, wallowing like a sick bird. A hatch in the fuselage opened and Moss saw a small machine gun swing towards them. Their main armament might be down, but they were still intent on butchering them! He ducked behind the rock as bullets ricocheted off the stone. Grabbing the rifle he popped his head up and attempted to let off a burst at the gunship. He pulled the trigger but nothing happened. He ducked back down again and released the clip. It was empty. They were out of ammunition and defenceless! The chopper circled Stonehenge looking for the best position to finish off its grisly work.

Moss was about to drag Jenson to the cover of another monolith, when the girl desperately pulled at his sleeve and pointed to one of the tall standing stones. There, standing in what seemed to be a doorway built into the very stone itself, stood a child, beckoning and calling Moss's name. The light behind him seemed to shiver and dance, but Moss recognised the child. It was Ambrose, the boy who'd given him the map and food back in Surrey! For a moment Moss wondered what the hell the boy was doing here in the middle of a fire-fight, but the approaching gunship rearranged his priorities as it closed in for the kill. He threw caution aside, hauled the heavy body of Jenson over his wiry frame in a fireman's lift and staggered towards the child.

'This way! This way!' Ambrose called, beckoning them to the strange orifice that pulsed with a warm light. What was a moment ago a solid monolith had become translucent, glowing as if it had some sort of internal energy. Given the choice of waiting to be mown down by the gunship, or taking his chances with Ambrose, Moss knew which way the cards were stacked and moved as fast as he could under the weight of the groaning Jenson. The girl was close behind them, carrying the rifle and knapsack. The machine gun swung towards them, while the pilot of the gunship tried to steady his machine. It was going to be a close thing. Moss could hear the stutter of the gun and felt the dirt fly around him as, with a last burst of energy, he leapt for the entrance. The three of them collapsed in a pile inside the pulsating opening. Ambrose waved a hand and the monolith once more became opaque, cutting out the sound of gunfire from behind them. The shells impacted on solid rock…

Brabazon sat at the hatch of the gunship, wearily watching Gulag sweep through Stonehenge in a frenzied rage, pounding on the ancient stones.

'Where are they?' he screamed. 'I saw them. They were in my sights, powerless! Then they were gone! You saw it Brabazon!

Where are they now? It was this stone, you saw it glowing! It was pulsating, and they all ran inside it, it must be some kind of entrance. What's down there Brabazon? An underground bunker? Come on you bit of slime, you must know something?'

Brabazon just sat there, his shoulders hunched over, and looked at the Dyason. How he hated this alien bastard! This alien that had just killed his twin brother! When the resistance fighter swept in, he recognised the familiar thoughts of his twin. His brother was on board that plane and now, just as they had been reunited after such a long absence, this alien had destroyed the plane and his brother! He'd seen it disappear into the gloom, trailing smoke, felt the mind of his twin suddenly go silent. Oh God, to be separated for so long, then to be so close, yet so far! Even now he found it hard to grasp that he'd seen the death of his brother, but he saw the plane go down - what other conclusion could he come to? Brabazon was glad the youth and his friends had escaped, and he cared not how they managed it. It was the only good thing to have come out of this sickening series of events. Gulag strode up to him, grabbed him by the lapels, hauled him to his feet and raised him off the ground until their eyes were level.

'You know don't you?' he ranted maniacally. 'You know how they escaped! Tell me human, tell me or I can assure you your suffering will be long and excruciating! Is this some sort of illusionary trick?'

Brabazon stared back into the alien's eyes, his face clearly displaying the disgust and hate he felt. In a flat drained voice he said, 'I don't know where they are Gulag. This is Stonehenge, nothing more but an ancient collection of stones. They're gone and bloody good luck to them! Do as you will Dyason. I don't know how they got away and I care nothing, for you or for them! Do with me as you please. I am beyond caring. You've seen to that!'

Gulag stared at the man, anger sweeping across his features. He raised his hand as though to strike, paused then released his grip. Brabazon fell painfully against the fuselage of the chopper.

'Not yet human, not yet, I haven't finished with you. You will help me find this boy again. Next time, he shall not escape me, and when I have finished with him, your turn will be next! Death would definitely be too easy for you. I want you little fuckers to really know the meaning of pain!' Gulag stared at Brabazon with eyes filled with hate and madness, then turned and shouted to the gunship pilot, 'Call up regional group and get another helicopter here fast! I've had enough of this hovel.'

He strode over to the stones again, and continued to scratch and claw at the offending monolith. Brabazon leant against the fuselage, hugging himself miserably, as the rain washed away his tears.

CHAPTER TEN

BELOW SALISBURY PLAIN

The girl screamed and clung tightly to Moss as the floor suddenly fell away. Down a glowing shaft of amber light they rapidly descended. There was nothing supporting them, just the sensation of falling, their stomachs seeming to rise to their throats. Moss heard another scream and realised it was his own. They kept on falling and falling for what seemed an eternity. Then, gradually, the speed of their descent slowed and stopped. None of them moved, the girl still clung tightly to Moss and Jenson still lay on the floor hugging his wounded leg. The floor underneath became solid once more. Slowly, they looked up in awe.

They were in an underground cavern with smooth walls of stone that lit the interior with some sort of soft glow that emanated from inside the rock itself. The cavern was about the size of a small church, an effect heightened by a series of crystal structures that rose from the floor and stood at one end. The floor was a mosaic of a type of tile that gave out a gentle warmth and they could now see that they stood on a platform that had descended through the roof of the cavern itself.

A movement at the far end of the cavern grabbed Moss's attention and he turned to see the small boy walk out from behind the crystal structure, take several steps towards them and bow.

'At last the legend is reborn' the child spoke in a clear, strangely adult voice. 'Welcome, Arthur Moses Pendragan. Welcome Lady Jennifer Hampton, consort of the King. Welcome Paul Michael Jenson, knight and King's champion!'

The three stood there, mute with astonishment. After all that had just happened, ending up in a crystal cavern underneath Stonehenge, and being greeted by a child with an adult voice, was taking things just a little too far... Eventually, Moss broke the silence. He was in no mood for silly games, not after just being shot at...

'Very funny Ambrose. My surname is Paterson not Pendragan. Now perhaps you would like to tell us all the why's and wherefores?'

The child replied with an impish grin but said nothing. Instead he skipped up to Jenson who was still gritting his teeth in pain. He reached out to him, but Jenson pulled back in alarm.

'Keep away kid! Moss who the hell is this, and where the bloody hell are we?' he demanded.

For some reason Moss couldn't quite put his finger on, he didn't feel the child was any threat to the three of them. After their last meeting, he'd suspected there was something strange about the boy, and now it looked like his suspicions were about to be confirmed.

'It's okay Squadron Leader, his name is Ambrose and he's helped me before. I'm not sure why he's here, or where we are, but I'm sure he means no harm'

'I can assure you,' the child spoke again in an adult-like manner, 'that all your questions will be answered in good time, and indeed, you are in no danger from me, or this place. However, Paul Jenson, you have a wound that I feel needs attending to.'

Then the child placed a small hand on Jenson's brow and whispered something inaudible. There was a small rushing of air in the cavern as though a vacuum was being filled. Jenson looked down at his leg in astonishment as the bloody wound closed up and seemed to fade away until only the ripped material of his flight suit remained. His eyes rolled to the back of his head and he quietly passed out. The girl dropped to her knees and cradled Jenson's head in her arms. She looked in astonishment at the healed wound and quickly placed two fingers on his neck and felt for a pulse.

'He's unconscious, but with a strong pulse,' she said with some relief looking up at Moss.

'How did you do that Ambrose?' he demanded of the child. 'Just what the hell is going on here? Come on, I want some answers boy!'

The child looked him right in the eye and said levelly, 'In much the same way as you killed the Dyason... You should be the last person to be surprised by such an event.'

'How do you know about that?' Moss asked suspiciously, thrown off guard by the small child's manner.

'Questions, questions,' came the reply, as the boy skipped away from the group again. 'You're all exhausted. There'll be plenty of time for answers later. Rest is needed first.' The child waved his small hand in their general direction.

Moss suddenly felt incredibly tired, his eyes became heavy. He willed his body to fight the exhaustion, to stay awake. Through half-shut eyes he saw the girl sway and gently collapse next to Jenson. Then unable to stay awake any longer, he also collapsed onto the floor as darkness swept over him.

Images swam past, like ghostly scenes from an old movie. Sometimes the images were in colour, but mostly they were in monochrome, like the faded films from the early twentieth century. Always the scenes were from afar, as though he were sitting in the audience, invisible to the participants. Yet, somehow, Moss knew these were more than just normal dreams. Usually, when he dreamt the images were confused and indistinct. These were clearer, followed a theme, as though he were watching newsreel of past events.

First there was the image of a young man, about his own age, living in a land devoid of cities, roads and Dyason. The youth entered a stronghold, not really a castle, more a stone building surrounded by earthwork defences. Then he saw the youth talk fervently with other men dressed in dented and tarnished armour. They sat at a huge round table. Moss didn't need a history book to know he was dreaming about the legendary King Arthur, but his dream was very different from the films he'd seen of the legend. Camelot was a stone fort in the middle of desolate moors, and the knights of the table were short and scruffy for a start. The scene faded to a bedchamber where the youth lay in animal furs beside a young girl, who seemed somehow familiar.

The scene faded again, to be replaced by a battlefield, littered with the dead and dying, tattered pendants flying in the breeze. The image zoomed in on a group fighting on top of a small hill. Swinging their broadswords and battle axes, the men from the earlier scene fought off hordes of red-haired assailants swarming around them. Bodies were piled high at their feet. Most wore furs and kilts. Some wore chain mail and armour.

A cry went up. The figure in the centre of the battling knights fell to the ground and the savages let out a great cheer. The banner of a dragon was ripped from its standard and set alight. The remaining defending knights broke and ran, only to be cut down by the victorious savages.

Atop two nearby mounds stood two figures, one dressed all in black, the other dressed in grey robes. The dream showed the face of the grey-robed figure. His face was old and wizened his expression one of great sadness. Across from him, astride an opposing mound, the figure in black swept the robe hood away and long jet-black hair flowed out. Her face was one of incredible beauty, but also strangely cruel. She stared at the old man then lifted her face to the heavens and let out a long evil laugh. The scene faded.

The Earth floated below him, the continents blurred by the mass of clouds that swam across the globe, contrasting greatly with the deep blue of the oceans. Over the curve of the planet, a distant object approached. At first its shape was indistinct, but as it grew nearer it emerged as a craft of huge proportions. The front of the craft was of complex curves, like the head of an exotic bird, attached to the main body by a long, slender neck. The body was again made up of complex curves, but was roughly a low wedge shape that led to a small tail unit that seemed to mount some sort of power unit. Two small stub wings at the rear of the body carried similar power pods. Even though Moss knew he was dreaming, he could not help thinking that the alien craft was both beautiful and graceful. Somehow, he knew it was at least three kilometres long. The black finish reflected the sunlight as it emerged from the dark side of the Earth. Markings in a language Moss didn't understand were highlighted in red and gold. Silently, the vessel came towards him until, once it nearly filled his vision, it began to slowly lower into the Earth's atmosphere. As the vessel came in contact with the first few molecules of the stratosphere, a bright glow began to emanate. However, it was not the craft itself that was glowing, but a conical zone around it. Moss came to the conclusion that this was some sort of force field, protecting the hull from the heat of re-entry. Soon the craft was nothing more than a blazing meteor leaving a fiery trail as it sped towards the Earth's surface.

The vision swam and changed. Now Moss saw a rain forest, a mass of green and lush vegetation, with trees that reached up hundreds of metres towards the heavens. Birds sang and unknown beasts lurched through the rotting vegetation of the forest floor, where the sun never shone. The view changed and closed in on two small rodent creatures that ran up a tree trunk. Their faces had two round eyes that faced forwards, and they had small gripping arms, and legs with toes, and fingers. The pair stopped at some bright berries and began to pick at them with their tiny hands. So intent with feeding were the two creatures, they failed to see the large bird of prey greedily viewing the pair from a branch higher in the forest tops. The bird spread its wings and launched itself towards the pair, talons stretched out. It swooped down eager for a meal, almost certain in its tiny mind of catching the nearer of the two. Something alarmed the female of the pair of tiny animals, and she looked up from her feeding, just in time to see the swooping bird heading for her mate. She chattered urgently in warning, but it seemed her warning would come too late. However, before the talons could grab the small furry creature there was a flash of light and the bird cried out in pain, then fell, its wings crippled, to the forest floor, where it was quickly ripped apart by the animals that inhabited the ground. The two small creatures fled into the dense tree tops, chattering excitedly.

The small robot rose up from its position halfway up the tree trunk. It examined the remains of the bird of prey, matching it with its internal library of Earth life forms. Then it searched the trees around the fleeing rodents for further birds of prey. Satisfied that the experimental specimens were in no further immediate danger, it shut down the small laser and blended its structure so that once more it became just another part of the forest vegetation.

The baby let out a howl as it was slapped on the buttocks, then placed, still wet from the womb, in the mother's arms. The young woman, not much more than a girl herself, looked at the baby with joy, then carefully wrapped it in animal skins, before passing it back to the attending woman, who approvingly took it, and walked out of the low tent.

His skin was dark and heavily weathered by the blazing sun. His robes were loose and at his belt he carried a bronze dagger. The man took the child from the elder wife's hands and looked into its face. It stared back with large brown eyes. He smiled; it was a boy, his heir at last. The man dropped to his knees, raised the child above his head and began the chant of thanks to his god. Behind him, the herd of camels, his measure of wealth and stature, snorted and grunted as though welcoming the new human child. The dream faded and Moss slipped into a deep slumber.

His eyes flickered then opened. For a moment, he panicked, unsure of where he was, unable to recall recent events in that half world between sleep and being awake. Then he felt a sense of well-being wash over him. Slowly, he raised himself onto one elbow and looked around. He was lying on a low bunk made of some sort of material that molded to his form. In turn, the couch was inside a room smaller than the crystal cavern, but still of gentle curves, and a rock that gave out low warm yellow phosphorescence. On other bunks spread around the room were Jenson, the girl, and two others, both wearing flight suits. Beside the bunk stood the child Ambrose.

'Welcome back 'came the thought into his mind.

Moss ignored it. Instead he swung his legs off the bunk and onto the marble floor. His tattered leather jacket lay folded at the end of the bunk and he reached for it, more out of habit than for any other reason. He stood up carefully, still feeling a little groggy, turned and looked at the smiling child. He paused for a moment then asked a question, using his mind.

'The others, still sleeping?

'Yes' came the reply.

'And dreaming?'

'Yes.'

'But you woke me first?'

'Also correct.'

'I think it's time for some answers. Don't you?'

'Perhaps, but I think you first need some nourishment. Follow me.'

The child turned and skipped to the other side of the room where a door appeared, like the one in the stone somewhere above them. He skipped through the door.

After a moment's hesitation Moss followed, cautiously prepared for the floor to suddenly disappear, as before. But his fears were unfounded and he stepped through into a room similar to the one he'd seen before, except that this one was simply furnished with a large round table. The child sat at a low stool and waved his hand. Two plates of steaming sausage, eggs and bread appeared in a small receptacle built into the wall, together with a pot of what smelled like coffee.

Somehow this wasn't what Moss had expected. This place seemed more like a grape and fruit joint than sausage and eggs. He wasn't about to complain though, his stomach led him to a stool where he hungrily tucked into the food. He wasn't surprised that it tasted as good as it looked and most definitely wasn't an illusion.

'I hope you don't mind if I join you? If there's one thing I like it's sausage and eggs with fried mushroom. I just need to get comfortable first,' came the thought into his head.

Curiously Moss looked up. 'By all means go ahead,' he said between mouthfuls.

The child seemed to shimmer and become insubstantial, as though another body was trying to replace it. Before he was even aware of what was happening, Moss found himself sitting opposite a wizened old man complete with white beard.

'Ah, that's a bit more bloody like it!' said the new body out loud, picking up a sausage with one hand and noisily devouring it.

For some reason, Moss was once again, unsurprised to suddenly find himself sitting opposite an old man instead of a young boy. Of course, he recognised him from his dreams. He chose not to say anything; instead he concentrated on finishing his first decent meal in weeks. They finished the food in silence, except for the old man's noisy slurping. Then he poured them both some coffee, sat back expansively and said. 'Ah... that's better the world always seems brighter after a decent breakfast. Now, I imagine you have a question or two to ask me. So now is the time. Fire away lad!'

He leaned forward elbows on the table and grinned at Moss. Moss sat and thought for a moment before speaking. It was difficult to know where to start.

'Perhaps,' he began, 'You should start by telling me who you are? I take it you're not a small child called Ambrose living on a derelict farm in Surrey?'

The old man chuckled then looked at Moss with steely grey eyes. 'Ambrose is indeed one of my names, but I'm afraid the boy was an illusion I created. It was necessary to gain your confidence. After all that has happened to you lad, it seemed unlikely you would trust an old man like me. So I created that illusion. Rather good wasn't it?'

Moss ignored the quip, held him in a steady gaze and demanded, 'So old man, who in hell, are you really?'

'Well I've been called many things over the years,' he replied, returning Moss's gaze. 'Not all of them complimentary, but the one I've liked the most is Myrddin.'

'Myrddin is another name for Merlin the Magician, so we're still running with the Arthur theme are we? They are nothing more than a bunch of old fairy tales... Come on old man, you'll have to do better than that!'

The old man looked a little crestfallen. 'Lad! Come on now, you must have heard of the immortality of Merlin the Magician? You've just seen the dreams, and you're still questioning my authenticity?'

'Yes, I saw you in those dreams you placed in my mind, but I have to say, you don't look a thousand years old. You'll have to do better than that to convince me.'

'Oh by all the gods!' exclaimed Myrddin. 'What's wrong with the youth of today? Back in the good old days, a simple materialisation would have been sufficient to convince a kingdom! I blame it on too much social media myself. I guess I'm going to have to tell you the whole story aren't I?'

'It might help,' replied Moss.

Myrddin made himself more comfortable, seemed to look inward, then began his tale. 'The dreams you saw were not dreams, but replays of past history, ingrained in the very structure of these caverns we sit within. The order you see them in, can be a little confusing, and the clarity depends on the dreamer's ESP potential, but what you saw was accurate enough. I've spent many years studying these dreams, and what I tell you now is my simplistic interpretation of what you saw.

'Long ago, when the planet was young, a craft appeared in the solar system. This craft carried the genetic seed of intelligence. It was an unmanned craft - it was programmed to find a suitable Earth life form in which to implant the seeds of intelligence. As you saw in your dreams, the craft landed on Earth and planted its seeds. Life had already existed on this planet for millions of years, the age of giant lizards had been and gone and mammals were now the dominant species. There was no spark of civilisation though, not yet. Mankind was just the twinkling in the eye of a small monkey. In the early years, robotic sentinels kept watch over the mammals they impregnated as they struggled for survival. As the eons went by, the sentinels disappeared and the mammals were left to develop on their own. The result was man.'

'How do you know this for sure?' interrupted Moss.

'I don't,' replied Myrddin. 'Like you, I have only seen the dreams this place creates. But over the many years I've seen them, I feel I've come to understand, at least part of them. Anyway, please don't interrupt me...'

'Sorry,' said Moss dryly, a look of interested disbelief on his face.

'I was born many *thousands* of years ago,' continued Myrddin, 'when the first civilisation evolved on the plains of Mesopotamia. As a youth, of about your age, I discovered, like you, that I possessed unusual powers. I could listen to conversations of people many leagues from where I stood and I could light fires without flint. As I grew up my talents diversified, they became more powerful and I wandered the known world, trying to quench my insatiable thirst for knowledge. In the beginning, I looked on my talents as a gift from God, but as those around me began to shun and fear me, I realised my powers were more a curse than a gift. Worst of all, I aged to the extent that you see me now, and no further. Those I loved and cherished died around me and as my powers grew I became an outcast from my own society.'

Myrddin's face took on a look of pain. 'For years I travelled the world, lost and without a cause, attempting to encourage civilisation whenever I could. Sometimes succeeding, sometimes failing. I must admit I was particularly pleased with Rome and Greece, though their collapse wasn't something to be proud of. One day, on my travels, I came across this place. That was back in the days when the Druids first built Stonehenge. Interesting bunch the Druids, liked their wine, had some small gift of power, I guess that's why they were attracted to this spot... Anyway one day, in the middle of an Equinox ceremony, the ground collapsed below me and I ended up here, much as you did. Like you, I fell straight into the dream world, saw wondrous things and more... much more. In short, this place became my home and it's been from here that I have watched events unfold in the outside world. It was here that I taught the young Arthur, the first man to unite the split kingdom...your great, great something grandfather.'

Moss, who until then had been listening with rapt if slightly unbelieving attention, couldn't help interrupting at this point. 'You called me Arthur Pendragon before. What do you mean by King Arthur being my great grandfather? According to the legend he died in battle without an heir, didn't he?'

Myrddin looked at Moss and smiled gently. 'How you remind me of him my lad,' he said. 'He was young and brash, but also a loner when I met him. Born of an illegitimate liaison between a Chieftain and a rival's wife.'

'I've always wondered,' Moss again interrupted, 'is that story about him pulling the sword out of the rock true? You know, what's it's name, Excalibur?'

'H'mm?' mused Myrddin, with a faraway look in his eyes. 'Oh yes, quite true. I admit I was a bit theatrical there, but how else was I to get everyone to pay attention to a skinny, spotty youth, a bit like yourself? Anyway, you're distracting me again. As the years passed by, he proved to be a great king, the first man to unite this land. Of course, that was back in the days before England, Scotland and Wales were one country, then it was simply a land run by chieftains, as Cumbria, Mercia, etc. To cut a long story short, Arthur was betrayed and perished in battle under the blades of mercenaries from the north. That was what you saw in your dream. It was after many wise years as the first king of England.

However, despite what legend may say, Arthur did have a son. Not from Gwenadere, but from a young maiden who worked in the castle. Lancelot wasn't the only one to dip his wick about you know!' Myrddin gave a small chuckle.

'I spirited the girl away from the castle, just before the final battle. She was looked after by a farmer who had recently lost his own wife and child to fever. The child grew strong and continued the Pendragan line. Over the eons, the inherited potential for leadership was kept latent, perhaps in some form of unconscious fear of appearing to be different. That is, until yourself! You, my boy, are a direct descendant of the Pendragon line and possess all the powers, and many more, inherited from your ancestor, Arthur Pendragan, first king of England!'

Myrddin sat back, folded his arms and looked expectantly at Moss with the expression of someone who's just given the world away.

Moss didn't react straight away. He sat quietly and thought for a while. It was a good story, but him, a direct descendant of the legendary King Arthur, who according to many history books didn't even exist? It seemed a bit unlikely,,. But, the old man certainly believed it was true, and it was equally true that he possessed some strange powers. Was it even necessary to believe the old man? The fact of the matter was, he seemed to have been led to this place for some reason, a reason connected to the Dyason and the resistance, regardless of stories from ancient history. Perhaps, it was better to humour the old guy rather than rattle his cage, after all this place was certainly possessed some sort of aura, he could feel it. So why not just roll along with things for the time being? At least he wasn't being shot at, and he was being fed.

Moss finally looked Myrddin in the eye and said simply, 'Okay'.

Myrddin's face fell and he looked crestfallen again. 'Okay? Okay? he muttered, 'I tell you that you are a direct descendant of one of the *greatest figures* in history, endowed with special powers undreamed of by most of humanity, and all you have to say is *okay?*'

'Well,' said Moss helplessly, shrugging his thin shoulders, 'It doesn't matter whether I believe you or not... We're still in this place, with no apparent way out. Surrounded by Dyason baying for my blood. I presume you're planning on helping rather than turning me over to them? So, what I believe is neither here nor there.

For the time being at least, I'm willing to go along with what you say. You're maybe nothing but a meddling old nutter, but I reckon there's more to you than that. We'll just have to wait and see if you really are Merlin the Magician, won't we? In the meantime I'm happy to roll along with whatever happens. At least I'm warm and being fed here, it's more than I ever got in the ghettos...'

Myrddin looked at Moss thoughtfully for a moment before answering.

'You know you're a real cynic, my boy. Arthur never dared question me! Still, I suppose that's what a few centuries of so-called civilisation does for you. It's obvious you're going to need some convincing.' With a sigh Myrddin extricated himself from the moulding chairs and stood up. 'Well don't just sit there lad, follow me!' He marched off muttering to himself about lack of respect and the youth of today.

Before he'd even thought about it Moss found himself following the old man. Another archway appeared in the wall and they walked through it and into a long corridor that sloped down, deeper underground. It seemed to take for ages to walk the length of the corridor, but it was in fact, only a few minutes. The walls glowed with the same warm amber light as in the other caverns and although they seemed to be made of stone they were as smooth as marble. Eventually, Myrddin and Moss passed through another doorway in the rock, which became translucent as they approached, and became opaque again once they entered the small chamber beyond. Unlike the other chambers that were lit by a soft amber glow, the crystal of this chamber gave out a green light. The interior was bare except for a round circle, made of some sort of dark smooth rock in the centre of the otherwise featureless floor. The stone was impregnated with small reflective gems that glinted and shone in every colour in the spectrum. Moss couldn't help but be impressed by its simple beauty.

'Step into the centre of the circle,' Myrddin ordered.

'Why? What's going to happen? The floor isn't going to drop away again is it?' asked Moss suspiciously.

Myrddin momentarily went red in the face, then after what appeared to be a battle of wills answered in exaggerated slowness, 'If you're ever to survive in this world lad, you *must* learn to know *who* to trust and when to trust them! This is one of those times to trust. Now step into the bloody circle as I told you!'

Moss hesitated for a moment, then without really knowing why, did as he was told. He stepped into the circle and was immediately bathed in a flickering bright white light that shot from the roof like the beam of a searchlight. He felt himself being held rigid by some unseen force. For a while he felt panicky and tried to move back out of the circle, but no matter how much he tried he could not will his legs to move. Then he felt something rapidly scan and probe his mind, not viciously, but effectively. Memories flashed past his eyes like a video rewinding, going further and further back into his childhood.

Images flitted through his mind of events that he'd though he'd forgotten, of his mother, father, of lying in a cot staring at the ceiling, of the pain and ecstasy of his birth, the moment he entered the world as a newborn child. The probing stopped abruptly and the white light vanished to be replaced by a warm red glow, like the glow of a heat lamp, gently massaging worn muscles. Once again he tried to move, but his muscles refused to respond. He was frozen to the spot, caught in the strange glow that spread through his tired body, healing, replenishing. The pain and agony of the past months seemed to be washed away, he felt himself getting stronger, the physical and mental scars of his recent past becoming less painful. It wasn't as if he were being brainwashed, he could still vividly remember everything that had happened. No, it was as if he was sharing the burden of his past with another person, and the load was halved. He understood better, felt more confident. Now a new presence entered the back of his mind, a gentle instructive presence. Images flashed past his eyes, not unlike those he had seen in his dreams not so long ago, but this time he understood their meaning, as though they were shown with a silent explanation. He saw an older man seduce a young bride, back in the dark ages of England's history. He saw a father watch his son grow from afar, and become King of England. He saw the Sentinel, a complex computer, develop its own living intelligence over the eons it guarded the development of the Earth's species. Moss felt the anguish, pain and pride the Sentinel felt at each of mankind's triumphs and failures; just as a parent felt for its child.

The dreams faded and Moss found himself directly linked to the mind behind this strange underground cathedral. It was an alien mind, but not like the hate-filled Dyason. This was a gentle mind, thoughtful, sensitive, but definitely alien. And yet somehow familiar. It was like the rapport between old friends. They needed no language, it was something far deeper than that. They understood each other so well words were unnecessary. Moss realised that in some bizarre unexplainable way, he was now, had always been, and always would have a rapport with this strange semi-sentient alien mind. They belonged together.

Something momentous had happened. He understood that he had been guided here. Not manipulated, not coerced, but guided. It was a subtle, but important difference. He was now and always had been free to pursue his own destiny, but at some time the two of them had to meet face to face. Now this had been done Moss knew the course of his life had changed forever. He knew that, he felt it in the very core of his soul. Two minds had come together, and the universe applauded. Quite what had happened he didn't understand, but for some reason he felt strangely fulfilled as though he'd been heading for this moment all his life. Above all he knew, in his heart, that he had returned to where he truly belonged...home!

He understood the past, and was clear about the future. Myrddin had been telling the truth, but knew only half the answers. The rest was for him to discover. His family had been butchered by the Dyason and he had been cast adrift, but not anymore. Now he had a home, a place where he belonged and a new family. Like a lost child returning home he had been greeted. The match was made, the bond renewed!

The light faded, and the presence drew away until it was only a familiar tingle at the back of his mind - still there, simply dormant, waiting for his command. Myrddin smiled at the youth and said quietly, 'It's done! Welcome home lad. Now do you believe?'

Moss looked at the old man with a new understanding, prompted by the presence that gently guided him from the back of his mind. He stepped out of the circle, walked up to Myrddin and embraced him. 'Yes great grandfather, I do believe,' he said.

With a sharp intake of breath Myrddin returned the embrace and exclaimed, 'You *know.*'

Moss held the old man at arm's length, looked at his lined and worn face then said, 'Yes Myrddin I do know now. I saw you sow the seeds that became Arthur, your son, my ancestor. In my dreams, the mind here explained that. You're right I should learn to trust. What you told me was the truth, but what or who is it? The mind I mean. You feel it also?'

Myrddin looked back at Moss, his look of astonishment changed into a broad smile. 'Yes my boy, I feel the mind also. It's been my friend and guide for many eons. What or who it is I don't know. It's not really sentient, not as we understand it. More like a silent friend, it shows intelligence and loyalty to our family, but what it really is I don't know. It's never shown me.'

Before Myrddin could explain further the light in the cavern began to change, to pulse from blue to green and back again. They looked around in surprise and wondered what was going to happen next. They didn't have to wait long. The wall furthest from the marble circle began to glow and become translucent, much as the monolith on the surface had.

'It's never done that before!' exclaimed Myrddin. 'The Sentinel has been waiting centuries for your arrival lad! I think we're about to be shown its innermost secrets!'

They stood side by side in rapture as the far wall became more and more translucent as if the very rock itself was fading to nothing. Eventually, it disappeared completely, and although there was nothing but darkness beyond, Moss could feel a whisper of air move past his face indicating that there was another cavern. Gradually he could make out the shape of a small balcony where the wall once stood, so together, they stepped onto it, despite being able to see nothing beyond. Slowly the dark was replaced with warm light, like the dawn of a spring morning. At first it was difficult to make anything out, but as the light increased shapes grew from darkness. The cavern was of enormous dimensions, so big Moss couldn't even see the far end, which he guessed must be at least several kilometres away. The unsupported roof was about one hundred metres above them, made of solid rock, but it was what was inside the cave that held them rooted to the spot.

From their position they looked down on what appeared to be some sort of craft, gigantic in dimensions. Moss guessed it must be at least twice the size of the biggest battleship. Its nose was like the head of a swan, a mix of complex curves that blended in a long elegant neck, which lead to a fuselage that was like a long low triangular prism, with some sort of intake blended into the underside and the top rear the fuselage. Its skin was a deep black that seemed to sheen in the golden light. Far in the distance, the rear the fuselage rose into a sweptback fin, on which sat a small tailplane that was again blended into some sort of intake. All across its body were markings, totally different to any language Moss knew of. They resembled hieroglyphics found in videos of ancient Egyptian tombs. All in all, its appearance was of a sleek marine animal, like a shark or dolphin, lying dormant waiting to be freed into its element again.

'Sweet mother!' Moss whispered in awe. 'What is it?'

'All this time!' Muttered Myrddin, 'All this time it here and I *never* knew! I *never* knew!'

Moss turned to the old man, it looked like he was in some sort of shock. The colour had faded from weathered complexion and he suddenly looked very frail.

'You never knew what? What is it Myrddin? What is this thing? It's bigger than anything I've ever seen before. Tell me!' he demanded grabbing him by the shoulders, shaking him to get some sense out of him.

Myrddin turned to his descendant and returned his grip, gazing into the youth's eyes.

'It's the ship Moss..., the mother ship..,' he said in hushed reverent tones. 'This is the ship that crossed the galaxy to bring sentient life to Earth, all those millions of years ago. This is the vessel that sowed the seeds of humanity...the Sentinel. Here it's lain, cocooned, preserved since the dawn of history, waiting... waiting for a time when it was needed again! For a time when human kind was once again threatened. For a time when its knowledge could mean the difference between survival and extinction for homo-sapiens and I never knew it was here! This is why you were brought to Stonehenge lad. It has been shown to you! This is humankind's inheritance!'

Moss turned and looked in awe at the mothership once more. It was too much to handle, an ancient alien craft, cocooned under the English countryside for millions of years, waiting for a time when it was needed again. A time like the present! Something entered his mind, but it wasn't the mind that had probed before. This was from beyond this place, from somewhere very far away. It was a mind of omnipotent power, a mind from the depths of the universe itself.

'MAN-CHILD, YOU HAVE BEEN SHOWN THE VESSEL KNOWN AS EXCALIBUR. THIS CRAFT CONTAINS KNOWLEDGE FAR BEYOND THAT OF HUMANKIND. IT IS YOUR SPECIES' INHERITANCE AND IT CAN BE USED FOR GOOD OR EVIL... USE IT WISELY AND IT WILL BRING THE SALVATION OF YOUR RACE. USE IT UNWISELY AND IT WILL BRING EXTINCTION UPON YOU ALL. IT IS FOR YOU TO DECIDE!'

CHAPTER ELEVEN

TOKYO INTERNATIONAL AIRPORT

The air was thick with a mixture of ash and soot from the thousands of small fires the humans lit in their hovels. The hovels surrounded the slave factories which once supplied people with cars and electronic goods, but now produced products for the Dyason Empire. A Dyason senior officer peered into the gloom, unable to see more than a few metres in front of him. Behind him, the guard of honour, immaculate in their dress uniforms, fidgeted uncomfortably.

From somewhere deep in the smog a pinpoint of light slowly emerged. As it came nearer it gradually took on the shape of an Imperial shuttle. It approached the landing strip in a wide curve then eased onto the tarmac. It rolled to a halt in front of the band and two troops ran a decorative gangway up to the craft's hatch. The band struck up the Dyason Imperial anthem and Marshal Mettar stepped forward expectantly. Nothing happened...

After several minutes the band came to the end of the anthem, leaving an embarrassing silence hanging over the airport until, after frantic motions by the conductor, they began all over again. Mettar stood stiffly to attention, unmoving, though Gulag noticed with some satisfaction, that his face was beginning to turn red and perspire. Just as it seemed the band would have to play the anthem for a third time, the hatch opened and out stepped two Imperial security men, bulging at the seams of their special service uniforms. They took station at either side of the step-way and after peering in all directions, nodded to someone unseen standing in the shuttle hatchway. There was the barest hesitation before a figure swept out of the shuttle and down the step-way. Gulag and all the officers lined up behind Mettar, stood to attention and gave the formal crossed chest salute.

Marshal Mettar fell to his knees and took the hand of the person who stood before him. He gave it a kiss, then his bowed his head. The figure beckoned him to rise, which was the cue for Gulag and the other officers to finish the salute with a flourish. The figure stood several centimetres taller than the stocky Mettar. Gulag tried to make out the face, but the hood of a full length cloak hid it from view. For some reason Gulag felt great unease at the presence of this Dyason. Not just because it was a high ranking from the Motherworld, but because it created some sort of disturbance in the back of his head, in the mind place, which was strange, because until now he'd never felt the presence of another Dyason operant. Was this about to change?

With a flourish the figure pulled the hood away to reveal a woman's face, beautiful in a harsh chiselled manner, with long shiny black hair that fell to her waist. But it was her eyes that startled Gulag the most. He felt inexplicably drawn to the deep, black, bottomless pits, that stared, not at Mettar, but straight at him! Nimue, the envoy of the Emperor, had finally arrived on Earth.

Gulag felt very uncomfortable at the evening function held in honour of the envoy. He found the ornate interior of the Japanese parliament buildings intimidating, and despite attempting to make light conversation with the staff officers, he found that talk faded away as soon as he approached any group. Even Mettar seemed to be going out his way to avoid him. In fact it seemed he made a point of not, chewing him out, for yet again losing the English brat. Which was suspicious, considering just how much Mettar loathed him. The old bastard would usually be delighted of any opportunity to crucify him.

So, Gulag found himself standing alone in a corner of the large hall while everyone else socialised in groups awaiting the arrival of their guest. He almost wished he was back in the lab with that wimp Brabazon. At least there, he didn't have to pretend to be pleasant. They'd been making good progress on studying Gulag's operancy, and even the goal of navigating the universe through the other dimension seemed less like a madman's dream. While Brabazon kept an eye on his brain patterns, Gulag had explored the parameters of his talents. He knew that the knowledge gained from the minds he'd taken had merged with his own, and it was this accumulation which fuelled his rapid progress. Brabazon was worried that the amalgamation could lead to some form of psychosis, but he wasn't having any of that bull. He knew *he* would stay in control. Others might succumb, but not him, he was made of sterner stuff.

So why was he being treated like a leper? Why was he being so obviously ostracised by his peers? He should be hailed as a hero by these bastards. After all, who had, and was still, doing more for the Empire, than him? They were scared, threatened, that's what it was... They were jealous! As he became more powerful, they became weaker, until one day, they would all have to bow and scrape to *him*, not that git, Mettar. He had thought of probing Mettar's mind, to discover what was going on in that thick skull of his, but as yet, he wasn't confident enough that he could probe without leaving any trace. The last thing he needed right now was for Mettar to discover just how far his powers extended. Let it be a surprise.

Gulag's train of thought was interrupted by a fanfare. Everybody stood to attention as Envoy Nimue and her entourage swept into the banqueting hall. She wore a formal Dyason dress that was cut low over her firm breasts and tight around her narrow waist. Her dark black hair was braided all down her back, leaving the nape of her neck exposed, whilst her aristocratic features were made up subtly, to highlight her steely dark eyes and somewhat thin lips. From the appreciative looks of other officers, Gulag was sure he was not the only officer present, admiring her cold beauty.

She moved silently up to the platform and greeted Mettar formally, and perhaps a little curtly too. There then followed the usual speeches by Mettar and his cronies, waxing lyrical about the honour of the Empire and the importance to the Motherworld of this new colony. Gulag switched off after the first sentence.

However, he was quick to notice that Envoy Nimue did not rise to respond to the Marshal's speech. Instead she simply stood to one side of the platform and smiled in a slightly disarming manner.

Again, Gulag felt that same unease he had noted at the airport. There was something about the Envoy that set off alarm bells in the other dimension, but he couldn't put his finger on what it was. He felt no signs of probing, but the nape of his neck tingled and the hairs stood on end, just the same as when that English brat was close by. Instinctively, he knew there was something inherently dangerous about Nimue, and he ought to keep his distance. Unfortunately, however, his instinct for survival was in direct contradiction to what his loins were telling him, and if it came to it, he knew which would come first...

Once the speeches came to an end, the officers once more split into smaller groups, the largest of which surrounded the Envoy like worker bees around a queen. Gulag found himself alone once more. After about half an hour, by which time Gulag was beginning to feel very sorry for himself, one of the Envoy's entourage worked his way through the hall towards him. He stopped in front of Gulag and gave a short bow from the waist.

'Group Leader Gulag' he said looking imperiously down his nose, 'the Envoy to the Emperor, Nimue, wishes the pleasure of your company.'

Gulag was so surprised, that when the Dyason turned sharply on his heels, he had to march rapidly to catch up. The hangers-on surrounding Nimue parted at his arrival and quickly dispersed, so that only Gulag and Mettar stood before the Envoy and her entourage. Close to, the Envoy was even more beautiful, with skin like porcelain that made his pulse quicken, with a mixture of anguish and desire. He snapped to attention, clicked his heels and gave a short bow from the neck. Mettar reluctantly gave the introductions.

'Envoy Nimue, may I introduce Group Leader Gulag.' Mettar looked at Gulag as if he were flotsam in a toilet.

The Envoy slowly looked Gulag up and down and gave an appreciative smile that made his pulse race even faster. Then she turned to Mettar and said, 'Thank you Marshal. You have been most kind and shown me great hospitality. However, without wishing to appear rude, I have Imperial matters to discuss with the Group Leader here'.

Mettar's face flushed with embarrassment and rage. He was being snubbed in front of all the assembled officers, by the devil's child Gulag! Damn the bitch! Barely able to contain his rage, Mettar snapped to attention, clicked his heels, turned and marched to the other side of the hall, followed by his senior officers. The Envoy's narrowed eyes bored into his back. When she turned and gave her full attention to Gulag, he felt as though his legs would give way as those steely dark eyes stared into his. By all the gods the woman was possessed of formidable power! It was almost a tangible thing that he could reach out and touch! It was all he could do to keep his composure.

The Envoy smiled and said pleasantly, 'I have heard many things about you Group Leader! Not everyone in the Imperial forces approves of your methods. First in that place in Europe... Ah yes, Britain I think it is called. Then in the research you now lead... I, however, can only applaud your work, and am eager to learn more. The Emperor is also very interested, and has instructed me to inform him of your progress as soon as I return to the Motherworld. But, these matters can wait until the morrow. Perhaps you would be so kind as to entertain us now with your experiences of this savage world?'

At last! He was right, the other bastards in the room were merely jealous - his work had come to the attention of the Emperor himself! Gulag's chest swelled with pride and he nervously cleared his throat, but before he could open his mouth, there was a loud bang and the sound of gunfire from another part of the parliament buildings. All heads turned and Gulag saw a small plume of smoke rise from the entrance to the banqueting hall. A squad of security troops ran towards the commotion.

One of the Envoy's private Imperial security team strode up to Gulag and Nimue. 'Envoy,' he said urgently, 'it appears that a small group of humans have carried out a successful attack at the entrance to the halls. The situation is under control, but I feel it would be wise to leave immediately. We have your car waiting at the rear. If you would follow me?'

'Indeed!' Nimue replied coolly. 'It would appear that the humans are not yet completely subjugated, as the good Marshal would have us believe! Group leader,' she said turning to Gulag. 'Would you be so kind as to escort me to my quarters?'

Gulag attempted to suppress a smile. Things were looking up! Mettar was now looking a complete idiot. Serve the bastard right!

'It would be a pleasure Envoy' he replied heading with the Envoy towards the rear exit, knowing everyone was watching.

The passions of the Envoy drove Gulag wild. Her wandering fingers entered his every orifice and manipulated his erection with an expert touch. She controlled his every movement, but as he screamed for release, she remained cold and calculating, her eyes always dark, bottomless pits. After what seemed an eternity she guided him inside her, and Gulag thrust deeply, with a frenetic energy he didn't know he possessed. He could feel himself reach a climax as he gripped her firm breasts and thrust at the same time. He gave out an animal growl and as he collapsed spent onto her body... She drew him into her arms and whispered into his ear, 'Come to mother.. child!'

Like an explosion going off inside his head, Gulag felt another mind enter his, and he realised the full horror of what had happened. From the depths of his soul came a long and terrible scream.

CHAPTER TWELVE

Jenson sat in the reclining couch that moulded to his form, and looked around him. If it wasn't for the fact that he kept pinching himself till it hurt, he would swear he was having one of those weird dreams. He was, there could be no doubt, in the control room of this huge spacecraft, surrounded by a myriad of controls that resembled the crystalline structures they'd seen when they first entered the underground chambers. Similar couches to the one he sat in were positioned at stations around the edges of the elliptical room, and in front of each were panels of opaque crystal and what appeared to be touch-sensitive screens and switches.

'I'm sitting here,' he said in wonder, 'but I still can't quite believe it! This is the control room of an alien spacecraft, cocooned here for centuries...no millennia; if our friends, Moss and the old man, are to be believed.'

Sandpiper, sitting in another couch, with his feet propped up on a control panel, as if he owned the place, looked at Jenson from the corner of his eye.

'All I know Skipper,' he remarked, 'is that one minute Brabazon and I were clambering from the wreckage of our FZB, with me badly concussed, and with several cracked ribs, and him, with a huge gash in his shoulder, and the next thing I remember is waking up in Santa's grotto, with no mark on me, except a slight headache. Oh yeah, I nearly forgot, a bearded old man introduced himself to me as Myrddin. So, I ask myself, after all that, why not an alien spacecraft to boot? May as well make a mass hallucination a good one after all!'

Jenson smiled wryly at his friend. You could always rely on Sandpiper to come out with a witty comment, no matter how bizarre the situation.

'I can assure you both, this is no hallucination,' stated Josh Brabazon rising up from behind the panel he'd been closely examining. 'The technology is well beyond our own present capabilities, but quite workable'.

Jenson sat up in interest. 'Go on Josh,' he urged.

'Well,' Brabazon continued, 'from what I can make out, these controls are part of a very large computer-operated system. The operator sits in front of the panel and receives information through a three-dimensional display panel. And, by placing their hands on the controls, a link is made directly to their mind. It's something we've been experimenting with for some time, but we've never made anything this advanced. Anyway, the operator is directly linked with the central computer, and can give it instructions, either through the touch-sensitive display panel, or by thought alone. At least that's how I think it's meant to work!'

Jenson looked at him thoughtfully. 'That's a rather astute observation Josh. At least one of us doesn't think this is all one big hoax. Have you got any other info for us?'

'Well,' Josh continued, 'it's obvious from the layout of the controls and couches that the original occupants were humanoid. These controls fit the human hand perfectly, which would raise some interesting questions as to what the definition of human is... Once we thought of Earth being the only home of homo-sapiens. What with the Dyason, and now this, we're going to have to reappraise that view.'

'Either that, or whoever built this machine were expecting us', interrupted Sandpiper. '

'That's a good point you know,' said Jenson. 'This all seems a bit too pat to me... On top of everything else here, it just happens, that the bug-eyed creatures that built this thing were almost exactly the same height, weight and had the same number of digits as humans. I mean, can we really believe this story that the old man is Myrddin the Magician, the kid is his descendant and this place is the cocooned hangar of a great spaceship that once colonised the Earth? If it were all true, why make an appearance now? Why not when the Dyason first invaded? That was when we really needed the help! I just can't quite accept it... In fact, more than just not being able to quite accept it ; I can't believe any of it period. Regardless of any dream brainwashing!'

'I can sympathise with you skipper, but I can assure you that this craft is quite real. Either that, or we're having one hell of a hallucination. Mind you...having said that...those dreams we all had in the catacombs seemed pretty real,' said Brabazon thoughtfully, 'but perhaps we shouldn't be questioning whether the old man and boy really are figures out of mythology. May I put it, that the question is not why, but how? This craft and its technology may just be the advantage we've been searching for to defeat the Dyason. Surely, the question is, how, are we going to make the best use of it?'

The sound of the control room door sliding open made Jenson look around. Myrddin entered the room looking decidedly unwizard-like in a pair of faded denim overalls. Only his white beard and strangely bright eyes bore any comparison to the story book images of Myrddin the Magician. He strode into the centre of the room and faced the three of them.

'He has a very good point, Squadron Leader' he said to Jenson. 'It really is immaterial whether you believe my story or not. I hope in time that you will. The youth respects you and looks up to you, even though he may not show it. In the events that are to come, he will need your help and encouragement. However, Dr Brabazon is right. For the moment the most pressing problem, is how to make best use of this vessel. It is, as it has already been pointed out, the best advantage we have over the invaders. It is for you and your friends to decide how to use it!'

For a moment Myrddin's eyes glazed over, then with a hint of a smile he said, 'I believe a mutual friend wishes to talk with you Squadron Leader...'

Without warning, the control panels around the room lit up, causing Sandpiper to jump to his feet in surprise. Display panels showed strange geometric shapes and patterns, lights winked on and off, while at the far end of the control room one whole wall lit up with a three-dimensional view of the entire vessel sitting in its cavern. Across the craft lights were coming on, systems starting up. The alien vessel was coming to life.

From nowhere came a quiet female voice which addressed them all in perfect English. 'Good day, Squadron Leader Jenson, Flight Lieutenant Sandpiper and Dr Brabazon. I am ready to begin your familiarisation with Excalibur."

The three men looked at each other with astonishment.

Jennifer Hampton tentatively held Moss's hand, as they explored the huge corridors and passageways of the alien ship. She'd changed out of her tattered rags and now wore a simple jumpsuit and jacket that highlighted her slim figure. Her hair, washed and combed, was now a golden blonde, that tumbled down her back in curly locks. Jennifer now found that it was very important to her that she looked her best. When she was working in the slave factory, she didn't care how she looked; she was more concerned about staying alive. But now, in her sixteenth year, she was discovering a whole host, of new emotions. To anybody watching, it would have been obvious who, the focus of these new emotions was.

Being operant, Jennifer had felt the intrusions in the mind dimension that all other operants shared. To her young mind, the potential power of the strange youth, about whom all operants talked, was like a myth. He was a character out of an old film; the hero who no villain could stop, the knight who saves the maiden! Never in her wildest dreams had she expected to actually meet, let alone be rescued by, the most notorious human being on the planet! Ever since her family had been butchered, she'd dreamed of an avenger who would rescue her, and bring justice to the world. It was a teenage fantasy, but it was a fantasy that had helped sustain her in her darkest moments, alone and hungry, in the slave quarters. Then, a few weeks ago, flesh was put on the fantasy, with rumours of an operant more powerful than any other on the planet, and this operant was giving the Dyason bastards a run for their money. He was a thorn in their sides, which they were desperate to remove, but nobody could catch him. The resistance was obviously irritated by this freelance activity. They considered his uncontrolled actions to be dangerous, and the myth surrounding him was raising the expectations of the holocaust survivors. They also knew there was nothing they could do to stop the rumours and the stories. The people needed a hero, a saviour, and they were determined to have one, regardless of the truth.

The cause of all this commotion? The boy called Moss. He'd swept into her life and rescued her from slavery. The fantasy had become reality, but the reality was beyond even her wildest dreams! She was in this strange place, being told by a man, who called himself Myrddin, that she was the king's consort, whatever that meant, and walking hand in hand through an alien spacecraft! Part of her refused to believe it was really happening, any moment she would wake up and find herself back in the squalid dormitories of the slave factory.

She stole a glance at Moss when he wasn't looking. From the grime had emerged a handsome young man, with strong chiselled features, startling eyes, and a generous mouth. He was such a complex mixed-up bundle of emotions. Sometimes he was quiet, thoughtful, then without warning, he would become excited and animated. Then he would be strong, decisive and confident, but when something happened he was unsure about, he would be like a boy; worried, confused and unsure. He would try not to show it, be cold and aloof, not show any emotion, pretend to be like a block of ice, but underneath, he was soft, warm and compassionate. It was funny, he pretended not to like the resistance leader, Jenson, but when he thought nobody was watching, he would copy his walk, his actions. Intuitively, she realised he was using him as a role model, of how to act like a man. He could do far worse; she liked and respected Jenson... Jennifer had found her hero, her knight, her avenger; and she was determined to hang on to him.

It was strange, she thought, but she was sure that in some way, Moss had changed in the short time since they'd escaped the compound. Then he'd been a somewhat awkward, gangly youth, but now he strode down the corridors of this craft, as though he'd been here before and knew every centimetre. Every now and then, he would stop and point something out to her, explaining what its function was, while she listened spellbound. He'd shown her the vast engine rooms and individual crew quarters. She'd been amazed at the vast shuttle hangars that housed numerous strange craft; some as large as jet liners.

Yet, Moss was never surprised by any of this, and he spoke about things she could never understand. And all the time he walked upright, shoulders back, striding along in a confident manner, all of which made him very different from the awkward stooping youth she first saw in the resistance hideaway. There his eyes were sunken with a hunted look about them, his hair greasy and matted. Now, his eyes had a sparkle and his physical presence seemed larger, more potent. Like herself, his rags had been changed for a simple flight suit, but he still kept his familiar well-worn leather jacket.

Somehow, this place, this cavern and spacecraft had changed them both, but despite that, Jennifer knew, with all her heart, that she loved this youth and they were destined to spend their lives together.

They walked up to another doorway, Moss placed his palm on the door plate and it disappeared. They stepped through and the door reappeared behind them. What she saw next took her breath away. They were standing in what could only be described as a huge garden. A single source of light from above imitated a sun and shed a soothing warmth on the plants and trees that grew in abundance as far as the eye could see. Streams filled small ponds and lakes, while strange birds chattered and flew from tree top to tree top.

'Is it real?' she asked in awe.

'Oh yes,' Moss replied with a sigh and quiet smile. 'It's quite real. You can touch and smell it.'

'What is this place?' Jennifer asked in hushed tones.

'It's a self-contained biosphere,' he replied as his eyes took on a strange inward-looking glint, as though he was listening to someone inside his head. 'Some of these trees, plants and animals come from the home world of the people who made this craft; some come from Earth. Here they created a self-contained garden which has its own little ecology, watched over by the ship's computer. Trees and animals have lived and died in this garden for millennia... a world within a world.'

Jennifer turned and looked Moss in the eye. She hesitated then asked in a rush, 'This computer, it talks to you and the old man?'

'Yes,' he replied the faraway look entering his eyes again, 'it has an intelligence of its own. This craft is not just a collection of parts from another world. It is really a sentient being with feelings and emotions of its own. The computer is its brain, the sensors, engines and controls, its arms and limbs. It wasn't like that in the beginning. When it first arrived on Earth it was just a computer, with no thoughts of its own. However, lying in hibernation for millennia, it has had time to evolve, just as we have evolved. All the caverns above us were created by the craft for our use.'

Jennifer looked at him. If she wasn't standing here, where she could clearly read his more accessible thoughts, she wouldn't believe any of this was true. As it was, she had no choice but to believe.

'What does it feel like? You know, an alien in your mind?' she asked.

'To be honest,' he replied, sitting down on what looked like grass, pulling Jennifer down beside him, 'it's a bit like having a puppy. Although it's immensely intelligent, its emotions are undeveloped. It tends to become overexcited and you have to be very firm with it to keep it under control.'

'What does it feel at the moment?' Jennifer asked.

'Excitement and curiosity. It's been waiting for all of us to arrive here for some time now. The recent events, us being here together now, seem to have been set in motion by the Dyason invasion and Myrddin. It's a bit like when a dog sees its master for the first time after being away. It runs around yelping excitedly. It's not much help to us at the moment, but once it has calmed down, we can get things moving!'

'What things?' she interrupted. 'What does it *want* of us?'

'To set it free from its cage. To roam the universe again,' he replied. Then, as Jennifer opened her mouth to ask yet another question Moss placed his finger on her lips and said, 'That's enough questions for today. I brought you here for a reason.

He leant over and kissed her firmly on the lips. Jennifer felt a hot flush rise up inside her and all her senses reeled. Not only could she feel his physical embrace, but the embrace of his mind, as he gently drew her to him. Excalibur glowed with pleasure and watched the two humans intensely...

Jenson sat in front of a holographic monitor and watched with fascination as the alien computer led him, and the others, on a holographic tour of the craft, including its propulsion systems. It was quite amazing. From what he could understand of what they were being told, the whole vessel was made of a material not unlike carbon fibre, but infinitely stronger. Each fibre was less than the width of a human hair, but had the strength of hardened steel more than six inches in diameter.

The propulsion was, as far as he could gather, something called two captive 'nodes'. Nodes were pea-sized balls of intense dark energy, that existed both in the three-dimensional universe and the multi-dimensional universe. Consequently, their reaction upon each other, and the universe around them, was to generate vast quantities of heat and power. However, their most important quality was to exist between dimensions, affecting time and space in an area around them. It was this effect that the craft ; which according to the computer was named Excalibur (a name Jenson suspected was given by the old man Myrddin to maintain his myth) ; used to transverse the universe.

How it managed to navigate through star systems was beyond him, but Brabazon, who had a better grip on such matters, said that the computer was able to visualise beyond the three physical dimensions into the fabric of space-time. In the same way that he, and his research team, had been attempting with human operants. It was also the method the Dyason were so desperate to emulate.

In fact, there was something odd about the computer that ran this craft. When they first came on board, everything was closed down, but without any input from themselves, systems seemed to be coming back on line, as though warming up after a long period unused. When the monitors first came on in the control room, the symbols on the screens were completely alien to him, but over the past few hours there had been some remarkable changes. First the screen information changed from the alien symbols to international English, then the displays changed to standard micro PC graphics. Now, the computer spoke to them in perfect English, in a pleasant conversational voice, gently fielding the hundreds of questions asked by Sandpiper and Brabazon, who were poring over a large holo-monitor.

Obviously, the computer's ability to learn on its own accord was phenomenal, but Jenson couldn't help thinking of the classic novel *2001* by Arthur C. Clarke, where the ship's computer HAL becomes paranoid and starts killing off the crew. This computer was far more advanced than the fictional HAL; he just hoped it was on their side and not paranoid!

The bridge door opened and Jenson looked up to see the girl Jennifer and Moss enter hand in hand. Jenson smiled quietly to himself. Well, there was love blooming and another mystery. Was this youth really related to the old man? Just how far did their strange powers go? What was their link with this place and this machine? So many questions, so little time... Maybe Josh Brabazon was right, maybe he shouldn't look a gift horse in the mouth. They should simply accept that these people and this place were perhaps the key to defeating the Dyason. He looked up at Moss, casually waved a hand and said, 'Hi kids, been having fun? Hope you didn't break anything, we don't want to upset the host.'

Jennifer smiled shyly, but Moss strode over to Jenson holding a data fob in his hand.

'I'm sorry Squadron Leader, but I forgot to give you this before. I guess it slipped my mind, in all the excitement of the past few days,' he said.

'What is it?' Jenson asked curiously.

'The resistance leader at the slave factory gave it to me to give to you, but I'm afraid I don't know what's on it,' he replied with a serious look on his face.

Jenson took it from Moss and called over to Sandpiper and Brabazon.

'Hey guys, I think you'd better come and take a look at this. Is there anything round here we can use to view this data?'

The reply didn't come from his friends, but from the alien computer.

'If you would kindly place the data fob on the panel in front of you, Squadron Leader Jenson, I would be happy to read and display the information for you,' it said in polite tones.

Jenson, quickly getting over his initial surprise at being addressed by the computer, placed the disk in a small niche in the main panel in front of him. Up on the main screen of the control room, which took up the whole of the far wall, an image of a blueprint and figures appeared.

'If you wish Squadron Leader," said the computer, 'I would be happy to analyse the information for you.'

Jenson looked at Josh Brabazon with a quizzical expression. Josh just shrugged and said, 'What the hell!'

Jenson looked at the panel in front of him and said, 'Thank you Excalibur, please go ahead'. Almost instantaneously the image changed to a brightly coloured three-dimensional image of a Dyason Dome.

'The craft,' said the computer, 'is an improvement on the standard Dyason design. The blueprints have been sent from their home world to Earth and replicated, so that they may be built in large numbers. The design is very basic. The Dyason do not have the electronics, which have become such a part of Earth life in recent decades. However, the Dyason have been using humans to update the plans using Earth computer technology. The plans you see have been so created, and according to the information on the fob, copied at great personal risk to the operator.

The design of the Dome is crude even by human standards, but effective.The shape is evolved from the use of heavy gauge metals crudely welded together. You could compare it to the production of a tank from Earth's last world war. The method of propulsion is simple nuclear technology. The base plate of the Dome is several feet thick. This is to protect the life support areas from the ejectors that fire very small projectiles below the plate. These projectiles are very small fission bombs which explode behind the plate and propel the vessel forward. The heat caused by this process is used to create electrical power for the craft's systems. The design and construction of these vessels would indicate that the Dyason are a heavily industrialised race, who have developed nuclear power to a greater extent, than humans. However, they have not developed sophisticated electronics, or computers. Indeed, there are many similarities with German and Russian engineering from the period 1900 to 1945.' The computer declared, then continued,'The resistance cell at the slave factory, where this information was collected, indicate that two Domes are under construction at this plant. They estimate that there are at least, another fifty craft in production at other plants around the globe. The estimated time for completion is six weeks.'

'May I point out,' the computer continued, 'that radiation and debris from a large number of these vessels leaving the Earth, will make the launch sites uninhabitable and have an adverse effect on the Earth's biosphere. Which is even now, struggling to recover from the debris thrown into the stratosphere during the initial invasion by the Dyason.'

'This is amazing,' exclaimed Josh Brabazon excitedly, 'NASA scientists in the last century considered using this method to launch space stations into Earth Orbit. The point being, that weight is not a problem when you have so much power, but the idea was dropped because of the pollution factor, and the adverse effect such acceleration would have on equipment.

It would also support my theory of a space-time fault in our Solar System. Without an interstellar drive, they couldn't have travelled independently from another star system.'

'You may be glad to know Doctor Brabazon,' intoned the computer, 'that I can confirm your observation of a fault in the space-time fabric, within the solar system.'

'Excuse me for my ignorance,' interrupted Jenson, addressing Excalibur, 'but how do you know all these things, when you've been cocooned underground all these centuries?

'Squadron Leader,' replied the computer, 'several of my probes are still functioning. One is placed on the moon. Another is in orbit between the Earth and the moon. These probes are the last of many, but are still able to send data. Also, I have numerous sensors able to receive radio and microwave signals from around the planet.'

'You should realise,' interrupted Myrddin, who had been listening to the conversation, 'that our friend here, has had centuries to study and observe the universe and Earth, albeit from the confines of these catacombs. I should point out that over the millennia Excalibur has developed its own level of sentience...'

Jenson said nothing, just looked thoughtful. Moss stepped forward and addressed the group, 'This discussion isn't addressing the main problem here. Whether you trust Excalibur or not, the Dyason are going to launch another fleet of Domes in just six week's time. If they achieve that, they may well also achieve their aim to navigate between Earth and Dyason without needing to use the unstable fault line, as described by Dr Brabazon. Either way, humanity will never release itself from the shackles of slavery if the new fleet is successfully launched.'

'So what do you suggest kid?' asked Jenson, who was looking at Moss with interest.

'The resistance is already planning a massive attack on Dyason installations in the near future. Am I correct? asked Moss.

'I won't ask you how you know this,' said Jenson pointedly looking at a reddening Jennifer, 'but yes, you're right. Go on...'

'This attack must be brought forward before the launch of the new fleet of Domes. Also, we must set Excalibur free and use it to defeat the Dyason fleet already in Earth orbit,' Moss continued.

'That's impossible!' exclaimed Josh Brabazon. 'This craft has been lying here for centuries, it would take years of study to figure out how to run it, and make repairs to any damage that may have occurred over such an immense time. Even if we managed that, we have no way of being sure that this thing is space-worthy. Then once that had been achieved, there would be just the small matter of half a kilometre of sheer rock above us to shift...'

'Perhaps, I may intercede at this point Dr Brabazon,' the computer interrupted. 'I am well aware of what is needed to restore all my functions to operational level. There are a fleet of nano-robots that are designed to carry out essential maintenance to my systems. Unfortunately, due to a virus in their software, all have succumbed over the centuries. Therefore, work must indeed, be carried out to some of my systems, but with my guidance and the current state of Earth technology, it should be possible to restore the fleet of nano-robots and effect repairs. I estimate five weeks, before my systems could be fully operational.'

'And,' interrupted Moss 'there is a ready source of technicians and equipment nearby'.

'Where?' asked Sandpiper.

'The slave factory.' Moss replied.

'Okay sure," said Jenson standing up. It was time to get things in order, before the kid convinced them all to go off on some wild goose chase, that was going to get them all killed. 'So, let's say we manage to spring the technicians and PCs out of the factory and manage to get this thing working. And it's one very tall if! There are still two small problems. One, as Josh said, is how do we get this thing out of this cavern? Two, does this thing carry any armament, or are we planning on ramming the Dyason fleet?'

'Squadron Leader," said the computer, 'in answer to your first question, the caverns have been designed with a future launch in mind. I can assure you that when the time comes, this vessel can leave without damage. In answer to your second question, although Excalibur is a research vessel, it does carry laser armament for the purpose of destroying rogue asteroids. Their power, once on line, should be sufficient to punch holes in the Dome hulls, if they are produced according to the plans given to us.'

'I don't know. I still find the idea of raising an alien spacecraft from below ground to Earth orbit, and then shooting down the Dome fleet in just six weeks time, is hard to take seriously,' said Jenson dubiously.

'I can appreciate your cynicism Squadron Leader' interrupted Myrddin, speaking for the first time, 'but without the advantage Excalibur may give the resistance, the chances of victory are far more remote. Besides, do you really have much choice? If the Dyason manage to launch their new fleet and solve the problem of inter- dimensional navigation, it is unlikely that humanity will get another chance to break free of its shackles for generations to come. *Any chance* is better than none at all.'

'He's right skipper,' said Hanson Sandpiper. 'I've seen enough here to know that there are things going on that we have no chance of understanding. Without something special to clout the bastards with, the resistance is unlikely to be ready in six weeks time. We had all been planning for six months from now. I say we go along with these guys. At least for now.'

'What do you think Josh?' Jenson asked Brabazon.

'I've no doubt that the technology on-board this vessel is far in advance of our own, and therefore leap years ahead of anything the Dyason possess,' replied Brabazon, 'However, as I've already said, bringing an alien craft to operational status in just five weeks, seems to me, an almost impossible task. Even taking into account, no doubt, the vast abilities of Excalibur's computer. Certainly, without personnel and equipment, I wouldn't even know where to begin.'

Jenson sat and thought for a moment. The key here was getting men and machinery into these caverns. They could ship some equipment by air from their Arctic home base, but the stealth aircraft could only carry so much, and there was always the risk that, even though they may evade the Dyason radar, they might be seen by a patrol or similar. However, attacking the nearby slave factory would be killing two birds with one stone. If they destroyed some of the factories key facilities, then the completion of the new Domes, at that location at least, would be delayed, perhaps indefinitely. If they could then, release some of the technicians who'd been forced to work there, and bring them here, there was just a slight chance, that they might discover something useful regardless of whether they really could fly this beast again, or not. Jenson felt it was unlikely that this ancient vessel could be raised from its tomb, but the technology could be put to their advantage.

The only question then, was could he trust the kid and the old man? Was their story true? Strange things had certainly been happening recently. The girl, Jennifer, truly believed in the lad, but then, love is blind. The problem was, the kid was a wild card. A youth of awesome mental power, but without the maturity and guidance to control himself. Could he be trusted, to do what he was told? Then, there was the old man who called himself Myrddin. He too, seemed to possess extra-sensory powers, but as yet, they had no way of knowing how far they went. What was his scheme? Did he really want to help them rid Earth of the Dyason, or was he part of a much greater conspiracy, that included this alien vessel and its almost sentient computer? For a man who liked to reduce all unknown variables to a minimum, he was faced with making decisions based upon nothing but variables. However, it didn't matter which way he looked at it, he really didn't have any choice. Hanson was right in saying, that it was incidental whether the kid and old man were really on their side or not. For the time, being their destinies were intertwined, and necessity made allies of them all. At least for now...

'Okay,' he finally announced to them all. 'We go along with the raid on the factory, and try to bring some personnel in here, to look at this machine. In the meantime, we alert all the resistance cells to be ready for a major offensive in six weeks time.'

'Josh,' he said looking at Brabazon, 'I want you to start working with this computer to figure out what makes this vessel tick. If you think it's impossible to get the thing working, then forget it. Just look for any new kit we can use against the Dyason. Figure out what these defensive shield things are, and what the armament is. Shit, this all sounds like a Buck Rogers episode!'

'Okay skipper! Said Josh with a smile, and immediately disappeared behind a monitor panel.

'Hanson,' Jenson continued looking at his friend, 'I need you to help me organise this raid. We're going to need kit from home base, and technicians to look at this thing.'

Sandpiper nodded. 'You got it skipper.

'Jennifer, I need you to make a sketch of the factory layout, and perhaps look at ways we might get in. Okay?' The girl nodded.

'What about us?' asked Moss.

'No disrespect kid,' said Jenson carefully, 'but you seem to wreak havoc wherever you go. I would feel a whole lot happier, if I knew you were somewhere safe. I'd like you to stay here. And that goes for you too old man,' he said looking at Myrddin.

Moss was about to say something but caught sight of Myrddin, who gave a small almost imperceptible shake of his head, but said nothing. He decided to let the matter ride.

'In the meantime, we need to find a way to make contact with Greenland. Jennifer, are you sufficiently operant to contact the telepaths there?' he asked the girl.

'That won't be necessary Squadron Leader,' interrupted Excalibur. 'I can arrange telepathic contact for you.'

Jenson looked at Brabazon who stood up in astonishment and raised an eyebrow.

'I'm sure you can Excalibur,' he said cautiously, 'but how can we be sure that the contact is secure?'

'If you wish, Lady Jennifer can monitor the proceedings. However, I can assure you, that there is no chance of the telepathic contact being overheard by the Dyason.'

Jenson hesitated for a moment, not wanting to rely on this alien computer, who now added telepathic ability to its long list of talents. Then he shrugged and thought, sod it; in for a penny, in for a pound.

'Sure why not? May as well add telepathy to all your other bizarre talents Excalibur!' he said. 'In the meantime, you guys pull your fingers out. We've got an enemy to defeat!'

ESP RESEARCH FACILITY
DYASON GROUP HEADQUARTERS , TOKYO

Brabazon looked up with lifeless eyes, as Gulag and the envoy entered the laboratory. He'd been expecting them. Since leaving England, sure of his brother's death, he'd thrown himself into his work. Convinced the Dyason were on Earth to stay, he felt his only option was to do their bidding as best he could, in the hope that he might eventually, be allowed to return to live with his wife in peace. That is if the guilt of what he was doing didn't kill him first.

MINDS OF THE EMPIRE

Gulag marched up to him, a haunted look in his eye, followed closely by the Envoy Nimue, a woman of cruel beauty and deep pitiless eyes, that sent a shiver down Brabazon's back.

'So, have you made any progress? Gulag demanded, waving a hand in the direction of the hapless human operant who lay strapped to a couch, gibbering and foaming at the mouth.

Brabazon wiped the sweat off his brow with a sweep of his hand then said in a tired voice, 'No. As you can see, we tried entering the fourth dimension again, but the subject reached the same obstacle as before. Yet another brilliant mind has been turned to jelly'.

'How fascinating,' said the Envoy in reptilian tones that appeared to make Gulag cringe. 'Please, do explain further professor.'

Brabazon looked at Gulag for confirmation. Somewhat reluctantly, he nodded his head. Brabazon wondered what was going on between him and Nimue but this wasn't the time or the place.

'Well Envoy' he began clearing his throat, 'we have been attempting to break what we are calling, the dimension barrier, for some weeks now. We know that the fault through which the Imperial fleet passes between this solar system and your own will not remain stable for much longer. Therefore, it is important for the Empire to find alternative methods of navigating between Earth and Dyason. Our research is looking into the possibility of navigating by using the extra-sensory powers of operants who, can visualise and guide vessels through the fault lines, that make up the fabric of time and space.'

'What are these faults you talk of professor?' said the Envoy with a cold smile. God, but she was an ice queen! Brabazon reckoned she knew everything about the project already, but wanted, for some reason, to hear it from him. Brabazon found himself drawn to her bottomless cold eyes, like prey mesmerised by the dancing of a snake before it strikes.

'Well,' he continued uncomfortably, 'if you can imagine a sheet of paper with grid lines drawn on it. When laid flat, the lines on the paper run straight and true both vertically and horizontally; parallel and at equal distance to each other. In a perfect universe, this would make up the weave of space and time, being orderly and in two dimensions; length and height. However, as we all know, in our world we see three dimensions; length, breadth and depth. To make our sheet of paper fit into this universe, we must turn it into a globe, so that all lines are continuous curves. Since the Big Bang, the universe has been expanding in all dimensions and in this manner the universe is similar to our sheet of paper which has been folded into the shape of a globe. Now, we have length along one axis of the globe, width along another axis of the globe, and depth through the diameter of the globe. Our sheet of paper is now a three dimensional-universe similar to our own.

If the material of the universe was consistent, then that would be the end of it. However, unfortunately, or fortunately, depending on how you look at it, the universe is not that orderly. If we imagine that the material that makes up our globe is thinner in some spots than at others, then we could put a small hole in the globe at one side, and another hole at the other side. If we fell through this hole we could travel through the centre of the globe, and exit through the other hole to another point on the globe. Your exit point could be anywhere. This is a poor explanation, but imagine the paper globe is the three dimensional universe and the stuff in the centre of the globe are the other dimensions. When you travelled here from Dyason, you went through a pin prick in the three dimensional universe, passed through the other dimensions, and reappeared in another sector of the three dimensional universe.'

'Yes, I know all that! But how does this relate to your experiments here?' the Envoy asked with impatience.

'Because,' he replied, 'the universe is full of thinner areas and holes that make up, what we call, the other dimension. Human ESP is part of this dimension. So in theory, it should be possible for someone with such powers, to see where all the faults and holes in the fabric of space are, and therefore guide a vessel through them.'

A look of cunning rose from the envoys eyes, 'So what you are saying, Professor, is that it is possible to guide a vessel through these faults, to almost any point in the universe?'

'Well,' said Brabazon carefully, 'Not everywhere, but certainly anywhere where a fault occurs.'

'And how many faults do you estimate there are?' she asked breathlessly.

'Oh,' said Brabazon almost flippantly, 'there must be at least as many faults as there are stars in the universe. There are probably more than one in many systems, including our own and Dyason. It's merely a question of locating them and navigating to them!'

Brabazon suddenly halted as he saw the look of pure evil glee that swept over the Envoy's face. She turned to bore through Gulag with her cold beautiful eyes.

'So!' she hissed in a strangely intimate voice at Gulag. 'It may indeed, be possible, to travel to any system in the universe, in no time at all! We wouldn't even have to travel far. All we would have to do is find where these faults lie, and let an operant astro-navigator move our craft into the space-time fault. The Emperor will be most pleased! A new opportunity to expand the glorious Dyason Empire!'

She stopped abruptly as a thought struck her. She turned back to Brabazon. 'But there is a problem. All your operants turn into mental vegetables as soon as they try to manipulate the other dimension, why is that?' she demanded.

Brabazon tried to look away, but was drawn like a magnet to her face. My God, she was even more evil than Gulag! He could see the madness of conquest in her eyes, and knew instinctively, that she would destroy anybody who stood between her and the expansion of the Empire. His hands shook with nerves, but he managed to stammer, 'Un. . .Un....Unfortunately we have not managed to visualise this, other dimension, yet. You are correct; so far all the subjects have become mental vegetables as soon as they reach the boundaries of 'N' space.'

'You mean you humans are too weak! Your minds are disorganised and like soft putty. This is a job for a Dyason. Have you tried a Dyason subject yet?' she shouted.

'Er... no...no, your Highness,' he stammered, wringing his hands anxiously. 'We haven't had any Dyason operants to work with.'

The Envoy turned and looked at Gulag. Brabazon followed her gaze. Gulag seemed to shrink within himself, he stared around the laboratory, as though looking for a place to run to, his eyes wild and twitching.

'Well?' she demanded of him.

'No...No I haven't. It's far too dangerous. I don't want to go there. You've seen what it does to them,' Gulag said pointing to the now insane human, still strapped to the couch.

'You must!' she said, 'For the good of the Dyason, for the Empire, for me! You know your powers are far greater than those of these weak humans. You must try and break this so-called barrier!'

Brabazon looked at Gulag. His face was a mask of torture, beads of sweat appeared on his brow. It was obvious, he was afraid that what had happened to the human subjects, would also affect him and turn his mind to jelly. Which, as he appeared to be already dancing a fine line between sanity and madness, was a real probability. Yet, as he tried to avoid the stare of Envoy Nimue, it was clear that he feared this female Dyason, almost as much as entering the other dimension. The question was, why? Now that Gulag made no pretence to hide his awesome extra-sensory powers, he had little to fear from anybody. Certainly, none of the human operants here in Tokyo were a match for him. As for the rest of the Dyason High Command, they regarded Gulag as a necessary evil. However, that didn't mean that they had to like them, and Brabazon had noticed Gulag was now nearly completely ignored and feared by his fellow officers. Even Marshal Mettar appeared to want to avoid him, if at all possible, despite making his dislike for Gulag quite obvious.

So why was the Envoy so interested in Gulag? Certainly, their relationship went beyond the attempts to break the navigation problems of N space, Brabazon, could see it in their eyes and body language. Gulag was both attracted and repulsed by the beautiful Dyason woman, but above all, he feared her! Brabazon had never seen him in fear of anybody or anything before. What was going on?

'You've seen what it does to them!' Gulag mumbled to the Envoy in an almost pleading tone. 'It's impossible to break the barrier! It can't be done...'

The envoy took Gulag's hands in hers, and stared him straight in the eye.

'Yes it can! There is no such thing as impossible' she almost spat at him. 'Those humans were all weaklings. Not like you... You can do it! I know you can. Break the barrier and we can rule the universe together, you and I. You must succeed! It is our destiny!'

Brabazon pretended not to understand this tirade, which was in Dyason, but his pen shook slightly when he heard the last sentence. Indeed, there was more going on here, than first met the eye!

Gulag seemed to be lost for a while, in that vacant place his mind seemed to wonder to so much these days, but after a few moments he pulled himself together, turned to Brabazon and with a pale drawn face, said to Brabazon, 'Prepare the probe!'

'But...but... you saw what just happened,' Brabazon started, pointing to the gibbering man who still sat in the sealed room. 'Surely it would be wise to wait until we have analysed all the data. Perhaps in a few weeks we will have cracked the barrier, then it won't be necessary for you to attempt this. It would be madness to try now!'

For a moment, it seemed as though Gulag might change his mind, as uncertainty swept over his face, but one glance at the Envoy told him that he had no choice in the matter. With a resigned voice he said, 'Don't argue with me human. Get rid of that gibbering idiot and prepare the data. I shall try immediately.'

Behind him, Brabazon could feel the Envoy smiling smugly.

Brabazon stood before the computer console watching the pattern of Gulag's brain waves. Gulag himself lay on the couch, in the specially prepared room, beyond the large pane of glass, that separated him, from the control centre. Any casual observer would have thought he was asleep, but Brabazon knew that this was simply the state the body was left in, when the mind roamed the other dimensions. He checked his monitors again. Gulag's heart was beating at a very slow rate, as if he was in deep sleep, but his brain waves were beginning to peak higher and higher. The Envoy stood behind Brabazon watching the proceedings with a strange almost vacant expression on her cold, beautiful face.

Brabazon could only judge by the information he received from the various probes on Gulag's head as to his progress. For several minutes everything seemed to be going okay, when without warning, Gulag's pulse rose to alarmingly dangerous levels, his brain patterns leapt up and down the monitor and through the glass Brabazon could see his body jerk against the restraining straps of the couch. Gulag began to scream out in Dyason.

'No! No! Please, I didn't mean it, please no more! *Oh God!*' he screamed.

The envoy grabbed at Brabazon's arm. 'What's happening? *Do something!* She demanded.

'There's nothing I can do!' replied Brabazon. 'He's hit the barrier - the same as all the others. They all go like this!'

Desperately he looked at his monitors feeling helpless under the stare of the Dyason woman, as Gulag screamed on and on.

'No!' he screamed, suddenly coherent again. 'MOTHER! MOTHER!'

'I'm coming. *I'm coming!*' Nimue called out, and to Brabazon's shock, she opened the door to the room and ran to Gulag. She placed her hands on his temple as his body writhed below her. Raising her face to the ceiling, she shouted in barely understandable Dyason, 'By all the gods, give me your power *now*. In the name of the Lord of the peaceful night and all embracing dark!'

Brabazon stood rooted to the spot. As he watched, the Envoys hand's seemed to glow from some sort of internal light, as if a myriad of stars swam in her veins. They then lost all colour, until they were the deepest black he had ever seen. It was as though they absorbed all the light in the room. The blackness spread like a cloak from her hands and into Gulag's temple. Papers and cups flew around him as a berserk wind whipped through the laboratory.

Gulag's face began to ease its painful grimace and the monitors showed his pulse and brain activity rapidly fall until they reached a state of deep, almost catatonic, sleep. Brabazon looked at the bizarre scene in the room before him. Light returned and the blanket of dark faded and disappeared. Gulag fell into a deep sleep, while the Envoy tenderly kissed his brow. With a cold, but exhausted look, she turned and faced Brabazon. In his mind, he clearly heard her say *'You saw nothing, and heard nothing human! If you ever say anything to anyone, I will know. Then you will beg for death!'*

Brabazon shook uncontrollably, more afraid than he had ever been before. He had seen, and felt, pure evil! He knew that what he'd witnessed made him a part of that evil, and it was the final nail in his coffin. There was no doubt now, that his soul would bc sent to an eternal hell, worse than the one he was in now. It was only a matter of time. He sobbed uncontrollably as a warm trickle spread down his legs.

CHAPTER THIRTEEN

TENSION MOUNTS

Moss stormed into Myrddin's private chamber and found him sitting cross legged on the floor in meditation. The room was made of a crystalline material, like the rest of the chambers that surrounded Excalibur. The walls gave out a warm soft glow, that gently lit the library of books, filling the shelves along one wall. From the look of the well-worn binders, it was obvious that some of them were hundreds of years old, while others were recent holo-books that stored their information digitally, and had their own built-in viewers. Along another wall sat a Louis XIV style writing bureau, that looked for real, while in contrast, on top, sat a very modern tablet computer. At the other end of the room stood a large pine bed, tidily made up. Unlike Moss and the others who had chosen to make themselves at home on-board Excalibur, Myrddin preferred the comfort of his familiar chambers.

'Myrddin!' he blurted. 'Did you feel it? It was intense, like a physical pain that lanced through my head, and there was that Dyason bastard and some woman. What was he doing? And who is she? What happened? What did they do to cause such a disturbance?'

'Yes lad, I felt the disturbance also, now calm yourself.' Myrddin replied without turning to look at Moss.

'*Calm*, how can I be calm? That Dyason bastard has done something to the mind dimension! I can *feel* it!' he exclaimed loudly, walking into the centre of the room.

'For God's sake, be still lad!' Myrddin snapped in irritation. 'If you're ever to learn to use your powers properly, you must learn to control these wild impulses of yours! If I hadn't stopped you, you would have confronted the Dyason there in the other dimension, which as I have already explained, is definitely *not* allowed. Now sit down next to me and be still! Learn to reach your inner calm, or I'll bloody clip you round the ear!'

Quietly fuming, but having already learnt that to argue with Myrddin was entirely futile, Moss strove to submerge his impatience and anxiety, and sat down crossed legged next to him. It was a full ten minutes before the old man spoke again.

'Now then my lad,' Myrddin finally said. 'I am aware of what took place and why. For the time being, the Dyason Gulag, is being prevented from breaking the barrier. The danger is that in his unstable condition, he may attempt something rash next time.'

'But what is it, that stops him, Grandfather? Why is the barrier there? Who, is stopping everybody from seeing the place beyond the boundary? Is it you?' Moss asked.

'Good *God* no, lad!' exclaimed Myrddin, 'My *own* talents are far short of that ability! No, I guess for want of a better description, you could call it nature itself. What they are trying to breach, are the very gateways of the multiverse itself. Nobody knows quite what is beyond the boundary, only that using force against it results in the destruction of the aggressor. That's why, we must never, attempt to use our talents in anything, but a passive form, on the steps of the gates. If we were to batter the gates, as they are, we may upset the delicate order of the multiverse itself! It is a delicate and fragile flower they are trying to crush! No lad, there is someone or something greater than ourselves watching the gates to the multiverse!'

'So what happened? And who is the Dyason woman? I thought he was the only Dyason operant, but when the boundary threw him back, it was her, who stopped his mind from being destroyed entirely,' Moss queried.

'I don't really know what happened Moss. Gulag was stopped at the gates as were the others, but the woman who dragged him back from the brink must have been even more talented than he, but I'm almost certain she's no Dyason; she's as human as you or I. No lad, she's an enemy from the distant past, who I thought was banished forever. I had hoped never to come across her evil soul again, but that was obviously too much to ask for...

If it is her, then her presence explains a lot of things, and you can be sure she knows I'm here now, and she'll stop at nothing to try and destroy me.' At that Myrddin lapsed into deep meditation. Moss knew it was pointless to try and get more answers for the moment, so he quietly got up and left the chamber. He had a feeling that Excalibur would have the answers he needed, locked up in her libraries.

He lay naked in her arms, curled up in the foetal position as she gently stroked his hair. He whimpered softly in the dark, letting the night embrace and smooth his tortured soul. She was also naked and felt a mix of motherly instinct, and sexual arousal, as she comforted Gulag. Outside her chambers, her security staff mutely guarded their privacy.

'There my son,' she cooed into his ear. 'There, there. You're safe now... Mother will protect you... They can't reach you here.'

Gulag whimpered in reply.

'I should have known,' she continued. 'It wasn't your fault son. I should have known he was still here. And begot a brat no less! They think they can stop us from breaking the secrets of the universe! But I know better! Never fear my son, we are far stronger than they can possibly imagine. It was simply the surprise of the attack. We were unprepared. Next time we shall pass through, but tomorrow we shall return to that accursed country and I shall face him for the final time. Nothing can stop us my child!'

For several minutes she continued to rant quietly into Gulag's ear, then feeling her urges rise, she slipped down between his legs and took his manhood inside her mouth. Gulag gave out a low groan, a mixture of tormented mind and animal lust.

Squad leaders ran around shouting at the young people busily unloading boxes of equipment from lightweight transports, in the age-old manner of all non-commissioned officers. There was no real need for them to shout, each resistance fighter knew exactly what he or she should be doing, but dwarfed as they were by the huge alien craft, the shouting made them feel better. It was a familiar sound in a very unfamiliar surrounding.

Jenson strode up to Captain Black, gripped his old friend by the shoulders and greeted him warmly. 'Peter! Welcome to the twilight zone. Are we glad to see you guys!'

Black dropped his kit bag on the hangar floor of the Excalibur and returned the greeting. 'You're a sight for sore eyes mate!' he quipped. 'We thought you were a goner for a while, but I guess we should have known better. Like a phoenix, you and Sandpiper rise from the dead, holding out on a giant alien spaceship, straight from the stage set of a bad *Star Trek* video, with the kid and some lunatic who calls himself Myrddin! Shit! Can't you guys ever stay out of trouble?'

Jenson laughed and replied, 'You know us! Never a dull moment! Get your lads bunked down, and we'll tell you all there is to know. Did you manage to get in undetected?'

'Yeah, no problems,' Black answered more seriously. 'We came in two VTOL transports with full stealth. For the last hundred clicks we were guided in by your friendly alien computer, and landed in some underground cavern, that appeared on the plains near Stonehenge. Then, we were sort of, guided to this place. I tell you man, there is some *weird shit* going on here!'

'That's the understatement of the century!' replied Sandpiper, and the three friends headed for the hangar exit, leaving the squad leaders to supervise the unloading of the hardware.

Moss stood at the back of the room being used to brief the fifty or so, resistance fighters. Holding the hand of Jennifer, he listened while Jenson, Sandpiper, Black and Brabazon talked.

'Well,' said Jenson, 'that pretty well covers what we know at present. Your task here is two-fold. The technicians among you, will work with Dr Brabazon here, in an attempt to get some of the functions of this vessel operational. The on-board computer reckons it's possible; we have our doubts, but will try none the less. Even if you don't manage that task, the knowledge gained will be invaluable in our fight against the Dyason.

'The combat squads are to accompany myself, Flight Lieutenant Sandpiper, and Captain Black, on a raid on the nearby Dyason slave factory at Lyneham. We've gained access to information that indicates that several new Domes are being prepared for launch there. At all costs, the launches *must* be stopped. Therefore, your first objective, will be to disable or destroy them. If the opportunity arises, your second objective, is to release as many technicians as possible, and bring them here to Excalibur. The raid will rely upon surprise for its success.'

'We're only a few miles from the factory, so we'll use the VTOL capability of the transports, to get right into the heart of the compound, make our attack, and get out before the Dyason can mount any sort of organised counterattack. Sandpiper and Black, will brief you on the details, while Dr Brabazon will brief you technicians.'

'Finally, I know just how hard it is to concentrate, in such unusual circumstances. However, may I assure you this place is for real, just as the Dyason are for real. We've *all* had to accept the impossible as possible, ever since the invasion. This place, is

265

just one more, to add to your list. The difference is, that the possibilities here, will lead to the downfall of the Dyason. You, are the *cream* of the resistance movement, and this raid is *vital* in our struggle against the slavery of humanity. So, listen up, and take notice! We leave at 2300 hours.' At that, he sat down and Black took the stand. Moss quietly slipped Jennifer's hand and left the room.

Jenson lowered himself into the pilot's seat, on the left-hand side of the cockpit and began his pre-flight checks. Behind him, in the main cabin of the VTOL transport, he could hear the resistance fighters strapping down their equipment, in preparation for the short flight to the Dyason factory. Outside the aircraft, another squad of resistance fighters blackened their faces and carefully checked their weapons.

They were inside a cavern, smaller than the one which housed Excalibur, but large enough to house the two transports, that had flown here with Black and his fighters, from Greenland. The roof of the cavern opened like an iris, enabling the transports to get in and out of the cavern. However, from the outside, it looked nothing more than a section of the plains, that surrounded Stonehenge. Brabazon had told him that this was once the place from which Excalibur had sent its probes out to study the newborn life on Earth.

The familiar knot of apprehension welled in Jenson's stomach. He always felt slightly nauseous before an operation, a mixture of fear, nervous excitement and a strange dread, that in some way, he may fail. He wasn't afraid of defeat, every one of them knew what defeat was and had learnt to live with it. No, his dread was that when the time came for him to perform, he might just crack-up. Worse than the fear of death, or injury, was the fear that he might fail his troops. He often wondered if all the heroes he read about as a child, had felt the same way. The joke now, was that Jenson knew that the resistance fighters saw him as a hero. If asked, they would follow him to the gates of hell itself, which was quite possibly, where they were going.

Sandpiper climbed into the co-pilot's seat interrupting Jenson's thoughts. 'We've got a small hitch skipper,' he said as he adjusted his straps.

Jenson looked up. 'What sort of small hitch?' he asked suspiciously.

'The sort that involves an old man and a youth,' replied Sandpiper. 'Nobody's seen them since the briefing. Neither of them are in their quarters and they don't seem the type to ignore an event like this!'

'Oh shit,' said Jenson in an exasperated voice. 'Well if they're not about, you can almost guarantee they're up to something. I wonder sometimes who's the greater threat, the Dyason or wonder boy and the magician. Well it's too late to worry about them now. So long as they don't jeopardise the operation I don't care.'

Captain Black's voice came over their headsets. 'Okay, we're ready to move, you guys,' he said.

'Right,' Jenson said into his throat mike. 'Now remember, you've got twenty minutes from the time you leave this cavern, to get to the factory and dig in around the perimeter fence. After the twenty minutes, we will take off and head for the centre of the compound. We will drop off the squad, then Han will clear the transport. Whilst the rest of us head for the main complex. At exactly 23.30, you and your squad will hit the perimeter fence with everything you've got, and make the biggest distraction you can. That should give us time to place charges against the Domes, before the opposition gets too organised. Have you got that?'

'Roger that,' replied Black, 'Everyone knows exactly what they've got to do. Let's get this show on the road!'

'Break a leg!' said Sandpiper.

Outside the cockpit Jenson saw the other squads climb a stairwell. Then, once the roof hatch had opened sufficiently, they slipped into the stormy night. He started the stopwatch and silently wished them luck.

The convoy of vehicles sped up the access road, through the outer perimeter and into the inner compound of the factory. Dyason troops poured out of the rear of the two escorting armoured personnel carriers and immediately took up positions around the limousine, at the centre of the convoy. Gulag stepped out of the car and braced himself against the howling wind and rain. He cursed loudly. In the short time away from this damned country, he had almost forgotten, how bloody awful, the weather was. His helicopter had been grounded, and they'd been forced to take this cross-country hike, despite the risk of renewed attacks from the human terrorists. As it was, they hadn't reached the factory until after dark. The Envoy Nimue had sat in silence throughout the journey, increasing the strain on Gulag's already well-frayed nerves. Gulag knew her well enough now, to realise when her black moods meant trouble for someone, and her mood had become ever deeper, as they neared the complex. Why, he wasn't sure, but he knew it had something to do with the human boy and the old man he had seen on his 'trip'. The mere thought of that nightmare still made him weak at the knees.

He put that thought out of his mind, turned and helped the Envoy out of the car. The human, Brabazon, got out of the car in front, together with the new North European Dyason leader, Colonel Brandrith. Gulag ordered the troops to form around them, and together the group headed for the hangar containing the new Domes. Nobody noticed the two figures that slipped past the gates before they closed, then disappeared into the shadows.

After waiting twenty minutes, Jenson fired up the engines of the VTOL transport. By now, Black and his squads should be positioned around the perimeter of the factory complex. That left him with ten minutes to get into position himself. As he opened up the turbines, he turned to Sandpiper beside him. 'Are you clear on what to do Han?' he asked.

'Sure skipper," Sandpiper replied with a nonchalant grin. 'We've been over it a hundred times already. We get to the compound, you and the squads drop out the hatch, while I cover you with the nose cannon. Then I get the hell out and hold in a waiting pattern, until I get your call to come in and bring you all home. Which, of course, means that I miss all the fun! Don't worry skipper, it'll be a breeze!'

Jenson smiled at his friend's flippant reply. He knew that Hanson Sandpiper was completely on the ball. Certainly, if anything went wrong, it wouldn't be because of him. He just liked to hear the sound of his friend's voice. It was like a ritual they performed every time, before they went into combat. He would always ask if Han knew what they were doing and Hanson always replied "It'll be a breeze skipper." He shot a grin at his friend, then opened the throttles wide, until the aircraft was shuddering under the power of the four turbines.

Hanson switched channel and spoke into his throat mike. 'Okay Excalibur, This is angel one. Please open the cavern doors'.

Looking up through the plexiglas of the cockpit, Jenson saw the cavern doors open like the petals of a flower, embracing a new day. As soon as he saw there was enough clearance for them to pass, he rotated the vector thrusts and the heavily laden machine began to slowly rise into the air. He kicked the rudder pedals, which opened the tail thrusters, and the transport turned on its axis through ninety degrees. They carried on rising and cleared the lip of the cavern. As soon as they were clear the iris began to close behind them.

Hanson quickly turned on the canopy deicers and wipers, as they were immediately hit by torrents of pouring rain, and began to side slip, from the gale force winds. With a steady hand, Jenson counteracted the effects of the storm and gradually turned the vectors back to the horizontal position. The huge transport began to pick up forward speed, gaining lift as it did so. Within seconds, they were ploughing their way though the storm at two hundred knots, just metres above Salisbury Plain.

From the viewing balcony near the ceiling of the huge hangar, Gulag could clearly see the work being carried out on the two Domes, directly below him. They were smaller than the ones, which brought them all here from Dyason, but thanks to the use of human technology in metallurgy and electronics, they'd managed to fit in twice as much capability, in only half the volume of the older types. They were a marvel of Dyason engineering. They could go faster, navigate better, and contained more fire-power, than anything that had gone before.

From the comer of his eye, he could see that the Envoy was listening to the moron Brandrith, with rapt attention. He wasn't sure if she lusted after these machines and the power they promised, or the body of the Dyason male. Gulag was uncomfortable with the feelings of jealousy this brought out in him. How dare she give her attention to anybody but himself? Damn the woman to hell! Making an effort to suppress his anger, Gulag tuned in to what the Dyason chief engineer was saying.

'Your Highness,' he said to Nimue in an ingratiating voice, 'as you can see, the nearer of the two Domes is, in fact, completed. We just finished installing the last equipment this morning. Now, she's all set and ready to go. However, we will of course, have to wait until the second Dome is also complete. Then, we shall launch the two vessels simultaneously. Otherwise, the power of the nuclear charges will destroy the uncompleted dome, and of course this whole complex, and anything within a twenty klick radius.'

'What will happen if you launch them together? enquired Brandrith.

'By launching them simultaneously, Colonel, the combined effect will be of mutual advantage, increasing the velocity upon launch and reducing the size of the booster charge, needed to obtain escape velocity from the planet. However, the timing will need to be precise to the nearest millisecond,' the engineer replied.

'What will happen to the factory and the human workers?' asked Nimue.

'Unfortunately, they will all be vaporised at the launch Envoy. However, as we will have no further use for the complex after launch, this is not seen as a problem. Indeed, we will be cleansing the area of native savages, in preparation, for later Dyason colonisation,' said the engineer with a smile.

'I greatly admire your professionalism,' said Colonel Brandrith.

Yeah I bet he does, thought Gulag, turning back to look over the hangar.

Through the cockpit windscreen, Jenson could just make out the lights of the Dyason factory on the horizon. However, that was about all he could see. The storm was so intense, he had to fly the transport on manual, as the auto pilot couldn't handle the severe gusting and wind shear. With no visual reference outside the cockpit, he was forced to rely on the infrared image on the head-up display. Beads of sweat broke out on his brow, from the intense concentration. They were only minutes from the drop zone.

Sandpiper flicked on the intercom and spoke to the squad in the hold of the aircraft. 'Okay everyone,' he said in even measured tones, 'drop point coming up in four minutes. Make sure your kit is strapped down tight and you're ready to leave in a real hurry'.

Hearing this, the squad sergeant stood up and yelled, 'You heard the man, now *move*! Two columns behind the rear hatch. Hang on tight to the supports provided. Paterson, if you don't move your ass and stop feeling sorry for yourself, I'm gonna feed you to the Dyason personally! Shit! Anybody would think you've never flown in this crate before!'

Hanson Sandpiper grinned at Jenson, 'Sounds just like the academy days!' he said.

Jenson smiled slightly, not looking away from the HUD display. They were almost on top of the factory now. 'Better switch on the gun-sight and arm the cannons,' he said to Sandpiper out of the corner of his mouth. 'Hopefully, we'll take them by surprise. Our stealth capability should take them unawares, but even so, things are going to get pretty hot around here any minute now!'

Then, he was hauling back on the vector thrust, slowing the aircraft down. From two hundred knots to a vertical hover, in a matter of seconds. At the same time, they began to descend vertically. Jenson had to frantically fight the controls, to overcome the effects of the turbulence, from the nearby factory structures. The compound was directly below them, thankfully empty of humans and Dyason, all of whom were sheltering from the storm. Jenson turned the aircraft around ninety degrees, so that the rear hatch was facing towards the hangar complex. With a hefty jolt, they touched down and Sandpiper immediately hit the door release. With a shout, the squad of resistance fighters hit the ramp at a run and began to disperse in small groups around the compound.

Jenson hit his seat harness release, piled out of the cockpit and headed for the ramp himself, but as he hit the ground all hell broke out around him. From the perimeter fence, explosions lit up the sky as Black and his team made their diversionary attack. However, the Dyason were waking up to the fact that they had visitors. Automatic weapons opened up from the widely spaced watch towers and tracer arced towards the compound where Jenson had landed and also towards the perimeter fence. Jenson saw one of the resistance fighters raise a blowpipe to his shoulder and release a missile towards the nearest watch tower, which promptly exploded in a blaze of pyrotechnics.

Jenson made a dash for the cover of a low building, where several others were waiting for him. He got there just before a group of Dyason troops opened fire. He spoke into his throat mike. 'Sandpiper haul ass out of here!' he yelled. 'The shit's *really* hitting the fan!'

'Roger that!' came the reply and Sandpiper immediately began to raise the transport off the ground, but not before he gave the Dyason troops pouring out of the hangar complex a withering burst of fire from the nose turret.

At first, Gulag thought the noise outside was caused by the storm, but the pounding of mortars and the staccato rhythm of automatic weapons fire, were sounds he was very familiar with. Any Dyason, who had been part of the original invasion forces, would know their particular type of macabre music. When a young Dyason lieutenant came pounding up the gangway towards them, his fears were confirmed.

'Sir, sir!' the lieutenant spat out at the captain in charge of the Envoy's security, 'the factory is under attack sir! The perimeter fence has been breached by a strong force of the resistance, and more have landed in the main compound area!'

What! That's *impossible!*' exclaimed Brandrith, suddenly looking up from his intimate conversation with the Envoy. 'There are no resistance cells of any strength, anywhere near this installation. They would be mad to attack us when our defences are so strong!'

'Shut up Brandrith,' Gulag snapped, then stared at the shaking young Dyason officer. 'Tell me what you know trooper.'

'Sir, an aircraft landed in the compound and set down many human terrorists. I don't know how many. Then, there were explosions at the fence. My platoon sergeant was killed. The humans seem to be attacking from all sides. What should we do sir?'

As the trooper babbled on, Gulag took the opportunity to quickly scan the young Dyason's mind. He cursed the mentality of the conscripts and their officers, who defended such an important site as this. Regular troops would never allow an aircraft to get within fifty klicks of this place, let alone land inside the compound. He saw directly from the trooper's mind, that unless he acted quickly, there was a real risk to themselves and the Envoy. Most of the factory's company was in position around the perimeter, where the main thrust of the human attack seemed to be targeted. Gulag felt it unlikely that they would manage to get past the outer defences, so the real threat must come from the smaller force dropped into the compound. They could be here for only one reason, and that must be to sabotage the two new Domes.

Then, from the back of his mind, came a strange, familiar, tingling sensation... At first, he couldn't pinpoint the feeling, but then it came to him in a flash. By the gods, they were back! He was sure of it! Only the human youth and his band of renegades would dare such a thing. Nimue had ordered this visit to the factory, in the hope, that they could pick up the trail of the youth and the strange old man he had seen in his dreams. Now, they wouldn't have to go in search for them. The prey had come to the predator!

Clearly, he saw what had to be done. He would personally, take charge of the troops within the compound and destroy the human attack from inside. Those attacking the perimeter he would ignore. The youth was bound to be among the humans in the compound, and when he found him, he would enjoy killing the wretched human slowly and painfully. He cut the lieutenant off in mid sentence then turned to the security captain.

'Captain,' he said crisply, 'take the Envoy and Colonel Brandrith to the office complex and wait there for further instructions. I will go with the lieutenant here and see to the rabble in the compound. I am sure there is nothing to be concerned about. I shall have this interference settled rapidly and we can continue the inspection as before.'

The captain snapped to attention, 'Of course sir, I will make sure the Envoy comes to no harm!'

'I'm sure you will Captain,' Gulag replied absently, his mind already on the prospect of finally killing his human opponent. 'I'll keep in close radio contact. Go now.'

The captain turned and motioned for the Envoy and entourage to follow him and the four escorting shock troops. Before she turned to follow, Nimue look straight at Gulag. *It's them isn't it?'* she directed a thought at him. *'I can feel their presence close by'.*

'*Yes'* he replied simply.

'*Go carefully son. Do not underestimate their power',* she cautioned.

Gulag didn't reply, he simply set off at a jog down the stairway to the hangar floor, a machine pistol taken from the security squad cradled in his arms. The lieutenant followed behind. Back up on the balcony, Luke Brabazon dropped behind the Dyason group, and seeing that he was unnoticed, slipped quietly into the shadows.

Jenson ducked back below the level of the wall, as a withering hail of fire, chewed up the brick and mortar, sending dust and vicious shards of brick in all directions. There was now a real danger of their surprise attack turning into a massacre, if they couldn't reach the interior of the hangar, on the other side of the compound. Unfortunately, the Dyason were reacting far quicker than he'd anticipated, and their positions on top of the hangar roof, gave them a clear field of fire over the whole, central compound, pinning down the four squads of resistance fighters. They'd already suffered casualties, with three men injured, two seriously. He knew they had to break clear, and soon. The clock was ticking, and every wasted second allowed the Dyason to organise their defences.

To the platoon around him, he yelled, 'Cover my arse! I need to get to the other side!'

Nodding their heads grimly, the four young men and two women, raised their short-barrelled automatics over the low wall and let loose short, staccato, bursts. Jenson sprinted for the small concrete bunker on the opposite side of the square compound, zig-zagging all the way. At one point, he nearly lost his footing on the wet concrete, just as the automatic fire from the rooftops, was finding his mark. Somehow, he managed to stay on his feet and with a burst of adrenaline, covered the last few metres in a few huge bounds. He collapsed in a heap, at the feet of the squad of fighters, taking cover there, breathing heavily. The resistance squad leader, a young, heavily muscled woman with dark skin, made her way to him and dragged him upright.

'Nice of you to join us sir!' she yelled with a grin over the sound of gunfire and howling wind. 'Bit of a tight spot we're in. What do you want us to do?'

Jenson pulled her face down so that it was level with his. 'Get your blow-pipes trained on the spotlights and take them out.' he yelled back, 'I don't reckon they've got any night sights up there. These are only conscripts and usually, poorly equipped. Once the lights are out, use your infra-red scopes to find their posts and take them out one by one. Got it?'

'Roger that!' she replied.

'Okay,' he continued. 'Now, get onto the others and give them the orders, then find me the girl Jennifer. Is she with you?'

'She sure is skipper!' replied the squad leader. 'Yo Jenny! Get your small white arse over here!' she yelled to a small slim figure crouched behind the wall at the far end of the bunker. The girl looked up then crawled over to where Jenson was. The squad leader moved off to find the rest of her group, muttering into her throat mike as she went.

Jennifer crouched before Jenson, a look of fear on her face. Jenson hated having to bring the poor girl back into this place, but her intimate knowledge of the plant made her invaluable. She had knowledge they now, badly needed.

'Jennifer' he said, yelling into her ear, in an attempt to be heard over the noise around them, 'is there another way into the main hangar complex without having to storm the main compound? If we stay here we'll get slaughtered!'

'There's a vent duct just over there,' she yelled back, pointing to a low concrete shaft with a metal grating on it. 'I made straight for it when we got out of the transport, the others followed me. If we go down it, it eventually leads to the lower galleries below the complex itself!'

'Good girl!' he said enthusiastically.

They were suddenly interrupted by the sound of several blowpipe missiles taking out the surrounding searchlights and plunging the compound into darkness. Now, the only light came from tracer rounds and the glow of fires, started by the action at the perimeter fence. Jenson could clearly hear the Dyason guards yelling out to each other in alarm, until some officer told them all to shut up.

Jenson spoke into his mike.'Strike group one, this is Foxtrot zero. Peter, what's the situation at your end, over?'

'Foxtrot zero, from strike group one,' came the crackling reply. Jenson could clearly hear the sound of gunfire in the background behind Black's voice. 'We've managed to take the outer towers and guard posts, but we're bogged down in the outer compound. The Dyason are getting over their surprise. Over.'

'Roger that, Strike one,' replied Jenson, 'Try and hang on as long as possible. We're going to attempt to enter the main hangar complex. Do not, repeat *do not*, attempt to link up in the inner compound. The fire is a little too hot here. Over.'

'Okay skipper, but we've managed to locate the main slave labour compound. We feel we can reach it and release. Can you authorise? Over.'

Jenson thought for a moment. He didn't like the idea of Black and his team penetrating too far into the factory complex and possibly cutting off Black's own escape route, but then, they had come in the hope of releasing technicians. Shit, he had to give the poor wretches some chance of escape.

'Okay Peter,' he said into his mike. 'Be careful and make sure that your route back to the rendezvous point remains open. Good luck. Out!' Jenson changed channels to his squad's broadcast band. 'Listen up, people,' he started, 'D platoon will follow me and Jennifer into the ducts in an attempt to reach the main hangar complex. The rest of you are to hold this inner compound area for as long as possible. If we lose it, there'll be nowhere for the VTOL to come in and get us. Do not take any unnecessary risks. Just keep those bastards' heads down. Acknowledge in squad leader order. Over.'

'Alpha platoon acknowledged.'

'Beta platoon acknowledged.'

'Charlie platoon acknowledged.'

'Delta platoon acknowledged.'

'Echo platoon acknowledged.' The different platoon leaders answered in order.

'Okay. Good luck everyone. If we're not back by the rendezvous time, call in the transport and leave without us. Out.' Jenson turned his attention to Jennifer. Behind her he could see D platoon gathering together.

'Right then young lady,' he shouted over the sound of the storm and gunfire. 'Lead the way!'

Jennifer moved over to the vent duct, being careful to keep below the level of the bunker. Which, protected them from the Dyason gunfire, coming from the top of the hangar. With the help of one of the platoon, she levered off the cover and nimbly slipped inside. Jenson took one last look around, then climbed inside, closely followed by the rest of the squad.

Moss followed Myrddin up the gantry-ways of the hangar; following the group of Dyason officers. They were making best use of the available cover, in addition to their mental cloaking. Myrddin had been busy in the past few days, instructing Moss on some of the finer uses of his skills. Rather than emitting a blanket denial of his existence to all and sundry, as he'd done previously, Moss had learnt to, gently, scan the minds of those within his possible viewing area. If someone happened to see him, Moss would encourage that person to quietly forget, exactly what it was, he was looking at.

The difference between this and his previous method, was subtle, but important. Giving out a blanket denial was a bit like a war plane carrying a radar jamming device. It worked great, scrambling the enemy's radar screens. Except that once the enemy knew their radar was being scrambled by a plane, they had warning that an attack was imminent and could take other measures to locate the intruder. So it was with Moss. Now that the Dyason knew he could blanket their minds they would be prepared for it.

So the youth and old man slipped silently, through the shadows. Moss saw the Dyason group stop at a viewing gallery and look over the apparently completed Dome. Warned by his scanning senses, Moss ducked back deeper into the shadows as a clearly alarmed, Dyason lieutenant, ran past him, pounding along the gantry. Moss turned and looked at Myrddin, raising an eyebrow quizzically. Myrddin frowned, shook his head, lay his hand out palm downwards and motioned towards the floor. His other hand quickly, went through several rapid motions. Moss knew this meant, wait, lie low.

Moss could guess what the conversation was about. He could hear the gunfire from outside, which meant that Jenson and his resistance fighters were somewhere inside the compound. He resisted the temptation to open his awareness to allow him to hear the conversation. There was too much risk of Gulag, or the Dyason woman, becoming aware of his presence, if he dared open his mind.

He saw Gulag take an automatic rifle off one of the group's guards, then follow the lieutenant back up another gantry, towards the hangar roof. Followed by four, of the Dyason shock, space marines. Moss got up to follow, but felt the restraining hand of Myrddin upon his arm.

'No Moss, leave him,' whispered Myrddin intently.

'I'm going after him Myrddin...We've got a score to settle,' Moss hissed back.

'Not here, not now, it's the woman we're after. Gulag can wait, but I must know who the woman is,' Myrddin said, keeping a firm grip on the youths arm.

'Fine!' Moss retorted hotly, 'You go after the woman. I'm going after Gulag, he's mine!'

With that, he tore his arm away from Myrddin's grip and set off at a jog up the gantry, towards the roof. Myrddin cursed violently under his breath. Knowing it was useless to try and stop the youth, he pulled his ancient cloak closely around his body and determinedly headed off towards the Dyason woman and her group, who were moving to the elevators.

Jenson looked down from his position on the ladder, at the top of the ventilation shaft. The twin beams of his helmet LED lit Jennifer, waiting below him. He guessed the shaft to be around twenty metres deep. Which meant that it ran well below the level of the ground complex. Once he reached the girl, she pointed to one of several, low horizontal shafts, that intersected with the vertical vent and went off, in the rough direction, of the hangar. It was going to be a tight squeeze. The roof of the tunnel was only a metre and a half high.

'It's a bit of a wriggle,' said Jennifer taking off her kit bag and placing it on the lip of the tunnel in front of her, 'but it leads directly to the basement below the hangar itself. It was built when this was RAF Lyneham, before the war. The Dyason built the complex on top of the old hangar. So they don't know about the existence of all these vents.'

Jenson also took off his pack and gestured for Jennifer to lead the way. She set off down the tunnel, pushing her kit in front of her. Jenson followed close behind, telling himself that he definitely, did not, feel claustrophobic... The curses of the squad behind him indicated that he was not the only one feeling uncomfortable, in such a small space.

For about ten minutes, they crawled on their hands and knee. Following the tunnel through several tight bends, seemingly designed to bruise limbs and catch clothing. Eventually, they arrived at a small opening, covered by a wire grille. Jennifer motioned for Jenson to switch off his lamps. She peered intently through the mesh, looking in all directions. Then, using a small blade, she undid a screw, which released the mesh. Carefully, she opened the grille and lowered herself onto the floor below. After checking up and down the corridor, Jennifer motioned for Jenson to follow. Jenson threw down her pack, followed by his own; which nearly knocked the girl off her feet. Then, he lowered himself down. The rest of the squad followed close behind.

'This corridor leads to a stairwell that goes up to the hangar level,' Jennifer whispered. 'It's used only rarely, so should be unguarded.'

'Well done Jennifer.' Jenson said, then commanded. 'Abrams, split the group and move up the sides of the corridor, buddy-buddy method, someone covering all the way.'

The female squad leader split her platoon up and they began to make their way cautiously, up the corridor. They met no resistance on the way and were soon moving up the stairwell. Jenson hoped the Dyason were too busy dealing with the attack from the compound and outer perimeter to consider the possibility of attack from such an unlikely route. When they reached the last couple of steps, Jenson motioned for the squad to hold still while he took a look. Carefully, he turned his head around the corner of the concrete pillar, only to move it back again in a hurry as several Dyason ran past carrying automatics. He lay flat against the wall until his heart slowed, then looked again.

The stairwell was situated at the far corner, away from the complex and entered straight into the hangar. The hangar itself was a scene of confusion. Humans working on two huge Domes were being herded together by guards, whilst other Dyason were dashing for the other side of the hangar. Obviously, going to reinforce the troops tackling his fighters in the compound. Jenson ducked back into the stairwell and spoke to Abrams.

'The two Domes are in there,' he said urgently. 'The nearest is only half complete, but the far one looks as though it's ready to go. The Dyason are in disarray, so surprise is on our side. You and half the platoon head for the nearest Dome and lay your charges. The rest are to follow me and head for the other one. Set the charges to go off in exactly fifteen minutes time. Once, they're laid, head for the main hangar doors. There won't be time to get out the way we came in, so we'll have to fight our way out the front door. Got that?'

'Roger skipper,' replied Abrams with a curt nod.

'Kwoloski, Paterson, Metzner and Sweeting follow the skipper. The rest of you come with me!'

'Okay let's go!' cried Jenson, and they set off into the hangar. Abrams and her group headed straight for the first uncompleted Dome, while Jenson and his team, including Jennifer, hugged the wall and ran for the further, completed Dome.

Abrams managed to get as far as the main ramp, leading up into the heart of the Dome, before a cry of alarm from a Dyason guard went up. Jenson saw her run into its heart, while the remainder of her team lay down covering fire. Three Dyason immediately crumpled to the ground. Two from the group herding the humans together and a third from a gantry halfway up the wall of the hangar. Unable to watch any longer, Jenson ran hell-bent for the second craft. They ran from pillar to pillar, making use of the cover offered by the massive steel supports, that held up the acres of roof. But, they were still some distance from their goal, when they were pinned down, by gunfire from two directions. Sweeting was hit as he ran for cover, falling to the floor motionless. The rest of them managed to reach the pillar, despite bullets ricocheting off the concrete and steel all around them. Jenson raised his weapon, pumped a grenade into the lower launch tube and launched it at three Dyason, firing from some scaffolding to their left. It hit its target with a satisfying crump, throwing two of the three off the platform. The third collapsed onto the metal, screaming loudly as blood pumped out of his severed arm.

'Abrams talk to me,' Jenson called into his throat mike. 'What's your situation? Over.'

'Skipper, I'm inside the Dome now, just about to place the charges. It appears to be empty. The Dyason shunted everybody out when the fighting started. Shit!'

Jenson clearly heard the sound of gunfire in the background. 'Abrams! Abrams! What's happening? Talk to me! Come on you bitch, don't quit on me now!'

The channel opened again, but Abrams voice was weak and barely audible. 'Oh God, I didn't see that one skipper. Got the bastard, but I'm afraid he got me too. I'm laying the charges now. .Uh. . .There! That's it they're set. You've got fifteen minutes skipper, then this baby goes up like the fourth of July. Uh...Jesus it hurts...think I'll just lie here and rest a moment...Bye skipper, it's been a blast... kick shit out of the basta...' the transmission abruptly halted.

'Abrams, haul your arse out of there. Come on move! Abrams! Abrams!' There was no reply, just static.

'Oh shit. Now we're in trouble!' Jenson muttered. The concrete a few feet in front of him erupted in a hail of splinters and ricochets. There wasn't time to feel loss. They had just fifteen minutes to lay the second set of charges and get the hell out of there... Only, it looked right now, like they weren't going anywhere...

Gulag had just reached the upper gantry that led to the rooftop, when he heard gunfire behind him. From inside the hangar itself. He turned and peered over the railings towards the two Domes. He could just make out figures scurrying across the floor. One group went straight for the uncompleted craft, while the other headed for the newly finished Dome. By spreading his awareness out towards the figures, he could perceive that they were resistance terrorists. He didn't need to take a guess what they were after, that was obvious.

'Incompetent *fools!*' he screamed at no one in particular. 'They've let them get inside the hangar! I'll skin some bastard alive for this!'

He turned and jabbed a finger at the space marines standing behind him. 'You, you and you...take that side of the gantry, follow it round until you've got a got field of fire below, then take out those human scum. The rest of you follow me, down the opposite side!'

Gulag cocked his automatic and set off at a run, the Dyason marines close on his heels. As he ran, Gulag made contact with Nimue, preferring a mental link rather that trying to use his radio as he ran.

'Mother!' he called in his mind.

'Gulag! What is it? What's happening? We're in the offices, but we can hear gunfire from within the hangar.'

'The humans have got inside! He replied. *'A group have already managed to get to the uncompleted Dome, and another group are heading for the second. We're on the upper gantry where we can pin them down, but they may have already set charges in the first Dome. Get Brandrith to move you and the others into the completed Dome and seal all the hatches. The humans won t he able to get in then, and their weapons will he ineffective against the hull. Once there, wait until I have cleared the area. I will tell you when it is safe to come out. And get*

Brandrith to send a squad to find the charges in the other Dome, before it goes up!'

'It will be done son!' came the reply. 'Have you located them?'

'No, but I am sure they are with this group of humans somewhere!'

'Be careful Gulag, don't underestimate their talents. They have got this far…We are going now!'

Gulag broke the mental contact, leant over the gantry railings, and let off a long burst of fire at the humans below.

Moss wasn't surprised when the fighting broke out in the hangar below. He knew Jennifer had planned to take Jenson and his fighters through the tunnels they'd used, when they first made their escape. It gave him a certain satisfaction, to see Gulag curse and pound the railings in rage. The bastard was certainly surprised, but Moss had to stop the Dyason marines opening fire on Jenson's team below. He was scared Jennifer would get hit, so he would have to take out the marines, before he could tackle Gulag. The Dyason lieutenant and two space marines ran past Moss who hid in an alcove. They moved down the far side of the gantry, placing themselves in a good position to lay crossfire on Jenson's team, pinned down on the hangar floor.

Moss followed, pulling out a small sub machine gun, from inside his leather jacket. The marines were too busy firing on the resistance fighters below to notice Moss creep up from behind. He didn't even have to mentally cloak his movements. Once he was within five metres he called, 'Hey mothers, surprise, surprise!'

The three Dyason turned in alarm, trying to bring their weapons to bear on the human youth, but they were far too slow. With a grin, Moss let off just three rounds and a neat hole appeared in the chest of each Dyason. The lieutenant was thrown backwards, over the top of the gantry railings and plunged towards the hangar floor. He was dead before he hit the ground. Moss quickly gave the other two Dyason a quick kick, to check they were both dead, then ran on, down the gantry. He stopped when he was opposite Gulag and his remaining marines. They were still firing at the resistance below, unaware of what had happened to the others.

Moss checked his weapon was still on single shot only and took careful aim across the width of the hangar. He squeezed off a single round and one of the marines collapsed. The Dyason next to him looked up in alarm, trying to gauge from which direction the shot had come, but it was too late. Moss had already adjusted his aim and with another squeeze of the trigger took him out too. This time Gulag did take notice, and with what Moss had to acknowledge was lightning speed, rolled away and let off a burst in his general direction.

Moss dived for the cover of some metal sheeting, as bullets impacted around him. He switched his gun to full automatic and in a rolling burst, fired at the last marine, who was levelling his gun at him. The Dyason dropped his weapon and screamed loudly. Good...that left just him and Gulag in the game.

'Hey shit head!' Moss called out in his mind, knowing the Dyason operant would hear. *'Remember me?' Thought I would come and pay my respects! I owe you for the murder of my family and thousands of innocent people. Now, I've come to even the score, you alien bastard. Make peace with your god 'cause it's time to die!'*

Nimue followed Brandrith onto the hangar floor, closely surrounded by the escorting marines. While they lay down withering fire-power, that kept the human terrorists occupied, Brandrith led Nimue the short distance up the ramp of the completed Dome and into the interior of the craft. He led her down access ways that looked like the interior of an ocean-going ship, with light grey walls and conduits of brightly coloured cables strung along the ceiling. Brandrith stepped through a hatchway and Nimue followed, carefully stepping over the seal, while ducking to avoid banging her head. Once through, she looked up again, only to see Brandrith sink slowly to the floor, a long blade protruding from his neck. As he hit the deck, his body rolled over and unseeing eyes stared at the walls, his death mask a look of surprise.

Her heart beat furiously and a cry of shock rose from her throat. Quickly, she fumbled for the small, single shot pistol, she carried within her robes. But, before she could reach It, a figure came through the doorway and stepped over the body of Brandrith. The figure wore a cloak of black, that absorbed all light. His grey hair and eyes seemed to belong to a man of great age, but his eyes shone bright, while his posture, was ramrod straight.

Nimue hissed in recognition 'Ssssssss...Myrddin!' I knew you were behind all this somehow!'

'As charming as ever I see!' replied Myrddin in a voice as cold as steel. 'It would appear, you have been weaving your evil spells again. Not content with destroying one civilisation, you now wish to eradicate another!'

Nimue curled her lip in contempt and spat at the old man. 'You old fool! You always were such a weakling! We both know it's my destiny. The lord has decreed I shall rule *all* in his name! You think you can stop us now, with these few feeble humans! Or do you intend to set your great grandson upon me? I shall crush him between my fingertips, like an insect, just as I destroyed Arthur!'

Myrddin was unmoved by the outburst. His face remained set like stone. 'I see you still talk too much, woman. You never seem to learn, that the forces of light, will always keep the eternal night at bay. Neither you, nor your bastard son, can change that. In any millennium or universe, the laws still apply. You know that. Why must you *always* try to break the laws that cannot be broken?'

'Laws made by your feeble God, not mine, old man! My lord has the might to take what he wants, and I am his tool and weapon!' Nimue ranted.

'This conversation is getting boring... I would have thought, that after all these centuries, you could at least, have entertained me with fresh fanatical gibberish. Time for me to leave.' Myrddin turned and headed for the hatch. 'Until next time little sister. Until next time..' he called over his shoulder.

She tried to raise her pistol at the retreating figure, but her arm wouldn't respond to her commands. 'Myrddin!' she screamed as he disappeared out of view, 'you cannot win! It is my destiny! Join me! Together we will rule the universe. As brother and sister, together for all eternity! Myrddin! MYRDDIN!'

A single thought entered her mind: *'Don't be pathetic little sister...'*

Nimue collapsed to the deck, hugging herself tightly around her knees. Spittle collected at the comer of her mouth as she rocked herself back and forth, muttering under her breath. She was still like that when the Dyason marines found her some minutes later...

As he let off a long burst of fire at the human youth, Gulag also let out a mental blast, that should, have fried the human's mind and turned it to jelly. Instead, Gulag found a mental barrier equal, if not superior, to anything he himself, could produce.

'You'll have to try better than that Dyason!' shouted the human out loud. Gulag cursed and braced his own mental shields, as the human sent a tremendous blast, in counterattack. He managed to block it, but was shaken to his very core. God, but the human was strong! It was taking all his concentration, to hold his barriers together. He would have to rely on more traditional means, to kill his adversary. Gulag rolled on the gantry and let off another blast of automatic fire in the human's direction.

As he rolled again, back behind the cover of some heavy steel sheeting, the ear-piece of his radio crackled into life. 'Commander Gulag! This is Marine Captain Zhevesoky. Do you read over?' Gulag cursed again, and flicked on his mike. 'What is it Zhevesoky? I'm busy being shot at right now!' he said in a voice laden with sarcasm.

'Sir! I'm inside the completed Dome. Colonel Brandrith has been killed, we have found the Envoy, but she appears to be in some distress...'

'What do you mean, by "distress", Zhevesoky?' he demanded in alarm.

'The Envoy keeps muttering to herself. The only word we can make out is "Myrddin".' Gulag knew that name. It was what she had called the old man, who she claimed, was an ancient adversary. So, he was here, together with the human youth and the terrorists! For the first time, Gulag felt fear. For them to have got this far, meant they were far more dangerous, than the usual human rabble he had dealt with in London. Briefly, he considered reaching Nimue by mental link, but he dared not release his barriers for a moment. The human was strong enough turn his mind to jelly in an instant. Another short burst of fire from the far side of the gantry made Gulag duck down lower.

'Sir,' continued the Dyason marine on the radio, 'the humans have also laid charges in the interior of second Dome. We can't get at them to defuse them, because the terrorists are in strong defensive positions around the outside. What are your orders sir? Should we seal the completed Dome? The terrorists' light weapons would be ineffective against the armoured hull.'

Gulag cursed, the situation was getting out of control. Damn these pathetic factory guards! He would have somebody's testicles for this! Suddenly, an idea came to him. He called the marine captain. 'Get me the engineer, is he there with you?'

'He is sir. Hang on...' 'Yes Commander?' the engineer asked as he reached the radio.

'Engineer,' Gulag demanded, 'you told me that the Dome is ready for launch. How long would it take to prepare to leave?'

The engineer thought for a moment, a little confused then replied. 'Well, we would have to secure the equipment, prepare the site and make last checks and calculations...'

Gulag interrupted, 'Never mind all that. I'm talking about now! We can't risk losing that Dome, the terrorists have already laid charges in the other craft . It may go up any time, unless we can defuse it. How long engineer? How long from now?'

'My God! You're *serious!*' exclaimed the Dyason engineer. 'Well, we have enough technicians on-board and your marines are here...' Gulag heard the engineer swallow hard before saying, 'We can rush the pre-flights and launch within fifteen minutes. But sir, you'll be killing all our own troops outside the Dome, in that area, in the hangar and compound!'

'We'll also be killing all the human vermin'. And that cursed youth, he thought to himself. 'Do it engineer! I'm on my way down now. Prepare your craft. It's time to leave!'

The firing from the upper gantries, abruptly stopped. Jenson looked up to see a solitary figure, letting off short bursts, from a small sub machine gun at another figure, on the opposite side. Jenson thanked the lone fighter and, not wanting to let the opportunity slip by, gestured for the others to follow him as he broke cover and ran full tilt for the next vertical column, halfway toward the furthest Dome. As he ran, he let off short bursts of gunfire from the hip. Two Dyason, standing behind a forklift truck, caught a packet. One of the squad behind him took out another alien, standing on a box of crates to their left. He made the cover of the column and pile of crates, and was grateful when the rest of the squad also made it without anyone being hit. Jennifer collapsed beside him. 'You okay?' he asked.

The young woman looked pale and frightened, but nodded in acknowledgement. Jenson smiled in encouragement. One of the resistance fighters tapped him on the shoulder. Jenson recognised him as corporal Paterson. The corporal pointed to the completed Dome. 'Look skipper!' he said.

Jenson looked to where he was pointing. Dyason troops in the uniform of the space marines, were climbing aboard the craft in a hurry, deserting their posts from which they'd been firing at Jenson and his squad. At the far end of the hangar, a group of human slaves, seeing what was happening, turned on their two captors and clubbed the luckless conscripts to the ground. They then picked up the fallen weapons and began firing on the retreating Dyason. The tables were turning.

Jenson got up and set off at a run towards the craft, urging the rest of the squad to follow. They ran for the boarding ramp, taking out another two marines on the way. But, before they were halfway across the hangar floor, the ramp began to close. Jenson cursed and let off the rest of his clip at the closing hatchway, but his weapon was useless against the armour plating. By the time they reached the base of the huge vessel it was closed, forming a near seamless seal against the outer hull. The hangar became strangely silent, except for the sound of gunfire coming from the compound outside and a strange tapping, from inside the hull of the vessel.

'Shit!'Jenson swore loudly and kicked at the armoured hull.

Moss could see Gulag talking into his radio. He was obviously mad at what he was hearing. Moss just wished he could listen to what was being said, but he too, was having to keep his mental shields in place. The Dyason had already launched a mental bolt that was far stronger than he'd expected. Despite all that he'd learnt under the guidance of Myrddin, the alien was still more than a mental match for him.

He raised his sub automatic over the metal sheeting he was sheltering behind, and let off another small burst in Gulag's direction. Sparks flew off the scaffolding on the other side of the hangar, where his bullets impacted, but none seemed to hit the Dyason. Moss checked the magazine on his weapon, there were only a dozen rounds left and he had no fresh clips. As much as he hated to admit it, this situation was rapidly degenerating into stalemate. He couldn't move or strike at Gulag, and the Dyason couldn't move or strike against him. It all amounted to who ran out of ammo first, and at the moment it looked like it would be him. Another burst of fire made him duck below the heavy sheeting again. So much for the quick assassination of his arch enemy!

Myrddin swept across the hangar floor towards Jenson. The human slaves who'd picked up the guard's weapons, followed close behind. His face was set in a grim expression, as he approached the resistance group, who were in defensive positions, around the edge of the Dome.

'Squadron Leader Jenson!' he boomed in a voice that reverberated across the massive structure. Jenson looked away from the ominously sealed and silent Dome and turned to face Myrddin.

'Hello, old man,' he greeted wearily. 'I should have known you would turn up at some stage, but I'm afraid you've arrived too late. They're all in there,' he gestured towards the Dome. 'It'll take more than what's left of us to winkle them out. The charges are set in the other vessel to go off in ten minutes, but unless we can get the other explosives into the heart of this one, I'm afraid we're not going to do it much damage. It would take a nuke to get through that armour plating.'

Myrddin ignored what was being said to him, instead he placed his hand on Jenson's arm and said in a voice that broke no argument, 'Squadron Leader, it is *imperative* that you break off this engagement *now*! The Dyason in that Dome are preparing to leave!'

Jenson looked at Myrddin quizzically. 'That's fine by me,' he said. 'There's only one hatch on this thing, so when it opens again we'll make mincemeat of them all...'

'No!' Myrddin interrupted. 'You don't understand my meaning. They are preparing to *launch* that craft! In less than fifteen minutes they will release the launch charge. When they do, this whole factory and everything within a four kilometre area will be *vaporised*!'

Jenson's face paled. 'That's impossible! They can't have gotten this thing ready that quick...' his voice trailed off as he saw the expression on Myrddin's ancient face. 'How do you know this old man? No hang on that's a stupid question, I know the answer to that one.'

Before he could finish his sentence, there was a rush of steam and smoke from the base of the alien vessel that filled the hangar.

A look of panic crossed his face. '*Oh crap*, now we're in trouble! How long have we got!' he asked Myrddin.

'About twelve minutes!' came the reply.

'And less than that till the other charges go off! Is there any hope the other charges exploding, will stop this Dome?' Jennifer asked from behind Jenson, where she'd been listening to the conversation.

'Not much chance of that. The armour plating on these things, is several feet thick in places. We'd be lucky even to dent it... Right!' he said decisively. 'Let's get the hell out of here!' Jenson switched on his throat mike, and called up Captain Black, and the perimeter attack force.'Strike group one from foxtrot zero, what's your situation Peter?'

'Foxtrot zero, this is strike group one,' came the reply. 'Skipper, we've managed to reach the worker's quarters. I'm afraid it became a bit of a blood bath, they decided to have a bash themselves, and turned on the guards, securing their huts. A lot of them got killed, but they'd overrun the Dyason by the time we got there. We've loaded the survivors aboard the APC's we've taken, and are now disengaging. We struck a bonus; two trucks in the outer compound, were loaded with computer gear, waiting to be unloaded. They should give you all the hardware you need, for that ship of yours. What's the situation at your end? Over.'

Jenson clicked the transmit button, 'Peter, listen, this is of *vital* importance!' he said urgently. 'We've managed to set charges in one of the Domes, but the Dyason have entered and sealed the second craft. We believe they're going to attempt a launch! I repeat; they are going to attempt a launch! We have ten minutes to evacuate! That is one zero minutes, to evacuate, before this whole area gets *nuked*. Return to Excalibur immediately... Return to Excalibur immediately... Do you copy that strike group one!

'Roger that Fox Trot Zero. Oh *Christ* skipper, you *really* know how to spoil a great party! There's no chance, we can get these vehicles, back to Excalibur in that time... hang on a minute.' Jenson heard Black talking hurriedly to one of his squad in the background, 'Okay, skipper; one of my guys says, there are three heavy lift C37 choppers, on a pad, just on the other side of the compound. The Dyason conscripts have pegged it, and left them there all fuelled up, and ready to go, he reckons. We're going to take a risk and head for them. If we can get to them in the next couple of minutes and fire them up, we might just make it in time!'

'Okay Peter, go for it! I'll make sure Excalibur is waiting for you! Good luck mate!' There was a double click from Strike group one acknowledging them, then Jenson called up Sandpiper in the VTOL.

'Sandpiper did you get that?' he called.

'Roger that skipper' came the reply. 'Am descending now. ETA two minutes. Haul arse, out of there skipper! I'll pick you up from the central compound.'

'We're on our way', Jenson replied. 'Okay people let's go!'

The resistance fighters picked themselves up off the ground, and headed for the exit to the central compound, backing out all the way. Keeping their weapons trained on the Dyason vessel, that hissed and glowed. The sound of gunfire from the galleries above them, attracted Myrddin's attention. Even though the steam and smoke, now filling the hangar obscured the view of the scaffolding, he knew instinctively, the source of the sound. He tried reaching the youth mentally, only to find the lad had created a solid barrier around his mind, and there was an equally solid barrier around the Dyason, Gulag. With no other option, he cupped his hands to his mouth and bellowed.

'Moss... they're going to launch the vessel. We must get out of here! Moss do you hear? *Moss!* '

Suddenly the gunfire stopped but there was no reply. '*Moss...!*'

Jenson took hold of the old man's arm. 'There's no time,' he said. 'If it's him he'll have heard. Come on, we've got to get out of here!'

Myrddin hesitated. The mind barrier he recognised as the youth's was still there, but why was there no reply? Reluctantly, he followed Jenson and his group towards the hangar entrance. He was right, there was no more time... He would have to rely on the youth's innate ability to survive, and hope he was on his way.

Up on the gallery, Moss had just ducked back below the level of metal sheeting, when he heard Myrddin call out from below. Could it be true? Were the Dyason really going to try to launch the Dome? He took a chance and peered over the rim of the metal, just in time to see Gulag make a dash from the opposite gantry, to the stairwell heading for the hangar floor. Well, that answered that question; obviously it *was* true...

Saving his precious last twelve rounds, Moss broke cover and also ran for the stairwell. Gulag turned as he reached the stairs, and let off a short burst in his direction. Moss fell flat on the gantry, as the bullets ricocheted around him. When he picked himself up again, Gulag had disappeared from view, although he could hear his feet pounding on the metal stairs. Somewhat more cautiously, Moss followed, pausing at each turn of the stairwell, to peer around the concrete central column, automatic raised, before carrying on. At the last turn of the stairs Moss looked around the corner, only to be met by a hail of fire. Instinctively, he pulled back and fired his own weapon, emptying his final clip. Well, that was that, Moss thought; until the Dyason also, abruptly, stopped firing. Perhaps he was out of ammo as well. Moss lay flat on his stomach and took another look around the central column. There was nothing there. He pulled himself forward, discarding the automatic and pulling out his ancient Webley revolver, from the top of his boot. Step by step, he moved down the stairs, until he finally, reached the ground level. There he found Gulag, collapsed on the floor, a pool of blood expanding from a wound to his head. Over him, stood a small thin human, grimly holding a metre-long steel bar.

The Dyason defences had collapsed, with most of the conscript guards fleeing, once their officers had disappeared into the completed Dome. Jenson met very little resistance, as he linked up with the rest of his group in the compound. Casualties among his fighters had been fairly heavy, with several dead and half a dozen wounded.

As good as his word, Sandpiper landed the VTOL transport in the central compound, within two minutes. As quickly as possible, the resistance fighters climbed aboard, carrying the wounded with them. Jenson reluctantly, ordered that the dead be left where they lay. There really wasn't any time to load them on board. He was just about to close the rear ramp, when through the smoke, wind and rain, two figures emerged. One small and thin, the other bent under the weight of a body. Jenson waved for them to hurry, as the sound of the turbines increased to maximum thrust. The figures ran for the aircraft and Jenson literally pulled them on board, and toggled the ramp switch, as Sandpiper turned the vectored thrust, and the plane began to rise into the air. The taller figure dropped the body he was carrying onto the floor of cabin. Jenson immediately recognised it as being the Dyason, Gulag. He turned and looked the youth straight in the eyes.

'Hey kid! You're full of little surprises!' he said. 'You nearly missed the ride... Next time, you walk home!' He patted Moss on the shoulder then headed for the cockpit. Jennifer leapt up from her seat, threw her arms around Moss's neck and smothered him in kisses.

Jenson clambered into the cockpit as Sandpiper vectored the heavily laden craft, in the direction of Stonehenge. Rain pelted against the canopy, reducing visibility to only a few metres. Sandpiper was relying on the infrared scope, which was displaying an image of the outside world, to an optical device attached to his flight helmet. Jenson donned a similar helmet and said, 'Head for the where those choppers are located at the edge of the compound. Let's make sure the rest of the group get away. We've room for a few more if necessary.'

'We'll be cutting it fine skipper. There's only seven minutes left!' said Sandpiper.

'Time enough..' Jenson replied.

The transport swept over the complex to the concrete apron, where three Sikorsky C37 heavy lift helicopters sat. Jenson looked out of the cockpit, and the infrared scope followed. He could see several APC's and men, clambering into two of the choppers, which had their blades turning, but the third machine lay motionless. Jenson clicked on the radio. 'Strike group one, we're above you. Black, I can see two of the choppers fired up, but what's the situation with the third over?'

For a moment there was the familiar crackle of static then Black's voice came over the headset.

'Skipper, we've managed to start two machines, which are loaded and ready to go, but the third machine got hit by a stray round and is inoperative. The other two machines can't carry all of us as well, as the released factory workers. Can you assist over?'

Jenson looked at Sandpiper and told him to take them down.

'Roger that! We're descending now. Get the other two machines into the air, and heading back for Excalibur as fast as possible!' he transmitted.

They rapidly descended onto the concrete apron. Whilst the two serviceable C57's wound up their rotors, and left the ground; soon disappearing into the gloom. Jenson spoke to the squad in the main cabin and told them to lower the ramp, and help the remainder of Black's men on board. This they did as soon as they touched down. Black's men literally hurled themselves on board, and in less than a minute, the VTOL was rising up again. It headed after the choppers, for the sanctuary of the caverns, that housed Excalibur.

Jenson took back control from Sandpiper and pushed the throttles to their stops. As they left the factory behind, Sandpiper pointed to a column of vehicles moving along the road, away from the complex.

'Looks like the rats are trying to leave a sinking ship,' he said. 'Don't fancy their chances though...'

'Ours aren't much better replied Jenson.

There was a dull clump from behind them. Sandpiper switched on the rear view monitor and watched a small pall of smoke, rise above the main hangar, which was rapidly disappearing into the distance. 'I don't suppose there's much chance of that charge you laid, stopping the launch of the other Dome?' he asked.

'I doubt it,' Jenson replied. 'Those things have to withstand a nuke going off underneath them. I doubt that our puny charge will have much effect. Besides, it was laid inside the guts of the uncompleted Dome. The armour plating will have shielded the force of the charge from the other Dome. No, I'm afraid they're going to blow pretty soon now and take us with it. Unless we can reach the relative safety, of the chambers around Excalibur.'

A head popped into the cockpit and said. '*Shit!* Can't you guys make this thing go any faster?'

'Hello Peter... Looks like I've had to save your arse again!' quipped Sandpiper.

'It isn't safe yet!' came the retort. Jenson waved them to silence as the radio came alive.

'Squadron Leader Jenson' came the smooth female voice of Excalibur, 'you are one minute ten seconds from the cavern. Launch of the Dyason vessel, is estimated to be, in one minute thirty seconds... Please relinquish control of your craft, so that I may bring it in on the most rapid line of descent. I have control of the two helicopters and am bringing them in now. Their ETA is fifty seconds.'

Jenson hesitated for a moment, reluctant to hand over control to the alien computer, but he realised this was not the time to argue the merits of trust, and threw the VTOL over to remote instrument landing. Ahead, his infra-red viewer could just make out the opening and iris, that marked the entrance to the underground chambers. They were approaching fast, with no sign of slowing. In seconds, they were nosing downwards, towards the open iris. Jenson was about to switch back to manual control, sure they were going to impact, when the thrusters went into full reverse. With a nose-up pitch, that made them all groan with excessive G forces, they stopped forward motion and descended vertically into the chamber. As soon as they were clear of the entrance, the large crystalline iris closed above them, and they rapidly descended to the chamber floor beside the two helicopters, their rotors still turning as their turbines unwound.

Jenson hit the emergency kill switch and the jets died. To his amazement, small robots shot out from the sides of the chamber and grabbed the nose leg directly below the cockpit. He saw others, similarly grab the undercarriage legs of the two helicopters and secure them. It was just as well.. The next moment, the cavern suddenly swayed and rocked as if in the grip of a large earthquake. Dust filled the air, and an incredibly deep rumble, swept through the metal airframe from the rock floor below.

The Dyason had launched!

Once the launch sequence had been triggered, the Dyason couldn't stop the tiny nuclear pellet, from exploding with the force of a small sun, underneath the armour-plated Dome. Built over a deep shaft, that went below the floor of the hangar, the force of the atomic explosion within the first nano-seconds, was aimed directly beneath, the thousands of tons of steel and iron that made up the shell of the craft. The result, was that of a bullet inside a gun. Obeying the most basic of Newtonian laws, every action has an opposite and equal reaction, the Dome shot towards the heavens, accelerating at over nine times Earth's gravity. Below it, the nuclear explosion moved into the next stage of its brief life, and vaporised most of the factory site. Then, fire and winds swept across the plains, crushing the fleeing Dyason conscripts.

At an altitude of 15,000 metres, a second nuclear pellet exploded below the concave base of the Dyason vessel, and with another boost of acceleration, it reached escape velocity, slipped through the tendrils of the dust-filled upper stratosphere and headed for the black depths of space.

Chapter Fourteen

IN ORBIT ONCE MORE

Only when they were safely in orbit, did the Dyason space marines release the belts, that kept them in the deeply padded acceleration couches. Chief engineer Direstine floated over to the main control panel and fussed over the large traditional dials and knurled knobs, placed alongside the human monitors and holo-screens.

The marine captain drifted over to him and asked, 'Are we sound? I presume we are in orbit. Is this thing working as it should?'

Direstine finished checking the panel and waited for nods from other technicians, floating above other control panels, before answering.

'Yes captain,' he said with a small smile of satisfaction. 'You may rest easy. The hull is sound. Some equipment on level three became loose and is damaged, but it does not affect our operational capability. The new design of hull appears to work.'

'Excellent,' the captain replied. 'As the senior officer now on-board I am taking command of this vessel. It is too important to risk another skirmish with the humans. Therefore, you are to head for the gateway and return to our home-world where the new fleet will gather.'

'But what of the remaining new Domes which are due to be launched? The original plan was to assemble the new craft in orbit and all return to Dyason together. Leaving just the original invasion fleet and two garrisons on Earth. Surely, we should contact Tokyo command and ask for further orders?' Direstine enquired.

The captain thought for a moment. 'We've seen that the human resistance movement, appears to be strengthening, rather than falling apart, as some would like us to believe,' he replied. 'It cannot be ruled out, that similar attacks will be carried out against the plants building the other, new vessels. As this is the prototype of the new type, we must take it to Dyason. I agree that we must make contact with Tokyo control, but for the moment we shall move towards the fault as a precautionary measure.'

'You would rather run than fight it would appear Captain!' spat Envoy Nimue, pulling herself hand over hand towards the two males, her long hair wild and waving like angry serpents in the zero gravity. Make-up was smeared across her face, which was contorted in a mask of anger.

'Er...Envoy, you should remain in your couch for now... Please, do not over exert yourself. Matters are under control,' the chief engineer stammered nervously.

'Silence! You snivelling creature!' she spat at him. 'Captain, I am awaiting your answer!'

The marine captain, to his credit, held the Envoy's stare, and answered in a measured and level voice. 'Your excellency, I am relieved to see you are feeling better. In answer to your question; I have been charged, together with my space marines with the duty of protecting you and this prototype vessel. That is a duty I am going to carry out by returning us all to Dyason.'

Nimue stared at the marine captain, her eyes boring into his sweating face, her face reflecting anger and contempt in the dim glow of the control room. The corners of her mouth still had traces of dried spittle, left there from her earlier fit. Very slowly, with a voice filled with malice, she said, 'You were ordered by Group Leader Gulag to wait for his embarkation on-board this vessel before leaving, but you left him behind Captain! You preferred to run and hide, than stay and fight at his side! Now, you intend to run to your mother, rather than face the enemies of the Empire!'

The captain's face hardened and his voice carried a sharp edge of anger. 'With respect Envoy! I was ordered to ensure you were safely led on-board the vessel and the prototype was launched, to protect it from the attacking humans. This I did. I am sorry, that Group Leader Gulag has been killed in action, but my priority now is the safe return of yourself, and this craft to Dyason!'

Nimue leapt towards the marine captain, her hands tightening around his throat. Together, they began to float away from the control panel, spinning madly in the zero gravity. Trained in weightless combat, the marine instinctively hooked his foot under the ledge of a bulkhead conduit, anchoring his body, while trying to pull Nimue's hands away from his throat. Her grip was strong, but it was an attack from another quarter which killed him. His head felt like it was being crushed in a vice, squeezed of all thought accept for the voice, which exploded in his mind.

'You pathetic fool. He's not dead! Far worse than that... He's been caught by the terrorists, who managed to escape! I know, because he is my son, and you left him lo those savages!'

The captain gave out a sickening scream that reached the very roots of his terrified soul. Direstine pleaded with Nimue, grabbing her arms in a vain attempt to release them from their death grip.

'Envoy no! *Please No..!* It's not his fault! Once the ignition sequence was started *there was no way to stop it!* With Brandrith dead and the humans outside, he could not risk looking for the Group Leader. Please Envoy *stop!*'

The marine captain's eyes went wide and with one last convulsion became sightless. Nimue grabbed an anchor handle on the control panel and pulled herself down. With one last contemptuous look she pushed the inert body away from her. It floated away, bouncing gently off the upper bulkheads. She looked at Direstine and said, 'Make no mistake about this engineer.. I'm in command now! First, you will put me in touch with Tokyo high command. Then, you will move this vessel to the asteroid belt. There, you will attach a suitable boulder and prepare for launch against Earth. We have unfinished business with enemies down there, before we can return to Dyason.'

Not daring to argue or contradict, the chief engineer nodded and pushed himself towards the comm panel where the other technicians were watching in silence. Nimue looked inward and expanded her mind, broadcasting to one particular human on Earth.

'We have yet to complete our destinies brother of mine. If you hurt my son I shall hound you to the very fires of hell! Release him and give up the bastard youth, or I shall ensure that the remains of humanity perish on a barren and lifeless planet!' Her reply was silence.

Josh and Luke Brabazon sat around a small table, in the sleeping quarters on Excalibur, that Josh had claimed his own. In front of them sat a jug of liquid, created by the alien craft's food synthesis systems. It tasted exactly, like good mature scotch. They were both very drunk, having downed half the liquid. They sat in silence, glazed expressions on their faces and anybody entering the room would think they were too drunk to talk, but all the talking took place in their minds.

'I had to do it Josh, I had to! They've got Mary and...oh God! I've been such a fool, a traitor to my own race. How could I have been so stupid? I tell you, I hate the bastards, I hate them...' Luke thought to his twin.

Josh let his brother carry on. He needed to confess his sins. The joy they had both felt at their reunion, had soon, become overwhelming guilt on Luke's part. Like a priest hearing confession, Josh sat and listened patiently, while he unburdened himself. Eventually, Luke's head collapsed onto his arms and he fell into a drunken slumber. Josh went around the table and, with some difficulty, managed to put his brother onto one of the bunks.

Then he lay down on the floor himself, and fell asleep. Luke was still asleep an hour later, when Josh wakened and left for the conference.

The conference room was light and spacious, placed near the centre of the main wedge-shaped body of Excalibur. Some way behind the pod and boom, of the main control complex. It was part of a unit of support facilities, that included an extremely advanced medical and automated surgical unit, and a dining area. Which was large enough, to cater for several hundred people at one sitting. Like everything on Excalibur, it appeared to have been built with human needs in mind.

The conference room itself, was lit by panels built into the bulkheads, all of which were made up of complex compound curves. In fact, in the whole of Excalibur, there were no right angles to be found anywhere. Like the sensuous curves of art nouveau architecture, the structure was soft and flowing. A large round table sat in the middle of the room, surrounded by small chairs that moulded themselves to the shape of the occupant's rear and back. On the table, beside each chair, was a small holographic projector and controls.

Jenson sat nearest the door. To his immediate left and right sat Hanson and Josh Brabazon. Beside Josh, sat one of the scientists released from the Dyason complex. A Russian, by the name of Gorsky, he was the most senior human involved in the building of the Dome. He spoke in low tones with Josh.

Opposite him, on the other side of the table sat Myrddin, looking like an old fisherman in his ancient faded blue jeans and Guernsey sweater. Beside him sat Moss, clad as ever, in his ancient leather jacket. Somehow, he seemed more heavily built, than when Jenson first met the kid, but maybe that was just the effect of three square meals a day. Next to Moss, sat Jennifer wearing a simple jumpsuit, that did nothing to hide her obvious signs of blossoming womanhood. Jenson could just see that the couple were holding hands under the table. Finally, on the other side of Myrddin, sat Black.

Seeing everyone was seated, Jenson tapped on the table and called the meeting to order. He began, 'Okay folks... now that we're all comfortable, can we make a start please? It's been nearly forty-eight hours, since the launch of the new Dyason craft. As you know, much has happened since then, and important decisions must now be made. Therefore, I would like to crack on with a report from Josh Brabazon.'

Brabazon cleared his throat and said, 'I would like to start with a report on the state of this craft. I have been busy examining the data banks of Excalibur, together with Dr Gorsky.' Gorsky nodded his head in acknowledgement, to the rest of the group. 'The ship's computer led us to several learning terminals, set in what, we believe, to be the library area. These terminals access data, directly to the memory areas of the brain, and can feed information to the recipient, at an amazing speed. It feels, as if you're spending weeks studying a subject. Through graphics and holographic images, but in reality, a whole new language, for example, can be learnt and absorbed in only a few short hours. With the use of these terminals, we've been able to study vast amounts of information about Excalibur, and her systems. Years of study have been compressed into weeks. Although, we will still need far longer, to absorb all the information available. It is a gargantuan task. However, I would like to point out, that we weren't the first people to use the equipment.' Josh looked pointedly at Myrddin and Moss who remained poker faced then carried on. 'We've studied the construction and power plants of this vessel, and I must say that it is at least several hundred years, in advance, of our current technology. We now understand the basic principles, under which she works. Which we shall now, try to explain, in simplified terms. Perhaps, I can defer to Dr Gorsky here, who's studied the construction in depth.'

Dr Gorsky cleared his throat and spoke in English with only a slight Muscovite accent. 'Firstly, may I express my deepest gratitude to you all for releasing myself, and all the prisoners, from the evil grasp of the Dyason slave masters. We are all deeply indebted to you...

As to this wonderful vessel? After having spent so much time, welding together the simple, if effective, Dyason Dome craft, Excalibur is an engineers dream. A lady of beauty! Her construction? Well basically, Excalibur is built from a substance very similar to carbon fibre. Molecules of carbon are woven together to produce large sheets that, when combined with an advanced polymer resin, produce a material that is half the weight of an Earth alloy such as titanium, but has no less than eight times the strength, of our strongest steel. A three millimetre depth of this fibre is equivalent to eight centimetre thick armour plating!' Gorsky paused for breath and took a sip from a glass of water before continuing.

'The flexibility of this material enables complex compound curves to be created with ease. Hence, the shape of the Excalibur is almost like that of a swan in flight. A head, containing the necessary control facilities, is connected to a long slender neck, that blends into the main body. This body houses all the power plants, living quarters and so forth.

'We have looked at the reason for the streamlined shape of Excalibur. As you know, as space is a near vacuum, there is no reason to streamline a vessel, which will not encounter a planet's atmosphere. Excalibur though, does enter planet atmospheres. If she did not, she obviously wouldn't be here now! So, the streamlined swan shape helps Excalibur slip through the atmosphere, but this is not the main reason for the shape. The real reason, is that when entering into, what we shall call for sake of argument, hyper space, the time space fabric builds up into shock waves. In the same manner, as shock waves build up on the wing of an aircraft, nearing the speed of sound. So, as with a supersonic aircraft, the shape of Excalibur is designed to reduce the effects of these shock waves, to a minimum.

Obviously, my main interest is in the power source of this craft. A source that has provided power for perhaps, thousands of years. Certainly, there has always been power available, throughout the period that Excalibur has been cocooned in these caverns. Albeit, at a greatly reduced capacity.

'My first theory was that the power source had to be some sort of advanced fission, or fusion power, but I couldn't have been further from the truth. You see, our craft here, is driven by the very substance of space itself!

'What substance? interrupted Black. 'Space is a void, empty. How can Excalibur run on nothing?

'Ah my dear Captain,' Gorsky replied, 'that is the misconception most of us have about outer space, but it is in fact, totally inaccurate. You see, space is full of molecules,gases, dark energy and dark matter. It is these gases, that form together, to create the stars, including our own sun. So, at any point in the universe, you will find, that what may appear to be empty space, is actually full of molecules of gases, such as hydrogen, helium, strains of carbon. All the basic elements that make up the structure of our world are there. When large concentrations of these elements converge, stars and planets form. And on some of these planets life also forms; as has happened here on Earth and, unfortunately, on the Dyason home-world'.

'I appreciate the explanation Dr Gorsky,' said Jenson, 'but what has all this to do with the propulsion and power system, on Excalibur?'

'Please be patient Squadron Leader,' continued Gorsky, 'I am just getting to that.'

A holographic image of Excalibur appeared above the conference table and Gorsky pointed to the main wedge shaped body. 'As you can see, Excalibur's main body has two intakes. One is blended into the belly of the hull, whilst the second, is placed within the tail plane, mounted on the central rear fin. At first we were stumped as to the use of these large intakes, but after having studied the main library we have not all...but some, of the answers.'

The hologram expanded so that the rear of the main body filled the image and changed to a cut-away, showing the position of the main power plants.

'The intakes are divided into the port power plant and the starboard power plant, as can be seen. As to the purpose of the intakes...Well, it is in fact, very simple. Dark Matter, the very substance of space itself, is drawn into the intakes, accelerated in the main engines and expelled at the rear of the fuselage through a series of vectored nozzles.'

'You mean,' interrupted Black again, 'that these things are like huge jet engines, sucking in the junk of space and shoving it out the back?'

'Exactly captain'. I couldn't have put it better myself!'

'But what sucks in the junk and accelerates it? It can't be a giant turbine - there isn't enough density in space for that, surely?' Black asked.

'Well,' said Gorsky, 'this leads us to the next bit.. Which is a little harder, to explain. So, please bear with me a moment.' Gorsky paused again, while the holographic image changed once more. This time, a small ball of light, looking like a miniature star, hovered above the table. 'What you see before you, is something that scientists have often talked of in theory, but until now, have never had proof of it's existence.'

'What is it?' asked Jenson.

'It is called a singularity.'

'What the hell is one of them?' Jenson asked again.

'A singularity is a very small concentration of space itself. It's a ball of hot gases, and more importantly immense energy. A miniature sun, if you like.'

'Don't you mean like a black-hole?' asked Black.

This time Josh Brabazon spoke. 'Not really Peter,' he said. 'A black-hole is a star which has collapsed under the weight of its own gravity, folding in on itself time and time again, until it absorbs everything around it. Light itself, is absorbed into those gaping holes in the fabric of time and space.

No, a singularity is not a collapsed star, but is in fact a star itself. Only its size is different; it's about the size of a pinhead. Yet, despite its small size, the singularity has an immense gravitational field. Not as great as a black-hole, or even as much as the Earth or moon, but still very great. These singularities usually roam through the universe, powered by the forces of dark matter and dark energy. Which as we know, are energy sources in themselves. So, in short, although true understanding will take many more years of study, Excalibur uses the power of these singularities.'

'I'm not sure if I like the direction this is taking us.' said Jenson. 'How does Excalibur use this power?'

'Well,' said Dr Gorsky, taking over from Josh Brabazon, 'Excalibur has two of these singularities; one in each of the power plants. Once in space, Excalibur draws in the substances of the universe, through its ducts, past the singularities. Which, compress and condense the sub-atomic matter of space, then ejects them through the tailpipes. Mostly, at the speed of light'.

Jenson groaned, 'Holy shit! I knew I wasn't going to like this.. You're saying that we're sitting right next to two miniature suns, with enough combined power, to tear the planet apart...

Wonderful! And what did you mean by "mostly at the speed of light"?'

'You see Squadron Leader,' embellished Dr Gorsky, 'like the rest of space, singularities don't just exist in three dimensions. Such is their power, that they also exist in the other eight, and who knows how many other, dimensions of time and space. Excalibur uses this ability to traverse the universe, at greater than light speed. It allows the singularities to distort the space-time around us. To slip through the fabric of the universe...'

Silence descended upon the group as they tried to take in the enormity of what had been said. Then in a burst of irritation Jenson turned to Myrddin and Moss and said, 'You both know this already don't you? Why didn't you tell us? Why keep it to yourselves? You've been making use of the rapid learning terminals, but haven't shared any of your findings with the rest of us... I sometimes wonder whose side you're on?'

Myrddin rubbed his beard for a moment before replying. 'What if we had, told you, would you have believed us? I doubt it, Squadron Leader. Your reluctance to believe in anything, beyond your immediate understanding, wouldn't have allowed you to accept our explanations... Dr Gorsky has done a good job of explaining difficult concepts, but I fear, the same information coming from Moss or myself, would have been received with derision. No...this was something you had to discover for yourselves.'

Jenson thought this through for a moment. He still didn't trust the old man and the kid, but if they had come to him with this information, would he have believed it? Two miniature suns distorting the very fabric of time and space, and taking Excalibur along with it? Myrddin was right. If he hadn't had it explained to him by Josh and Dr Gorsky he wouldn't have believed any of it... So, leaving that aside, where did all this leave them? Well, perhaps he should be a bit more open minded in the future, but the inevitable question had to be, could this alien craft fly?

'Okay Myrddin, I'll try to be a bit more flexible, if you two agree to share your knowledge with Josh and Dr Gorsky. Okay?'

Myrddin nodded with a smile, then Jenson turned and addressed Brabazon. 'Josh, I don't understand totally what you're saying about singularities and the like, but let's take it as read that I get the drift, and the details can be filled in later... So, we know how this thing works. The question is, can we get it to work for us?'

Josh Brabazon looked at Gorsky who nodded silently, then said aloud, 'Yes, we can..'

'When?' demanded Jenson.

'Within five weeks,' came the reply.

'As short as that?' asked Sandpiper. 'You said that wouldn't be possible a few days ago.'

'That was before I was able to study Excalibur's data banks. Now, we have a clear picture of the work that needs to be carried out. Excalibur has been maintained over the centuries, by a team of maintenance droids. Unfortunately, many of these droids have succumbed to a deterioration of their memory boards over the eons, and become inoperative,' said Brabazon. 'Happily, our technicians are able to replace those faulty memory boards, with our own computer chips, under the guidance of Excalibur. That means we can get those droids operative again. With them, and the help of Dr Gorsky and his team, we can in turn, get this vessel operational again.'

'No Shit!' said Sandpiper expressively.

'Indeed!' said Jenson. He looked at Myrddin and asked, 'Do you go along with this Myrddin?'

Myrddin looked at Jenson and said simply, 'Why ask me? Surely your question should be directed at Excalibur itself? What makes you think I know all the answers?'

'You've been one step ahead of us all the way so far old man... Still...to save further argument,' Jenson looked toward the computer console in the centre of the conference table and said, 'Excalibur, please give me a report on the status of your repairs'.

Immediately, the soft female tones of Excalibur filled the room. 'Repairs are progressing well, Squadron Leader. Twenty-five of the thirty-five repair robots are now operative, and carrying out essential repairs, and maintenance. I am enjoying working closely with Dr Gorsky, Dr Brabazon and their team of technicians. The main power plants will be back on line in approximately, twenty-eight days and thirteen hours. Once pre-flight checks are complete, the re-launch may be carried out fifty-seven hours after, the main engines are back on line. I am looking forward to this moment Squadron Leader.'

'Thank you Excalibur, that will be all for now,' said Jenson. He looked down at his hands clasped together on the top of the table and thought for a moment. Delivered into his hands was a craft of immense power, centuries ahead of anything humans could currently produce, and vastly superior to anything the Dyason could produce. If what he was being told was correct, he had the means to defeat the alien occupiers. The ultimate weapon... Or was it? They'd already discussed the fact that Excalibur had no real offensive weapons of its own. However, it would be a fairly straight forward matter to fit laser cannons and a host of missiles capable of taking on the Dyason fleet. But what if they themselves were fatally hit in space? Would the two singularities escape their confinement and burst into a fireball that would not only obliterate them, but destroy much of the Earth as well? Did he have the nerve, or even the right, to make such momentous decisions?

They couldn't risk informing the other resistance cells of the existence of Excalibur, there was too great a risk that the Dyason would get to hear about it. That meant, the secret had to be kept among the several hundred resistance and ex-prisoners, that now occupied the vessel. Which, as senior officer, left the final decision with himself...

He had to make the decision to launch; or did he? What if he said no, what would happen? Would Excalibur agree to simply shut down and wait perhaps, another eon before being freed? And what of the relationship between Moss, Myrddin and the alien vessel? They knew all about the power source, long before Brabazon and Gorsky had figured it out, but said nothing. The kid especially, seemed to have a special rapport with the sentient intelligence of Excalibur. Since they'd arrived in the chambers, which felt like years ago, the kid had changed dramatically. Gone were the nervous shifting eyes, the hunched shoulders and haunted look... Now, he sat opposite a young man, with a confident look, shoulders pulled back, physique turning to lean muscle, at an incredible rate. Moss had become a man, almost overnight, and now, had the quality he recognised in himself... leadership. So, would the alien computer, that was essentially Excalibur, accept his leadership, or had that already passed over to this remarkable youth and his mentor? How long would it be, before the rest of the men and women on board, saw him as their leader also? He needed to know more, but a decision had to be made now. Yet what other choices were there really? None...that was the short answer.

Jenson lifted his head up and spoke decisively to those around the table. 'Ladies and gentlemen, there is only one course for us to take. We've been given the means and we must use it... Prepare Excalibur for flight, we shall launch at the start of the counter-attack.'

CHAPTER FIFTEEN

THE CALM BEFORE THE STORM

Jenson lay beside the small brook, that ran into the lake. At the centre of the several acres, of gardens and woodlands, that were part of the leisure deck. The crew had nicknamed the place "Sherwood Forest", after the place that hid Robin Hood and his merry-men. He recognised some of the trees and vegetation as being from Northern Europe and America. But, there were some plants and shrubs that were obviously not from Earth. There were huge flowers, that blossomed to over three metres across, and alien trees, with red and yellow leaves. He'd even discovered a bush, whose tiny flowers seemed to hum a musical tune, whenever the very normal-looking bees, pollinated them. It was a beautiful place, a self-contained eco-system thousands of years old. Built within the even more ancient Excalibur.

With his combat boots off, Jenson waggled his toes in the clear cold water, looking at the huge salmon which swam to and from the lake and listening to the chatter of the birds in the trees. The simulated sun warmed his tired body, as he lay back on the grass and almost immediately fell asleep. He wasn't sure how long he'd been dozing, but it must have been some time, for when he opened his eyes, he saw he had company. Myrddin had rolled up the legs of his ancient dungarees, and was walking up and down the brook, tickling the salmon with his big toe.

'Hello old man,' said Jenson. Myrddin looked up at Jenson, noting the tiredness in the eyes of the resistance leader. Over two years of fighting the Dyason, always cutting and running against the odds, had taken their toll, and it showed in his face. Myrddin smiled gently and said, 'So, I'm not the only one who comes to this place for a bit of peace. You've obviously been spending some time thinking Squadron Leader, a penny for your thoughts?'

'It's been a long time since I heard that phrase,' replied Jenson smiling back.

Myrddin scratched at his beard and said, 'Well you know how it is, as you get older, you can't keep up with all the latest fads in slang. I'm afraid all I know, are the old cliche's... but you haven't answered my question. Is there anything you'd like to talk about?'

Jenson looked at Myrddin's weather-beaten face and impossibly deep, blue eyes. Despite his usual reluctance to tell anybody his inner thoughts, there was something about the old boy that made him decide to open up. At least a little.

'I guess I'm just trying to come to terms with the strange circumstances I find myself in,' he began. 'When you sit down and think about it, it all seems so incredible. Before the war, all I wanted to do was to fly, and that's all I did. Sure, I was in charge of a squadron, but none of us ever thought we would see combat. With the formation of the WDF from the United Nations Security Council, we all thought that was the end of all wars. Then the Dyason arrived, and the rest is history. Here we all are, in a prehistoric alien spacecraft, about to take on an alien race. Sometimes I have to stop and remind myself that it's all for real, and I'm not going insane...' Jenson's voice trailed off and a heavy silence fell between the two men until Myrddin spoke.

'I can assure you Squadron Leader, as a man who has met many a madman, you are perfectly sane. Or at least as sane as the rest of us. You know, there's a tale of a wise man who once said, "if you can count all the stars in the sky, then you know that the universe is finite and only a certain number of things are possible." However, after trying for many years the wise man realised, that he could never count all the stars in the sky and so he had to come to the decision, that the universe was infinite. Therefore, the wise man came to the conclusion that in an infinite universe, anything is infinitely possible...'

Jenson looked up at Myrddin and laughed gently. 'A wise man indeed, and I get the moral of the story.. You're right, I should try to open up my mind to new possibilities,' he said.

'But tell me Myrddin,' he continued, one hand thoughtfully propping up his chin, 'why haven't you used your whizz-bang powers to influence events? I've seen what Moss can do, and that's frightening. Now you're teaching him even more. Which implies, that your talents are even greater than his. So as I said, why haven't you been actively supporting us against the Dyason?'

'Ah!' exclaimed Myrddin, 'Now I see the root of your mistrust in me, Squadron Leader, You feel that if, as you say, I am so omnipotent, I should have stopped the Dyason when they first arrived in our solar system. Am I correct?'

'Something like that," agreed Jenson.

'Well I hate to disappoint you,' Myrddin continued, 'but the truth of the matter is, that I'm not omnipotent at all.. Far from it, I'm afraid. You see, my powers are mainly telepathic. I can, to some extent, read others' thoughts. Although, like most telepaths I can only access a person's uppermost thoughts and feelings. Also, I can create illusions and produce a few other parlour tricks.'

'Like the illusion of the little boy? Interrupted Jenson.

'Yes, something like that. But Moss, on the other hand, has far more ability than me. Much of it, as yet, undeveloped. So, it's important that he learns to expand his skills gradually. To carefully explore the envelope of his performance; to use a pilots' phrase. That is what I am tutoring him in. The raw power is all his own.'

'That may be, but you claim to be centuries old. That's no mean feat. In fact, it's quite miraculous. How do you explain that?'

'Ah...' sighed Myrddin. 'So many questions, so little time. Let's just say, that God has had his uses for me, over the eons. And leave it at that'.

'God! Which one do you believe in Myrddin? The Protestant God, the Catholic God, Jewish God, Allah, Buddha...? Or perhaps, some Druid god, or other? I'm sorry Myrddin, but it seems to me, that the gods deserted us the day the Dyason entered the solar system!' exclaimed Jenson vehemently, repeatedly stabbing the soil with his index finger in agitation.

Myrddin said nothing, but stepped into the brook, hands in the pockets of his dungarees, hitching them up over the level of the water. For a few minutes, he stood there letting the cool water run over his feet. Eventually, he turned to Jenson, who was now lying on his back on the grassy embankment, eyes closed, hands behind his head.

'It seems to me,' he said in a low, but assured voice, 'that what is really at the core of your disquiet, is a crisis of faith. Up until the invasion, your life was an orderly, military world. Where you were never asked to believe in what you could not see, hear, touch or understand. But, in a short space of time, you've been thrown into a maelstrom of violence, against an enemy you can barely comprehend. You feel guilty that you've survived, when so many of your friends have been butchered. You carry the responsibility of the whole resistance movement on your shoulders. And now find yourself, as you say, inside a prehistoric alien vessel of awesome power. The mechanics of which, we can barely understand. To top it all, you're being asked to fly this untried, alien machine into combat. Which goes against all your military training. It's more than most mortal humans could bear... but you manage! A great feat in itself. But let me pose this question to you, Squadron Leader. Could it really be sheer coincidence, that a group of such diverse talents as those aboard Excalibur, should be gathered together, at such a crucial time in history? Is it chance that has brought Moss, the Brabazon twins, Jennifer, Sandpiper, you, myself, and even that scum Gulag to this place, at this time?'

Jenson opened his eyes and sat up, hugging his knees and looking thoughtfully into the water for a moment, before replying. 'You're right Myrddin, it does seem a little too convenient, and that's what worries me, more than anything... I can't help getting the feeling, that we are all pawns in somebody else's game. The feeling of not having complete control over my own destiny terrifies me!' He paused and looked up at Myrddin, holding the old man's stare with his own. 'But, what you're really saying old man, is that I should trust in fate... Is that right?'

Myrddin smiled and said, 'Perhaps, just a little. We must all try to take control of our lives, but we can only do so much. After that, we're in the hands of the gods, whoever and wherever, they may be.' Myrddin then turned and sat down on the embankment next to Jenson. Changing the tack of the conversation a little, Jenson asked, 'Tell me Myrddin, where do you and the kid fit into this great cosmic scheme? Are you committed to defeat the Dyason, or are you on crusades of your own?'

'Believe it or not,' Myrddin said with a laugh, 'I am now, and always have been, unequivocally on your side, Squadron Leader. It's simply been, that you've never entirely, trusted me. I hate the Dyason, every bit as much, as you do. In fact, I have some very good reasons to hate them more! Which perhaps one day, I'll tell you about... I have suffered constantly, from almost overwhelming guilt, at not foreseeing the invasion. Millions of innocent people are dead or enslaved, because I was too stupid to read the signs that were written all over the heavens. Of all the people on this planet, I am the one who should have known what was going to happen!'

Jenson looked sideways in surprise, at the old man sitting next to him. Seeing him in a new light. He was tempted to probe further, to get a greater insight, into this complex character, but something deep inside him told him not to push it further. He didn't want to risk the first shoots of trust and friendship. Instead he simply said, 'I'm sorry.'

'Sorry for what old boy?' Myrddin asked looking up in surprise.

'For not trusting you.'

Myrddin smiled, 'Nothing to be sorry for, my lad. If I were in your shoes, I would be even less trustful.' He placed his hand on Jenson's knee and squeezed it, like a grandfather would to a favoured grandchild.

Jenson smiled back then asked. 'What about Moss?

'What about him?'

'The Brabazon twins believe he is the key to the next step, in the evolution of mankind. That he has awesome mental ability. Most of which, is dormant at present. Even I can see, that being on-board Excalibur, is having an effect on him. When I first saw him he was a ghetto rat, fighting for survival, underfed and lacking any sort of self-esteem. Now he strides through the ship, as though he owns it. He seems to know more about the workings than Josh, or Dr Gorsky, put together, He's physically bigger, although three square meals a day would account for that. And I'm told, he's devouring educational clips from Excalibur's library, at an incredible rate. In fact, a rate, that would blow the mind of anybody else, who tried it. The only normal thing about him, is his relationship with Jennifer! He worries me Myrddin. The kid is an unknown element, rogue...Will I eventually have to confront him?'

Myrddin was quick to reply, 'No, I don't think so. Moss looks up to you, and respects you. Even though he may not show it. As to the changes he is undergoing, well you have to realise, he does have, extraordinary talents. Telepathy, psycho-kinetic energy and so on, have always been part of the human make-up. In the same way, that dogs can sense earthquakes, and birds can navigate over large distances, in the dark, or in complete cloud cover.

Over the generations, the extra senses in humans, have become redundant. Especially, in recent generations, when the machine became god. However, as we have seen, there is a revival of the talents. These talents are particularly strong in Moss. How strong, we are only just beginning to discover. Whether or not, he represents a new evolutionary step in homo-sapiens, only time will tell. But, because he is so talented, it is of vital importance, that he is guided and not simply allowed to roam free, using his powers indiscriminately. You know as well as I, what chaos he can cause. That is why I am acting as his mentor, and that is why, he is spending so much time in the ship's library.'

'That I can understand' interrupted Jenson. 'But there is still, something strange, in the affinity he shares with Excalibur's computer. Moss knows so much about this ship, it's got to the stage where Josh and Dr Gorsky aren't even bothering to study anything about Excalibur, but simply ask Moss instead. What's going on?'

Myrddin sat and thought for a moment, pulling at his beard with thumb and forefinger. Then he said, 'It goes back, to what I said, about us seeming to be guided to this place for a reason. We all have a purpose here, including Excalibur. In her case, if 'her' is the correct pronoun; it would appear, that she's been waiting for eons for the arrival of one person. That person is Moss. I can't begin to know the real reason why, but this craft came alive for him, not for us. If we come right down to it, this is his ship, not ours.'

'That's what I'm afraid of," said Jenson with concern in his voice, 'It's *his* ship! The troops are beginning to talk about Moss, as though he were some demi-god, come to the salvation of all. A whole aura of myth, is being built up around him. I mean, how can I lead these people when he's around?'

Myrddin gripped Jenson`s arm and looked straight into his eyes, with an intense stare, 'Look at me Squadron Leader,' he demanded. 'How do you know, that his purpose in life, *isn't* to save the human race? God knows, people need some icon to give them courage. Somebody to believe in!

'We've already established, that forces beyond our understanding, are influencing events around us. Those same forces, have a particular role for Moss. It's not a question of competing with him, but *working* with him. The time will undoubtedly come, when you will have to decide where your allegiance lies, but there will always be an important difference between you and Moss. *You* are a natural leader. A man that people follow because they admire you. They trust you, and believe in you, as a fair and strong man, at a time when such qualities are so badly needed.

'They *don't* see Moss the same way. You're right, people are beginning to see him as a demi-god of potent power, but they don't love him in the way they love you. They *need* to believe in his talents, *need* to believe he is the saviour. I believe, that Moss will be the leader the people will look to, to drag this planet back from the abyss, and into civilisation again. But in their hearts they will *always* fear him. After all, aren't they all *God-fearing* people? If you create a god, then you have to fear him... That is the difference between the two of you. The time *will* come, when you have to decide for yourself... Will you support him or work against him?'

'Do I have much choice? It seems that we are all pawns. Part of some huge game, in which we can only visualise a small part,' replied Jenson shaking his head.

'Don't underestimate the power of the individual. The forces of destiny can only bring people together, in the hope, that events will be affected in a certain way. The day-to-day decisions we make, are entirely our own.'

'I don't know if I believe in all this stuff about destiny and dark forces, but I can still see the writing on the wall. Don't worry Myrddin, when the time comes, I'll support Moss... You're right, people are going to need somebody to believe in, and I'm just not up to the job,' said Jenson.

'You shouldn't knock yourself Squadron Leader. Your troops would follow you to hell and back. The resistance couldn't exist without you.'

Jenson smiled at that and said, 'Well, I'm not sure about that, but thanks for the compliment anyhow. I'm glad we've had this chat Myrddin. Friends call me Paul.'

Myrddin smiled back, and took the hand of the resistance leader, 'You're a good man Paul.' Then he stood up, wiped the grass off his dungarees and headed into the woods, Jenson watched him thoughtfully for a while, then lay back on the cool grass and soaked up the artificial sun. Within a few minutes he was, once more, fast asleep.

Gulag lay on the cot and through half opened eyes, examined every corner of the cell. The walls blended into the ceiling, without any apparent join line and appeared to be made of some sort of strange resinous material, that gave off a dull glow. The fourth wall of the three metre by five metre cell was transparent, beyond which, he could make out a corridor. An armed human stood sentry, directly in front of the cell, looking in impassively at him. He had no idea how long he'd been unconscious. The last thing he could remember, was being hit over the head with a steel bar, by that snivelling creature, Brabazon. Curse his soul!

Carefully, he sat up and gingerly reached for the bruise on the top of his head, where the bar had impacted. It was covered with a gauze dressing and although tender, was not as large as he'd expected. The swelling had obviously gone down, indicating that he'd been under for some time, perhaps days.

He tried to stand up, but immediately regretted it, as a wave of nausea swept over him. He sat back down rapidly. For several minutes he cradled his head in his hands, waiting for the feeling of nausea to diminish. When it did, he attempted to stand again. This time, with a little more success. Somewhat shakily, he walked up to the transparent wall and pounded on it with his fists. The guard outside didn't react, his stare remaining impassive. With a last thump for good measure, Gulag gave up and turned round to examine his cell once more. As he watched, part of the far cell wall glowed, then became transparent. A man stepped through and the wall immediately became solid again. With a gasp Gulag recognised the man. His lips curled back and he snarled 'You!'

'Me' Moss replied in a deadpan voice.

Without thinking, Gulag gathered his will and hurled it at Moss, but in his weakened state, the mental bolt bounced harmlessly off the human's mental shields. Another wave of exhaustion swept over him and Gulag collapsed back onto the bunk.

'So!' he snarled through gritted teeth, 'you've come to gloat have you! Well I refuse to beg... Get on with it, kill me if that's what you've come for!'

Moss stood there with his hands on his hips and stared at the Dyason. He'd dreamed of this moment, ever since the death of his parents, at the hands of Gulag and one of his death squads. That was back in the ghettos of London, soon after the invasion and the failed rebellion.

God, but that seemed a long time ago. How he had changed! Could that really have had happened to him?

Yes, it could and here was the tormentor and executor of his family. His time had come... Yet, now he wanted more than the quick death of this Dyason bastard. Revenge was no longer sufficient, he yearned for something more... He wanted justice!

He'd learnt so much, since coming to Excalibur, and one of the things he had learnt about, was justice. Instinctively, Moss knew how to deal with Gulag, to make him suffer, in a manner that would make him beg for a quick death.

'What makes you think I'm going to kill you Gulag? Moss finally asked, his voice calm and even.

Gulag spat, the phlegm falling at Moss's feet. Then he scoffed, 'I might have known you wouldn't have the stomach for it... You pathetic fool. You'll never keep me here! The whole of the Dyason fleet will be searching for me, and you can be sure, when they find this bolt hole of yours, they'll eradicate it. Just like all the hideaways, you vermin have built. That is, if I don't break all your feeble minds myself!'

Moss stood and looked at his opponent, sitting in his filthy uniform, defiantly staring back at him.

'I wouldn't threaten anybody, if I were you,' he said. 'You might just piss somebody off, and you're hardly in a position to do that.' He paused for a moment then said, 'You know as well as I do, that I could easily kill you here and now with my bare hands. However, that would be too easy, too quick, for scum like you. I want you to suffer, just as you've made all those people suffer over the years. Tell me, what makes a creature like you, take pleasure in making so many suffer, such terrible deaths?'

'Who are you, to judge me?' spat Gulag, 'Your people were meant to be slaves... You've given up all interest in conquest. In expanding your breed. Look at you all...Before we came, you were destroying your weapons, in the name of so-called peace. Your economies were in shambles, nothing was being produced, nothing being done... Your leaders were senile old fools, incapable of making decisions. You're surprised we took advantage of the inherent weakness in you all? You're more of a fool than I took you for, human!'

'Stick around Gulag,' Moss said coolly. 'You're going to find the next few weeks interesting... In case you weren't aware, your precious fleet is preparing to evacuate. That's right, they're bugging out and leaving you behind! Don't worry though, 'cause were going after them, and were going to destroy them. At the very moment they attempt to flee... Then, when the time is right, we're going to put you on trial before the whole world, for crimes against humanity. After being paraded around, once your body and soul is broken, we're going to string you up like the animal you are... I can assure you, that death will come to you slowly and painfully!'

With that, he gave the Dyason a contemptuous look, then turned to leave the cell. A low animal-like growl came from deep in Gulag's gut, which rose to a crescendo until, with a scream, he leapt at Moss's back, fingers outstretched like clawing talons. But, before he was halfway across the cell, Moss turned and with a slight flick of his hand, sent out a bolt of pure mental energy. Gulag fell to the floor, screaming at the top of his lungs, holding his temples in his hands, the attack stopped in its tracks. Without another look, Moss turned again and left through the cell wall which opened, then smoothly closed behind him.

Jennifer entered Excalibur's cavernous hangar, just as Sandpiper and Black were overseeing the securing of several unusual aircraft, in-between the even more exotic, shuttles and craft that were already berthed there. Curious to know what was going on, she walked up to the pair, ignoring the admiring stares from of a group of recently arrived resistance pilots.

'Hi Hanson!' she called out to Sandpiper.

'Hi yourself kid,' he called back with a smile. 'Come to admire our new toys?'

'Yes, what are they?' she asked.

'These babies,' he said, patting one of the fuselages affectionately, 'are the latest state-of-the-art Sukhoi's. Capable of working both in the atmosphere and outer space. The engines are hybrid hydrogen and oxygen burners, and with the modifications made by Gorsky and Josh, their space flight envelope is vastly improved.'

'So,' interrupted Jennifer, 'armed with AP.598 Baron missiles, with armour-piercing warheads, you intend to launch them from orbit, against the Dyason fleet?'

Sandpiper smiled and said laughingly, 'You've obviously been doing your homework on the tutorial machines as well, young lady! Well, you're spot on... These lovelies, are ex-WDF Russian fighters. Twelve of them flew from a resistance stash in Siberia, to here. Those are the pilots over there, and it looks like you've got some new admirers!' he nodded towards the group of Russian pilots, of whom the eight male members were openly staring at her with fixed grins. The female pilots looked on, in obvious annoyance.

Black, who was debriefing the group, saw the direction of their gaze and said, 'You guys had better look elsewhere, if you don't want your brains frazzled by the Kid..'

Taking his meaning, the men quickly looked away. The legend of Moss had already spread far beyond the confines of Excalibur. Jennifer carried on examining the sleek, shark-like machines, with a slight blush to her cheeks. Hanson smiled to himself. The girl was becoming a lady, but a lady who was maturing into a match, for any trooper on-board.

Marshal Mettar was glad the communications link was voice only. Despite having access to the latest Earth technology, the rush to get the new fleet of cruisers operational, had meant cutting some corners. Vision and sound Com's was one of those corners. Still, just for once, he was pleased he couldn't see Envoy Nimue's face. Nor could she see, the look of contempt on his.

The central operations control room had been cleared of all other personnel, except for himself and his aide. Ostensibly for security reasons, but really, because he didn't want anyone to overhear the humiliating way the witch spoke to him.

'With the greatest of respect Envoy,' he tried to explain in exasperation, 'No one could have foreseen that the resistance would attack that complex. Our intelligence was that there were no, I repeat *no*, terrorists in that area. Regardless of that, the launch of your new cruiser obliterated the complex and everything within several klicks of the site. Reconnaissance shows the place to be nothing but a radioactive wasteland now. I'm convinced the terrorists and unfortunately, Group Leader Gulag, were terminated in that blast.'

Nimue interrupted Mettar and said in a voice dripping with malice, 'You say this, but no positive identification has been made of any bodies. So how can you be sure that they are all dead? I am telling you, I know they are still very much alive and still on the plains of Salisbury somewhere. I can feel it! Perhaps you are calling me a liar; is that it Mettar?'

Mettar went red in the face and his eyes narrowed. Damn the bitch, she was impossible!

'No Envoy, I am not calling you a liar, but I have no hard evidence to go on. I mean, for all the gods' sake, the place has been nuked! We haven't been able to identify where parts of the factory once stood, let alone take a body count! There's nothing left, but a bloody huge crater and tons of radioactive ash! The whole area for several klicks is now lethally, radioactive. Anyone who did survive, will now have a lethal dose of that radiation.

Nearly screaming into the mike, Nimue demanded, 'I *insist* you send ground troops to sweep the area. I tell you, Group Leader Gulag is alive! Can't you appreciate the *importance* of the man? The *very future* of Imperial Dyason may well rest with him! You *must* carry out a detailed search, no matter what the cost!'

This nonsense was more than Mettar could take. He slammed his fist down hard on the console and shouted into the mike.

'You insist *nothing* Envoy! *I* am in command of the occupation forces, not *you!* We lost hundreds of troops in the destruction of that complex, and I don't intend to lose more, because of radiation exposure! On top of which, we don't have the manpower to carry out such a search. You know as well as I do, that the portal is now critically unstable, and may close completely, at any time. In case you hadn't noticed, we're trying to organise an orderly withdrawal from this fucking awful planet! Cruisers are evacuating nonessential personnel every day, but we're coming under constantly increasing pressure from the Earth terrorists. As it is, we're having trouble holding the areas of the planet we still occupy. We're spread dangerously thin everywhere and the last thing I can afford, is to send my men off on some wild goose chase to look for your *bloody lover!*

'Be advised Envoy, within the next month, the remaining vessels will launch together, for the return to Dyason. Even if your toy boy is, by some miracle, still alive, we aren't in a position to get him back. And to be frank, they're *bloody welcome* to the bastard! Now, I am ordering you, to turn your cruiser around and return to the portal. The prototype vessel is too valuable to waste on some futile gesture! I repeat, *return to Dyason Nimue!* Those are your orders and this conversation is ended!'

Before she could reply Mettar cut the comm link, turned, and angrily stomped out of the control room. His aide close on his heels.

When Mettar cut the comm link, Nimue said nothing and moved not a muscle. Only the faint gravity, caused by the cruiser's steady acceleration, stopped her from floating away from the console. The crew around her however, knew the look on her face. They'd seen it several times during the past days. That look meant danger... On the surface her face appeared calm, almost serene, but underneath this facade she seethed in anger and when the Envoy was angry, those around her suffered. She stood motionless for several minutes, while the tension on the cruisers bridge became so intense, it was almost a palpable, physical thing. Finally, she turned to Direstine, the engineer. Now given a field promotion to captain, to replace the terminated marine officer.

'Direstine,' she said in a quiet, icy voice, 'you will remain on course for the asteroid belt. We shall continue with the plan to retrieve a suitable, piece of rock. I'm sure I don't need to remind you, that the improved power plant of this vessel, enables us to acquire a much larger asteroid, than before.'

The engineer looked up from the Earth-made navigation computer and said nervously, 'But.., but.., Envoy, with respect...I mean, well, you heard the Marshal. The portal may close at any time... Even now, it will take some thirty-five days to reach it. Surely, we should be trying to get there before we are trapped here perman...'

He got no further. His head felt like it was being squeezed by a clamp; being crushed. God the agony! He began to foam and gurgle at the mouth, as he collapsed to the deck.

'No. I think we shall continue on course for the asteroid belt, engineer. I'm sure, you wouldn't like to disappoint me now, would you? After all, remember what happened to your predecessor,' Nimue said casually, her voice quiet and icy, dripping with malice. 'Now then, navigator?'

The navigator nervously stood up from his console and faced her, 'Yes ma'am?' he answered quietly.

'How long do you estimate it will take us to retrieve a suitable asteroid and return Earth orbit?' she demanded.

The navigator quickly looked at his notes then answered, 'Approximately twenty-five days ma'am'.

'Excellent, just in time to leave a farewell present for Earth, before we rejoin the fleet. Now, I want you to calculate an asteroid strike against Salisbury Plain,' she purred.

'Salisbury Plain Envoy? Where we've just come from?' the navigator asked in confusion.

'Yes navigator, if you please. In fact, to be more precise, the strike point is the ancient monument of Stonehenge.' With a flick of her hand, she released the engineer from the mind block, then without a second glance, swept out of the bridge, heading for her quarters, humming tunelessly.

Moss sat cross-legged opposite Myrddin in his mentor's chambers, sipping at the brandy, without great relish. He'd yet to develop a taste for such things.

'It's strange Myrddin,' he said conversationally, staring into his glass. 'He was there helpless before me, I could have easily killed him with my bare hands, but I didn't. He's the bastard who killed my parents, and thousands of other innocent people in the London ghettos. If anybody deserves to die, it's him. But, for some reason, simple revenge, is not enough anymore.'

Myrddin knocked back his tumbler of brandy in one gulp, then smacked his lips noisily.

'Yep, I know,' he replied between belches.

'How do you know?' asked Moss, 'Did Excalibur tell you what happened?'

'She didn't have to,' replied Myrddin, 'the guards saw and heard what happened, and they've told just about everybody on-board. Yes, your mythical reputation, did well out of that stint, my boy.'

'Oh come on Myrddin. You know I didn't stage that event to enhance my reputation.' Moss said a little hurt. 'I'm serious... Before, I would have just killed the bastard outright. Now...I dunno, I guess I'm looking for something more.'

Myrddin looked up at his prodigy and said, 'I know Moss, and I'm proud that you didn't kill him. It's right, that he should stand trial for his crimes against humanity. There's no doubt in my mind that he'll hang, but it's important for you, and the world, that his death comes from a judge's sentence, not from revenge.

You see, just as you're beginning to realise lad, anger and lust for revenge, are the two things that will eat away at your soul. Until you become no better, than those you despise. If you're to remain above those you condemn, you must suppress these two emotions. Above all others.'

Moss looked over the top of his brandy glass and said, 'You mean like when you met Nimue, or should I say, your sister, you could have killed her then, but you didn't?'

Myrddin sat thoughtfully, with a faraway look for a moment, before replying.

'So you know about that do you? Well, I guess you had to find out sooner or later.. But you're right, it's just like that. That woman, is filled with hate and anger, and it warps not just her own mind and soul, but those of all around her.'

'Don't you think it's about time you told me about her?' asked Moss quietly.

Myrddin sat without speaking for a minute, his eyes still glazed, with that faraway look. Then he nodded and said to Moss, 'Yes I guess its time for you to know...

Long ago, before the fall of the Mesopotamian civilisations, I was born to a rich nobleman who owned many camels and cattle. He was proud to finally have an heir, a male child to carry on the family line. My mother had been barren for a long time, before finally becoming pregnant. My father loved my mother dearly, and never really recovered from her death in childbirth. You see, there were no problems with my birth, but she died giving birth to my twin.'

MINDS OF THE EMPIRE

'Your twin?' said Moss in surprise. 'You never mentioned a twin before.'

'It was a very, very, long time ago, Moss,' replied Myrddin.

'So Nimue is your twin sister? Is that what you're saying? I mean, what happened? How did you become such enemies?' Moss asked.

'With the death of our mother, we were largely brought up by an old priestess, who arrived one day at my father's encampment. Soon after our birth. My father found it hard to show affection to my sister, for two reasons. Firstly, because she was a girl. He saw no active role for her in the family tribe. As was the way, in those days. Secondly, he got it into his head, that she was touched by the devil, and that was the reason, for my mother's death, in childbirth. My father, overwhelmed with grief, spent most of his time travelling across Mesopotamia buying and selling livestock. Only occasionally, did he return to the encampment, that was our home.

'The priestess Mammat was wise, in the ways of the ancient religions. So, wasn't surprised at the rate of our growth. Both mental and physical. She did her best to educate us, in the methods of the ancients, and I loved her, as the mother we never had. Yet, as we grew older, even she, was unable to control my sister. Frustrated, by the lack of respect accorded to her being a girl, and the almost open hostility, showed by my father towards her, she became warped, twisted with anger and hatred.

'One night, when we were fourteen, my father's tent caught fire. I rushed to waken my father, who having just returned from months of travelling, was asleep inside. Braving the flames, I entered to find my sister, standing over the bloodied remains of his body. Flames leaping all around her, but not touching her. My father's head had, quite literally, exploded. His brains spread all over the carpets.

'Nimue had exacted her revenge, with talents fed by the flames of hate. Seeing me, she tried to destroy my mind also. We stood there, in the burning tent, my father's body being consumed by the flames, mentally committed to mortal combat with each other.

By dawn, there was nothing but a pile of ash in the desert. The rest of the family household, had fled during the night. Fearing the curse of the gods. Knowing evil deeds, were taking place.

'Nimue and I stood facing each other, untouched by the fire, one unable to defeat the other. It was a standoff... By the time we unlinked our young minds, we were both exhausted, to the verge of death. Nimue turned and walked off into the desert. I went in the opposite direction. Later that morning, I came across the body of Mammat. She had plunged a knife into her own heart.

'Since that time, we've been adversaries. Knowing neither of us is sufficiently strong, to mentally defeat the other, we have faced each other across battlefields littered with the armies of many civilisations. That is until the time of King Arthur. Your direct relative... My son..

'Arthur linked all the kingdoms of this land, to form the original, United Kingdom. His reign was to herald a new era of peace, stability and civilisation, an end to the dark ages. Unfortunately, it wasn't to be, my sister saw to that... Like all she touches, Nimue corrupted those around Arthur, and the kingdom fell apart, in a sea of jealousy, and mistrust. Outlanders finally killed Arthur in battle, and the country dissolved into chaos once more.

'I went in search of her. For years, I followed her trail across deserts, moors and mountains. Across Asia and Europe, and the Americas. When eventually I found her, I banished her...forever. Or so I believed...'

'How did you do that?' said Moss leaning forward in rapt attention.

'I led her to the gates of the cosmos and forced her through!'

'Jeez!' exclaimed Moss, 'You mean, those gates we saw Gulag attempting to enter? So, it *is* possible to enter the fabric of the space-time continuum?'

'Yes,' replied Myrddin simply. 'I've never attempted it since, and have no intention of doing so, but yes, it is possible. I believed, she would be lost in hyperspace for all time. But, somehow, she must have found her way to another world. A world very similar, to Earth. There ,she must have corrupted their civilisation, to create the Dyason Empire. Now, she has returned to her birth place.'

The buzz of the entry phone broke the silence that hung between them. Putting his brandy down, Myrddin walked to the phone, flicked on the monitor and said, 'Yes, what is it?'

The face of Jenson appeared on the screen. 'Myrddin, it's Paul here. May I come in?' he asked.

'Yes, of course, Squadron Leader,' replied Myrddin, and with a casual wave of his hand, a doorway appeared in the wall. Jenson stepped through and took the chair offered to him.

'Brandy?' asked Myrddin.

Jenson looked hungrily at the bottle, standing on the Louis XIV table.

'As much as I would like to Myrddin, as I'm on duty, I don't think it would be a good example to the troops. Thanks anyway. I'm sorry to disturb the two of you, but I was hoping to have a word with Moss.'

Myrddin got up to leave. 'Of course, Squadron Leader. I'll leave the two of you to talk in private.'

'No it's okay,' interrupted Jenson. 'I think you should hear this as well.'

Moss turned to look at the resistance leader with interest, as he continued, 'You see, I've been talking it over with Sandpiper,

Black and Josh Brabazon, and we all agree. Basically, Moss, as you have such a close rapport with Excalibur, and know this ship better than any of us, it would be foolish, *not* to have you as an active crew member. So, we would like you to start training with us... There's a position for you, as an officer on the bridge. If you want it that is...'

Moss was so surprised, he said nothing for a moment. Only a few weeks ago, he would have held up his hands in horror, at the thought, of becoming an active member of the resistance. In fact, he would have run a mile, or more likely several miles. But, things had changed dramatically since then. He knew instinctively, as perhaps Jenson did also, that his future, was intrinsically linked, to the alien vessel and those now aboard her. He looked at Jenson and smiled, 'It would be an honour Paul!'

Jenson smiled back, and offered his hand to Moss. Who pumped it enthusiastically.

'It's good to have you aboard. Welcome to the resistance kid! If you report to Black, first thing in the morning, training can begin straightaway. Until then, I'll leave you guys to it... Have a nice evening.'

He turned to leave, but before he stepped through the doorway, Moss said, 'Paul?'

'Yeah, what is it Moss?' asked Jenson turning to face Moss again.

'Thank you,' Moss said simply.

Jenson said nothing, just smiled back and left the chamber. The doorway closed and Myrddin stood there beaming at Moss. 'Well, well, well...about bloody time!'

The auditorium buzzed with anticipation. For weeks, they'd all toiled to bring Excalibur to operational status. Technicians had poured over computer monitors, checking over the thousands of kilometres of optic fibres, that were the electronic lifelines of the ship. Engineers had worked alongside the repair droids, restoring Excalibur's numerous systems. The most vital being the vast engines and status fields, that held the singularities in position. At the same time, the squads of resistance fighters had trained constantly in simulated combat. And the pilots had flown hundreds, of simulated missions in their Sukhoi fighters.

Now, the preparation and training was at an end. Excalibur was ready - as was her crew. At least, they fervently hoped, everything was ready, because it was too late if something, or somebody wasn't. The Dyason were preparing to evacuate within twenty-four hours and resistance units around the globe, were preparing to launch the final offensive.

Exhausted technicians sat with their eyes closed, grabbing a few moments rest, before the briefing began. Veterans sat slouched in their seats, their postures those of studied casualness, Whilst those who'd never been in combat before, sat bolt upright, note-pads at the ready to take down every detail of the brief. The environment may have been different, as was the war they were fighting, but regardless of these things, it could have been a briefing room on the eve of any battle in the history of humanity. 'Ladies and gentlemen, your target for tonight is...'

'Room atten...tion!' called out a flight sergeant from the front of the auditorium, and in stepped Jenson flanked by Black, Sandpiper, and a few steps behind Moss, Josh and Luke Brabazon. The group took seats on the raised dais, facing the rest of the auditorium. Jenson stood at the podium and winked to Jennifer and Myrddin sitting in the front row. Then he looked up and addressed the rest of the assembly.

'Good afternoon ladies and gentlemen, please be seated,' he said with authority. 'Firstly,' he began, once they had all settled down, 'I would like to congratulate you on a magnificent job well done. I am proud of every man and woman aboard Excalibur. In a few short weeks, you have turned an alien artifact, into an operational fighting machine!'

From his position Moss could see, and noted with interest, how just about everyone sat up a little straighter in their seats, as pride swelled their chests. Once again Moss admired, and learnt, from Jenson's skill as a leader.

'You have achieved what I believed was impossible!' Jenson continued. 'Now we're going to use this incredible vessel against our most hated enemy - the Dyason - and they're going to get their arses kicked, aren't they!'

The auditorium erupted as with one voice, 196 resistance fighters shouted, 'Yes sir!'

'Good!' he replied. 'Okay, so let's get down to details, time is precious. Firstly, a general overview of the situation. As you all know, the hyper-spatial tunnel the Dyason have been using to travel to our solar system, is threatening to close at any time. Without sufficient manpower, and with the threat of their lines of communication and supply being cut, the Dyason have had no choice, but to initiate a withdrawal.

'Over the past month, all nonessential personnel have begun the return journey to Dyason. Under constant attack and harassment from our resistance units around the globe, their ground forces have been forced to pull back, to a few easily defended, key areas. These include Tokyo in Japan, which is still their main base of operations; Pearl Harbour in the Pacific; London here in England and several other smaller bases. The areas most heavily defended are, the launch sites, and the factories which have been building the new fleet of cruisers.

'Our latest intelligence is that the Dyason intend to launch these new cruisers, and evacuate the remainder of their forces, within the next twenty-four hours. This will be done under the umbrella of a flotilla of Domes, currently in Earth orbit.

'At 0100 GMT, resistance units will launch an all-out offensive on the factory sites holding the new cruisers, and all current launch sites. Their job is to stop the launch of the new, higher performance cruisers and put a halt to the evacuation.

'Our job, ladies and gentlemen, is to engage the flotilla in orbit, and stop them with any means, from disrupting the offensive. Now you may ask, "If the Dyason are leaving anyway, why bother to attack at all, why not simply let them go?" Well, the answer to that is very simple. We cannot let them leave in a state, where they can possibly, *ever*, pose a threat to Earth again. The new cruisers, built here on Earth incorporate technology new to the Dyason. As you know, the Dyason Empire never developed the sort of electronic and microprocessor technology that we have. If any of these new cruisers were to reach Dyason, the equipment installed here on Earth might give them a technological boost that would threaten other civilisations, not just our own.

'However, of greater concern than this, are the experiments the Dyason have been carrying out in interstellar navigation. They've been experimenting with changing the space-time fabric, using human operants. We know they've had some limited success with these fantastic experiments. So, we cannot take the risk that they may now, or in the future, manage to enter hyperspace without the use of stellar faults. Such as the one currently, in our solar system.

'Therefore, it is imperative that no human operants leave with the Dyason. In fact, if we are to ensure that there can be no future invasion, then the remainder of the fleet must be destroyed! No more Domes must be allowed to return to form the basis of a new invasion fleet. Their defeat must be total!

'Now with details of the attack plans, I hand you over to Flight Lieutenant Sandpiper.'

Jenson turned and sat down with the others at the back, whilst Sandpiper took the podium.

'Okay people listen up! This is the way it's gonna be!' he began.

CHAPTER SIXTEEN

TIBOOBURRA, NEW SOUTH WALES, AUSTRALIA
00.55 HOURS GMT, 10.55 HOURS LOCAL TIME.

Zanthuman scanned the horizon with his binoculars. With less than twenty-four hours before the new cruisers were due to launch, he was nervous. Reports had been coming in from all over the planet of increased activity from the human scum. Some bases had already been under attack.

So far, the factory complex here in the Australian outback, had been unaffected by these attacks. Who the hell would want to come to this godforsaken part of the world?

The sun had broken through the thinning cloud cover some ten days ago, turning the desert into a furnace devoid of all life. It was a bloody awful shit-hole, and as far as he was concerned, the humans were welcome to it... He couldn't wait to leave the sodding planet!

Once again, he turned in his command position in the APC and scanned another section of the horizon. Nothing, as usual. There was nothing out there now, there was nothing out there before, and this patrol was a complete waste of... hold on a moment... What was that? He'd nearly missed it, a flash of light on the horizon. It could have been just the sun glinting off the wreck of some old vehicle, but then it might not.

Zanthuman kicked the driver with his foot and ordered him to stop. He swung his binoculars back to where he thought the glint had come from. There it was again. He held the image in the centre of his viewfinder, unable to make out what it was he was looking at, until it came closer and became clearer.

Shit! It was a vehicle of some description, with four low-pressure tyres attached to an open-frame chassis, some metres off the ground. It was bounding over the scrub and rock of the desert at an incredible speed, and as it came closer he could see that the strange buggy was bristling with Gatling guns and what looked like, anti-tank missiles. Then he saw another of the vehicles speeding through the desert, then another and another, until the whole horizon was filled from left to right with speeding desert buggies!

By the gods! This was it! The human attack, this must be it! Zanthuman flicked on the comm link to base, but before he could speak, he felt several pairs of strong arms haul him bodily out of the APC and throw him onto the desert. He fell heavily, badly twisting his ankle and screamed in pain. Another body fell on top of him and pinned him to the ground. A sharp blade dug into his neck, and the only sound he could make was a gurgle, as his blood drained into the desert soil. The last thing he saw was the rest of his crew being terminated in a similar manner, and the deep black eyes of the Aboriginal resistance fighter, before darkness arrived for the final time.

TOKYO BAY
00.58 HOURS GMT

The thing flew above the waves of Tokyo Bay, at a height of just ten metres. The ramjet engine kept it at transonic speed, while the short stub wings gave just sufficient lift to allow it to fly at an ultra-low level. Its guidance system compared the optic, infrared and radar image it received from its sensors, to a detailed map, embedded in its memory. Occasionally, it either popped up another ten metres, or took a detour to avoid the masts of the commandeered Dyason vessels in the harbour. Despite these obstructions, the cruise missile was accurately on course and time.

The harbour shot below it, and the missile was forced to fly a little higher, to avoid lampposts and telegraph wires. However, it kept on towards its target flying, between buildings and up streets, the faces of the Dyason troops below barely able to register surprise, before it was gone. The target was coming up... The electronic mind compared the image supplied by its sensors, to the information in its memory. It homed in on a ventilation shaft, at the base of a tall, modern, multi-storey office block. It flew into and down the shaft, cutting its engine and allowing momentum to force it in. To the accompaniment of ripping and grinding metal it came to an abrupt halt, at the bottom of the shaft. The artificial intelligence unit thought for a moment, then decided it was in the required position and ignited the heavy explosive charge at exactly 0100hrs GMT.

Those inside the Dyason main battle command centre either died with ruptured lungs and eardrums instantly, or a little later, when the roof caved in, burying the underground chambers and their occupants, in thousands of tons of concrete and rubble. Above ground the multi-storey block collapsed like a pack of cards, and with it went the Dyason command headquarters.

From across the city came the sound of other explosions, as wave upon wave of cruise missiles found their targets, at the heart of Imperial Dyason's new colony.

WEST END OF LONDON
01.00 HOURS GMT

They poured out of the sewers onto the streets of the West End in their hundreds, all armed to the teeth, all highly trained, and each and every one of them, with a score to settle. The Dyason troops, more concerned with the forthcoming evacuation, than with the security of the small pocket of London they still held, were taken largely by surprise. They were soon being forced back towards their barracks in Chelsea, and the shuttle craft, lined up in

222

Regent's park. Mortar shells fired from the resistance-held ghettos, landed all around them. Several found their mark, destroying one shuttle and damaging two others.

On the dark swirling water of the Thames, a flotilla of small craft, made up of anything from crudely made rafts, to fast dinghies with outboard motors, began to cross from the South Bank to Westminster. Each carried several people, all armed with guns of various description from "liberated" Dyason automatics, to crude underground-made rifles, and ex-WDF forces light arms. Many never made it to the other bank, as the now alerted Dyason troops, lay down a lethal curtain of fire over the small vessels. Hundreds fell into the Thames. Some dead, some badly wounded, their bodies slowly carried sea-wards by the tide. But, sufficient numbers made it to the far side, to add even more pressure on the beleaguered Dyason troops.

Under the overwhelming onslaught of a desperate and bitter enemy, Dyason organisation began to collapse at the huge fortified battlements, that separated the West End, from the ghettos. Panicking troops fled their positions in the watch towers and gun posts, leaving their weapons behind, in their rush to escape, the hordes of resistance fighters, and ghetto dwellers, who poured through several breaches in the boundary defences. Deep in the heart of the West End, the fighting was reduced to hand-to-hand combat as the more experienced and disciplined Dyason bitterly contested every metre of ground. Even so, house by house, street by street, they were forced further and further back towards their last circle of defence.

DYASON SPACEPORT - TOKYO, JAPAN
01.30 HOURS GMT, 10.30 HOURS LOCAL TIME

The impacts from the explosions could be felt through the plates of the Dyason flagship *Emperor.* Marshal Mettar didn't need to be told that their last stronghold was under full-scale attack. Fortunately for him, he hadn't been at the command centre when the cruise missile had struck. Instead, he'd been overseeing the final preparations for the launch of his flagship, and the new fleet of Dome battle cruisers.

The loss of the command centre had been a serious blow. Packed with the latest in Earth communication and intelligence-gathering equipment, it had been the nerve centre of their operations. With its loss, they were reliant upon the equipment installed on the Emperor and her sister craft in orbit. This equipment, although functional, was crude and basic in comparison. Not that any of it was working at present... They were having trouble making contact with the rest of the fleet, as some source of local jamming, scrambled most of their transmissions.

Mettar leant over the shoulder of the battle group commander, who was busy adding plots to a large-scale map of Japan and the Tokyo area. 'What's the situation commander?' he asked.

The Dyason commander turned and looked at the Marshal with a serious face, 'It's very confused sir, but I'm afraid that if we stay here much longer, we are in grave risk!'

'That bad huh?' commented Mettar in a deadpan voice.

'I'm afraid so sir,' continued the commander kneading his brow. 'The first wave of cruise missiles took out our command and communication centres. The second wave caused considerable damage and casualties, to the fifty-ninth battalion's barracks, and many of the aircraft at the air force base. One missile was heading for the space port here, but fortunately an alert anti-aircraft gun crew managed to blow it out the sky, just as it crossed the port boundary. So far, all the warheads have been conventional, rather than nuclear. I guess they want to keep casualties among their own people to a minimum, but that could change at any time. Since then, all units report coming under heavy attack from human troops entering from the city outskirts. We're holding them in check at the moment, but everyone's under considerable pressure. The humans are fighting like maniacs, devoid of any concern for their own lives. We're even getting reports of suicide attacks, by local people carrying home-made explosives!'

'By the gods!' swore Mettar pounding his fist in frustration on the console. 'I thought they'd handed over all those missiles at the armistice, and where the hell, are all those bloody human troops coming from? We had no indication, that the resistance were so strong in this area.'

'From what little intelligence we have sir, it would appear that the local terrorist cell is being supported by forces from unoccupied areas of the Pacific Rim. Our hasty evacuation has left a vacuum, which the terrorists have filled. My guess is they've been gradually building up their forces on the Japanese islands over the past several weeks, maybe even months, in parallel with our own withdrawal,' replied the commander.

'So, do you believe this to be an all-out attack? Do they intend to delay us, or destroy us?' Mettar asked already knowing the answer, but looking for confirmation from somebody else.

'Marshal, all the indications are that this is a major offensive! There can be little doubt that their aim is to wipe us off the face of their planet! There are some garbled reports that have come through the communications jamming, of similar attacks upon all our remaining bases across the planet. I'm totally convinced, that these combined attacks, amount to a worldwide offensive by the humans. They know we're getting ready to leave, and it's their plan to destroy what's left of us! At the moment, the space port is under no immediate threat, but it can only be a matter of time before they direct their attention on us. It'll only take another cruise missile to actually hit us and we're *history!*'

Mettar thought over the commander's prognosis for a moment before saying, '*Damn* it all, but I'll have to agree with you commander. This has all the hallmarks of their final push, and we're sitting ducks if we stay here.' He turned to the captain of the

Emperor who was conferring with the engineering officer on the other side of the bridge.

'Captain!' he bellowed.

'Sir!' the captain replied, dismissing the engineering officer and moving to where Mettar stood beside the battle group commander.

'Captain, prepare the *Emperor* for an emergency launch. We're going to have to bring the launch time forward. Seal the hatches and order the communications room to give the general order to *all* Dyason craft to evacuate!' Mettar ordered.

'But sir!' the captain appealed. 'That means deserting all our troops still fighting the humans. Shouldn't we wait to evacuate them also?'

Mettar gave the captain a withering stare and said, 'I admire your concern Captain, but we're not going to be much use to anybody, if we get a cruise missile up our arse, are we? If you're that concerned, you have my permission to stay behind with them... If you want to get the hell out of here, then perhaps you should leave the thinking to me! Now prepare for launch and try to get through to the fleet. If you can get a message through the jamming, tell them we're on our way to rendezvous in orbit, and they're to lend what assistance they can. As to the remaining troops fending off the human vermin, we'll use the shuttle craft to evacuate the survivors once we're in orbit. *Now do it!'*

Without another word, the captain scurried off to carry out the marshal's orders. Outside, the hatches were sealed, the umbilical cords detached and the unfortunate technicians being left behind fled in their vehicles to the bunkers, on the other side of the launch site.

EARTH ORBIT

01.33 HOURS GMT.

The bizarre combination floated in orbit across the night side of the Earth, little stabs of flame shooting out from guidance thrusters. Twice the size of the craft propelling it, the asteroid seemed to shimmer and change shape, as light played across its pockmarked surface. Placed carefully at one end of its axis, the cruiser was attached like a limpet. With its curved surface against the hard rock and its main engines pointing rear-wards. For twenty days, the mated craft had travelled from the asteroid belt beyond Mars, and back to Earth. Pushing the thousands of tons of rock, that made up the asteroid, in front of it. Now its journey was nearly completed. On the bridge of the cruiser Nimue presided over the proceedings, as the delicate final adjustments were made to their orbit, before the asteroid was released. To begin its trajectory towards the Earth's surface. Technicians poured over human-made computer monitors, as the various factors of mass, drag, inertia and trajectory were calculated. They whispered into their comm links, and numerous small thrusters, built into the hull of the Dome, made minute adjustments to their orbit.

The communications officer came over to Nimue and whispered in her ear, 'Envoy, I've received a message from fleet. They want to know why we didn't continue with the return journey to Dyason. They're demanding that we rendezvous with them and rejoin the fleet. What should I say ma'am?'

Nimue didn't even bother to look away from the situation board she was watching. 'Ignore it,' she snapped.

'With respect Envoy, I have already accepted the message. I cannot ignore it,' the comm officer replied urgently.

Nimue turned to look at the officer and gave him an icy stare. 'I said *ignore it*. That will be all!'

For a moment the officer opened his mouth to reply, then thought better of it. Silently, he returned to his communications station. Nimue turned back to look at the situation board. The technicians had begun the countdown to release. Five...four...three...two...one... With a jolt, the Dome released from the asteroid. Video monitors showed the asteroid drifting away. Then there was a short burst of flame, as the attached guidance thruster pack, kicked in.

'How long to impact?' Nimue asked Direstine, the captain.

'Eighteen minutes, thirty-four seconds,' replied Direstine.

'Excellent!' Nimue purred and in her mind called *'Time to come up and play Myrddin!'* Out loud, she ordered, 'Move to a holding orbit on the opposite side of the planet from the fleet.'

Direstine exchanged looks with the navigation officer. Why weren't they joining the rest of the fleet? He opened his mouth to question the Envoy, then changed his mind. Instead, he simply replied 'Yes Envoy', and passed the order on to the helmsman.

Outside, the asteroid began to tumble slowly, as gravity gripped its huge mass. Then it began to glow, as it hit the first wisps of atmosphere. The rock glowed dull red, then yellow, then white, then burst into flames, as it shot across the night sky like a fiery comet, heading for an inevitable impact, with the Earth's surface.

SALISBURY PLAIN
01.37 HOURS GMT.

'Systems all read functional. We have no faults at this time.'

'Engine room reports full operational power. Singularities are on line. All status fields are go.'

'Navigation command...go.'

'Fire-power control...go.'

'Communications...go.'

'Damage control...go.'

'All equipment is stored and in take off positions.'

'Sixteen minutes to launch...'

The bridge of the Excalibur was thrumming with activity and tension, as the crew ran through the preflight checks. At each control station sat a man or woman, who'd spent all their waking moments, over the past thirty days, training for this moment. Their hands lay on the touch-sensitive panels, as information was inputted directly to their minds. Monitors before them flashed confirmation of the orders they were giving and receiving. The verbal acknowledgement of the take off check list wasn't a necessity - it was merely a tradition, that went back to the birth of powered flight. It was psychologically important.

Moss sat in the helmsman's acceleration couch. He appeared to be watching the proceedings with half-closed eyes, but it was his mind that was active, not his eyes. His mind was linked to the sentient computer that controlled Excalibur, and as the human crew ran through the check lists, he mentally raced through the alien vessel, initiating the necessary ignitions sequences, checking circuits and finally bringing the ancient craft to life, after eons of hibernation.

Beside him sat Jennifer, her hands flying over a control console, following Moss through the many systems of Excalibur. She double checking everything he did and passed on information to the other technicians on the bridge. Jenson sat in what was dubbed the "Admiral's chair" flanked by Sandpiper and Black, watching the alien vessel come to life. Only Myrddin was without a station. He chose to observe proceedings from the rear gallery. The Brabazon brothers and Gorsky roamed from console to console like worried hens, checking and rechecking the information on the monitors.

Throughout the ship, men and women carried out their assignments, working as a coherent team, as one by one all the ancient systems came alive. Navigation equipment so far advanced, it was only partly understood, came on line and began feeding information on the Earth and the solar system to the awed human navigators. Communication equipment hummed and scanned the airwaves feeding radio communications, both human and Dyason, to the battle command centre. Where, recently installed Terra computers absorbed and analysed the information. Indeed, it was one of these computers that raised the alarm first. Jenson was informed of the threat over his comm-link, and despite his alarm, remained calm and gently tapped Moss on the shoulder. Moss lost his faraway look and focused on the resistance leader.

'Hey kid,' Jenson said quietly, 'we've got a problem.'

'What sort of problem?' Moss asked, rubbing his eyes and stretching his neck. Which had become stiff, whilst his mind was wandering.

'A large lump of rock, sort of problem!' replied Jenson pointing to a monitor on a nearby console. Which showed the progress of the flaming asteroid through the atmosphere. 'One of the Dyason cruisers let that thing go a few minutes ago. Its impact point is calculated to be right on top of Stonehenge - which means right on top of us!'

Moss said nothing, but looked at Myrddin questioningly. Myrddin nodded and said, 'Yes, it's her... I heard her call...'

A shout came up from the bridge floor, 'You got that skipper? Eighteen minutes to impact. We'd better haul arse out of here on time, or that mother's going to gives us all a terminal headache!' called Josh Brabazon.

Jenson looked at Moss intently and said, 'We're cutting things fine. Are you sure we can get away in time?'

'I think so, but I can't be sure, you'd better ask Excalibur,' he replied.

Jenson addressed the console in front of Moss and asked, 'Excalibur, what about that large asteroid entering the atmosphere? It's too large to break up and we calculate the impact point to be on the surface above us. Can we launch in time? And what damage do you estimate it would cause if we don't get away in time?'

The calm female tones of Excalibur's computer filled the bridge. 'I have noted the approach of the asteroid, thank you Squadron Leader. Our launch is scheduled for two minutes before impact. At present the countdown is on time. It will take approximately forty-three seconds to clear the cavern site, and a further thirty-two seconds to engage drive and clear the impact area. We therefore have forty-four seconds leeway. If the asteroid were to impact during launch we will be destroyed, and the release of the singularities will destroy much of the northern hemisphere. If we delay launch, the impact is estimated to be the equivalent to several megatons of explosives and would cause severe damage to the caverns. Although designed to withstand natural disasters, the caverns were not meant to survive a direct impact of such a large object.'

'Things are *that* good huh!' Jenson said worriedly. He looked back at Moss and said quietly, 'Well we haven't got any choice but to try and launch, or be buried under tons of rubble. It's all down to you kid... Go to it!'

Moss simply nodded and took on the faraway look, as he once again, coursed through the ship's circuits. Above them in the stratosphere, the asteroid fell to Earth, trailing a flaming tail nearly a hundred kilometres long. The countdown continued. All nonessential personnel strapped themselves into acceleration couches, which moulded to their forms as they sat in them. Large, energy-absorbing arms gently restrained them.

In the hangar, the ground crew gave the Sukhoi fighters one last check over, to ensure all the tie-downs were secure, before running to their launch positions. Anxiously, they watched the countdown taking place on the bridge, via internal monitors. At T-minus one minute fifty-two seconds, the countdown stopped. Moss, rushing through the preflights with Excalibur, noticed it first. To the credit of the engineering officer, she noticed one second later.

'*Oh shit!* Moss shouted out loud on the bridge, 'we've lost a superconductor in engine one!'

Josh Brabazon rushed over to the engineer's position and expertly glanced over the monitors. 'Roger that! We have a superconductor down in the power exchange unit of engine one! I've got a robot-repair unit on its way now. Estimate time for repair...oh *fuck it!*...One minute three seconds.'

'Christ!' exclaimed Jenson, 'Come on guys, we've only got forty-three seconds leeway to mess about with here. No...make that thirty-four seconds!'

'I know, I know!' replied Brabazon, 'but we're going as fast as we can! There's no way we can bypass that circuit, and if we continue to launch, we'll blow ourselves to a thousand small pieces!'

'Well it's that or we get buried to death,' said Sandpiper who unusually for him, was showing signs of stress. Beads of sweat were popping out on his forehead.

'Just get on with it as fast as you can. If you have to...launch anyhow!' shouted Jenson.

'We can't!' shouted back Brabazon. 'We can't override the countdown. She's gone into fail-safe!'

Moss wasn't listening to any of this. He was lost inside the circuits of engine one, examining the fault at the speed of thought. The information being fed directly to his brain, through the console link with Excalibur. He looked at the circuits from all angles, examined the failed unit, considered the problem and saw a solution. If he just rerouted the power to here.. so this superconductor shared the load with this one here...that is, if they didn't all blow at once...now, by re-engaging these two circuits. Hang on... that wasn't right...bugger it! What if he tried sharing the load, with the power exchange unit of engine two...using that bypass circuit and that system ...yes, that might just work...come on, come on baby, nearly, nearly...there it was done!

The countdown began again, forty-two seconds later.

Josh Brabazon turned and stared at Moss who still had that glazed faraway look. 'Bugger me! How the hell did he do that!' he exclaimed.

'Not now!' said Myrddin. 'There will be plenty of time for explanations later. If there *is* a later!'

The countdown continued. Whilst above them, the fiery comet became larger and larger. Its flames filling the entire sky, until night was turned into day. At T-minus thirty seconds, small charges detonated across Salisbury Plain, almost insignificant in comparison to the chaos that was approaching from above. The ground shook and trembled and a small fissure appeared right through the centre of Stonehenge. The huge standing stones swayed and fell with a crash. The ancient monoliths which had stood for thousands of years, collapsed like a house of cards, as the fissure became wider and wider. It was as if something was consuming the Earth, as rocks and boulders disappeared. Leaving nothing, but a smooth, metallic substance, that reflected the angry reds and yellows, of the flaming asteroid above it. More and more of Salisbury Plain rolled away, to expose vast tracts of the smooth metal. Until, an area two kilometres wide, by three kilometres long, shone in the angry, artificial dawn.

MINDS OF THE EMPIRE

At T-minus eleven seconds, the metallic shield stopped, reflecting the light of the approaching asteroid. First, it became opaque, then gradually, turned translucent. Becoming thinner and thinner, until it was no more than a membrane, several molecules thick. Then, it disappeared completely... For the first time, since before humankind walked the surface of the planet, Excalibur was exposed to the world. Her hull duly reflecting, the flames of the nearing asteroid. From her deep slumber, the ancient vessel had been awoken by Dante's inferno!

On the bridge, Jenson gripped the arms of his acceleration couch so hard, blood was seeping out from under his nails. On the main viewer, that stretched across the entire front of the control room, he saw the incredible material that had covered Excalibur, all these centuries, disappear. All he could see now, was the whole sky aflame with the approaching asteroid. *Christ!* There was *no way*, that they could get out of there before the thing hit! They were doomed, and there wasn't a damned thing he could do about it. Never, had he felt so helpless, as he did now! All their lives lay in the hands of the strange youth and ancient machine. And the machine had already gone wrong once! He desperately wanted to scream out - to tell the kid to launch the beast, and get them the hell out of there! But, he knew that would achieve nothing. He sat there mouth clamped tightly shut. With sweat dripping into his eyes. Whatever else happened, he must not let the crew think he was losing it. They were just as scared as he was, probably more so. If there was one time he needed to appear calm and in control it was now... It was just a bit difficult with that asteroid bearing down on them all!

'Thirty-three seconds until impact' intoned Brabazon.

Moss said nothing, he still had that faraway look in his eyes.

Jenson felt a tremor ripple through the ship, like that of a liner leaving port. He felt the plates vibrate gently, as they absorbed enormous power. Slowly, painfully slowly, as if moving through treacle, Excalibur began to rise from her ancient resting place. There were no roaring rocket engines. No smoke and flames. Just the gentle rising, of thousands of tons of spacecraft, defeating gravity for the first time in several millennia. Like a phoenix rising from the ashes, Excalibur cleared the lip of the caverns. Then rose above Salisbury Plain. At two hundred metres she stopped rising and paused.

'Twelve seconds to impact!'

Excalibur paused... The bridge became deathly silent, as Moss closed his eyes, and breathed deeply. Nobody moved, nobody dared say a word. All eyes were fixed upon the youth, their own consoles forgotten. He was the pilot, he was the navigator, he was...*Excalibur*.

'Five seconds to impact!'

Jenson closed his eyes. They weren't going to make it! There was something wrong... The ancient vessel had risen from its grave, but could go no further! To have come this far and fail now! Defeat swept over him...

Well, at least it would at least be a quick death. They wouldn't feel a thing when it hit them, just four seconds from now...

He felt a surge gently push him into his couch, then it was gone. There was just the gentle throbbing of the engines, being transmitted through the material of the acceleration couch and...no collision! He opened one eye first.. then the other. Expecting to see the flaming asteroid bearing down on them, moments before impact. But, what he saw on the viewer were the stars becoming clearer and clearer, as Excalibur sped through the atmosphere, reaching for her home environment. The depths of outer space!

He turned and looked at Moss. Who in turn, was staring back at him, with a grin that stretched from ear to ear.

'Well bugger me kid! The bitch *flies!* exclaimed Jenson.

Below them, the asteroid collided with the Earth. Vaporising what remained of the ancient caverns, and sending flames and debris high into the Stratosphere. In London, night became day for an instant. But, the fighting never stopped...

CHAPTER SEVENTEEN

EARTH ORBIT
02.13 HOURS GMT.

'So...here they come, out of the fat and into the fire. You thought I didn't know, that I wouldn't find out Myrddin, didn't you! You old fool... Nothing escapes me - nothing. The final hour approaches brother of mine!' Nimue ranted, spinning wildly in the zero gravity of the cruiser bridge, while the rest of the crew cowered from her. Eventually, after bouncing off several bulkheads, she caught hold of a chart table and pulled herself back onto the Velcro floor. Which connected with her deck shoes and stopped her from drifting off again.

'Battle officer!' she yelled, 'what is the status of that vessel now?'

The battle officer looked over his monitors, checking the speed and vector of the human spacecraft. 'Envoy!' he snapped back, 'the human vessel has accelerated to escape velocity and is heading for an orbit that will intercept the rest of our fleet! Their craft is of *huge* dimensions! Over two klicks long and one wide. Our intelligence has no knowledge of the humans building such a craft... From the orbit it is taking, I can only presume that they intend to engage our fleet!'

Nimue hissed and spat like a cat, '*Hsssss*...So, as I thought... that's what the old bastard's been up to. Well, we'll see about that! The slimy moron! Open the frequency to the fleet commander, and tell him to prepare to engage the human craft. That is, if the weakling has the *balls* to do it! We shall remain here in higher orbit, at a safe distance from the rest of the fleet. And...' She stopped in mid-sentence, her eyes closed and face relaxed. The Dyason crew around her looked on in bemusement, not daring to approach. She could feel him, *he was alive!* She'd known it all along... That pathetic fool Mettar believed he was dead, but she had *known* all along he was alive! Her son! He was there - on the human spacecraft - *alive!* Nimue opened her mind, reached out across the thousands of klicks of space and touched the mind of Gulag.

The tranquillisers they'd been pumping into his body had kept him unconscious, but they hadn't stopped the dreams. He had lots of dreams - dreams about reaching the gateway to the cosmos, only to be confronted by his own nightmares. Dreams of floating through the universe pursued by the human youth. Trying to run away, but his limbs having no effect in the vacuum of space. Dreams of lying in his mothers arms, as she aroused his manhood and he entered her again. Memories, that he knew weren't his, kept invading his mind. Memories he knew, belonged to the souls he'd raped. He desperately tried to shut them out, but they kept intruding, forcing their way in. Then there were dreams of... an alien spacecraft emerging from a cavern, whilst a sun fell towards them. Dreams of... *'Mother...Mother... is that you? Mother where are you? Where am I?'*

'Son, son. . .I knew you were alive!'

I am alive, but I can't wake up'

'Son, they left you for dead...but I never gave up...I would never desert you. ..'

'Get me out of here Mother! Get me out of these dreams, before I go mad! I've got to escape! They're trying to destroy my mind!' 'There, there son. . .do not fear...I am here...this is what we shall do...'

Gulag's eyes snapped open. He awoke. He knew where he was, and what he had to do. He sat up, his head was finally, crystal clear. Turning he looked at the back of the single human guard in the corridor, then he lay back down again and closed his eyes once more. He knew *what* he had to do.

The hangar of Excalibur was a hive of activity. Pilots sat in the seats of the Sukhoi fighters, whilst ground crew checked their straps, and fussed over the start-up trolleys. Weapons attached to pylons below the stub wings, were secured and armed. Small electric vehicles manoeuvred the fighters, that were to be launched first, over to the catapults. Josh Brabazon stood in the deck officer's control room, overlooking the whole hangar, discussing the final details with Jenson and Sandpiper.

'Are you sure these things are going to launch properly?' asked Sandpiper doubtfully.

'Yeah, no problem,' replied Brabazon. 'It's simple really. We've adapted the nose-leg links of the fighters so they can be attached to the catapult dollies. These catapults are like those found on aircraft carriers, except these work with electromagnetic fields instead of steam. The net result is the same. We simply place the fighters in the launch tubes and the catapults fire them clear of the ship - couldn't be simpler.

'I'll say one thing though. It's a godsend the gravity fields of the singularities create an artificial gravity on-board ship. There's no way we could have trained the crew for weightless conditions!'

'Let's hope it stays that way,' said Jenson, 'otherwise, we're gonna find ourselves floating all over the place and useless with it.'

They were interrupted by the buzz of Brabazon's comm unit. 'Yes what is it?'

He listened to the anxious voice on the other end for a moment then said, 'Oh bugger it! Okay, do what you can. Get my brother Luke to give you a hand. What do you mean he's not there? Well he was a minute ago.. .okay, okay never mind, he'll turn up. I'm on my way down' and cut the link

What's wrong?' asked Jenson anxiously.

They've got faults with two of the Sukhoi's. One is unable to hold tank pressure. And the fuel systems computer, on the other, is down. I'm pretty sure we won't get them back on line, in time for the launch.'

Oh sod it!' swore Sandpiper. 'That means that two pilots are gonna have to stay behind. We haven't got that many fighters to start with... Is there no way they could be jimmied in time?'

'They're doing the best they can, but it's not looking good Han' Josh replied, 'Unless of course...I wonder?'

He turned and headed for the deck elevator. 'Follow me guys I might just have the answer to our problems,' he called over his shoulder.

They followed him down the elevator and onto the hangar deck. Walking between the huge alien shuttle craft, and the Sukhoi fighters, they followed Brabazon to a corner of the deck. There, hidden under the wing of a shuttle craft, was a smaller machine. Obviously made from the same resinous material, as Excalibur herself, it was the same size as one of the Sukhoi's. There was no tail as such, just a rectangular streamlined nozzle at the rear, that looked as if it could vector. The body blended into a very small delta wing, that drooped in a complex curve, toward the hangar floor. These wings in turn, blended at their root, into what looked like, the canopy and nose. Which was short, and had two prominent bulges on the underside.

'What is it?' asked Sandpiper.

'We discovered it in one of the launch tubes, all ready and waiting to go. We haven't had time to examine these larger shuttle craft, but I got Excalibur to give me the lowdown on this thing. And guess what. . .?' said Brabazon as he walked over to the fuselage. He pressed a panel, just below the dark canopy. Which then opened, with a slight hum of servos.

'It's a fighter! stated Jenson. 'Or at least, that's what it looks like...'

Brabazon pulled over a set of steps, climbed up, then peered into the cockpit. He turned and grinned back at Jenson.

'Very nearly,' he said with a smile. 'In fact, it's designed to destroy rogue asteroids. It's armed with two laser cannons, which are those bulges under the nose. When moving through asteroid belts, Excalibur's own laser cannon removed most obstacles. And this baby removed the ones she missed, for whatever reason. That's why we found her in one of the launch tubes. This little beauty was always armed and ready to go.'

'Are you telling me that this thing is ready to fly now?!' asked Jenson incredulously.

'As far as we can tell,' replied Brabazon.

Without another word Jenson climbed into the front seat of the two-seat cockpit. The seat adapted to his form, in the same manner as the acceleration couches on the bridge, and a seat harness automatically wound around his upper torso. The controls seemed almost too simple. What would normally be the instrument panel was still there, but instead of the numerous monitors and traditional instruments he was used to, there was a single large monitor. An arm rest on each side of the cockpit led to not one, but two, small joysticks. One on each side. Behind him, Jenson heard Sandpiper climb into the rear cockpit and give a low whistle of appreciation. Flicking on his personal comm unit, Jenson called up the computer.

'Excalibur,' he said. 'Is this machine in serviceable condition?'

Immediately the smooth female tones filled his head. 'Yes Squadron Leader. The Flyship you are in, is operational, and has been kept in a constant state of readiness. It can be launched at any time.'

'What about an instruction manual?' Jenson heard Sandpiper call from the rear seat.

'If you would care to take hold of the control columns and close your eyes, I shall furnish you with the information you need,' replied Excalibur. Jenson hesitated - he hated the forced learning the alien computer was capable of. The others had all spent long periods buried in the learning machines, that fed information directly to the brain, but not Jenson. He kept having visions of having his mind fried. As if reading his thoughts Excalibur said, 'Please grip the controls Squadron Leader. The process is quite safe.' Jenson took a deep breath and gripped the controls.

Immediately, images flashed past the back of his eyes. Explanations of the various controls flooded into his mind. Three-dimensional views, simulated flight, months of training entered his mind in an instant. It all happened so fast, he wasn't even sure *what* he knew and what he didn't. Abruptly, the images stopped. He let go of the controls and kneaded his brow. From behind him Sandpiper said in a hoarse whisper, 'Oooh, my *head...* It feels like I've got a *mother* of a hangover, without the benefit of knowing you had a good time. Don't you just *hate it* when that happens!'

Jenson smiled to himself and gingerly gripped the controls again. Did he really now know how to fly this machine?

'What do you reckon Han?' he said to his chum. 'Can we fly this baby?'

'As my favourite hero once said,' replied Hanson, 'if you can fly a Sopwith Camel, you can fly anything! Besides there's the "F factor"'.

'The "F factor"?' asked Josh Brabazon, from the top of the steps looking in at the pair. 'What the hell is the "F factor"?'

In unison Jenson and Sandpiper looked at Brabazon and shouted 'The *fuck it* factor!'

All three laughed. 'Okay Josh,' Jenson then said. 'Move this thing into one of the launch tubes ahead of the Sukhoi's. We'll launch first, and providing nothing goes wrong - we don't blow ourselves up, and we can actually fly this thing - then we'll call in and you can launch the others behind us.'

'Okay skipper you got it!' grinned Josh, then leapt off the steps and called to the ground crew, still feverishly trying to fix the two inoperative Sukhoi's. 'Leave those mothers for now! All they're good for is the scrap heap... Get that trolley over here and move this baby into launch tube one. Come on people, *move* it!'

The battle command centre had been set up in what was originally, so far as anyone could make out, the science-probe control room. Here, monitors and equipment were specifically setup to analyse and interpret the vast gigabytes of information, that came in from Excalibur's many sensors. With the addition of some Terra-made battle computers, the control room was easily transformed.

Black sat before the central holographic monitor. The planet Earth floated in the centre, in lifelike high-definition. Whilst a single red light marked the progress of Excalibur towards the group of blue lights, which marked the flotilla of Dyason craft. As he watched, another three blue lights moved up into formation with the others. Those were the Domes which had managed to launch from various points on Earth, despite the efforts of the resistance ground forces. One single blue light held a position on the far side of Earth. For the time being, Black ignored it as a rogue element. There would be time to worry about that one later. His main concern at the moment was the rest of the Dyason fleet and their amassed fire-power.

His headset clicked as a channel opened. 'Black, this is Jenson...'

'Reading you skipper, go ahead,' Black spoke into the throat mike.

'Okay Peter, we're all done here. Ready to launch on your mark. I suggest you open the channel to conference and give everybody the low down, while there's still time.'

'Roger that skipper,' Black replied, then clicked onto the ship-wide channel. 'Okay people, listen up, this is your *last* briefing before the shit *really* hits the fan!

'This is the situation as it stands at present. Our ground forces have taken several factories and launch sites.However, four... I repeat four, of the new Dyason cruisers have managed to launch. Three of the older types, have also managed to get away. The flagship *Emperor* among them. That means we're up against nineteen of the mothers!

'The situation on the ground is that Dyason resistance has collapsed in many areas, but in a few key positions, our troops are taking serious casualties and having a hard time of it. Tokyo, London and New York are the worst spots with hand-to-hand fighting on the streets. Our guess, is that if their fleet is blown out the sky, then the rest of the bastards will give up the fight. At the moment they're hanging on for grim life, in the expectation, that their shuttles are going to come to evacuate them. They'll soon give up, when they realise they've got no chance of getting off Earth.

'Now, the fleet and their shuttles are armed with nukes and conventional armoury. So they could *still,* screw things up nicely for our people on the ground. However, they're going to have to deal with *us* first. By now, they'll be aware of our approach. So the element of surprise has gone. As we approach, we can expect them to split up the flotilla. Whilst the cruisers take us on, with anything they can throw at us, we can also expect them to launch their shuttles against us. That's where you boys in the Sukhoi's come in... Your job is to take out those shuttle craft and get at the Domes, if you can. Watch your propellant. You've only got a short time to engage.

'Excalibur's job, is to use the main laser cannon to blast the Domes. Just as if they were the asteroids, the thing was designed for.'

Jenson then came on line and said, 'Remember people, this thing hasn't flown for a few thousand years. We still really don't know what she's capable of, but there is one thing we can be sure of - *no* Dome can be allowed to return to Dyason! You all know what you have to do... If we fail, more of our people on the ground will be slaughtered. We owe those bastards! Go to it and let's kick some arse!'

'Squadron Leader,' came the quiet calm voice of Moss piloting Excalibur from the bridge. 'Three minutes until we come in range of the Dyason fleet. I suggest you prepare for launch.'

'Roger that,' replied Jenson. 'Okay people, this is it! Our moment of history is upon us. *Let's do it!'*

'The craft is at two thousand klicks and closing fast Marshal,' the battle group commander called out to Mettar on the bridge of the *Emperor*. 'The vessel is slowing and matching orbit with our fleet sir. Our stealth systems do not appear to be working against this craft. We're obviously still visible to them. I recommend we launch the shuttles sir!'

Mettar slammed his fist against the bulkhead, making it ring. 'Damn! How the *hell* did they put such a large vessel together, without our knowledge? It's over two klicks long! Where did it launch from?'

'As best as we can make out, England, in the northern hemisphere sir.'

'I might have known! Right from where that piece of slime Gulag, was *supposedly* running things. May his soul suffer eternal torment in the fires of hell…

'Right then Captain, launch your shuttles and place them between us and the human vessel. Tell the pilots to engage as soon as that thing comes in range. Then, get the fleet to break formation as it approaches. They're to allow the craft to pass through their ranks, then encircle it. Once it's snared, they can give it a full broadside and blow the bastard to a hell and back!'

'But Marshal, if we launch all the shuttles, we risk losing them and not being able to recover our troops, still on the planet. Surely, it would be wiser to keep some in reserve?' asked the captain, looking at Mettar and the battle group commander with anxiety.

'Stuff the grunts!' shouted Mettar. 'If these humans are packing some weaponry, that we don't know about, and blow us all out of orbit in some mad suicide mission, then *none* of us will see Dyason again! Whose arse are you *more* concerned about Captain? The grunts on the ground or your own? Now launch the bloody shuttles and prepare for combat!'

The order went out to the fleet. Nineteen Dyason shuttle craft left the Domes' launching bays and sped toward the rapidly approaching Excalibur. Nineteen payload bays opened and nineteen weapon pallets, carrying cannons and missiles, began to track the human vessel.

The corridors to the brig were nearly all empty. Without a full compliment, the crew of Excalibur was stretched to keep the ancient craft flying, let alone engage in combat. Everyone was at their posts, making it easy for Luke Brabazon to find his way to the cell holding his tormentor, without being seen. He knew his destiny was to kill Gulag. So long as the Dyason monster was alive, he posed a terrible threat to Excalibur and all those on board. He *owed* it to them, to his brother and above all to his young wife, to kill the creature he'd helped to create. Terminating the alien had been on his mind for weeks, but until now, he'd held back. The time hadn't been right, but he knew *this* was the moment. His role in the coming battle was clear to him, he *must* destroy Gulag.

He approached the door leading to the cells. He laid his palm against the identification pad and the door opened silently. He marched past empty cells, until he came to the only one that was occupied. Through the transparent wall he saw his mortal enemy, lying unconscious on the bunk.

The single guard patrolling the corridor saw Brabazon and said in surprise, 'Dr Brabazon? Shouldn't you be at your post in the flight hang...'

The guard never finished his sentence. Brabazon hit him smartly across the temple with a heavy wrench and he fell to the deck unconscious. Not wasting any time, the doctor bent down and took the card-key and the automatic pistol from the guard. Then he moved to the electronic lock and inserted the key. Part of the cell wall before him became transparent, then disappeared. He stepped through the doorway, turned to face the comatose Gulag and raised the weapon. It clicked audibly, as he released the safety.

Gulag's eyes suddenly snapped open, causing Brabazon to step back, with a sharp intake of breath. The Dyason was meant to be under heavy sedation! Gulag turned his head to look at the doctor. Then, slowly raised himself off the bunk and stood up to face him.

'Well my friend,' Gulag hissed quietly. 'It's taken you a long time to come to pay your respects!'

'You... you...you're meant to be under sedation!' Brabazon mumbled.

'Come now, Brabazon! Did you *really* think their feeble drugs could keep a mind, as powerful as mine, under sedation for long?' replied Gulag with a sneer. 'You helped make me what I am. So *you*, of all people, should have realised that I cannot be kept from my destiny!'

Despite the hammering of his heart and an overwhelming urge to turn and flee, Brabazon held his gun level at the Dyason and said through clenched teeth, 'You've destroyed enough lives Gulag! I *know* who you really are. You're the devil incarnate! I'm telling you *now* that your rampage of destruction is at an end. As we speak, this craft and those on-board, are preparing to *destroy* the rest of your evil fleet, and as *they* die so shall you! It is time to answer to God, Dyason!'

He levelled the muzzle at Gulag's chest and squeezed the trigger. Nothing happened...

He tried again, *nothing!*

He willed his finger to squeeze the trigger, but it wouldn't move...

He couldn't control his hand!

Again, he tried with all his might, to squeeze the trigger and kill the Dyason. Still his trigger finger refused to move. All his muscles had locked solid. He had no control over any part his body! Gulag laughed loudly, a mad *evil* glint in his eye.

'Now Brabazon,' he giggled insanely, 'Is this *really* any way to treat an old friend? I'm deeply hurt. I thought you were here to help me...Ah, I see, you *thought* you were here of your *own* volition, to kill me!

'No, no, no old friend! You're here because *I* called you. I simply let you *believe* you came of your own accord! Now, it's time to reward you for such loyalty, and the gift of this *wonderful* ship. With which, *I shall conquer the universe!*

Gulag stretched out his arms expansively and laughed shrilly. Brabazon stood rooted to the deck unable to move, mumbling, 'Oh God no! What have I done? Please Lord, have mercy!'

'Mercy? mercy!' snarled Gulag, his face suddenly contorted in rage. 'I offered you the universe, to work alongside me! All I asked in return was loyalty, but what did I get you treacherous, worthless, human? You expect mercy from me? All you can expect is what you *deserve!'*

Brabazon screamed and fell to the floor, as Gulag entered his mind and began to rape it mercilessly. The doctor could feel his memories and knowledge being ripped from his head. Leaving nothing, but a bare, arid, lifeless, soul. The pain was indescribable - it felt as if his very innards, were being pulled out of his body. With a last surge of willpower, he concentrated his remaining free mind on the gun. Painfully slowly, the muzzle turned and despite the agony, he managed to force his finger around the trigger. The gun fired a single shot. Which entered through his chest, in a blaze of agony, before blissful darkness overcame him.

Gulag laughed maniacally. 'Too late. . .*too late* human! I've got it, *I've got it!* You're far too bloody late, you pathetic creature. You've given me *everything* I need to know about this vessel. It will be mine and with it I shall *rule* the stars!'

The Dyason leant over Brabazon and dribbled some spittle onto his upturned face, before grabbing the card-key and prising the gun from his fingers. With a parting kick to the inert body, he left the cell and ran with a giggle, up the corridor towards the main deck.

CHAPTER EIGHTEEN

ORBITAL DOGFIGHTS

Five...Four...Three...Two...One... Launch!

The catapult propelled the Flyship down the launch tube at over four 'G' shoving Sandpiper and Jenson hard into their seats. The lights of the tube flashed by faster and faster, until they were clear of the hull and accelerating rapidly away from the huge mass of Excalibur. Jenson took hold of the two small joysticks and came close to blacking out, as his senses were overwhelmed by the flood of information that hit them. He could feel the craft around him - no, more than that - he'd become at *one* with the small alien fighter! Information was being fed through the control sticks *directly* to his mind. No longer was he a man of legs and arms, he was a flying machine of wings, thrusters and awesome power plants. He could *feel* the wisps of space moving over his skin, he could *feel* the force of the Earth's gravity opposing the power of the engines.

Experimentally, he flexed the short stub wings, as one might flex muscles, and the 'Flyship' rolled neatly around its axis. With glee and a surge of adrenaline he plied on the power, as a runner might pump his legs, and pulled the craft into a zooming loop. *My God what a machine!* Never had he felt such power, So at *one* with a craft. This was real flying - flying in the boundless regions of space!

A voice entered his mind and intruded on his thoughts. *'Wow skipper,'* thought Sandpiper, *'this is some spacecraft! I can feel every centimeter as if it were part of my own skin!'*

'You're not the only one Han. I've never felt anything like it. This isn't just piloting, it's real flying!' replied Jenson doing another

roll. *'Give Excalibur a call and tell her to launch the Sukhoi's. It's time to get serious and see what this baby can really do!'*

Behind them the Sukhoi's accelerated down the launch tubes and burst into space. Their small fuselages glinted in the sun, looking as if they were falling towards the bright clouds, dirt brown land masses and blue seas of Earth's southern hemisphere below. Jenson reversed the thrust of his Flyship to decelerate and waited for the Sukhoi's to formate on him. Just visible above the curvature of the Earth were the Domes of the Dyason fleet and approaching rapidly, marked by small spurts of flame, were their shuttles. The first ever orbital dog-fight was about to commence.

On-board Excalibur, Josh Brabazon watched the launch of the last of the fighters from the hangar deck control room. With a sigh of relief he saw it join the formation, led by the strange craft flown by Jenson and Sandpiper. For the moment at least, his job was done. He flicked on the intercom and spoke to the deck crews. 'Well done everyone, they're all away and safe.' A cheer floated up from the deck.

'Now clear the deck and prepare for recovery. Remember, when those birds come back on board, some of them are likely to be badly shot up. So, clear away any unnecessary kit, and crash crews stand-by!'

Josh changed channel and spoke to Peter Black in the battle centre. 'Okay Captain, all the birds are away safe and heading for intercept.'

'Good work Josh,' came the reply. 'Hand over to someone else for a while. We need you up on the bridge.'

'Wilco,' he acknowledged. He then left the hangar control and headed for the elevator, that would take him up to the bridge, at the very prow of the Excalibur. He stepped inside, then without warning collapsed to the floor in agony, his headed ringing as if it were being hit with sledge hammers. He screamed in pain. His contorted body writhing on the floor, hands squeezing his temples.

It felt as if the innards of his skull were being ripped out by a huge hand. The pain was incredible, it went on and on until... It stopped abruptly. Fighting for breath, Josh gasped *'Luke...it was Luke!'*

There was something wrong with his twin. It wasn't his mind that was under attack, it was his brother's! He could feel the pain as if it were his own!

Weakly he dragged himself to his feet and whispered into the elevator control panel, 'Brig.'

The elevator moved off smoothly.

Gulag - that was the only answer. Gulag must have attacked his brother's mind and he'd felt it too! But now he couldn't feel anything! *'Please God, don't let him die'*, he thought, *'please don't let me be too late!'*

He pounded on the elevator wall. 'Faster, faster! Don't let it be too late!'

It seemed to take a lifetime, but it was only a matter of seconds before the elevator came to a halt and opened. Josh pounded down the corridor, placed his palm against the door control and entered the brig area. Immediately, he saw the guard lying on the floor, bent down and checked for a pulse. It was still there - weak, but steady. He looked up and saw the open cell door and leapt through it. There, lying on the cell floor, surrounded by a pool of blood was Luke Brabazon. Josh gave out a low moan and fell to his knees in front of his brother's prone body. He felt for a pulse. At first he could feel nothing, he tried again - there, very weak, the faintest sign of a pulse.

'Luke...Luke...' he cried. 'Hang on in there brother. Please hang on in there, I'll get help, you'll be okay...!'

Ripping off part of his jumpsuit he pushed the material against the bullet wound in a vain attempt to staunch the flow of blood.

Luke Brabazon's eyes flickered then half opened. 'Josh...Josh...' he gurgled, blood coming from his mouth.

'Luke....don't try to talk. Just hang on in there...It'll be alright!'

'It's too late for me,' Luke Brabazon gurgled, barely audible. 'He got me. I always knew he would in the end...'

He spat out a mouthful of blood. 'You must stop him... he'll destroy you all if you don't. I'm sorry Josh...Find her and tell her I love...' His eyes rolled to the top of his head, and Josh felt his body go limp. He gently closed his brother's eyelids and cradled his head in his lap sobbing violently. Black and three troopers found them like that a few minutes later.

The sun glinted off the silver skins of the Dyason shuttle craft, as they closed rapidly on Jenson and the Sukhoi fighters. Their weapon pallets moved on servos to lock onto the human craft. Then there were three brief bursts of flame, as missiles were fired. Jenson spotted the incoming missiles first, making good use of the Flyship's sensors. He opened the comm link and called, 'Phoenix Squadron, we have three incoming Atolls. Red flight prepare to break to eleven o'clock high. Blue flight follow me.'

A thought struck him. 'Hey Han!' he called to Sandpiper in the rear cockpit, 'Do you reckon you could take out those incoming with the laser?' Sandpiper thought for a moment then replied, 'Yeah I think so. Can't be sure, but my implant says I can. Hang on, I'll give it a bash.'

'Okay but make it quick, they're closing fast!'

Sandpiper engaged the laser armament and immediately information flooded into his mind. He saw a view of space before him and mentally chose the three incoming missiles. With his hand on the small guidance joystick, he selected the missiles as targets and in his mental image three lock-on circles were illuminated. He waited a breath, until the lasers fully charged, then squeezed the fire button. Three brief flashes of light emanated from the bulges under the fuselage and the incoming missiles dissolved into balls of flame.

'Yo! Good shooting Han', called out Jenson. 'God, but this babe is one hell of a machine!'

'Piece of cake!' replied Sandpiper with a laugh.

Jenson flicked open the comm channel and said, 'Okay red flight, incoming are clear. Prepare to break and engage the shuttles. Use your Gatling guns and keep the missiles for the Domes. Blue flight stick with me, we're going to blast straight through and take on the big birds. On my call!' Jenson watched the silver shuttle craft closely and when he judged they were just outside of the Dyason's gun range he called. 'Break, break, break!'

The five Sukhoi's of red flight broke high to the eleven o'clock position in a long accelerating curve, their main engines blasting a trail of flame. The remaining fighters stayed in formation with Jenson accelerating straight towards the approaching Dyason.

'Okay blue flight, one pass only. Pick your targets, blast through the formation at full throttle, then head up towards the Domes.'

While blue flight chose their targets, red flight peeled in, their Gatling guns blazing. Tracer flew like fireflies in direct lines towards the shuttle craft. Two of them immediately disintegrated into huge fireballs, as cannon shells found their mark. The Dyason scattered in all directions, all hope at keeping formation gone, as they attempted to avoid the more maneuverable human fighters. Jenson led blue flight straight on and a shuttle appeared directly ahead. Sandpiper engaged the laser cannon, causing a stabiliser of the Dyason craft to disintegrate. It tumbled away out of control, trailing burning propellant, until the flames reached the weapons bay, whereupon it exploded, sending shrapnel in all directions.

Jenson felt the small impacts against the skin of the Flyship, stinging like mosquito bites, until they zoomed through the cloud of gas and debris, and out the other side. He willed the machine to turn. It banked and headed for the main fleet.

Using the information input to his mind, Jenson saw that five shuttle craft had been destroyed on the first pass, with another two tumbling and trailing plumes of propellant. The five Sukhoi's of blue flight had come through unscathed, but red flight were less fortunate. As he watched, two of the Dyason shuttle craft loosed off a volley of missiles, that sped toward the Sukhoi's. One struck a direct hit, obliterating the fighter. The other exploded, just under the tail of another, causing it to tumble out of control for a time. Until the pilot skilfully used the thrusters, to bring it to an even keel.

'Phoenix leader, this is red three, I've been hit! My panel is lit up like a Christmas tree!' called the stricken fighter.

'Roger that,' replied Jenson. 'Haul ass back to Excalibur, over!'

'Negative Phoenix leader. I'm losing propellant fast. I don't think I can make it back to Excalibur, but I might be able to make an emergency re-entry over!'

Damn! The pilot must have lost nearly all her fuel. In his mind's eye, Jenson checked over the stricken craft with the Flyship's sensors. Sure enough, there was a metre-long gash on the underside of the fuselage and propellant was streaming out. Causing a plume of crystals to form behind it, as the fuel hit the absolute zero of space.

'Okay red three' he called. 'You're losing fuel through a gash on your underside. I recommend you eject your propellant, then use your emergency thrusters to initiate a re-entry. Once you hit the atmosphere head for one of the reoccupied territories in Australia. Good luck red three!'

She clicked her transmit button twice in acknowledgment. Then there was a brief spurt of flame from the fighter's retro-thrusters. Slowly, the crippled Sukhoi sank towards the spinning Earth. Red flight peeled away for a second pass, tracer from the remaining shuttles following them, but not finding their mark.

Jenson turned his attention to the huge Domes looming ahead. 'Okay Han, now the fun really begins' he said grimly.

'No worries skipper,' came the reply. 'Let me at the bastards!'

Excalibur bore on towards the Dyason fleet, her engines throbbing with power for the first time since her voyage to Earth. Then she arrived in peace, but now she was on the attack, reaping revenge against the molesters of her children. Moss sat in the helmsman's seat on the bridge, his mind linked to that of the Excalibur. He could feel the power of engines, the numerous systems alive and humming as if they were part of his own body, which in a way they were.

He was now an integral part of Excalibur. He didn't steer her, so much as fly with her, through the vacuum of space. It was a shared experience, a partnership. Part of his mind registered what was happening on-board the bridge, aware of the information and commands that were going on around him. He was aware of Jennifer sitting at the navigation station beside him and Myrddin behind, but the rest of him wasn't there. It was coursing through the void, heading directly for the Dyason fleet.

He watched the opening exchange of fire between Jenson's fighters and the shuttles. He ignored the resultant debris and flew on. The dull black Domes came nearer and nearer - nineteen of them, ugly evil machines. Back on the bridge his body flicked on the comm link and spoke to the battle-centre. 'Fleet in range in forty-three seconds, arm laser cannon'.

Inside the battle-centre the crew engaged the circuits for the single laser canon. Beneath the chin of the forward section, that made up the prow of Excalibur, a sphere extended on a short arm. Like Cyclops it had a single eye that swiveled and locked on the nearest Dome. Moss guided her toward the selected Dome, at the centre of the Dyason fleet. As they approached all nineteen Dyason cruisers gave out short spurts of flame, as they changed their attitudes. The formation split up, breaking away from the approaching craft. The target turned and exposed the underbelly. They were in range...

'Fire cannon,' he called to the battle centre.

There was a brief, blinding light, as the laser struck the underside of the Dome. It began to tumble - thrown out of position by the enormous bolt of energy, but seemingly, otherwise unharmed. Damn it, he thought they'd struck the armoured part of the Dome. There was no way they could bore through that.

'*Come on* battle-centre!' he shouted down the link. 'Not the *bloody* underside... It's heavily armoured! Aim for the top of the Dome, where the skin is at its thinnest'.

Hurriedly, they realigned the laser and recycled it. The single eye swiveled and blinked. A burst of light struck again, but this time near the very top of the tumbling Dome. At first, nothing appeared to happen. Then slowly, bits of metal and what appeared to be rivets, flew off the shell of the Dome and span away into space. More and more debris split away from the skin, until the whole top of the craft blew outward, with a cloud of gas, flying metal and what appeared to be bodies. The remains of the Dome span away, wildly out of control.

Moss pulled Excalibur around, banking and turning at the same time, until she was clear of the crippled Dome and was heading towards another. But the second cruiser was quicker off the mark and launched a salvo of missiles, which accelerated rapidly, tongues of flame trailing from their liquid fuel motors.

'Three fireworks inbound. Impact in fifteen seconds!'

'Realign and charge laser.'

'Target acquired and locked, laser ready to fire.'

'*Fire!*'

Once again Excalibur's laser cannon blinked and one of the incoming Dyason missiles disintegrated. It blinked a second time and another missile exploded. It blinked a third time, but the beam struck a piece of spinning debris, missing the third missile which carried on closing fast.

'Third missile has not been hit! It's still inbound. Impact in nine seconds!'

'Re-acquire target!'

'There's no time. It takes ten seconds for the laser to recycle! Impact in seven...six... five...'

'Prepare for impact!'

Moss tried to roll Excalibur away from the incoming missile, but it followed the turn, remaining locked onto the heat of the engine exhaust. He braced himself for the inevitable impact and saw everyone else on the bridge do the same. Then he was aware of a sleek machine dive and bank within the arc of the Dyason missile. There was a flash of light and the missile exploded, just before it hit Excalibur.

'Yeee-ha!' shouted Sandpiper over the comm unit. 'How's *that* for shooting? Eat your hearts out guys!'

'Heh kid!' called Jenson, pulling the Flyship up and away from Excalibur and towards another Dome. 'That's another one you owe me!'

'Roger that!' replied Moss with a tight smile. 'Thanks guys, that was a bit *too* close for comfort. Okay people, let's take out that other Dome before it fires again!'

He flexed his mind, rotated Exalibur back toward the attacking Dyason and fired the laser. It blinked and the cruiser exploded in a massive fireball. Ignoring the expanding gas cloud and shrapnel that peppered the hull, Moss swept the ship through the extremities of the fireball and on toward the next target. Across Excalibur the crew cheered wildly at their posts. Finally, the day of reckoning had come!

The evasive manoeuvres of the *Emperor,* moving away from the oncoming human vessel, threw Mettar uncomfortably in all directions, despite the restraining straps of his acceleration couch. Not having spent anytime space bound since the invasion, he was unused to the sudden unpredictable 'G' forces caused by the thrusters kicking in, followed by the sickening weightlessness. He was going green at the gills, and despite the red combat lights of the bridge, he could see that many of the crew were suffering also. He dared not think what state the crews of the other cruisers were in. Too sloppy, too complacent, they should've continued space combat training, rather than deem it unnecessary, after Earth's capitulation. Now they were all paying the price for it. And the price was badly reduced efficiency and morale that was falling through the floor.

'Marshal the *Miyaka* has just exploded and the *Shanote's* hull has been breached,' called the battle officer from his station. 'They're losing atmosphere rapidly and have lost the guidance thrusters. The captain reports they're tumbling out of control and are falling into a decaying orbit! He reports they were hit by a powerful laser from the human vessel which punctured the upper hull!'

Mettar cursed, 'By the gods! How could they have built such a craft? There is nothing I would not give, to command *such* a ship!'

'Marshal, we must either destroy that ship *now* or disengage. This spacecraft is faster, more maneuverable and has sufficient fire-power to decimate our fleet! I strongly recommend that we disengage and head for the gateway!' urged the captain.

Mettar looked at the captain with slit eyes, while trying to ignore the bile of space sickness in his throat. 'And return to Dyason with our tails between our legs like *cowards? We will* engage the enemy captain! Now, what of the shuttle craft - have any of them begun their attacks yet?'

'They've been intercepted by two flights of human fighter aircraft, adapted for space operations, Marshal,' answered the battle officer, reading the battle computer monitor, and listening to reports coming in on his headset. 'Five have been destroyed and the remaining three flights are having to fend off the fighters on their approach to the human cruiser.,'

Mettar slammed his fist down onto the acceleration couch. Which caused his bloated body, to rise painfully against the straps in the zero G.

'I don't believe it! This situation is *ridiculous*. We are Dyason warriors! What is *wrong* with you all? Has your time on that pathetic planet turned you all into old women? *Enough* of this! Weapons officer!'

'Sir!'

'Order the launches to be loaded with nuclear-tipped missiles and fire at will. It's time to finish this *once and for all!*'

'But sir!' appealed the battle officer, 'at this range those missiles would not only destroy the human vessel, but ourselves and half the fleet! Our hulls are designed to take the force of a small charge at the epicenter of the under-shield, not across any other point!'

'Fine, then order the fleet to disengage and move away to a safe distance!'

'They *can't* sir,' said the Emperor's captain tiredly. 'The human vessel is faster and more manoeuvrable. It can engage us at will.'

'Then by all the gods!' thundered Mettar, 'move us away and fire those missiles. Do it now!'

'Sir, sir!' called out the communications officer.

'What!'

'I have a link with envoy Nimue on the *Kineriez!*'

'What's that *bitch* doing here? I thought we gave her the order to make for the gateway? *Damn* the woman, haven't we got enough on our plate already, without her meddling? I suppose you'd better put her on.'

Mettar reached for the mike clipped on the console above his couch, and flicked the transmit button. 'Nimue, just what the *hell* do you think you're doing? You were ordered to head for the gateway weeks ago. You should be back on Dyason by now. What the *blazes* are you playing at?'

'Never mind what I've been doing!' came the static-ridden reply. 'I have important news!'

'It had better be *bloody* important! In case you didn't know, we're under attack by a human ship at present. We've just lost two cruisers. So it could be said we are just a *little bit busy*,' Mettar snapped.

'That ship is what the news is about!' replied Nimue. 'Now, just shut up and listen, you blithering idiot! Group Leader Gulag is alive and on-board the human space vehicle! He's been held prisoner there, but has in the past few minutes escaped and believes he can disable the vessel. So, hold off your counterattack. I repeat *hold off* your counterattack!'

Mettar stopped in surprise and said nothing.

'Mettar did you copy that message?' hissed the amplifier. 'I repeat, do *not* counter attack!'

He clicked on the transmit button. 'How did you get in contact with him? We've heard *nothing* from him!

'Never mind how, we have our ways,' Nimue replied. 'Listen Marshal, if you return to Dyason now it will be in disgrace. You've fled from the enemy, and given up a world that was conquered for the Empire. They'll string you from the highest tower and roast your intestines! Unless... unless *you* capture this craft from the humans. What a prize that will be! A prize that once it's given up, its secrets will enable the Empire to traverse and conquer the universe! It's *your* choice. Either you return empty handed and be branded a coward, or return with the *greatest prize of all!* '

Mettar thought it over. He had no faith in that slime Gulag at the best of times, but the idea of capturing the human vessel intact was worth considering. She was right, even if they managed to disengage and return to Dyason, his life was over. The Emperor didn't treat lightly those who failed him. At best his career was over, at worst he was a dead man. However, possession of that craft would alter things dramatically. He knew the bitch and her bastard had powers he didn't even want to think about; it was unnatural. But, he would have to trust in those powers now. Their ground forces could only hold out for so long without the support of the fleet. If he took out the humans craft with a nuke, he would also take out half the remaining cruisers. Very few of them would reach the gateway, which in its unstable state didn't guarantee taking them back to Dyason. But, if this human vessel was only half as potent as it appeared - well, things would certainly be different!

'Okay Nimue. We'll play it your way for now, but Gulag had better do something soon or there *won't be a fleet* left to save. He's got just twelve minutes, if nothing happens by then I'm going to nuke the bastards. Then once I've done that, I'm going to come after *you!*'

Using the information supplied by raping the mind of Brabazon, Gulag moved down the empty corridors of Excalibur. He knew exactly where he was heading and what he had to do. Now was the time for his revenge and glory! He felt rejuvenated. Knowing that the fleet was out there boosted his confidence, while entering the doctor's mind had been like feeding. The experience left him feeling stronger, revitalised - more powerful than at any time since his capture.

He was nearing his destination. From his mental map, he found the entrance to a service tunnel and began to descend, using the hand holds built into the wall alongside the fibre-optic cabling. At the bottom, the tunnel took a ninety-degree bend, which he followed to an access hatch. Carefully, he opened the hatch and slipped through. He was there, inside the main engine room.

It was like a huge cavern, the roof seeming to disappear into the heavens. In the centre of the cavern were two large plants that stood side by side. Their casing was transparent and inside were two of the largest crystals he'd ever seen. They reached halfway to the ceiling and glowed with a pulsing light like an aura. From the knowledge obtained from Brabazon, Gulag knew these were the units responsible for regulating the massive power of the two singularities. Which themselves, were placed in status fields, further back in Excalibur's body. But it wasn't the regulating crystals that Gulag was interested in.

He looked around. The walls were covered with the strange alien control panels and holographic display monitors. In front of the largest control units sat two human technicians, intent on their work. Good! They hadn't seen him. Stealthily he moved behind them, then quietly raised his stolen automatic. He pulled the trigger twice and the two technicians collapsed to the deck. Shock on their faces and blood oozing from bullet holes in their backs.

Gulag moved over to the control panel and hit one of the touch-sensitive switches. Wiring diagrams flicked onto the holo-monitor. He ran through them quickly, comparing them to the image in his mind, until he found a match. There! That was what he was after. He noted the location and set off at a jog to the regulator on the port side. It took him a minute, after several failed attempts, to find the right access panel. He pulled it open and without hesitating emptied the automatic's clip into the fibre-optics and micro-circuitry.

Jenson banked and thrustered tightly, until he was heading straight for the Dyason cruiser. He jigged wildly to throw off the gunfire coming from blisters on the craft's upper hull. Behind him, Sandpiper worked the laser gunsight. He locked onto one of the blisters and fired. The beam struck, silencing the gun emplacement and melting some of the metal plates.

'Blue two, this is Phoenix leader. Concentrate on the gun emplacement on your pass. Blue three, aim to lob your load where we've just struck. Those plates will be weakened,' said Jenson pulling away from the Dome's surface.

'Roger that Phoenix leader. Commencing attack.' Blue two did a half roll and pulled in towards the surface, strafing a gun blister with cannon fire. The shells exploded on contact with the hull, ripping holes in the skin. The Dyason gun emplacement went quiet and wisps of atmosphere blew out of the punctured plates. Blue two pulled a hard bank and swept away from the Dome.

'Okay blue three, you're clear for your run,' said Jenson.

'Blue three heading in!' came the pilot's reply. She also did a half roll and headed for the Dome's surface. Ignoring the incoming tracer from the last remaining gun emplacement, she switched on her laser target designator and locked one missile where Jenson had made his pass and another, where blue two had made his pass. Her finger lightly squeezed the fire button on the joystick, just as the Dyason gun emplacement found its mark. The damage control panel lit up like a Christmas tree and the smoke and ozone of burning electrics filled the cockpit.

'Blue three pull up! Pull up! You've been hit... You've been hit! Disengage!' Jenson screamed over the comm link.

'Negative Phoenix leader' came the barely audible reply. 'This mother's mine!'

Blue three ploughed straight into the hull of the Dyason. There was a blinding explosion as the Sukhoi's propellant ignited. Followed a moment later by a second explosion, as a large wedge of the cruiser blew away, sending the remainder of the craft spinning and tumbling into space.

With grim expressions set on their faces Black, and Josh Brabazon approached Myrddin on the bridge of the Excalibur. Jennifer looked up from her console when Black said, 'Myrddin something's happened.'

'What sort of something?' Myrddin asked in a low voice so as not to disturb Moss who was still in the pilot's couch, throwing the ship around the Dyason fleet.

'Gulag's escaped' Josh replied.

'What the...! How?' Myrddin blurted.

'He tricked Luke into opening his cell.Then destroyed his mind, before making his getaway, with the guard's passkey and gun,' Josh answered.

'He's dead?' Josh nodded.

'Oh blast, I'm sorry Josh...And Gulag's probably got all the information he needs on the internals of Excalibur from Luke's mind... There's *no* excuse. I *should* have foreseen something like this would happen! Have you started a search?'

'We have, but we can't spare many people and this is a big ship. So far there's no sign of him. He could be hiding anywhere,' answered Black.

At that moment, the engineering officer called out from his console. Which had turned into a riot of colour, as flashing warnings lit up his monitors. The bridge lights went out and yellow warning lights pulsed on.

'The port regulator has gone down. Something just blew the fibre optics. We're gonna have to shut down number two compressor! He called out anxiously.'

'Not *now* Chief!' called out Moss urgently as he swept Excalibur past another burning Dome. 'We've got three cruisers closing in on us. I need *full power* to manoeuvre.'

'There's *nothing* I can do sir!' the engineer pleaded. Frantically, he input commands into his console, in an attempt to hold down the runaway regulator. 'The second regulator can't handle the power surges alone. If we don't shut down the singularities will rip away from the status fields and turn us *all* into space dust...!'

'Warning, warning' intoned the female voice of Excalibur's computer. 'There is damage to the power regulating units. Melt-down imminent. Automatic shutdown commencing...'

'No wait! Not yet! Excalibur *not yet!* Just give me a few more seconds!' yelled Moss.

'Shutdown completed. Emergency power only.'

With a mind wrenching tug, Moss was pulled back into his own body. No longer could he feel and control the ship. No longer was he the pilot. Excalibur had shut down the engines and cut the thrusters. Throughout the ship systems went down, monitors became blank and red emergency lights cast haunting shadows. Excalibur began to drift helplessly.

'I think we know where Gulag is now,' said Myrddin ominously.

'Marshal, the human craft appears to be in trouble. Her engines have shut down and she's drifting... The *Kaloll* and *Jakazon* are closing in from opposite vectors to ourselves!'

'Yes...*Yes!*' shouted out Mettar excitedly. 'We *have* them! The bastard *actually* did it! The ship will be ours! Close in to three clicks and hold. Bring all guns to bear, lock and hold the missile battery. We've got the human scum!'

'Marshal I have the Envoy on channel one sir.' The comms officer opened the frequency and Nimue spoke to Mettar.

'Marshal, I trust your faith is renewed? As you can see the human craft is incapacitated.'

'Excellent work Envoy. *Excellent work!* We need now only to talk to their captain, to accept his surrender and their ship is ours!' enthused Mettar.

'I feel you're being a little over optimistic Marshal,' replied Nimue. 'The humans aboard this craft are desperate people. I think it unlikely that they will give up so easily. They will probably try to scuttle the ship, rather than let it be captured. Group Leader Gulag tells me that although there aren't many humans on-board - fewer than two hundred in total - they're all highly trained resistance fighters.'

Mettar thought over what Nimue said for a moment. 'Perhaps you're correct Envoy. Although, we have them surrounded and out-gunned, they are clearly fanatics. Other than blowing them to pieces, do you have a suggestion to encourage their surrender?'

Nimue's voice purred over the comm-link as she said, 'Indeed I do Marshal. Gulag informs me the craft has a large hangar area. He's confident that he can open the space lock to let in several of our shuttles. We're moving in to formate on you, and have our shuttle prepared and ready to leave with a full complement of troops. If you have any shuttle craft left, I suggest you recall them and have your troops board also'

'You say there are fewer than two hundred on-board?' asked Mettar.

'That is correct.'

Mettar kneaded his brow in thought for a moment then called to the battle commander, 'What's the status of our shuttle craft?'

'Ten destroyed outright. Three have returned to cruisers with damage. Four are still engaging the human fighters, and two have returned low on propellants, including our own.'

Mettar reopened the link to Nimue. 'Okay Envoy, we'll do it your way.' he said then turned to the battle commander. 'Have the two shuttles refuelled and rearmed. Then load battle squads, kitted out with pressure suits. With three shuttles that should give us over five hundred and fifty men. Excellent! We're going to board the swine!'

'Phoenix leader this is red one. I am Winchester. All munitions gone and fuel level low, over.'

'Phoenix leader this is red three. Winchester and fuel low, over'.

One by one the surviving five Sukhoi's called their low fuel status and expended munitions. Jenson broke off his attack on another Dome and called back.

'Roger red one and three. Phoenix leader here. Okay people, good work,' Jenson told the surviving pilots. 'The Dyason shuttles are bugging out and five Domes are history. Outstanding work! Red one take lead and disengage. Return to Excalibur, over.'

'Roger that,' replied red one. 'Hang on - Phoenix leader, Excalibur appears to be in trouble! Her engines appear to be dead and she's floating, over!'

'Shit!' Using the Flyship's sensors, Jenson moved his vision to Excalibur. The ship had just decimated another Dome, which was spinning away. But, instead of thrusting on to engage two more Dyason cruisers, her engines had indeed stopped and she was beginning to tumble slowly.

'Skipper' called out Sandpiper, 'Excalibur has just called. That bastard Gulag has *escaped* and wrecked one of the regulators in the main power plant. The computer has gone into failsafe and shut everything down. Engines... laser... sensors... the lot, only the life support systems are still functioning on backup power. They reckon the damage will take at least four hours to repair, and there's no sign of Gulag!'

'Oh shit,' swore Jenson. 'Okay red one, there's nothing more you can do here... There's no way you can get safely back on-board Excalibur. Without power you can't refuel and launch. So, lead the flight and go for re-entry. There should be a window any minute now. Head for 'Table Top' airfield in New South Wales. It's back in our hands.'

'I hate bugging out on you now skipper.'

'You've done more than anyone could ask red one. Now push off. We'll take it from here!'

'Roger and good luck Phoenix leader,' and with that, the remaining Sukhoi's joined formation and began to drop back towards the Earth's surface.

'Now what?' asked Sandpiper from the rear of the cockpit. 'It looks like those three cruisers are closing in for the kill, and one of them is the flagship *Emperor*. They've still got twelve Domes left here and my scopes read another closing in fast from a higher orbit. That makes thirteen in total!'

'I guess that leaves just us in the game Han. The first thing we have to do take out those cruisers closing in on Excalibur Jenson replied, hauling the Flyship round towards one of the three Domes. 'Thirteen to one. My favourite odds!'

'Jenson, this is Moss, over,' Jenson's comm unit clicked on.

'Go ahead kid. What's the situation?' Jenson replied.

'We've got the Dyason flagship hailing us. I'm gonna patch them through to you as well, hang on...' the voice of a Dyason came over his headset, speaking in heavily accented English.

'Unidentified human spacecraft, this is Marshal Mettar of the Imperial Dyason fleet. We know you're vessel is without power and helpless. Your fighters are out of fuel and weapons and are fleeing. We have your ship surrounded and can destroy you at any time! If you surrender your vessel, you shall be treated well. Despite murdering so many of my men, in your unprovoked attack. You have three minutes to submit. If you don't we shall take all necessary actions.' The link broke as the Dyason stopped transmitting.

'What do you make of that Han?' asked Jenson.

'That last sentence, *"take all necessary actions"* makes me think they don't intend to blow Excalibur out of the sky at all. They want her intact for themselves. They realise what she's worth. Somehow, that slimeball Gulag, has managed to get in touch with them and given them the low down.'

'I reckon you're right Han' said Jenson. 'That means we might be able to buy some time, in the hope, they can repair the regulators and get the power back on-line sooner, rather than later.'

'Paul, this is Moss over.'

'Moss, we believe the Dyason intend to attempt to take Excalibur intact for themselves.'

'That's what we think also. There's something else you should know... When Gulag escaped he took half of Luke Brabazon's mind. We reckon that's how he knew which bit to wreck, without causing any long-term damage. But, it also means he must know that if Excalibur is destroyed and the singularities are released from their status fields, then the resulting explosion will take them out with us,' said Moss.

'That's a good point kid! So what do you think we should do?' replied Jenson.

'Well, if you can keep them busy for as long as possible we'll try to repair the regulator. They're working on it now, but the estimate is still over three hours before we can bring the power back on line. In the meantime, we're gonna tell them to stuff their vocal chords up their anus!'

'Okay kid you do that. We'll do what we can.'

With that Jenson cut the comm link, opened the engines wide and flick rolled toward the approaching Dome. Once again they zoomed towards the surface jinking wildly to avoid the incoming cannon fire. Sandpiper locked onto the nearest gun blister and blasted it with the laser cannon. It exploded in a blaze of pyrotechnics. Jenson thrustered away from the debris and drew a line on another emplacement. Once again, the lasers blasted out, destroying the gun position and puncturing a hole in the cruiser's surface. Jenson pulled the Flyship up away from the surface, did another half roll and came in again for a second pass at the weakened hull. Hopefully, they could punch a bigger hole in the plates and do some terminal damage.

Behind them, moving through the floating metal debris, a Dyason shuttle closed in on the Flyship. So intent were they on their attack, that neither Jenson nor Sandpiper noticed its approach. Again they lined up for their run and headed for the surface. Sandpiper blazed away with the laser cannons, and saw with satisfaction several large plates buckle and rip away. The cruiser began to keel over, just as the shuttle opened up with its Gatling gun. The tracer crept towards the fighter and drew a line across the port wing. Jenson's mind screamed out in agony as the craft's sensors sent a shaft of pain through him. It was as if it were one of his own limbs that had been shot. They span away from the Dome out of control.

'Ah...*Shit!* We're hit. We're hit!' Jenson cried out, desperately trying to bring the tumbling machine under control. 'Han can you see what got us? My sensors have blown.'

'Skipper we've got a shuttle on our tail! It's hit us with its cannon and looks ready to take another pot shot. You've got to get us under control or we're history!' yelled Sandpiper craning his head round to get a padlock view on the Dyason.

'It's bloody difficult! We've lost the port stabilising thrusters. It's like trying to fly a bucking bronco without a control stick. Hang on...I'm trying to compensate by pulling back on the starboard power unit. Come on, come on baby...*Yes!*' The Flyship snapped out of its three-axis tumble and decelerated rapidly causing the faster-moving shuttle to overshoot. Jenson cautiously added the power again and they set off in pursuit.

'Nice one skipper! Okay let's get the bastard! Damn…laser cannon guidance is down. I'll have to sight manually!'

'Make it quick Han, I can't keep control for long. It's taking everything I have to fly a straight course!'

'Okay just close in a little more, just a few seconds more…'

Ahead of them the Dyason ignited his thrusters and began to roll to the left in an attempt to turn back towards the Flyship, but he was too late, Sandpiper opened fire with the lasers. The first salvo went wide as the shuttle rolled away. He shifted his aim and fired again. This time the lasers bore a hole straight through the rear fuselage, igniting the propellant and turning the shuttle into a flaming ball of gas.

'*Yes!* Got you, you mother!' shouted Sandpiper excitedly. He was cut short by a loud bang from behind them. 'Skipper port engine's given up the ghost!'

'I know Han. This is where things become tricky. She was barely flyable before - now it's gonna be almost impossible! Call up Excalibur and tell them to have the landing pad ready for an emergency recovery. We'll be coming in fast so strap in tight.'

'Okay skipper. I'm not worried - you'll do it like it was a piece of cake!'

'If only… Not this time I fear, chum!'

Fighting with the nearly failed controls, Jenson guided the crippled machine towards the slowly tumbling Excalibur. He knew his chances of guiding the alien fighter in for recovery, when Excalibur herself was crippled, would be hard enough when he had full control.

Now he reckoned their chances, in an almost unflyable state, was less than one in a thousand!

'There's just not enough of us to do a proper sweep. He could be anywhere. I've got as many people as possible on it, but Excalibur is vast - it'll take hours to complete a full search.' said Black despondently.

'By which time he could achieve all sorts of mischief,' added Jennifer. 'Myrddin, can't you locate his mind? I've tried but I'm coming up blank.'

Myrddin sighed, eased himself out of his couch and paced around the bridge. 'No, I've tried Jennifer, but I can't track him either. He's become very adept at cloaking his thoughts... It's obvious now, that the Dyason intend to take Excalibur for themselves. So my best guess is that Gulag's next step, will be in aiding them to take us, but I haven't figured out *how* yet.'

'Is there no way we can get the power back on line, if only for a short time? So we can get out of here! I mean, *surely* it would be worth the risk rather than just sitting here helpless?' she asked.

'No I'm afraid not. You see Excalibur is designed to shut down completely, if there's a risk of the status fields, which hold the singularities, collapsing. If they were to break free, not only would they destroy the ship, they would rip an enormous hole in the fabric of space. These safeguards cannot be overridden until repairs have been made. No, Gulag did a good job all right... We're stuck until the regulator can be put back on line. Josh and Dr Gorsky are working on it now, but it's going to take some time,' answered Myrddin.

From the communications console one of the crew called out, 'The Flyship has just called in. They've been hit by one of the Dyason shuttles. They've lost an engine and the port guidance thrusters! Squadron Leader Jenson is going to attempt an emergency landing. He requests guidance coming into the retrieve pad.'

'How badly are they damaged?' demanded Moss stepping over to the comm console. 'Can they make it back?'

'It's going to be touch and go sir,' replied the engineering officer, Paterson. 'Excalibur is rotating slowly, and if they haven't got full control themselves it's going to be very hazardous.'

'Damn, it never rains it pours! Okay Paterson, you take the bridge, there's nothing I can do here for now. I'm going down to the hangar to guide them in,' Moss said, then headed for the ship transporter.

'Wait Moss, we'll come with you!' said Myrddin. 'I've got an idea...'

Myrddin, Black and Jennifer stepped into the transporter with Moss and the four set off down the neck of Excalibur, towards the main body, where the hangar and retrieve pads were located.

'If we were in the Dyason's shoes what would we be doing, to try and take Excalibur in one piece?' Myrddin asked of Moss.

'I haven't thought about it,' Moss replied, 'but I guess if I were them, I would want to ensure we didn't try to scuttle her. The only sure way of doing that would be...*to board her!* I see what you're getting at Myrddin. Gulag is in touch with Nimue isn't he? She's on-board that other Dome, heading towards the fleet now, isn't she?'

Myrddin nodded.

'Would you boys please enlighten me? What's going on?' asked Jennifer.

Moss turned to her and said, 'Gulag is Nimue's son.'

'Her son!' exclaimed Black in surprise.

'That's right,' replied Myrddin. 'She tried to keep it secret from everyone, but that's the score all right... Somehow, she used their mental link to pull Gulag out of his sedation and together, they hatched the plot to sabotage and take Excalibur for themselves. With Excalibur they'll be able to traverse the stars at will, without needing to break the hyperspace barrier.'

'Gulag took the information he needed from Luke Brabazon before he died. So he knows how Excalibur operates. Given that their plan must include boarding Excalibur in sufficient numbers to subdue us, that means to complete this plan, there's only one place he can be...'

The penny dropped in Black's mind and he said, *'The hangar!'*

'Exactly,' confirmed Myrddin.

Black clicked on his comm link and said, 'Zimmerman, this is Black. Round up the squads and meet me at the entrance to the main hangar. Make sure everyone is armed and you've got spare hardware for the rest of us. The odds are Gulag is hiding out there.' He closed the channel looked up at Moss and said, 'If he's there then he's dead meat!'

'Maybe,' Moss replied quietly.

CHAPTER NINETEEN

THE CLIMAX

Sweat dripped off Jenson's brow. It was taking all his concentration to control the Flyship. It kept wanting to flick away and spin on a diagonal axis. Through the alien craft's interactive flight system, it felt like trying to support a dead weight at arm's length. In the rear seat, Sandpiper was doing what he could by juggling the thrust from the single healthy engine and the remaining operative guidance thrusters.

Above the top of the canopy loomed Excalibur. Slowly, they matched her rotation with small spurts of power and retro thrusters until they hung with the retrieve bay directly above them. Lights ran along the short strip, acting as a guidance reference in much the same way as landing lights worked on a Terran airfield.

'Flyship this is Excalibur,' came the voice of Moss over the headset. 'Remember, that as you come closer to the pad, Excalibur's gravity field will start to take effect and you'll have to compensate. You're now in position over the landing pad. Initiate your roll *now'*.

'Roger that,' replied Jenson, his face furrowed with concentration. Carefully, using the remaining thrusters, Jenson began to roll the Flyship so that Excalibur moved from the top of the canopy, in relation to their position, to below the nose.

'Okay Paul, now begin your descent. You're at 1,000 metres and closing,' Moss called calmly.

Trying to control the shaking in his limbs, Jenson lowered the nose of the Flyship and thrustered towards the surface of Excalibur. Behind him, Sandpiper said nothing, knowing better that to interrupt his concentration at this stage. The flashing lights of the retrieve pad came closer and closer.

'Your attitude is looking good, but a little low. Decrease your descent path, Flyship.'

Jenson eased the nose up slightly, aligning it on the guidance beacon at the end of the pad, but he was having trouble holding in opposite roll. Gradually, almost imperceptibly at first, they began to roll to port. Below them the lights of the pad got bigger and bigger.

'Paul you're beginning to roll to port. Correct the roll. I repeat, *correct the roll*,' warned Moss.

Jenson willed the starboard thrusters to compensate for the roll, but in doing so lost the match with Excalibur's slow rotation. They were now only metres above the short runway and pad and moving forward too fast..

'Reverse thrusters, use your reverse thrusters! You're coming in too fast. Paul you're *too fast!*' shouted Moss urgently, but it was too late.

With a sickening crunch, the short landing legs impacted on the strip. The starboard leg collapsed first, followed by the port and nose-leg a moment later. The Flyship slew along the runway in a shower of sparks heading straight for the retrieve bay. The port wing hit the edge of the entrance ripping off the tip completely. The remainder of the ship spun round 360 degrees and entered the bay backwards, still moving at a rate of knots. Jenson pulled his arms over his face instinctively, to protect himself from the impact. But, just as it appeared, they would hit the rear of the bay, a large wide net, like those on aircraft carriers, sprung up from the floor and brought the wrecked Flyship to a rapid halt. The bay doors closed behind them.

Inside the cockpit, Jenson slowly lowered his arms, still in a daze. Behind him Sandpiper said with a groan, 'Bugger me skipper, we're still here! Not the most gentle of arrivals but I ain't complaining. You know what they say...'

In unison the pair shouted out loud, *'Any landing you can walk away from is a good one!'*

They both laughed a little hysterically. Black ran up the fuselage side and hit the emergency canopy release. It sprang open and he peered in at his friends.

'Nice landing guys. Are you all right? The pair hit their strap releases and eased themselves out of the cockpit, both of them groaning slightly, as the tension eased out of their bodies. Jenson stood with his hand against the fuselage of the now wrecked Flyship and shook his head.

'Yeah we're okay. A little shook up, but everything appears to be working.'

'Do you need a medic?'

'No, we're okay.' replied Sandpiper stretching his limbs with a moan. Technicians poured over the damaged machine, securing the systems and powering everything down. The three men headed for the bay exit where Jennifer and a squad of heavily armed fighters stood.

'What's going on?' Jenson asked as he and Sandpiper were relieved of their flying kits and given a machine pistol each.

'Glad you're still both in one piece. That was some flying boys! We've got visitors on the way,' Jennifer answered as they set off at a jog down the corridor. She then gave Jenson the low down on what had been happening.

'So where's Gulag now?' he asked Black.

'He's in the hangar control room. From there he can operate the other retrieve bays and bring the Dyason shuttles on board.'

'And you're going to let him do that? asked Sandpiper.

'Yes. It's Moss's idea. We're letting Gulag think we don't know what he's planning. Nobody is to use their comm links, in case he has one himself. So were relying on runners, and mind link between myself, Moss, Myrddin and Josh. The plan is to let the Dyason land with only a token resistance. We'll fall back from the retrieve bays and lead the Dyason into the main hangar. That's where our main force will be sited, and we can contain them until Josh and Gorsky can make the repairs to the regulator and get the power back on line. Then we can get the hell out of here.'

'In the meantime the rest of the fleet won't make moves against us 'cause half their troops are trapped on board Excalibur,' added Sandpiper catching on to the scheme.

'Moss thought that one up?' Jenson asked, slightly surprised. 'I'm impressed.. Heh, maybe there's hope for the kid after all!,' He winked at Jennifer, who blushed.

They arrived at the small control room at the rear of retrieve bay four. 'We've cut the intercom monitors, so Gulag can't see us,' Black informed them. 'He'll think they just went down when the main power went off. Myrddin and Moss are with squads in the other two retrieve bays preparing *reception* committees.'

Jennifer looked at Black and said, 'They're on their way now.'

'Okay people,' Black said to the squad, 'take-up your positions and keep out of sight until the shuttle lands. Open fire only when the Dyason have disembarked, and aim well clear of the propellant tanks, or you'll blow us all to pieces. When I say, start to pull back to the main hangar.'

The resistance fighters duly took up their positions. Whilst from out in the retrieve bay, came the sound of the atmosphere being vented as it became un-pressurised. Then the main doors eased open.

'Right on the button,' said Jennifer, 'At least Gulag is predictable.'

Jenson peered carefully over the main console so he could see through the open doors. Beyond, he could see the landing lights flash and coming in on approach, the unmistakable shape of a Dyason shuttle.

It came in on the guidance beam, descending steadily. Little spurts of flame emitting from its guidance thrusters. The undercarriage lowered and the shuttle touched down on the short runway, then rolled into the retrieve bay. It braked and came to a halt. Immediately, the bay doors closed and it began to re-pressurise. A ramp dropped from the rear of the craft and out poured Dyason troopers, who quickly took up defensive positions around the shuttle. Once they'd disembarked, a tall arrogant female strode down the ramp and spoke to the troop commander.

'I know that bitch,' Jenson said with feeling. 'It's *Nimue!'*

'And Myrddin reports that Mettar has landed in one of the other shuttles,' added Jennifer.

'All the baddies coming to visit eh? Wherever Gulag is, evil follows like flies to dog turd...'

What a ship! She'd taken the opportunity to examine the vessel as the shuttle had landed. Furnished with the information supplied by Gulag, she knew what to expect, but even so, she was still awed by what she saw. Given such a vessel there was nothing she couldn't do!

Whatever ancient civilisation had created this spacecraft, their technology was light years in advance of human, or Dyason science. They'd mastered interstellar travel without needing to resort to mind tricks, in an attempt to navigate hyperspace. With such awesome power at her fingertips, she could conquer the stars! They would subdue Earth again, and use the slave labour to build a whole fleet of such craft. Then the universe would be *hers!*

'Gulag, my son' she called in her mind, *'we have landed in the retrieve bay. There appears to be no opposition as yet. We shall make our way to the main hangar where we shall be reunited!'*

She felt Gulag respond. *'Mother we must act quickly before the humans can block us. The other two shuttles have landed. Mettar is aboard one of them. '*

'We're on our way son,' she responded.

Just as she was about to give the troop commander the order to move out, gunfire erupted from the control room and doorway. The troop commander leapt on top of Nimue, forcing her to the ground and opening fire with his assault rifle. For several minutes there was a vicious fire fight, in which several of the more exposed troopers were hit. Then, without taking any casualties themselves, the human resistance fighters backed out of the retrieve bay and fled down the corridor.

Nimue picked herself up off the deck floor and ordered the commander, 'Well don't just *stand there,* you fool. Get *after* them! Group Leader Gulag is in the hangar on his own. Get your men down there!'

'Yes Envoy!' The commander snapped, and set off at a jog, followed by the rest of his squad. They met little resistance on the way. The humans apparently preferring to retreat and run, rather than stand and fight. This encouraged the Dyason troopers and by the time they met up with the companies from the other two shuttles, they could feel victory within their grasp.

'Envoy!' Mettar called when he saw her, a big grin spread all over his chubby face. 'Well met! This is some vessel, eh! And the humans don't have the stomach for a fight... We'll sweep through and round them up no trouble.'

'So it would appear,' Nimue replied coolly. She had hoped Mettar would remain on-board the Emperor. His presence made things more complicated.

'Where to from here then?' Mettar asked.

'We must go through the hangar deck to access the rest of the ship,' she replied. 'There Gulag will join up with us and act as our guide. Half our force must head for the engines and power plants to safeguard them. Whilst the remainder of us must take control of the bridge, placed at the prow of the ship.'

'Excellent. Then lead the way!' Mettar chortled.

The Dyason troops poured onto the hangar deck, spreading out in small groups as they went, taking up defensive positions and making a sweep for humans. Once the deck was secured Nimue stepped into the centre of the hangar and called out loud.

'Gulag, we are here. You're safe now. Come down!'

The elevator to the hangar control room descended to the deck. It's doors slid open and Gulag stepped out. His uniform was gone, replaced by the sweat-stained jumpsuit he'd worn in the cells. In his hand, pointing at the deck was the automatic pistol he'd taken from the guard. He walked slowly up to Nimue, past silent Dyason troops, who watched him with curiosity. He stopped in front of her, opened his fingers and let the gun fall to the deck with a clatter. Then, she threw her hands around his neck and hugged him urgently, squeezing hard.

In her mind she said *'My son! My son! I never gave up! I knew you were alive, and now this! I knew the dark gods hadn't deserted us, that destiny still had her cards to play. You have done well my son. With this machine we shall conquer the universe!'*

Gulag pulled himself away from the embrace and held her at arm's length. 'Yes mother, destiny has decreed that we should have such power! The fools thought we could be vanquished. How *wrong* they were, victory is ours!' he said aloud, but from somewhere in the back of his mind a familiar voice said, '*Think again... arsehole!'* Gulag whirled round looking for the source of the thought, his lips curled back in a snarl. From galleries around the edge of the hangar, dozens of resistance fighters appeared. Each one armed to the teeth. More stepped out from the interiors of the strange craft, that were docked in the hangar. Still more moved out from behind plants and machinery. Gulag grabbed Nimue's arm and dived behind some heavy metal crates, just as the whole hangar erupted in a hail of gunfire...

Mettar dived for cover and snarled into his battle comm unit, 'Open fire all units! Take-out those rebel scum!'

His company commander collapsed in a heap beside him breathing heavily and said, 'It's a trap Marshal! All the exits have been sealed and we're being fired upon from the galleries and gantries. There must be at least sixty or seventy of them!' '

Sixty or *seventy* of them!' snapped Mettar, 'What are you talking about you sniveling coward! We've more than *double* that number! We're not going to be stopped now! Take the vermin out or I'll shoot you myself...'

With that, he snatched up a machine pistol and sprayed the galleries above. The company commander never got a chance to reply. A neat hole appeared in his forehead and he collapsed, stone cold dead, onto the deck. Across the hangar the Dyason took what cover they could, or died where they stood. Within seconds half their number lay dead or wounded, but the resistance fighters didn't have it all their own way. Some of the Dyason were experienced veterans. They began to organise themselves as soon as the fire fight broke out. Squad leaders snapped out orders over the battle comm units, pulling their men back where they could. Laying down fire zones against the humans with speed born of desperation. Sheltering under whatever cover they could find. Those who were equipped with grenade launchers began to lob the small explosives at the humans. Who inevitably, began to take casualties.

Jenson lay next to Moss and Jennifer up on one of the galleries letting off short, well-aimed bursts, from his assault rifle. From his vantage point he could see that despite the initial surprise, the Dyason were recovering rapidly and had taken up good positions behind the strange flying machines and equipment, that littered the hangar floor. When the grenades began to go off, he knew that it was only a matter of time before they were overrun. The Dyason badly outnumbered them. At the moment it was stalemate - they didn't have enough manpower to finish the fight and the Dyason weren't in a position to organise a proper counterattack. However, as the resistance fighters began to take more casualties, he knew it was a battle of attrition they couldn't hope to win. They'd gambled that the element of surprise would be enough to secure victory. However, they hadn't been prepared for the fighting ability of the veteran Dyason. He was personally still reeling from the recent dog-fight. Talk about out the fat and into the fire!

'How long until Josh can get the power back on line?' he shouted to Moss over the sound of gunfire.

'About another fifty-five minutes!'

'That's too long - we're going to be overrun by then! They've got over their surprise and we're beginning to take casualties. They heavily outnumber us kid!'

Moss nodded grimly and emptied another clip at the Dyason. Jennifer looked up from her gunsight and tugged at his arm, pointing with her automatic towards a lone figure, striding purposefully through the smoke of gunfire, to the centre of the hangar. A grim expression was set upon his face, his cloak trailing behind him, oblivious to the bullets flying all around.

'It's Myrddin!' she cried.

'What's the old fool up to this time?' Jenson exclaimed.

Another figure stood up from behind some crates and stepped forward to meet Myrddin. They met at the centre of the hangar floor. It was Nimue. They stood only a few metres apart eyes locked, completely ignoring the fighting going on around them. Imperceptibly at first, but with an ever-increasing intensity an aura of shimmering blue light surrounded each figure like a halo. As the intensity increased so did the size of the aura until the two combined, to form one glowing, pulsating mass of light. The gunfire around them eased and finally ceased as the fighters on both sides stopped, instinctively aware that taking place before them, was a *far* greater combat. Even Mettar put down his weapon to watch in awe what would happen.

'Dear brother' Nimue said in an icy voice through the blue aura that surrounded her body. 'How nice to see you again'

'I wish I could say the same' Myrddin replied.

'Is *now* the time?' she asked.

'Perhaps. Maybe you should find out...'

Nimue raised her hand and pointed it at Myrddin who also did the same. Additional blue-green light spread down their arms to the tips of their fingers and then out from their bodies, to meet in a blaze of light and pyrotechnics, at a spot equidistant from each other. There the light grew and waned, as if battling to overcome the other source, in a storm of sparks and power, that made the troops' hair stand on end.

From up on the gallery Moss silently watched the combat. He knew what was happening and why, but they were both wrong - this wasn't their time or their place. He placed his weapon on the floor and got to his feet. Jennifer grabbed for his arm, dropping her weapon with a clatter and stared deeply into his eyes.

'No Moss...please don't. You *don't* have to do this. You *don't* have to get involved. Haven't you done enough already? This is *their* battle not yours! You don't have to do this!'

Gently Moss placed his hand over hers and said quietly, 'No Jennifer, you're wrong. Everything has been leading to this moment. They're wrong, this is my time, not theirs, and this is my battle. I've got unfinished business to settle once and for all. I cannot avoid my responsibility, my destiny... Believe me, if there was another way I would take it. Whatever happens, I love you now and forever. *Remember that!'*

Then he carefully removed her arm and moved away. With one last look he turned to Jenson who gripped his hand and said. 'I know what you have to do kid... Go down there and finish it once and for all... I know you can do it...'

With a nod Moss released his grip and disappeared down the gantry.

Myrddin and Nimue stood rooted to the spot, their bodies unmoving, hands raised, blue light cascading and jumping around them. They stood like that for minutes on end, as everyone looked on. One moment the epicentre of flame would move closer to Myrddin, the next it would slip towards Nimue, but at no stage did it ever really move close to either. Eventually, from some sort of mutual agreement the light began to fade then die leaving Myrddin and Nimue standing untouched and unharmed.

In a voice touched with exhaustion Nimue said, 'The time has not yet arrived old man...'

'No Nimue,' he replied in a quavering voice. 'The time for us is not now. We're here for another reason - to fulfill another destiny. As well you know!'

'So be it,' she said icily.

Gulag rose from behind the cover of some crates and stepped forward. From the shadows behind Myrddin, Moss stepped forward also. The two stepped towards each other until they were nose to nose, staring with hate into each other's eyes. This time, the only aura was one of pure malice.

'This is it Dyason. This is the final showdown. The pay-off for the murder of my family and the thousands of innocent people your thugs butchered. I'm your judge, jury and executioner. This is your trial here and now and the sentence is death,' Moss said in a deadly quiet voice.

'You're no match for me scum. My destiny is already set and I shall dispatch you, as I did your weakling family, human. Then, I shall take this vessel and begin my conquest of all the star systems. Oh, and while I think of it, I enjoyed your sister very much...she suffered much pain before she died.' Gulag replied his eye glinting evilly.

'For that you'll die,' replied Moss icily.

The pair took a step away from each other. Moss dropped into a fighting stance. Gulag rocked back on his heels coiling his body like a spring. Simultaneously, they leapt at each other. Gulag went for a hand jab to the throat, but Moss got there first with a snap kick that winded the Dyason as he flew past. Despite the kick, Gulag landed and rolled straight into a defensive position as Moss came at him again. Gulag span into a reverse kick that stung Moss on the back, but Moss managed to sweep the kick partially away, causing Gulag to lose his footing. Falling to the deck he rolled and grabbed a length of pipe that lay next to some machinery. When Moss leapt at him again, he swung the pipe, catching him a glancing blow across the head. Moss fell dazed to the floor and seizing the opportunity, Gulag climbed onto his back and placed the pipe around his throat in an attempt to strangle him. Moss grabbed at the pipe and tried to stop it from squeezing his windpipe, but the Dyason was heavier and stronger than he was. He couldn't stop the pipe from gradually choking him.

In desperation, he threw his mind against the Dyason's mental barriers. Which held, but gave Moss the distraction he needed to heave Gulag over his back and onto the deck. Gulag let go of the pipe and scrambled away, while Moss fought to get his breath back.

'So that's the way you want it, is it human!' shouted Gulag maniacally. 'You think your puny mind is a match for mine! Is that what you think, eh? Well let's see what you're really made of... have a blast of this!'

Like Nimue before, Gulag raised his arm and an intense blue light flared around him, down his arm and out through his outstretched hand. Unlike Myrddin, Moss was unprepared, being on his knees, still spluttering and coughing. Without any sort of mental shielding the bolt of mental energy hit with the force of a sledge hammer. He writhed in agony on the deck, collapsing into a foetal position, his hands grasping his temples screaming in agony. His mind was being crushed, swamped, *ruptured...*

Sensing victory Gulag stood over Moss and with a gleeful smile, hit him with another burst of energy, laughing maniacally.

'You see human. You see just how *pathetic* you are. Look at you.. you're nothing! *Shit* that I would wipe off the soles of my boots. Like all the others, your mind is like putty. Just waiting to be squashed. This is your *end*, and *my* beginning!'

The blue light intensified, Moss again screamed out in agony. His muscles contorted uncontrollably and his head felt as if it would explode. He began to black out, wanting the release that death would bring him - an end to the *incredible* body-sapping pain. Death would be welcome - *anything* was better than this. His whole life had been nothing but pain and now it was nearly over. He was nearly gone, the darkness closing in all around, lights fading... Then he heard a voice at the back of his head.

'Please Moss...No...don't die...'

'I love you, please...'

'I know you can hear me...'

'You can do it ...you can win...you must.'

'I love you...I need you...'

'Please don't leave me...' the voice repeated over and over again.

He knew it was Jennifer, the one good thing in his existence. He loved her, but what was more important was that she loved *him*. If he died she would be defenceless and defeated, before this evil creature. She would - they *all* would, be back under the shackles of a race that showed no mercy. Gulag's words came to him: *'I enjoyed your sister...she suffered much pain.'* He *wouldn't* let it happen, not to Jennifer, not to *anyone*, never again. He could not, *would* not let it happen.

From the very depths of his soul came a renewed source of energy he didn't know he possessed. He *wouldn't* give in! He refused to die! He would fight back and he would win!

Like a hidden store, the power came from deep inside him and gradually filtered through his body and soul. His mental barriers slowly rose, blocking the Dyason's attack. The darkness began to recede. Weakly, he looked up at the evil stare of Gulag, raised his arm and released his mental energy. A flash of red light hit, the blue aura of Gulag, who staggered back in pain and surprise.

Painfully Moss got to his feet. Deep inside him his strength began to grow. Now he was *angry!* This motherfucker was *pure evil*. He'd killed his mother and father, raped his sister and murdered countless innocent souls. *Enough was enough.* He would torture no more. Cause no more suffering, never rape another soul. It was time to put an end to it. Time to finish the Empire. Once he wanted justice, now he wanted *revenge.* All his pent up frustration and anger burst in his mind, swelling his soul with pure energy until, with a surge of adrenaline, he released all his deep seated anger and power at the Dyason.

Gulag staggered once more, under the renewed onslaught, collapsing to his knees and crying out in pain. The blue aura surrounding him began to fade, while the red light of Moss's mental bolt increased in intensity.

'No, this *cannot be!*' Gulag ranted, rage contorting his face. 'I cannot, *will not* be defeated! My destiny is assured. I *shall* rule the stars...', but his aura continued to fade. Gathering up his will in a final desperate push, Gulag expended the last of his mental energy against Moss. For a moment the blue light intensified, pushing the red aura back towards Moss, but it couldn't and didn't last. Under the overwhelming onslaught of Moss's anger, Gulag's power faltered and died. The instant it did, he was swamped in the pulsing red energy.

'*No...No!*' pleaded Gulag as the mental energy enveloped him, twisting and contorting his body in overwhelming agony. 'No, this cannot be...I cannot die...*I beg of you*...please. This is not my destiny. It is not *meant* to happen!

With a face set in granite, Moss continued his onslaught, saying in a voice devoid of all sympathy, 'It's too late to plead Gulag. You're wrong, *this* is your destiny. The pain and suffering you have brought to others ends here... It's time to put a stop to it...It's time to make peace with your dark lord... It's time to *die!*'

Gulag's body erupted into flames which consumed him like a furnace.

Nimue screamed 'My son no!' and tried to run to him.

Gulag feebly tried to reach out to her as the flames consumed him, screaming 'Mother...*No...Please, no...*This is not the way it was meant to be...*NO!*'

Myrddin grabbed and pulled her away from the flames before she could burn herself. Gulag's flesh boiled and dropped away from his bones in charred lumps, his limbs writhing, ineffectually beating at the flames until he could move no more. With a last agonising scream that chilled every soul to the core, he finally, painfully, died. The flames went out, leaving nothing but an unrecognisable lump of charcoal. Nimue wrenched herself from Myrddin's grasp and ran off sobbing. Nobody tried to stop her. Nobody moved - their eyes riveted on Moss in awe and fear.

The red light faded and Moss lowered his face. He stood silent and motionless for several minutes. Then, he slowly raised his face and arms to the roof of the hangar. The aura of light returned and surrounded his body. However, this time it pulsed with a renewed intensity across all the colours of the spectrum. The lights of the hangar dimmed. As did those throughout Excalibur. As did those on-board the Dyason fleet. As did those of the cities on Earth - still fighting for the supremacy of one race over another.

As the lights faded the universe glowed with a strange, intense, multi-coloured aura. Everywhere on Earth the fighting paused as instinctively, both humans and Dyason raised their faces to the sky. All knew that something momentous was about to occur. Gunfire died, hand-to-hand combat ceased, everyone stopped what they were doing, wherever they were. They had no choice - something, someone had entered their minds and had something to say.

Moss held out his arms, lifted his face to the stars and let out a cry that could be heard across the world - into the minds of every living soul, no matter what race, creed or breed. There was a blinding flash of light. Night became day, as the solar system was swamped with an intense white light. There was a lurch that all living creatures felt. A lurch that felt like time and space had taken a sideways step and back again. A lurch as if time had paused for a heartbeat and then continued as before.

The light faded, the aura vanished and Moss spoke to every human and Dyason. Not verbally, but in their minds - so clearly, that no creature could mistake his meaning.

'It finishes here! The gateway is closed, our battle won. Let that be an end to the killing! There will be no more fighting on our planet. Not here, not in this corner of the universe! It's time to rebuild our shattered lands. The tortured souls of all those who have gone before cry out for this thing to end. AND END IT SHALL!'

Deep in the soul of every living creature, across the globe and above the planet, regardless of race or nature, came the realisation that Moss told the truth. The heavens returned to normal and the presence left their souls.

He lowered his arms and stared at the Dyason troops. Marshal Mettar climbed to his feet and with a manic glint in his eye addressed his men.

'Are you *all* mad?' he ranted, 'Can't you see this is *nothing* but a bunch of *parlour tricks* meant to frighten us like children? Are you all cowards or proud Dyason warriors? I'll show you how mystical he is!'

He raised his weapon cocked it and pointed it straight at Moss's heart.

There was a single shot. A neat hole appeared in the Marshal's head and he fell dead to the deck. A Dyason colonel lowered his smoking gun and dropped it to the floor. The hangar went silent, nobody moved... Everyone was waiting to see what would happen next.

For several minutes the colonel stood motionless, then as if coming out of a trance, shook his head and strode up to Moss. He saluted smartly and snapped, 'My name is Group Colonel Lambdan of the Dyason Imperial forces. Please accept our unconditional surrender...'

Across the hangar the Dyason troops dropped their weapons to the floor and stood up. Hearing the surrender over their comm links, the remainder of the Dyason fleet moved away from Excalibur and disengaged their weapons. They knew there could be no return to Dyason now. With the closure of the portal they were marooned. Now, their only hope was to plead for mercy and live with the humans in peace. They too, knew it was time to end the killing.

A chant rose from the throats of the resistance fighters.

'Moss...Moss...Moss...Moss!' they cried louder and louder stamping their feet. The chanting reverberated throughout the structure of Excalibur.

Incredibly, the Dyason troops in ones and twos, then en mass, joined in also, until the craft rang, *'Moss.... Moss.... Moss!'*

In the cities and towns of Earth, the Dyason troops put down their weapons and surrendered.

Across the globe from deep in everyone's souls rose the cry, *'Moss...Moss...Moss!'*

Jennifer ran down the gantry, threw her arms around his neck and kissed him passionately. 'I *knew* you could do it. I just *knew!'*

Moss held her at arm's length, looked deeply into her eyes and said, 'I couldn't leave you... I love you too much... It was *you* that brought me back from the brink. You saved my life.' Then he kissed her full on the lips.

Myrddin smiled, came over and tiredly, hugged the pair. Moss looked the old man in the eye and said simply, 'I couldn't take it anymore... it had to stop. So I stopped it... The war is over Myrddin.'

And so it was.

Unnoticed, the Sukhoi fighter shot down the tube and launched into space. It was one of the two fighters that had been unserviceable earlier, but had been repaired and placed ready for launch from Excalibur. Nimue sat at the controls, using the knowledge she'd taken from Gulag. Who in turn had taken it from Luke Brabazon.

Her son was dead, or at least his body was gone. However, his knowledge and experience lived on in her own mind. In the last few moments before his death she had reached out and taken it from his tortured soul. Now he lived on - in her.

The battle was lost, but the war was *far* from over. She would meet with Myrddin again, and when the time was right, one of them would die and the other would inherit the stars. Their destinies were yet to be fulfilled.

She opened the throttle wide, accelerating away from Excalibur and the Dyason fleet. Her mind reached out for the hyperspace barrier and as she came upon the gateway, she pushed with all her will. There was a slight displacement, a flutter in the time and space continuum. The Sukhoi slipped through a hole in the fabric of space and Nimue disappeared from the solar system.

EPILOGUE

Excalibur flew low over the oceans of the world. Moss sat in the pilot's seat, feeling the ancient craft slip through the atmosphere and soar like a bird. He banked and rolled the huge craft enjoying the sheer pleasure of flying - a pleasure he shared with the exhilarated computer that was Excalibur herself.

As she flew, pods released from containers under her belly and floated down to the ocean's surface. When they hit the water they blew open and thousands of tiny spores spilled out. Immediately, they entered the water and began to feed and multiply. They fed on the pollutants that people and war had deposited in the Earth's seas. They fed on the toxins and chemicals that polluted the atmosphere and in return, they pumped oxygen back into the skies. Replacing that which had been taken in decades of abuse.

Above Excalibur the clouds dispersed and the sun shone down on a world refreshed with hope and a reason for living.

So ends book one of the Dyason.
The story continues in book two.

Printed in Great Britain
by Amazon